WHEN WE WERE BAD

Claudia Rubin is in her heyday. Wife, mother, rabbi and sometime moral voice of the nation, it is she whom everyone wants to be with at her older son's glorious February wedding. Until Leo becomes a bolter and the heyday of the Rubin family begins to unravel...

His calm, married, more mature sister, Frances, tries to hold the centre together, but the stresses, for Frances, force her to re-examine her own middle way and lead to a decision as shocking in its way as Leo's has been.

Meanwhile, Claudia's husband Norman has, uncharacteristically, a secret to hide—a secret whose imminent unveiling he can do nothing about...

A warm, poignant and true portrayal of a London family in crisis, in love, in denial and—ultimately— in luck.

WHEN WE WERE BAD

Charlotte Mendelson

WINDSOR
PARAGON

First published 2007
by
Picador
This Large Print edition published 2008
by
BBC Audiobooks Ltd by arrangement with
Pan Macmillan Ltd

Hardcover ISBN: 978 1 405 68640 2
Softcover   ISBN: 978 1 405 68641 9

British Library Cataloguing in Publication Data available

Printed and bound in Great Britain by
Antony Rowe Ltd., Chippenham, Wiltshire

For Joanna, my love

ACKNOWLEDGEMENTS

Thank you to
Jane Craig, Lynne Drew, Rabbi Helen Freeman,
Mary-Anne Harrington, Ilu Kertesz,
Martha Lane Fox, Tejina Mangat,
Clementine Mendelson, Maurice Mendelson,
Theodore Mendelson, Rabbi Julia Neuberger,
Rabbi Elaina Rothman, Kate Saunders,
Gillian Stern, Simon Taube and most of all to
Gill Coleridge, to Maria Rejt and everyone at
Picador, and to Joanna Briscoe.

PROLOGUE

Sunday 18 February 2001

The Rubin family, everybody agrees, seems doomed to happiness.

*   *   *

Today is the wedding day of Leo, the first-born. He is thirty-four; he has not hurried, but now he is to marry and the next instalment of family history has been ensured. There is, in the jokes of his many ushers, his parents' smiling efficiency, the kisses and handshakes of his older relatives, a sense of relief.

The wedding will begin in fourteen minutes. Grandchildren frolic in the bright sunlight. Elderly and difficult cousins, naphthalene-scented in ancient Marks & Spencer's good winter coats, raise their chins and ignore each other, their cheeks wet with wind-tears. Despite the intense cold of this February day, nobody wants to go inside. It is much more fun to circulate, speculate, pretend to ignore the onlookers, wait for the photographers to look your way.

But they will not. No one is interested in you. There is one star of this show: tall and distractingly voluptuous in sea-green silk devoré. With her in their midst, this brilliant schtuppable pioneer, who could not be happy? Every one of the three professionals' cameras, the eighty-one amateur Nikons and Canons, points at that bone structure, that smile. Lean handsome old men, short dark sharp-suited young men, shrunken great-aunts with lizard eyes watch each other, watch the celebrities, but most of all watch her. Even the passers-by are unable to pass by. Whether or not they recognize her, their eyes are drawn in one direction, in her direction: at Rabbi Claudia Rubin, mother of the groom.

*   *   *

It is time to go in, but no one can quite break free. She shines amongst them, caramel-skinned, narrow-eyed, with a brain women envy and an opulent, maternal, fuckable body which makes men weak. Those guests who do not know her well mill cautiously in her direction, hoping for their moment. Those who do remain nearby, reluctant to release their hold.

Almost forgotten, the bride, Naomi Grossman, and her parents are approaching the synagogue in a car from Woodside Park. They are mute with excitement. Rabbi Rubin has been so good to them, letting their own rabbi lead the service, insisting on paying for the reception and flowers and photographers, for all that catering. What could they do but stand back and let her take charge?

'Nearly time,' murmurs Claudia's husband, Norman.

'Mm,' says Leo.

'Hooray!' says Claudia to one guest, then another. Her dress is tight: not unseemly, but it shows her at her confusing best. 'All the way from Newcastle with your sore leg! Thank God you've come. I have the most *unbelievable* blisters. You smell amazing. If it rains, we're screwed.' Even her youngest children are attentive, affectionate, as close as a family can be: tall handsome Simeon at her left shoulder, lovely Emily at her right. If this, the few minutes before the wedding, could be frozen and kept unsullied by the future—the Rubins in their heyday—their happiness would be complete. But it cannot be frozen. Things happen.

Part One

ONE

It is beginning.

'Come in!' says Claudia, waving her guests through. 'Sweetheart, how gorgeous you look. Hello! No, it's not me, couldn't possibly do it today—it's Naomi's rabbi, Nicky Baum, you'll know him. Oh, you hero—you made it! Hello, gorgeous, how are *you*?' They are all smiling as they approach. Her warm brown hand on their arms sustains them. The Rubins can be relied on. This will be a memorable wedding.

*   *   *

Beyond the railings the onlookers, dressed in their ordinary weekend clothes, begin to move away. Those who recognize Claudia or one of her friends will report their sighting later, proprietorially. Those who do not will ask themselves the same uneasy question as their day progresses: who *were* those people? The old women with their foreign accents, the young men with their suits: they make them think of the Mafia, of rich foreign families with their secrets and their power. Look at those expensive handbags, the sunglasses on a cold Sunday afternoon. Who do they think they are?

A few others, the most observant—a financial journalist, a French lawyer, an osteopath—notice details: the clip on a skullcap glinting in the sun; the discreet brass sign beside the gates. They start to look more carefully at the hair, the faces. And, as they move on, one thought unites them: 'Bloody

3

Jews.'

*   *   *

'Are you ready?' asks Leo's father, his sisters, his brother, as if he weren't the famously steady son, the memory-machine. They ask him anxiously, and so he reassures them.

'Yes,' he says, touching his pocket, his heart. 'Of course I am.' Out of the corner of his eye he watches his mother speaking to her buffoonish stand-in, Rabbi Nicholas Baum of West Finchley Liberal, his slender wife by his side.

*   *   *

Beneath the wedding canopy, Frances, the elder of Leo's two sisters, is trying to feel moved. This is, after all, an occasion. Her favourite sibling, after a life of diligent hard work and gentle correctness, has earned a clever moley wife who loves his mother almost as much as he does. She is his reward, as Frances's reward for instructing him in the ways of normal people is an embarrassing place of honour under the chuppah where, in a few moments, his married life will begin.

Look at him now, bending down from the bimah to correct the angle of his one goyisher usher's skullcap: at that stocky barrel-chested nervousness and extraordinarily square jaw and furry-eyebrowed frown. If anyone can be relied upon to make the cousins happy, to do his duty, he is the one. And he and Naomi, his bride, will be perfect together, testing each other on legal precedents, teaching their fortunate children to argue

4

Talmudic niceties, very politely. He has found the only woman in the world willing to spend her honeymoon visiting the observatory at Salamanca. Truly, Frances is glad for them.

But, oh God, the future. She loves her brother, of course she does, but the thought of the obligatory Friday nights ahead, the unabridged prayers and poached chicken and bathroom full of peach hand towels, fills her with a strange disloyal heaviness. Besides, her imagination is wringing every last possibility for tragedy from the joyous scene before her: heart attacks during the service, car crashes en route to the airport; even a sudden fatal flaw in the synagogue's foundations.

Relax, she tells herself, fiddling with the official pen for the signing of the Ketubah, but the truth is that she does not know how to. These huge family occasions are worse than shul. Everyone knows you, everyone wants to pinch your cheeks, remind you of the time you wet yourself at cheder, ask why you won't grow your hair or go to ophthalmology school like your uncle. There is no escape.

And, as several of them have helpfully mentioned as they pressed her to their bosoms, today of all days she does not look good. The dress her mother had offered to lend her, clinging, patterned, size fourteen, made her look like a flagpole in a sack. When she was summoned to the bathroom this morning to model her own choice, Claudia's face, framed in bubbles, made the scale of her error plain.

'Oh Lord, darling,' she had said.

It is, admittedly, only creased green cotton but she has always thought it a relatively successful student purchase, concealing her lack of bosom with an interestingly forties-style tie at the side. She had planned to wear it with a new blue silk cardigan and a pair of silver earrings from the Moroccan stall at Camden Lock: Land Girl with a touch of the Orient. Through the steam, however, it looked very different: a housecoat, a hospital garment for the insane. Her fifty-five-year-old mother, naked, looked better dressed than she.

Claudia had sat up, slick dark hair like an otter, breasts and shoulders shining: too monumental to be beautiful but beautiful all the same. 'Couldn't you,' she asked, 'at least have had a haircut?'

The truth is that no haircut could possibly help. After an unlovely doughy girlhood the wrong bones poked through and now she is like a Victorian spinster, a tall thin unbeautiful woman, with pale wrists like light bulbs, a skinny breastbone, long cold feet. Even on her own wedding day she had fallen short of prettiness, as if the dressmaker had drawn the outline and then cut a centimetre outside it. When she had moved towards her perfect husband-to-be, the fabric seemed to hang back.

The others compensate. Not Leo, of course; he is a lawyer. No one expects them to be handsome. But look at her mother; even her father, with his brainy forehead and eagle's eyebrows, his mighty nose, is growing into his face. Look at her little sister, Emily, plump-skinned and shining-haired as a French king's mistress, not a modern girl at all. Or her younger brother, Simeon, thick-lashed as a baby, his dark dreadlocks tied in a topknot for the occasion like a bandit prince pretending to be tame. The older guests can't stop kissing them: so charming, so naughty, so wonderfully talented, so prone to drama although, dear God, please not today. And, of course, their unwed state adds interest because marriage, apparently, is always a good thing.

'Never forget,' her mother reminded her only this morning, 'what you and now Leo have is the greatest gift of all. You're the lucky ones. Think of your brother and poor Emily. It's very hard for them.'

Frances knows she is lucky. It is emotion, purely, which makes her put down the glass she has been wrapping carefully in a double layer of napkin—how many stamping grooms have severed an artery?—and claw a fragment of tissue from her sleeve. Crying at weddings is normal. In the front row her mother's sisters, Rose whose husband left her and poor fat virgin Ruth, are already passing a handkerchief between them, their faces unbecomingly flushed. Or rather she assumes that this is normal. Every wedding she has ever attended, as a helper, as Claudia's proxy or, in the case of her friend Tamar, who married a Syrian ballet dancer, as a bolster, has featured broiguses, reconciliations and weeping long before the choir began to sing. But perhaps this is Jews. Perhaps, Frances thinks wistfully, in other parts of England, people marry their love-matches perfectly calmly.

Four minutes to go. She smiles nervously into the middle distance, catching no one's eye. Anything could happen, despite her seating plans and schedules. She has tried to brief the younger Rubins on their duties but Em is simply gazing picturesquely into space, while her brother is failing to direct guests to their seats, preferring to concentrate on their more attractive wives and

7

daughters. Sim has never been reliable, with his ropy money-making schemes and murky little habits. She was a fool to count on him, she thinks, and sees that she has shredded her tissue to feathers.

She tries to straighten the Ketubah but it is difficult to see. Cold sunlight is blazing through the western windows into her eyes. The makeup she attempted this morning, under instructions from her mother in the bath, will be creeping down her face already: vanity misplaced. This is not the time, she reminds herself, for angry worrying about lost rings and straying pensioners and her siblings' carelessness. She should enjoy being here, in this temple to her mother, surrounded by the prayer-books she helped to revolutionize, the new seats paid for by her fund-raising. Everyone wants to join New Belsize Liberal, where famous authors come to Chanukkah parties and the congregation seems to grow by the hour. As its senior rabbi herself has said, community, family, is the answer. Aren't they all so lucky to be part of hers?

And look how happy they seem: unfavoured relatives from her father's side; mysterious debonair old men from her mother's; Leo's hideous childhood friends from Parliament Hill and summer Kadimah at Tring, whose film options and accountancy promotions the other guests know by heart. Here, right on time, comes Naomi's mother, a poem in pleated fuchsia, taking her rightful place under the chuppah. The junior rabbis will make the day run smoothly, as they are used to doing, and so, of course, will Claudia, gazing down upon her people. She looks edible, a fertility symbol made of praline. With her in

8

charge, how could it not all be fine? Today is a wonderful day.

In the front row Frances's husband, stoically managing the children alone, is beaming. He is in his element. He gives her a merry little wave. She smiles at him with her lips, as if someone is pulling levers. She cannot make her face engage.

As she turns her head she notices an elderly cousin, whose powdery embrace she has been evading all morning, raise her eyebrows. They are watching her, the beady old ladies. She will have to be careful now.

*   *   *

The ushers have their hands full. The bride will appear at any moment and the guests will not sit still. They crane and shout and embrace each other, jumping up from their seats like toddlers at a matinée. Each of them seems to be on kissing terms with at least half the others: history, community, gastronomy unite them all. Only the goys are behaving, obediently taking their white satin skullcaps from a box by the door; turning the prayer-book pages left to right in polite confusion; or simply sitting, a little self-consciously, while around them roar the sounds of Jews at play.

The children grow more excited. The adults call louder and louder. There is so much to discuss. Claudia's new book will be published in April, they inform each other importantly. Didn't you see her on *Question Time*? It'll be all over the papers. She'll be touring America in the summer, and there's a big-shot lecture in Cambridge, very prestigious. Brenda told me. Hadn't you heard?

Our boys are very close. When were you last there for dinner?

Together they sit, in the centre of everything, watching the Rubins, delighted with it all. Their fears are numerous and no quantity of bomb-proof glass or burly cousins on security at the door can reassure them entirely. Nevertheless, a fragrant tide of flowers and good feeling envelops them now. It is cold outside but in here they are warm and jubilant. Today even the Jews are blessed.

*   *   *

At the front of Landau Hall, his back to the chuppah, the best man shuffles the orders of service with shaking fingers. Why, precisely, is he nervous? Is it the presence of a few distinctly famous guests: an old left-wing politician, a vice-chancellor, two still-beautiful actresses, several very familiar writerly faces whose exact names now escape him? Is it the Rubins themselves, in whose company he always feels the same mixture of excitement and heartache, welcome and faint exclusion, as if he were thirteen again? Is it Rabbi Rubin, that alarming brain, that photogenic face and tightly packed compelling body, before which he always feels rumpled and ashamed? Or is it memories of the previous Rubin wedding, the lovely jumpy Frances's, when the whirling-round of the happy couple in their chairs and the demented stamping music set him adrift and he almost kissed one of them, any of them but most of all the bride, before remembering his place?

'We're on.'

An usher is beside him, nodding at the choir. On

10

the far side of the room another taps Leo on the shoulder. The congregation's tone has altered, like a car changing gears.

The great wooden doors at the back of the hall are opening. Nervous but happy in unflattering ivory velvet, the bride-to-be, led by her father, is about to begin the slow walk towards her future.

*   *   *

Leo stands on the bimah with his family, his back to the hall. Everyone is smiling, their hopes heavy upon him: all those wedding-hungry relatives behind him, all his mother's friends. He knows precisely what is expected, has always done everything that they have asked: until now. Now his mind is full of his beloved: not, unfortunately, his bride-to-be, but the officiating rabbi's wife.

*   *   *

The doors swing closed behind Naomi. The choir begins its joyful song. As the guests fall reluctantly silent, Leo's mind sweeps clear. For almost a year, since he began to accompany his betrothed to Rabbi Nicky Baum's Saturday morning service—since he first came face to face with Helen Baum—he has been another man. Order, hard work, punctiliousness: all of these have evaporated, to be replaced by longing. And nobody has noticed. Any amount of short-tempered unreliability, it seems, is excused in the soon-to-be-wed.

And she, too, loves him. She is an older married woman, graceful, subtle, transfixingly clever, and she loves him. For the last six months they have

11

met on Tuesday evenings, each claiming a lengthy evening class, and have gone to a park or a square on the fringes of London or sat in his car on a side street, and kissed.

In less than a minute, his bride, the wrong bride, will be at his side.

He turns to his sister, Frances. She will help him.

'Listen to me,' he says.

TWO

Frances Rubin runs up the aisle, towards the foyer. Relatives and friends turn to watch as she passes, Claudia's elder daughter, too skinny, a worrier, but a good girl none the less. What on earth is she doing? Unnoticed, at least at first, Leo jumps from the bimah and runs towards the very end of the front row, where a slender dark-haired woman, the officiating rabbi's wife, stands alone. Then everything seems to happen at once. Frances is standing at the back of the hall, holding the solid velvet shoulders of Leo's bride-to-be who is, for the record, crying, but quietly. Leo is speaking urgently to Nicky Baum's wife. She is holding his hand. And, on the bimah, in full view of the admiring, the envious and the sceptical, the groom's mother—at whom most of the guests are still staring, as if she is the point of today—begins to weep.

*   *   *

It is Frances who does it. Somebody has to. She walks all the way back up the aisle to the front and turns to face them and has barely said the word 'unforeseen' before the hall has begun to clear.

*   *   *

Fortunately there are coffee shops nearby. There the guests begin to assemble, warm with cake and Schadenfreude. Such a scandal, in their synagogue? Their rabbi's son? Soon the kitchens and shuls of North-West London, of Oxford and Manchester and of further afield, will be in uproar. So few Jews, so many opinions. The national grid will spike.

As for the others, after a tearful conversation with the groom's mystified father, the former bride-to-be's parents sigh brokenly, wipe their daughter's eyes and lead her to the waiting car which was to have taken her to Gatwick after the reception and now will return her to Woodside Park and West Finchley Liberal. Her bridesmaid nieces, ululating, are smoothed and kissed, but will not be calm. Rabbi Baum, deserted, sweating, accepts one of many solicitous offers to drive him and his almost-adult son across the battle lines home, where Rabbi Rubin will not be welcome again. Leo, emerging from the anteroom into which his mother had summoned him, leaves the shul by a side door. Hand in hand with his mistress, he disappears down the street.

Then Claudia appears. Ignoring the excited loiterers, the remaining Rubins group around her respectfully, like bodyguards at a funeral. Only the younger children touch her. Emily, weeping, rests

13

her chin on her mother's shoulder like a loving pony. Simeon takes the car keys, manfully. Gently they usher her into the passenger seat and begin the drive home to Gospel Oak, past the spectators pressed against the coffee-shop windows, to face the future.

*   *   *

The house is so cold. Em sobs at the kitchen table, occasionally choking out reminders to Frances about back-stroking and tea and toast. The bell of All Hallows chimes the half-hour, then the hour. Frances's husband, Jonathan, tends to the children out of the way in the sitting room. He knows, as always, exactly what is expected of him. Claudia has withdrawn to her bedroom. After a short uncomfortable interval, their father follows.

It is, of course, a terrible evening. Only Simeon, paranoid and murderous, seems to be enjoying himself. He proposes that they interrogate the cuckolded Rabbi Baum, nominates himself to pursue Leo and 'bring back the fucker, wherever he's hiding', snaps at every concerned caller and claims to have friends who could 'scare the tits off that stringy cradlesnatcher. What is she? Sixty? Sixty-five?'

'Early forties, apparently,' says Em. 'Bloody lucky to have him. Give me some,' and she holds out a mug to Sim, who has opened the champagne semi-quietly to spare their mother's feelings.

*   *   *

Frances telephones the Grossmans to console

14

Naomi and discuss what to do. The aunt who answers will not help her; she only says, 'Oy. Oy, oy,' which seems to sum it up. Next she rings the synagogue, to check that the junior rabbis have dispatched the photographers and rerolled the unsigned Ketubah, that the caretaker will drive the flowers to the Czech Home in Willesden Green. She leaves a message for Mikey, her mother's tame travel agent, to inform him that although Leo and Naomi have paid for the honeymoon, they will not be going. 'Please don't ring us,' she says as, behind the fridge door, she hears Em's plaintive voice: 'Wish *I* could go to Spain.'

Then, at last, she raises the question of what happens next. In Primrose Hill tables are being laid; a student klezmer band from UCL, where Claudia is a favourite, is making its way up the Northern Line with hope in its heart. 'You know,' Frances tells her sister, 'we're going to have to do something about the restaurant.'

'What, cancel it?'

'Of cou—yes. I mean, if he's gone off . . .'

'He hasn't,' says Em. 'How could he?' Nevertheless, if one of them is to speak to their mother, apparently she is the one. '*I* know what she's like,' she says. 'You'll upset her.'

Braced for the sound of weeping from upstairs, Frances sets to work. She chips rye bread and cholent made by other people's grandmothers from the catering-sized freezer's frosty slopes. She arranges the fruit bowl in order of antioxidant potential. She removes the torn ham left by Sim on a plate and buries it deep in the outside bin. Next she stacks newspapers, polices the age and cholesterol level of their father's snack collection,

15

does the laundry, eyelids lowered in case of stains. She checks for disintegrating cables and windows left unlatched, listening out for her sister's feet on the stairs.

Em returns ten minutes later in a cloud of fortifying cigarette smoke and righteous indignation. 'How could he do that to her?' she says. 'She's gutted. Poor old Mum.'

'Did she tell you that?'

'Course not. But I could tell. And apparently that witch Barbara Stoner has already emailed to ask if she's OK. Can you believe her nerve?'

'But isn't that—'

'She's not family,' growls Sim. 'Not her business. Silly bitch.'

'So, look, sorry,' says Frances, stepping a little further inside the cage, 'what did she say about tonight?'

'God,' says Em. 'You're so heartless. Is that all you care about?'

'Of course not! But we've, I've got to tell the restaurant *something*.'

'She said she'd do it. She knows them, doesn't she?'

'But it'll still cost her thousands.' Not for Claudia the lox-and-cream-cheese quarter-bagels, the silver-foil trays of milchedik biscuits from Lyn's Kosher Katering consumed at other people's weddings. Tonight's reception at Balthazar's in Primrose Hill, even with her large local-celebrity discount, did not come cheap.

*   *   *

'Hey,' says Simeon to Frances, three fat spliffs

16

later. His heels rest on one of the new speakers which have mysteriously appeared in the run-up to the wedding. He is scratching his ear with a rusty skewer. 'It's like old times, you here in Motherland. Maybe you and your lot could move in. Kids could kip on the sofa. You and Jon-boy snogging on the stairs.'

She pretends to be inspecting a bowl of congealed fat in the fridge. Even at the idea of moving to Behrens Road, or home, or whatever she is supposed to call it, it is impossible to remain calm. She does not want to live here herself, not remotely, but the others' continued presence is strangely disturbing. Every time she hears that despite her flat Em has stayed the night here, or trips over yet more inexplicably afforded guitars, her wedding ring flies from her. She is squashed into the corner of the car seat, scratchy in hand-me-down corduroy, a furious girl again.

*   *   *

Evening. Night. Still no sign of Leo. They cannot unplug the phone in case he rings so they take it in turns to fend off callers: Frances; Sim; Frances; Em; Frances, Frances, Frances. Her husband takes the children home, leaving a sheaf of crayoned love-letters to grandmother Claudia, tucking into his pocket a list of awkward phone calls: their allies at the *Jewish Chronicle* to request privacy, Claudia's assistant about tomorrow's appointments. ('Tell her to remind the junior rabbis that the Burts are both survivors. And Joan Walton and her husband weren't speaking, and I don't blame him. And bring Monica grapes and

17

Tibor some old magazines and don't mention children to Miri Dresner.') Jonathan can be trusted, although he barely conceals his reluctance to miss this bonding family occasion. As they both know, he is the one who should be staying.

Such a good father, as Claudia always says. However, she is upstairs. Unwitnessed, Frances can wave them off with only the quickest goodbye kisses. In the circumstances, it is all anyone can expect.

Em, looking prettily distrait, is eating Bourneville. Snap. Snap. She is apparently between boyfriends, which never helps. Frances, who is so thoroughly married, cannot even remember which category her sister is currently exploring. Is it Greek? Older? Black? Teenage? Public school? Irritating as they are, these mute adoring boys, at least they keep her happy.

'Why didn't he tell us the other day?' asks Em. According to her oldest friend, Lucy, who turned up earlier with vodka but knows the Rubins too well to have come in, 'Loads of guys panic when they're called up at the auf ruf, but you can stop them. That's what it's for.'

'Well,' begins Frances, 'imagine saying something in the middle of a service, in shul, with half the guests there. Maybe he—'

'He just should've.'

'Yeah,' says Sim ominously. 'Should've done it at 'gogue. We'd have helped him remember how to behave.'

'He'll ring us, though, won't he?' Em asks again.

'I'm sure he will,' says Frances, wincing up at a new ceiling crack. She means it. How could he not? Don't the Rubins all telephone each other daily, because bits of flattery and advice and gossip are their lifeblood, their obsession? Even she does it. They take the smallest silence so personally. As Claudia says in her forthcoming book: 'Home is the mother-ship, the constant. In an ideal world, which this is not, it would always be home to them, wherever they live.'

Leo, however, seems to have forgotten this: *Leo*, of all people, with his calculator and his swimming nose-clip. One by one, as the night draws on, they go to the sitting room and take down his photographs—the sturdy scholarship boy blushing as he receives his third mathematics cup, the undergraduate picnicking awkwardly in the grass, the hard-working young barrister at his desk: a very small desk, crammed into a corner of a lowly chambers, but hard-won, well deserved. There is, in the nicest possible way, something slightly odd about Leo. Emotion, they had assumed, barely figures. He has always had a plan and, snail-like, infinitely determined, achieved it. Where does this fit in?

Sim opens another bottle. Frances's baby will be up at six; she has a scientist's TV tie-in to auction and publishers to chase but, for now, she is free. They pull on jumpers and make more tea and, warmed by Blitz spirit, debate reasons for Leo's absence:

—He is having a premature midlife crisis, caused by wedding pressure and the unreasonable expectations of his future in-laws, the endless visits to *Vood*side Park.

—The old and therefore experienced Helen Baum has seduced Leo with Kabbalah-based erotic techniques. 'It's always the quiet ones,' says Sim

19

knowledgeably.

—This is simply a puny and belated attempt at rebellion and at this very moment he is slinking back to his flat in East Finchley or, better still, back to his parents' house. Of course he is.

*   *   *

Norman Rubin, paterfamilias, stands on the stairs outside the dark little kitchen, listening. He would wish a day like this on very few of his enemies: five or six, at most. Noisy as they are, the Rubins rarely emote together. Today, as if at a death, this has changed. He keeps walking in on different combinations of heartbreak: his wife and youngest child, clutching each other and sobbing; his daughters wailing softly together; even Simeon blowing his nose unpleasantly into a tea towel. Hushed telephone conversations; confusion; he, Norman, creeps around his devastated loved ones, trying to do right.

'Is it the humiliation?' he had asked Claudia, he thought sensitively, on meeting her red-eyed outside the bathroom. 'Shul, and, and . . .'

She had actually flinched. 'God, not you too,' she said. 'Do you think I don't know what a field day they're having? The pitying visits? The gossip? The glee? Jesus, Norman,' and, chin quivering, she had shut herself back in their bedroom to wait for Emily, who understands.

As if undaunted, he is still trying to behave like an angry father. So long as he keeps muttering 'schmuck', snapping at callers, pretending to be too distracted to eat and doing his best to comfort Claudia, no one could guess that, unlike the others, he is not willing his elder son home. On the contrary. Although every day Leo stays away will be hell for his family, it has also created a diversion, a smokescreen. For the first time in Norman's relatively faultless life, this is exactly what he needs.

THREE

Despite the Rubin family's mutual reassurances, Leo does not come back. He does not even telephone. Like one of their father's jokes, they sit in the dark and wait for him.

Monday passes: nothing. Harassed by concerned friends and relatives and perfect strangers, Sim and Em leave indignant messages at Frances's office. She leaves soothing ones back. They ring her again.

'I do not *know*,' she says, when another meeting is interrupted by an urgent call from her brother. She is standing at the shared assistant's desk, two inches from his shoulder, but the sound of Sim's voice transports her home: the mildew, the paranoia. 'Honestly—how can I? I said I hadn't heard this morning and nothing's changed. Sorry, but I honestly do have—'

'But *why*?' he demands. 'Hey, come on. A quick chat? This is the real world, man. This stuff matters. Just tell your boss it's urgent. It's family. Doesn't he have family?'

She tries to explain, gently, that her partners at the agency come from families which are more restrained; that other parents, for example, allow

21

their adult children to live abroad, or to telephone only weekly. However, Sim, at almost thirty, still lives in his boyhood bedroom. Em, too sleepily fragile for independence, too passionately wedded to her brother, officially sublets a little flat in Belsize Park but spends most of her time in the house with him. Unlike Leo and Frances, the younger Rubin children do not exactly work, nor do they rent damp rooms on benefits because they are, as their mother often explains, creative, vulnerable. They live like teenagers preserved in a silt of comfortable squalor, bills paid, fridge full, heating soporifically high. Almost anything is more than they can cope with.

*   *   *

'Please come,' Em begs on the fourth night of no Leo. 'Why won't you come? The other light in the hall has gone. We don't know what's wrong with it. And the sodding radiator's busted *again*. And Sim said something so clever to the postman, I have to tell you. And this time someone has definitely nicked my coat.'

The truth is that they do need her. Someone might trip on the stairs in the dark. Em might catch pneumonia and her lungs collapse. It does happen. Frances could not live with the guilt. She will go this evening, through the frost. She will make herself do it.

*   *   *

'Of course you must,' says her husband when he comes home. 'Of all times—they are your family, love. You've got us, but think how hard it is for them. Poor Emily. You should be there. It goes without saying.'

She does not have time to walk even if she dared to, past the fat boys doing wheelies and the broken supermarket trolleys glinting in the night. She cannot drive because she is a danger to herself and others, braking for bookshops, forgetting to brake for walls. Every journey in her flimsy killing machine seems bound to end with someone's death, probably a child's. So, like the kind of harassed wholesome Heathmother so despised by the Rubins, she has bought herself a bicycle and, in fear and trembling, she rides it. At least, she tries to. Today she seems to be under a spell; her legs are stiff, her brain feels thick as dough. She arrives at Gospel Oak at last. She untangles the numerous bunches of keys which all good Rubins must carry around with them, because you never know. Then she pushes open the front door and a scent of cardboard, Barbour wax, custard powder, illegal woodsmoke and garlic swaddles her, welcoming her home.

*　　*　　*

'That you?' Em calls from the kitchen. 'God, I thought something bad had happened. We're freezing to death in here.'

The effects of abandonment are beginning to show. Em has apparently stayed the night again. She is wearing an old red T-shirt of Sim's which reveals the scratched eczematous skin of her inner elbows, and has drunk so much coffee that she shakes. In the short interval since Frances's last

23

visit they have broken the kettle. There is a pan of water boiling, almost dry. Even on the ground floor, where things are supposed to look civilized, chaos has settled more thickly, curling the edges of the cookery books, loosening the hinges.

Sim stumbles into the kitchen, scowling as if he has just woken up. His enmity with Leo is never mentioned; a stranger would assume that he is worried about him. Too late, as always, Frances remembers that she has entered a fairytale world, where one door leads to a golden hospitable land and the other to a black forest of unreason, where snapping creatures wait, grievances whistle past you, danger is well concealed.

'Did you bring milk?' he says, scratching his back. He is wearing pink translucent flip-flops and expensive new-looking low-slung jeans.

'I didn't . . . didn't have time.'

'Really,' says Sim, staring at her until she yields. He slams the fridge door shut.

'He's very depressed,' whispers Em, ripping at a cuticle as his big feet suck their way across the tiles towards the stairs. 'Want some cheesecake? Bit of a crap one. One of those stupid gossipy Lewises brought it round from number fifty-two. You wouldn't believe how much stuff's been turning up. It's not like he's *dead*.'

Frances stares at a deep groove in the tabletop, a festive seam of Christmas-card glitter and raisins and rainbow Chanukkah wax. 'How's Dad?' she asks at last.

'Barely eating. Hardly even meals.'

'Well, meals are something.'

'Yes, but not enough. He never leaves his study.'

'That's not like him.'

24

'I know. Don't tell me,' Em says, beginning to pout. '*I'm* here all the time, not like you. I see him. I know.'

'And Mum?'

'Working. Lecturing vicars at 'gogue tomorrow and she looks like crap. You've got to do something.'

*   *   *

Frances goes up to the first floor, bearing coffee and cheesecake. Their mother is sitting at her desk, gazing bleakly at the blank computer screen. Her dressing gown is half undone. Her skin gleams slick with moisturizer. This is the Claudia outsiders never see.

'No news?' she says, staring blackly at the window.

The cheesecake smells of gymnasium mats. Frances's skin begins to prickle, as if under a shower of tiny coals. 'Sorry. Not that I know.'

'I've unplugged the phone. Are they still ringing?'

'Well, ye—'

'Well, let them. I'm not talking. I'll go back in tomorrow and face the vultures down.'

'They're just concerned . . .'

'Rubbish. They want details. Probably going to print it up in the newsletter. Did you notice if he took his coat? What if he's cold?'

Frances has never known how to charm her mother. Their conversations are full of crevasses and rockslides and little velvety traps. 'Why?'

'He can hardly be trusted to look after himself, can he?' she says. 'And as for that woman . . .'

25

Frances stares at the back of her neck. 'But if he's with, you know, with her, he won't be wandering ab—'

'How *he* could do this to us, leave us . . . Anyway, they won't be happy,' her mother says. 'She's too old, she's too thin. Sorry, but it's true. And she'll be full of guilt about her son. I know he's at university but what kind of woman abandons her family, anyway? Hmm? Tell me that?'

'I don't—'

'Unconditional love, that's what mothers are for. Not love until you stop feeling like it. It's a child we're talking about, not a gerbil. Nothing matters more.'

There is a pause, in which her mother considers the astonishing fact of other people's failings. 'But,' begins Frances, remembering her fleeting impression of Helen Baum: dignified, elegant, discreetly stylish, 'I hardly saw her but she seemed, well, fine—'

'I'm not asking you for a character reference.'

There is a paperweight in Frances's hand, a dangerous egg of glossy marble. Carefully, she puts it down and reminds herself, yet again, that she is an adult and none of this should bother her. I have given birth, she thinks. I work at a respected literary agency, as an almost-equal partner. I have business cards. Profitable, if unglamorous, clients have chosen me. She looks for a flat surface on which to leave the plate, dislodging a multicoloured torrent of bris and naming invitations, a box of shul bookplates and a newspaper photograph of Claudia at the Cambridge Union, kissing a Palestinian playwright

26

on the cheek.

'It will be all right,' Frances says unconvincingly. She puts out a hand to touch her smooth shoulder and somehow misses, or her mother moves aside.

*   *   *

It is midnight before she has changed the light bulb, visited her monosyllabic father, found her sister's heavy purse and empty atomizer, reassured and promised and cleaned up enough to leave. The front door scrapes closed behind her, announcing its weak lock to passing burglars. She wheels her bicycle back down the path, the threads of family still tight around her neck, and slowly she begins to pedal towards the kebab shops and security grilles of Archway, where the children of North London live who cannot afford to move nearer their families, and do not dare move further away.

Her bicycle wheels skid on the icy tarmac. No one knows precisely where she is; it is her parents' nightmare but she finds it more exciting than she should. On an empty stretch of road she veers over to the wrong side and pedals quickly through the dark, willing the cars towards her. She is going home, which is not where her heart is.

*   *   *

'Are you awake?' whispers Norman.

Claudia, his wife of three and a half decades, is sitting in her alcove, her back to him. It is late, far later than he usually dares to work but tonight, it seems, he is in luck. In her distress and disarray she has fallen asleep at her desk and cannot ask him

27

questions.

He creeps through their bedroom towards her. Her hair is a soft dark nest stuck with pins. Her milkmaidy shoulders are bowed with the pain she feels about Leo and will not discuss with him, however much he asks her. She makes no sound.

'Bubeleh?' he whispers. Her desk never fails to move him. Its drifts of orange peel, engraved fountain pens, Hampstead Heath bat-walk schedules, reading glasses, bequeathed Belorussian grape-scissors, couscous recipes, charity council minutes, tchotchkes for local babies and notes in the universal elaborate handwriting of shaky Mitteleuropeans remind him of how one of their babies—Frances, maybe?—used to sleep in her cot, her body arranged possessively over everything she loved.

'Darling, you're schluffing. Poor girl. Come to bed.' He puts his hands on her shoulders, his thumbs on her warm golden skin, soft as flour. Nothing good can last.

Like a statue come alive, she turns her head.

'Oy!' he says, jumping away. 'You— God almighty!'

The balance of power flicks back towards her. 'Where have you been?'

'Ah,' he says. 'I . . . er—'

The senior Rubins' marriage is, he gathers, the subject of much speculation. That they enjoy each other's company; that they still so obviously have sex; that they somehow transcend the contrast between their worldly attainments; these facts fuel the imaginations of friends and readers of interviews, her congregation and the press. However, even facts can change. There is now

28

much that Claudia does not know about her husband.

'I've been, you know, pottering,' he says. 'Fiddling with that bloody computer.'

'Really?'

Does she suspect him? Despite, or because of, her job, she is not a woman who talks about how she feels. Obviously he must tell her the truth. It is, however, difficult, more and more so as the weeks progress, to imagine how he could justify what he has done; what he is about to do. *Now*, he commands himself sternly, not for the first time. You have to tell her now. He looks at her round shoulder where her silky dressing gown gapes, the nibbled skin around her thumbnail since Leo ran off, the thank-you letters and invitations which lie around her like litter, a testament to how much she is wanted. He is supposed to be her protector. That is what he is for.

'Of course,' he says. 'Of course really. Trust me.'

Claudia gives him her most promising smile. 'I know I can,' she says, her hand on his.

                    *   *   *

Frances has always tried to keep her family's oddnesses private. Once past the shameful difficulties of childhood she kept friends away, returning to their houses after school for hot chocolate and homework and the triumph of reason. However, now the Rubins are madder. Tonight, as she prepares for bed among the laundry and broken stair gates of her disappointing marital bedroom, she decides that it is time to talk.

She slips under the cold duvet beside her

29

husband. He is lying in a cloud of night-breath, warm and sane and adequately rested. After eight grainy months of broken sleep, it is impossible not to hate him. She fidgets until he is half awake and then, slowly at first, she begins.

'. . . It's, well, scary. Em's there all the time, which can't be healthy, can it? And Sim pretends to be busy and brings back women and drinks and smokes and turns up the thermostat, and you can't *move* for bloody bikes and camera lenses for his projects and hardback books because paperback print gives Em headaches, and it's stuff they already have, stuff still with price labels . . . anyway. It's falling apart there, isn't it? Everyone thinks they're the Incredible Performing Rubins but they're . . . they're not. How will they cope if something actually—I mean, what if Leo—'

'He'll be fine,' Jonathan mumbles. In the next room their baby, an impossibly light sleeper, stirs in his cot.

'Well maybe, maybe.' Anxieties are crowding in. Even if Leo is safe from beefy Nicky Baum, what about motiveless violence, the myriad accidents which threaten the unworldly? What about the lure of Beachy Head? As for the others, isn't it time that someone noticed all is not well with the Rubin family? There is a dark well of panic inside her, old and very deep, and whenever she goes home its cover slips.

He is unbearably calm. 'They're not . . . they're no good at looking after themselves,' she says, as one might discuss a litter of kittens. 'None of them. They seem to have no instinct for survival.'

'What do you mean?'

'I mean . . . they can't go on like this for ever.'

But her voice is mild and her true fears keep to the shadows: a slow slide into greater chaos, accelerated by disasters, sickness, death. Jonathan has no idea about any of it. 'Never mind,' she says and turns over. Then she turns back. 'One more thing, though. Everyone's so anti this woman. But if she's happy with Leo, and he is, apart from poor old Naomi do you think it's so wrong?'

'Of course it is,' Jonathan says. 'God, don't let your mother hear you say that.'

Frances looks at his slumped profile in the street light. After an adolescence yearning for married love, a perfect passionate understanding, she has discovered how little husbands really want to know.

*   *   *

There is so much she must not tell him. She has not hinted, for example, at the abject lunacy of her early teens when, after a mild scandal involving her mother, a prawn canapé and the Sunday papers, she embarked on a full-time campaign to please the Lord. She went from unfocused superstition to twenty-four-hour diligence overnight. It was her calling. Religious punctiliousness is wonderfully comforting. Besides, there was a thrilling amount to learn.

For the next two, three, five years she was the Rubins' full-time domestic vigilante, sneaking upstairs to examine her mother's Talmud and Halachah, repenting for every impure thought, inventing new exciting ways to protect her family from harm. In their mother's absence she had hours to devote to the purification of tap water; to

31

warding off the angel of death with strategically placed paper napkins; to tapping thresholds and raking the doormat for insects, predicting the future from her French dictionary, composting unholy garments, scouring her hands and then scouring them again. So much contamination, so little time. She grew expert; there was not a mitzvah, a b'racha she did not know, even the ones for seeing a king and his court, or a dwarf, or fragrant oils or the sea or lofty mountains. Bath times were exhausting. Newspapers took hours. And, oh, the fresh prayers she invented, the midnight supplications for everyone whom she loved, or knew from shul, or had simply glimpsed in the pages of the *Jewish Chronicle*.

She couldn't slow down. She didn't dare. However, there was a problem; it was becoming harder and harder to save her erring relatives from themselves. How her younger siblings would mock more observant teenagers, their davening during youth services at shul, the tefillin they would smuggle in their rucksacks to summer camp at the Royal Masonic School in Rickmansworth. It was not the Rubin way. Had they noticed hers? No one said a word. Then one day her father left a symptoms handbook open in her bedroom, with Obsessive Compulsive Disorder gently question-marked in pencil. Revelation. Appalled, enlightened, she simply stopped.

*   *   *

The adult Frances moves her foot away from her husband's, infinitesimally. Danger, to Jonathan, is something any fool can avoid, provided they keep

32

ropes and water in the boot, avoid underground car parks, extensively virus-check, measure carbon monoxide and stick an up-to-date list of emergency numbers on everyone's telephone. He has a monthly diary reminder to test the smoke-alarm batteries. He doesn't lie awake visualizing his siblings in a cluttered inferno, wrenching at the rotten sash windows, breaking their necks in a newspaper avalanche in the rush to escape.

'It's just—it was quite an odd childhood,' she says into the darkness. 'Whatever you think.'

He is awake, despite appearances. His voice gives her a little shock. 'If you say so,' he mumbles. 'But you have to admit—'

'I'm not saying,' she offers, 'that it didn't have its moments . . .'

'Frances, your childhood was one big moment. Anyway,' he says as he turns on to his side, releasing a puff of stuffy air, 'going home is healthy. Bit of stability. Of course you enjoy it.'

There is a smile in his voice. They were made for each other, the Rubins and her husband. Isn't she lucky to have them both? Really, she should be the happiest woman alive.

*   *   *

A little later, after Claudia has tried every trick she knows, Norman falls asleep.

At last. Quiet and still gratifyingly supple, she eases herself from their seamy bed. She cannot think with him grumbling and fretting beside her and there is much to worry about. Her cold quiet alcove is calling to her. Even in the circumstances, it gives her relief.

33

She sits at her desk and listens to the settling of her house around her. How grim and damp and cheap it was, she thinks, when she first found it. The ancient River Fleet soaking the garden, the smelly old Heath bridge over the tracks, the roof caulked with buddleia and pigeon shit. Nobody else could see its potential as dormitory, banqueting hall, fortress, least of all Norman. He does not have her vision. Cleverly, she won him round.

One, it was huge, an embarrassment of space: a house to erase the cramped flats of their childhoods. His eyes had widened at every new bedroom. They would have no embroidered placemats from the old country here, she saw him thinking; no carefully preserved 1950s trolleybus maps and tragic little guides to English idiom. This house would be filled instead with light and colour, feeding the infant geniuses who would bear his name.

Two was geography. Gospel Oak, then so run down and menacing, is only ten minutes' walk from Hampstead village, home of the Etonians and Wykhamists who were his deadly foes. She knows he pictured himself there amongst them with her— queenly, decorative, covetable—by his side. He had believed that this house was merely the first step. They do not refer to that now.

Three, it overlooks the Heath. Raised as he was in Paddington, with a view of grey bridges and joyless ironmongers, he enjoys proximity to nature, within reason. The Lombardy poplars and London planes, the scent of water, make him feel that he has arrived.

Four, they saw it on her thirtieth birthday when

34

she, a crusader, a communicator, had achieved what very few other women had dared to try. Thanks to her charm, her brains and her determination to beat the dull male rabbis at their own game she was hauling them all—Norman, of the sideburns and glorious ideas, solemn Leo, fretful Frances and delicious Simeon, all toddler-belly and feral teeth—from West Fulham, a two-bedroom flat and an education rabbi's pittance, to glory. The misleadingly named New Belsize Liberal might only have offered the shortest possible contract, a subtly reduced woman's salary but, faced with her knowledge and her certainty, offered it they had. She was turning their life around. How could he refuse her on such a day? Particularly when the last affordable house they had seen, in Chalk Farm, had had hens in the kitchen?

And fifth, it contains a vast long-windowed bedroom, and bedrooms have always been very important to Norman. When she opened the door and led him in he gasped. It was only on moving-day that he looked more closely and discovered her secret: the alcove round the corner where she could work late to the sound of his breathing, cold and focused and absolutely alive.

*   *   *

Usually she needs nothing more than this: the bright pool of a desk lamp in the darkness, the stretched hungry centre of the night, the little sighs and turnings of someone nearby who loves her, resents her, wallowing in sleep while she goads herself on. Even at her most difficult moments this

35

sound has strengthened her; husband, sisters, being left behind.

Now, however, she listens to his breathing and feels no comfort. She cannot work. She climbs back into bed and, tired as she is, she cannot sleep either. How can she, knowing that Leo is out there in the cold and dark? None of the prayers, no ritual for the comforting of troubled Jews can help tonight and, oh God, the meetings and visits ahead, the service on Friday night, however high her head, however sweet they are.

She must pray. She buries deep into almost forty years of knowledge and retrieves, of all things, the old-fashioned Service for the Redemption of the Firstborn, which she has endured for so many other families but, naturally, scorned for her son. She imagines the money held above Leo's little fluffy head, reciting the words with which she claims him: May this child enter Life, Law, the fear of Heaven. And then, because she can't face the bit about nuptial canopies, she fast-forwards to the blessing she longs to give him again, the one which, every Friday night, makes her eyes sting: May the Lord bless you and keep you. May the Lord's face shine upon you and be gracious to you. May the Lord's face be turned to you and give you peace.

Lord, she thinks, wiping the tears away, thinking of Norman: enough already. Bring him back.

It is lust, of course—she knows all about that. But for her own son to have put it first, before even family, is inconceivable. There is an ache in her heart because of him. It is, in its own way, reassuring, evidence that she feels as a mother should. The wedding fiasco has shaken her confidence. She does not want doubt, or change, or

36

horrible truths about the dark little wills of her children. She had always thought that if the surface were perfect, the rest would follow. Could she have been wrong?

The house is too quiet. Panic feeds in the dark. For God's sake, she thinks, what's wrong with you?

She turns over, freeing the flesh which has wedged itself beneath her arm. She has not examined her breasts this month, or the last. She loves them and so, with every passing year, she grows more frightened of what she might find. Death, however, is one of the many subjects she will not allow herself to discuss or even consider. No one has ever guessed how much she fears it, however many sickbeds and stonesettings she attends, the bereaved relatives embraced in cemetery car parks. Even now the very idea is speeding up her heart; it bangs on her breastbone impertinently. She makes herself take a deep slow breath, then another. As a girl she fantasized about, among other things, a seamless body made of steel, tight with perfection. But now here she is, full of rust at fifty-five, with much still to achieve and only two decades, if that, to do it in.

*   *   *

A cold wind is beginning to blow in from over the Heath, rattling the broken roof tiles. A long night train clatters past the end of the garden, then another. It is no use. She will not sleep. Her thoughts have turned, as lately they have begun to do, to money.

She grew up poor. There is no shame in this, or in self-betterment, as long as, from the outside, it

37

looks easy. Nothing is more unattractive than a struggling immigrant; nothing except her father, swaggering around Portobello while his wife and daughters bargained for bruised fruit. Her lip curls when she thinks of him, the hollow man of means.

Yet despite her hatred of the penny-pinching days, they are returning. When she closes her eyes she sees only bank statements: not only the wedding, an investment she could ill afford, but the astonishing sums paid out monthly for the roof, the subsidence and bubbling paint; the car Sim drains dry; the keys poor Emily lost, again; the women to whom she gives five hundred pounds a week to wipe her father's chin and pretend they understand his accent; the secret handouts to her sisters; the consoling treats for her younger children and the cash they require simply to exist; the too-few hours of cleaning she has tried and failed to do without; the train fares; the hair dye and clothes and makeup on which, at her age, a woman relies; the heat and light; the donations to the Carpathian League, the Mobile Library Service, the Immigrant Women's Shelter, the Israeli Peace Corps, the Home for Aged Jews and almost everywhere else; the endless insurance on which Norman insists; the expensive local shops and hopeless elderly tradesmen whom she supports because somebody must; the bank loans; and, most shockingly, the amount they seem to spend on the essentials, the abundant feeding of children and guests which is surely the point of it all.

Meanwhile the monthly paid-in column is down to this:

—seven thousand pounds, before tax, from the

shul.

—another four hundred or so, after tax, from the opinion pieces she writes at night, the prestigious but poorly paid lectures and modest library payments for her old books, set texts all over the world, as if that helps.

—here and there, a hundred pounds for one of Norman's book reviews. Unlike his brother, who was made to learn ophthalmology and will never forgive him for it, Norman was raised to be the educated man of culture his father would have been in another Vienna. However, he had hated students, hated Birkbeck and so when he hit fifty they had agreed that she would provide and he could leave. Theirs is not a confessional marriage. Of course she cannot admit that she was wrong.

—nothing else.

*   *   *

Norman is a dead weight beside her. Something, larger than a bird, scrabbles over the roof. There is hope but only that, not certainty. Their future depends on her new book's reception: on her reinvention as a family goddess, the soul of the nation, ripe for the papers to fall in love with one last time. When Leo comes back as, please God, he must, she will have to explain the importance of credibility. Even apart from her own views on setting a moral example, on fidelity however much she flirts, one thing is certain. Her elder son cannot be a home-breaker, simple as that.

FOUR

No one has rung Frances since yesterday morning and it is now three days since Leo's disappearance. Their silence means that he is lost, or dead, or worse. It is better to know. So she waits until her mother will have left for her Wednesday moaners' clinic and then, because he can be trusted not to cry, she dials her father.

Uncharacteristically, he answers at once.

'My God,' Frances says, 'what's wrong?'

'What's wrong? Nothing's wrong. Why, what's wrong with you?'

'It's . . . Leo, has he—?'

'No. Anyway, shouldn't you be working?'

'Er—well, yes. I *have* been,' she begins. 'Dad, the baby was up at two and five and twenty to seven. Please don't start.'

She can hear him scratching his beard in disappointment. He thinks she spends her working life having lunches and laughing at authors like him. 'You'll never make it if you spend your time chatting,' he tells her. 'Can't this wait?'

'I wanted to know the latest.' She is refusing to be irritated. Given his arteries, every conversation may be their last. 'So anyway, vy did you rush to the phone like that?' she asks, because usually nothing cheers him more than the accent he escaped from. 'Vot are you doing?'

He does not answer. Her tricks are not working. In desperation she exhumes a joke from childhood: Norman as sleeper, the Soviet agent time forgot. 'Are you awaiting instructions?' she asks.

40

The bristly sound stops short. 'I have no idea,' he says, sounding oddly formal, 'what you're talking about.'

'But we used to pretend . . . you know.'

'Nothing is going on! Where did you get that idea? What a nonsense. Do I interfere in your business? I'm perfectly entitled to answer the phone in my own—'

'Calm down. I didn't mean whatever you thought . . . What *did* you think?'

There is a long, dense silence. 'Oh,' he says at last. 'Right. Yes. I see.'

'What?'

'Nothing. Nothing. I just misunderstood.'

'Hold on,' she says. 'Something's up, isn't it? Has Leo—'

'No,' says her father. 'Not Leo. Don't get excited. I promise, Bubeleh, everything is fine.'

*   *   *

So where is Leo? Leo is in heaven. Helen Baum is lying on her side before him, naked on a big white hotel bed, and as he strokes her, he marvels. She is a thing of beauty and she is here, with him. Incredible, but he must try not to show his amazement. Again and again he moves a hand, recognizably *his* hand, over her long neck, her satiny shoulder, her slenderly curving back.

They are in Edinburgh, the coldest, wettest, least Jewish place they could think of in a hurry. However, despite the guilt about what they have done, despite the oppressively quiet tea rooms, it is perfect. No days were ever like these, sliding over icy pavements further into love. No nights were

41

ever so illuminating. Here he has been truly
certain, for the first time in his life.

* * *

Just after seven on Saturday evening, at the
miserable nadir of the children's bedtime, the
phone in Frances's hallway rings and rings and
rings. She stumbles towards it, gripping her furious
wet baby around his shiny stomach, noticing
another patch of mould above the fanlight. From
the kitchen comes the sound of escalating warfare:
a scuffle, the hiss of a threat. How long can she
justify staying away?

She picks up the receiver, braced as always for
the worst.

'Sis!'

'Oh God, not now—'

'He's here,' whispers Em dramatically. 'Now. In
the kitchen.'

The baby roars. She puts him, bare-bottomed,
on the carpet. 'You're joking.'

'He's been in *Scotland*,' says Em, who does not
travel. NW3 is world enough for her. 'I can't
believe it. Do you think he's . . . changed?'

The baby has wriggled precariously close to the
stairs, leaving a glistening perfectly shaped turd
behind him. She begins to clear up the mess at
once, to earn her escape. Kitchen towel and baby
wipes, however, are not enough. She retrieves a
bent aluminium spoon from beneath the kitchen
sink and scrapes at the carpet fibres.

Jonathan, sensing a Rubin update, has followed
her. He observes the fluffy faecal purée
dispassionately. 'You should go straight over,' he

says.

'Are you sure?'

'Of course.' He wipes milk from his son's soft chin with a crooked finger. 'In fact it might be better, me putting them to bed. The variety, I mean.'

She gives the girls bright goodnight kisses, as a stepmother should. Back in the hallway, Jonathan bends at the knees to rescue her gloves from the poo-patch, little Max clamped to his hip like a toy koala. When she turns to wave goodbye, rather than holding out his arms to his mother, he snuggles a little closer.

*   *   *

How quickly she pedals; how relieved she is. Nevertheless, storm clouds have gathered over Behrens Road. Simeon is standing in the kitchen in a brown knitted hat and precarious tracksuit bottoms, smelling hungover. She watches him uncork a half-empty wine bottle with his teeth. After a respectful pause, she speaks.

'What've you heard?'

He gives a scornful half-shrug.

She tries again: 'Isn't it great about, you know. What a relief.'

'Yeah. How super. Mum's been bricking herself and ickle barrister decides to drop in.'

Frances nods stiffly, as if face to face with a bear. Unlike Leo, she has learned not to argue with him. 'I'd better . . . I'll, er,' she says, eyes averted from the claws and matted fur and, smiling vaguely, backs away towards the sitting room.

43

*   *   *

Leo is wearing a thick grey polo neck more interesting than his other clothes. There are lines around his mouth that she has never noticed before, like those of an older, smilier man. A pathetic little holdall lies at his feet. After the embraces, when Em's tears have been dried and they have returned to the now-safe kitchen for something to eat ('He's thinner,' murmurs Em. 'Mum was right'), he shyly explains the situation.

'She's taking over the flat. We agreed. And the car.'

'Who?' asks Em, taking another bite of strudel.

'Naom—you know. My thingy. Former fiancée. It's the least I can do.'

'You spoke?' Frances says. 'Thank God, because her parents won't put her on to me and . . .'

'At work. It was horrible. So—'

'You are sweet,' Em says, in the indulgent voice with which she talks of her siblings' petty concerns. 'All that arranging.'

'Where will you live?' asks Frances.

'Here,' he says, holding her gaze so that neither of them can look in the direction Sim has gone.

'Really?'

'I have to,' he tells her. 'For a while. So I can keep paying the mortgage, until . . . She can't do it, not by herself.' His brow is furled with worry, like a big velvety dog in pain. 'It's only temporary. I don't know what else to do.'

Frances touches his shoulder clumsily. They are almost the same height, as shul acquaintances like to remind them. 'Why would you do anything else?' asks Em, tearing open a packet of crumpets.

44

'Home at last. Mum's always said you should. Frances, your turn next.'

* * *

Norman creeps around his study, treading carefully to avoid being heard below. He is searching for strengthening poetry: MacNeice; Larkin; Vickers. However, he cannot settle. Relieved as he is by the return of his first-born, k'nayn hora tu-tu-tu, it is extremely difficult to know how to behave. Should he admonish him for self-indulgence? Use his presumed rejection by Helen Baum to demonstrate hubris? There is, surely, a moral lesson to be derived from all this. It is simply a question of establishing what it might be.

Besides, Norman has a problem. He needs privacy. The others rarely trouble him. His wife's evenings and weekends are not her own. Emily no longer comes in search of hole reinforcements and highlighters for her audition scripts; Simeon emerges chiefly after dark. Leo, however, is clever and quiet and studious. It could be a disaster. The last thing his father needs now is another pair of eyes.

* * *

They install Leo in his old bedroom, among his Einstein posters and model dinosaurs. As Em inexpertly straightens the duvet Sim had borrowed, now reeking of smoke and unthinkably stained, it is easy to imagine never referring to the rabbi's wife again. However, when he and his elder sister

45

are left alone at last, he sits on the edge of his bed and looks up at her and Frances realizes that, for the first time in his life, dear wooden Leo actually wants to talk.

'It was wonderful,' he whispers. Two perfect tears start up out of his eyes and slide down to the fascinating squareness of his jaw.

'Oh, sweetheart,' she says, sliding uncomfortably towards him on the sagging little mattress. Her own eyes burn. 'Don't.'

'I can't not . . . I can't bear . . .'

She glances nervously at the door. 'What? What can't you bear?'

'I can't bear that I did it . . . and to Naomi. What a horrible, bastardy thing to do. Bastardly, rather.'

'No, it wasn't,' says Frances untruthfully. 'Well . . . but, you know, you had to.'

'I did have to. But I could have not, not—'

'I know,' she says.

'You do know I love her. Don't you?'

'Naomi? Well—'

'No. Helen. I . . . I . . .' He takes a crumpled handkerchief from his pocket and jabs it fiercely against his eyes. She cannot put her arms around him, here on his bed, with her little breasts and his big shoulders, so instead she takes the cloth and wipes tears awkwardly from his cheeks, his big but not unattractive nose, his big tense chin. His chest is heaving like a child's.

'I don't want to give her up,' he says.

'But—'

'But I have to. I know. She has a hus, husband, a son and a husband and we can't, well . . . It's Mum's work, his work, mine and hers, all of it. It's . . . sensible, I suppose.'

46

'Yes.'

'But I don't *want* to. Oh God, I can't—'

Frances wipes her own eyes with the handkerchief. She breathes in tear-soaked damp cotton: the secret scent of her childhood and, she suspects, of his. 'What are you going to do?'

He frowns. His profile is like a curly bracket, definite and tight. 'I don't know.'

'You can't stay here with Sim, can you? He's . . . he's very volatile.'

They both know. She puts her hand on his and they sit together for a few minutes longer: the good children, at least until now.

FIVE

'Well,' says Claudia's guest of honour. 'Everything they say is true.'

At that, Claudia feels herself begin to lighten. For the first time since Leo's return she allows herself to hope that the worst is over. In celebration of this, although she would never say so, she has persuaded Rabbi David to take her Friday night service, releasing her for a Shabbat dinner: a good one. So, in addition to a selection of loyal regulars and the usual bewildered newlyweds from shul, she has been making use of her Rolodex. In particular, she has invited Robin Buckley of the *Sunday Times* and his Sri Lankan architect boyfriend. Why not? To be witnessed in her element, with barely a month to go before publication, cannot possibly hurt.

And it is working. She has been watching him

47

watch her. When he arrived late, to be met with a wall of laughter and manly embraces and sociable argument; when Norman passed him the kiddush cup with a booming 'Am*ain*'; when she and Norman blessed their adult children in turn, kissing them as if they were still edible toddlers, not stubbled and tired; his blue eyes goggled with the usual anthropological alarm. But it was at her moments, singing the b'rachot alone in the candlelight, that she saw how thoroughly she had him, ablaze with curiosity and complicated lust.

'Would you like some more artichokes?' she asks. 'The servants have been de-whiskering them since dawn.'

He takes the spoon greedily as she tries to remember how artichokes grow: on a vine? From the soil? In any case, they require the seasonal b'racha; as she recites it silently she sees that, across the table, most of her guests are doing the same. How an abundance of food always cheers them: curvaceous challah and black Carmelli's rye; watercress soup to fill them up; vegetables roasted singly and in radical combinations; four lemony roast chickens and a huge nameless fish, virtually a dolphin, obtained by Simeon from God knows where and cooled on the garden step; stinking pounds of Camembert and Gorgonzola and those exorbitant lemon tarts loved by her younger children; figs and halva; artful jugs of tap water; and wine provided, thankfully, by previous guests.

However, although there is nothing she enjoys more than Friday nights, the combination of spiritual sustenance and social gratification, she cannot entirely relax. His eyes are still hungry, consuming them all. So many people do not want

48

her to be successful: the competitive; the bigoted; the envious; those who insist all English Jews must keep their heads down, in that crouching self-loathing way she cannot stand. Then there are the under-rabbis with their petty divisions of pastoral care, their resentment about her public profile, as if without her concerts and book groups and lecture tours, her dramatic sermons, this shul would have a single new member, let alone its stars. There is the new generation of woman rabbis, unfrumpy, feminist, charming to the last. She is not unique any more. They are hungry to dethrone her. If he has not heard about the wedding yet, he will.

So they must seduce him. Tonight, at least, the family magic is working. The Rubins are, after all, used to being on display, never more relaxed than when in the company of strangers, like actors at last allowed on stage. Photographs of their childhoods have illustrated each of their mother's stages: foxy feminist don; racy rabbi; moral crusader; mother to her flock. This time, however, it is different. Her book—

'So tell me, Rabbi Rubin,' says Robin Buckley, raising his voice against the roar. 'About your book.'

Claudia smiles. As ever, she and the press are one. 'Well,' she says. 'What do you know?'

'I know that it's about family,' he tells her. 'And that it's going to be huge.'

'I bet you say that to all the rabbis,' she replies but her hand is clenched with excitement. She is proud of her book. What no one seems to have realized, particularly since the wedding, is how badly she needs it to work. 'So, shall I tell you what the blurb says?'

'Go on.'

'Not that I wrote it, of course: "In part a selectively revealing memoir, full of complicated feasts and wry nostalgia and her own mistakes, and part a moral and ethical handbook for families of the new millennium." I'm the matriarch everyone thinks they need.'

'So it's not exclusively for Jews?'

'Of course not,' she says, with a look. 'Although obviously the Orthodox will denounce it, which will be wonderful for sales. But everyone needs encouragement, don't they? To think about other people, have the courage of their beliefs?'

'How, given their inner Oedipuses, could they not?'

She gives him her most knowing smile. However, as he turns to Frances, who does not understand how the press works, who is likely to admit all her authors are socially hopeless dullards unfit for interview, she begins to worry again. Could one of the children reveal something dangerous? Perhaps, thinks Claudia, I should have put him beside lovely Sita Joel.

*   *   *

Fear is nibbling at the edges of her pleasure. She will not let it. The sound of noisy enjoyment is a tonic, or used to be. She must bask in the flattering candlelight, the overlapping conversations, the speed at which the plates are being emptied. Besides, for the first time in weeks, all her children are here, as they should be. It is almost like old, less worrying, times.

50

So, are they behaving? First she checks on Norman, who is never much of a problem. He is as lovingly, grudgingly, wedded to failure as to her. He once told her that he thinks of their marriage as being like that grown-together pair of trees they often pass on their little walks around Parliament Hill. He has never noticed that one of them is clearly stronger, straighter. It is a private act of love that she has not told him so.

Now he is reconstructing, with salt dishes and wine spots, his favourite Stalin joke: there is the old-woman face, there the little lecture on Yiddish inflection ('*You* are the true heir of Lenin? *I* should apologize?') for the Buckley boyfriend, as if he cares. She sees Norman sense her gaze upon him. He glances in her direction and so, because it is what he would expect of her, she rolls her eyes and looks away.

She is trying hard not to think about Leo. The only way to deaden the shock waves, she has decided, to minimize the damage to her reputation and her shul, is to pretend it never happened. Norman may call this denial, but it works. In any case, ever since his homecoming Leo has been himself again. She can almost pretend, unless on a gruelling hospital visit, say, or struggling for sermon inspiration, that February's nightmare of humiliation and worry is beginning to fade. He has clearly given that woman up, as was his duty to both congregations, to his family, to Claudia herself. He is once again an elder son to be proud of. She can be sure of him.

Simeon is laughing loudly, but that is Simeon. People have always asked questions, stupid questions about drink and worse, but she ignores

51

them. So what if he is not as community-minded as he might be, if none of his creative projects have yet quite come off? He is her baby and she would not change him for the world.

She glances at Emily, who after recent wobbles—a failed audition, presumably, although she would never ask—has returned to her most purringly pettable self. She sees her look at her watch, then look again. Timekeeping is not her forte. Then she wipes the back of her hand absent-mindedly over her breast in its beautiful new black jumper, the gorgeous purple bra Claudia bought her just visible at the V, and smiles to herself.

'All right?' whispers Claudia because, with poor Emily, one never knows.

'Fantastic.'

No signs of tears, no sudden headaches: nothing to worry about. 'Are you having fun?' Claudia mouths.

'Of course I am, dear Rube,' and, simply at the sound of that childhood name, that proof of love, her mother feels herself relax.

Frances, on the other hand, is neither relaxed nor relaxing. She has always been this way, all elbows and seriousness, less succulent than the others, like a disappointing section of tangerine. There are spots of something on her tired blouse. Her hair needs urgent attention; she should go to the hairdresser Claudia and Emily always use. With that thin face she needs something more flattering, not those sawn-off messy waves.

I am, thinks Claudia, only trying to help you. Must this be so hard?

At Frances's age she had already taken on Oxford's smiling misogynists, her Rabbinics

52

teachers at Leo Baeck, the doubting matriarchs of Fulham and beaten them all. Once she had dreamed of founding a dynasty, sharp-witted daughters and granddaughters advancing knowledge, defiantly saving the world exactly like her. However, the closest Frances has ever come was a long teenage phase of impossible frumness: suspicious rituals in the lavatory, berets indoors. So obsessive—and now so bizarrely resistant. With her rented flat and her anxious face she has not proved to be her mother's mirror, after all.

*   *   *

Claudia shifts in her chair. Anxiety is pointless but there is no leeway for disaster, none whatsoever. They must all shine, all be a credit to her if this book of hers is to succeed. And it must, because the alternative is failure, and that she cannot bear. Everyone thinks they know her story: how she began as a young and fierce classics tutor at St Anne's, clever but, even then, no obedient little don, who met her first sniffy Hebraicist and decided to beat him at his own game. What they do not know is that she grew up with nothing: no Friday nights, no grounding in the Torah, no community apart from other silent scornful women like her mother, united by a shared language and a competitive interest in yeast dumplings. Who, from those origins, would not want to give their children another world? Who, having known her father, would not develop a strict moral code: think of what he would have done, and do the opposite?

The problem is that, however vigilant she is, there is scope for disaster.

53

She needs distraction. She presses a poppy seed on to her tongue but the taste evokes only thoughts of war, of hidden starving children, of whom to feed how many unnourishing seeds. There is a dark place in her mind and it is so easy to slide down into it; past her cold childhood bedroom, her father's empty chair, the damp sweet smell of candlewick. The room goes dark.

'Rabbi Rubin?' Robin Buckley says again.

*   *   *

'Stop it,' Frances tells her elder stepdaughter. 'You'll fall.'

'What?'

'The rocking. People . . . children hurt themselves like that all the time,' she says weakly. 'And you'll break it. Claudia will mind.'

'She won't. Anyway, I'm not.'

'I saw you.'

'Am not.'

'Oh, for God's sake.'

Rebecca's lips set. Her sister scowls in sympathy. Frances will never be able to deal with them. They look to their father for rescue, wondering, like her, when he will notice that she cannot do this. She is neither a mother nor a friend to them but rather an unwanted and interfering older sister, correcting, constraining, all the time. It is as if the fierce sentimental love she feels for her father, her elder brother, clots when she faces children; she does not know how she is supposed to be. It happens with Max. With the girls, because they so openly prefer their father and shrink from her, it has been less easy to love them than she

54

thought. Easier, in fact, to hate.

She cannot do motherhood. It is as simple as that. No one else can get enough of them. Her husband hurries home after work; her sister, if not boyfriending or tired, takes the girls and Max on subsidized trips to the Rubins' favourite café, where they are petted and given mugs of cappuccino foam. Her mother, crouching open-armed, adores everything about them; their lavatorial habits, their tiny bite-marks on apples, their scent of ammonia and scalp and Plasticine. Other women Frances knows read submissions as they walk along the street, set their alarms early to check contracts, solely in order to prolong their hours of playing time. Children are a delight, everyone says so.

*   *   *

She has been thinking, in the rare moments when she is not tending to her authors' egos or her baby's bowels or the understandably bitter little hearts of her stepdaughters, about what is wrong and has realized that she has nobody to consult. She cannot, of course, tell Claudia, the perfect grandmother, or Norman, who would be disappointed, or Em; despite all the noise and emotion, the discussion of painful subjects is not the Rubin way. However, although she knows endless mothers her age from shul or her stepdaughters' school, her real friends are still childless, suddenly well dressed, affluent, rosy with sex, living lives of unimaginable freedom and unable to comprehend hers. Only two have reproduced, and they are so cheerfully competent,

55

breastfeeding as they answer the door, lovingly disciplining toddlers, that she tries to avoid them. Besides, she is not in the habit of confiding.

She has looked online furtively at work, certain that at any moment one of her childless partners will stride into her office and catch her at it as if she is masturbating or sobbing, either of which they would prefer. She has found chat-rooms of such infernal complexity, sites so filled with sugar or streaked with the bloodiest despair, that her mind has shrunk to a little hatch of baby-harm and cake-baking and she does not want either. She has skulked near Self Help in bookshops; searched through Norman's family health manuals for references to agonizing maternal loneliness; smiled hopefully at harassed yet stylish women around the edge of the Parliament Hill sandpit: all in vain.

Once she had assumed that she would simply improve: begin to enjoy looking after them, feel manageable levels of fear and worry, invent games and initiate baking, know instinctively how strict, how kind to be. However, she has not. Nothing is changing; if anything, it is becoming worse. As her panic grows, shame helps her hide it. Truly, no one can know.

*   *   *

'So, Norman,' says Betty Lister. She married cousin Petey in December 1965 after a long dalliance with Norman, whom she dumped outside a night club on the Bayswater Road. Norman suspects she still regrets it. There is a bitterness to her, a beadiness; she knows she made the wrong choice. Petey may have become a very successful

56

hosiery manufacturer but, fond as Norman is of him, no one can doubt who has the fire in his soul.

Once he enjoyed baiting her. Lately, however, he is trying to be careful. He cannot risk having Betty Lister on his trail.

'What are you working on now?' she asks.

'Me? You know me. The same little books.' He makes his voice louder than normal. Claudia is close by and twice as sharp as she.

'But what?' Betty insists. She is trying to taunt him. 'I know your educated-man schtick but poets aren't exactly big business, are they? Surely there must be something . . . well, worthwhile?'

Norman, caught between fear and gurning delight, struggles to master his facial muscles. Time will tell, Betty Lister, he thinks as he pretends to inspect his fork. Time will most certainly tell.

*   *   *

Other people are warm right the way through, thinks Frances: full of love and interest and involvement, with tiny healthy wisps of annoyance. But I am freezing cold inside, burning and brittle on the surface. Could I be turning into a baked Alaska? What is wrong with me?

The others are so obviously enjoying themselves. Her husband has been gleaming with pride since he was allowed to carve the chickens.

'So how was the inter-synagogue quiz?' he asks his mother-in-law. Jonathan Edelstein has been a fixture at this table ever since he was a friendly local-history teacher with a nice young wife. Frances, eight years and a lifetime younger, had been simply the welcoming daughter, her mother's proxy, as uninterested in him as he was in her. He has been worn smooth and utterly unobjectionable. The Rubins love him. They barely notice him. He is their perfect match.

'Did Orthodox rabbis abseil on to the stage to stop you?' he asks. 'Bet you got all the answers.'

'Jonathan,' she says, 'what would I do without you?'

Thank God you don't have to, thinks Frances. She tries to catch her father's eye but Norman is arguing with Petey Lister about which of the Queen's sons seems most Jewish, and fails to notice her. This should be, as anyone would tell her, a delightful family occasion. Every aspect—the endless multigenerational hugging and kissing, the presence of happily dazed strangers, the sense that history is being made every time Claudia blurs God's gender—delights and inspires.

So what is wrong with Frances? She was born and raised as a perfect example but has not turned out as she should. Today she feels demented with irritation, like Rumpelstiltskin. If she stamped her foot she would burst through the floor. Are other families this pleased with themselves? Jonathan, the ardent convert, thinks the Rubins are right to be. What about their ridiculousness, their oddnesses, their frightening unfitness for the world?

If only she could stop fantasizing about sleep and novels, and make herself relax. The guests are basking, as if their presence alone is proof that they are loved. Her stepdaughters are not fighting. Baby Max is sucking quietly on a piece of challah, lids drooping, in his father's arms. And her siblings

58

are being themselves, uproariously. However, ever since this evening's tidying and cooking, her attempts to marshal them like an incompetent nursery helper, she can barely stand to look at them. The characteristics at which the family laughs fondly, or simply ignores, seem spotlit this evening: Leo's inability to ask polite questions of the first-timers or help clear up; Sim's hyperactive charm, the endless mythologizing about his novels and photography and daring escapades; the ongoing pretence that Em is frail and innocent and about to be discovered, her extraordinary statements about what constitutes a busy day.

But no one says anything, because of Claudia. She is this evening wearing one of her many sexy dresses, tight, midnight-blue and silky, which clings to her big breasts and hips and belly like wet sealskin. She could be a figurehead for whom sailors go to their deaths. A moment ago she brought in more bread, holding up the board as if she had ground the wheat herself. The guests, already high on Sim's mango daiquiris, were transfixed.

Frances alone remains unmoved. Here she sits, apparently still resembling a good daughter, her skin so tight with annoyance it could crackle into scales.

'So then,' she hears her father saying, 'I walked on to the stage. And I looked out past that first row of students and so forth, the lot I'd seen from the wings—'

'Go on,' grins Petey Lister. His bushy white hair trembles with anticipation. This is one of Norman's most popular stories. 'And then what?'

Norman's expression is comically baleful. The

sadness in his dark eyes, the deep lines around his mouth and silver muzzle make him look like a tragic bloodhound in need of sleep. 'And there,' he goes on, 'in the darkness, where I'd sensed my huge rapt audience waiting . . .'

'*Longing* to be told all about Rex Kenyon's inner voices—'

'That's right . . . who do you think I saw?'

'Who?'

'No one.'

How they laugh. Benji, Claudia's most sycophantic godson, is beating the table with his fists. Stony-faced, Frances watches. 'No one,' he tells them. 'Not a sausage.'

'So who were you up against?' prompts Petey Lister.

'Who was I up against? Only John Updike.'

'And no one had told him!'

'You think anyone had *told* me?' He lifts his shaggy eyebrows in mock-hopelessness. 'That front row consisted of the meshuggener Biography organizer, my introducer, my thanker, the lighting assistant and . . . oh, and someone who'd expected John Updike.'

'He got you?'

'Exactly. He got me. Oy, was he disappointed.' Norman scratches his grizzled beard in humorous resignation. Then, at Petey's urging, he begins a hilarious new version of the faith-healing joke from Sandy Tudor, which Frances has already heard three times. He never changes, she thinks with an uncomfortable edge of pity.

Then something horrible occurs to her. My God. Perhaps he does. She had forgotten that strange telephone conversation, his quickness to answer, his caginess. Is he ill? Something is wrong, as she has always known it would be. How could the others not have noticed? Why has her mother not taken better care of him?

*   *   *

Claudia is leaning close to Robin Buckley: close enough to lick his face. Her enviable skin is gleaming. Fatness has firmed her, like a statue. It is impossible not to covet that tight jawline, the pad of plumpness beneath her chin. She is saying, in that special emphatic voice she uses for gay men, 'I mean, have you *seen* her footwear? Please. Crêpe soles. I'm serious. She *rambles*.'

Robin Buckley giggles. 'You can't say that,' he exclaims. 'She's a Dame. A pillar of the community.'

'Quite. And a lesbian. Ask her husband, he should know.'

Petey Lister leans across his neighbour. He has three successful sons. His life is sweet. 'Isn't she,' he asks Frances for the ten thousandth time, 'wonderful?'

Frances is grinding her teeth. Her limbs are squashed uncomfortably; the air is soupy with boasting and insincerity and candle wax. Her lips are sore. Even her scalp hurts. She glances at her husband and notices, only then, that he and the baby have vanished, leaving behind them a careful pile of deadly fish bones, a bottle lid and one pale green sock.

'Excuse me,' she says to her mother's friends, who smile as only the middle-aged can smile at a young mother. Drowning in niceness, she pushes past them and heads upstairs.

SIX

Frances finds Jonathan outside her parents'
bedroom, a finger to his lips. The air is scented
subtly with mouse. Electric candle-flames blur in
his spectacle lenses. At the sound of her footsteps
Max stirs.

'Ga,' he mumbles. Or it could be: 'Pa.'

Jonathan smiles fondly. He would know what
the word was. She, the mother, can hardly ask.

'Did he—will he sleep?' she asks.

'I think so. He dropped off at nine twenty-five,'
he says. 'So he should have eight hours, give or
take. Give or take.'

He is wearing an old green jumper, matted at
the elbows. Because he is, according to Sim's strict
hierarchies, very nearly as good as family, his
numerous fashion errors can be overlooked.
Nevertheless, he is drab in the half-light, with baby
snot on his sleeve and a dot of yoghurt at the
corner of his mouth. She ticks off his good points
automatically, to remind herself:

He is a freakishly good father, a kind man, a
thoughtful husband. He does not shout at her, or
expect her to iron. He is never late.

He truly loves his in-laws. He fits in quite
naturally, cooking and telling jokes as they do, but
with exactly the right degree of deference.
('Probably wants to shag us all,' says Sim.) He fully
supports their beliefs about telephoning and
visits and makes Frances conform. On their

honeymoon—a week driving around Normandy reading aloud from guidebooks, while his daughters, at Claudia's house, had the time of their lives—he was the one who obeyed her parents' instructions, ringing before and after every leg of the journey, avoiding dubious pâtés and, because of Le Pen, rural areas. His own mother lives in suburban peace on Swain's Lane, where the freshly creosoted fences advertise talks by local historians and her neighbours are dignified, civilized, if too damaged to be truly content. He would join her there if he could afford it, in a house connected by well-sanded trapdoors. In the meantime, the Rubins are an ideal alternative.

He also, unlike her, knows exactly how to please them. He has read all Norman's remaindered biographies; he understands the calibrations of chivalrous flattery that Claudia needs. He takes Em's symptoms seriously and helps spread the myth that, like her younger brother, she is a creative prodigy simply waiting to be discovered. He is also Sim's fall-guy and cheerleader, co-archivist for his sacred collection of Rubiniana: an endless, pointless, heavily financed task. He even upholds Rubin traditions, producing little laminated song cards for Shabbat guests, walking his daughters all the way to Heath Hurst Primary because that is where Claudia's children went. Frances thinks of him as the true Rubin and herself as the difficult daughter-in-law. How relaxing, how releasing, that would be.

He is practical. This, too, helps them love him. They need it, while pretending that it is merely an amusingly alien hobby, like orienteering or exhibiting leeks. When a bookshelf collapses or a window sticks everyone has to pretend that Sim will fix it. The books crumple, the rain blows in and, eventually, Jonathan is secretly summoned, with his collection of wood glues and neatly ordered nails, and no one refers to it again.

He is like them: neither a so-called Anglo-Jew with class delusions, nor a glamorous Sephardi nor, God forbid, a frummer, with rude Israeli relatives and sisters in pancake wigs. Like them he believes unthinkingly in a cross but vaguely humorous God, and if he knows how entirely Frances has failed to believe, he has said nothing. A rabbi's daughter, particularly Claudia's, has considerable leeway with the Lord.

Best of all, he is sensitive. He has suffered. His first wife, kinder and more beautiful than Frances, died, of course, of breast cancer, three years ago. How vital, the community agreed, that they find him someone soon, as they brought him a lifetime's supply of brisket and chicken soup and drew up Shabbat rotas. Then Claudia started bumping him into her elder daughter: in shul in a suit; with his sweet girls in a double buggy; at her own kitchen table, where she fed him his lines. When he made the obvious, hurried, next step, Frances, who had expected spinsterhood but hoped for Mr Knightley, was the only person in her wide acquaintance to be amazed.

*   *   *

'Are the girls all right?' whispers Jonathan.

'Oh . . . yes.' She tries to smile. 'I've . . . I'm a bit sick of it down there, to be honest,' she confides. 'Maybe I'm not in the mood.'

64

'Come on, love,' he murmurs, patting her hand on the banister. 'They're only being themselves.'

She keeps her hand where it is, with an effort. 'Well . . .' she says. There is a gust of laughter from downstairs. It pricks her on. 'Normal people aren't like this, though,' she says, 'are they? So . . . extreme? It's exhausting. Does it never bother you?'

'No. Not remotely.' His voice is unnaturally calm and low. He is, she realizes, trying to stop her from shouting by example. 'They simply enjoy having people here,' he says. 'And *they* love it, the guests—'

'Yes, well,' she says darkly.

He gazes at his sturdy shoe: a kind father waiting for the tantrum to be over. Rein me in, she thinks. Shout back; agree; offer to carry me (and Max, mustn't forget Max) down the drainpipe and away from them all. Instead he waits, his dry fingers lying on her own, his Adam's apple dipping as he swallows.

'Did you ring the plumber?' he asks conversationally. 'We'll have to start looking at boilers. And there's definitely moisture under the girls' windowsill. Are we collecting my mother on Sunday? Oh, and Susannah needs new shoes again.'

It is like being smothered slowly, out of love. His list goes on: lost squash rackets and spelling books and hairline cracks and landlords and all the time she is thinking thoughts she should not be thinking, of accidents and rivers, peace at last.

She tries once more. 'This huge rotting house with bits falling off it . . . They're like a soap opera: all these hangers-on and idiots with bongos drifting

65

in and out, and fascinating bloody playwrights with perversions and no one to fix the loo seat . . . And it's as bad when there's no one here. More flouncing out and crying but just as bad. They can't do anything without showing off and drama and—'

'You're tired.'

'Well, yes,' she says. 'But you think so, don't you? I'm sure even you've said . . .'

He makes his demurring face. 'Well, no,' he says, reasonably. 'They're very good to me. I love them. And your mother is great. Shall we go back down?'

She feels her mind move away from him, as if she is lifting up a drawbridge. He smiles at her mildly from the other bank. The lives she had been aiming for—her father's brilliant biographical heir, a famously beautiful poet, a television pundit with multiple fields of expertise—have not happened and, she thinks now, perhaps she can live with this. But what she had always imagined were the two basic ingredients of happy adulthood, intellectual companionship and thrilling sex, are missing too.

'I'll just check on Max,' she says, as he would expect and he nods, satisfied.

*　　　*　　　*

Robin Buckley has picked up on something. He is, after all, a journalist. They are never fully tame. Claudia has seen him looking out for signs: Emily's flush, Leo's quietness, Norman's bitter little stories, as if any of it means anything, which it does not. Everything is fine. He may not see it but they are iron filings, all pointing in the same direction. They want what she wants. How could they not?

They will not let her down again.

Nevertheless, when Emily rushes back into the room from God knows where, she senses the need for action.

'Oh, Jonathan,' she says, quite coolly. It never does to spoil them, men, or children, or members of the congregation, and her son-in-law is pretty well all three. 'Have you two met?'

However, the moment he opens his mouth she sees from her star guest's expression that Jonathan is not the answer. He is too mild, too wholesome for Robin Buckley, who requires, as she does, something sharper. She turns the other way, towards her younger son.

'Simeon!' she calls. 'Come here, sweetheart.' If she and Simeon join forces, they are unstoppable. He hears the urgency in her voice, her golden boy, and so he comes.

'You've met, haven't you?' she asks Robin Buckley. 'That big photograph in the hall, that's one of his. He's very good.'

'So, Robster,' her son begins, 'are you ready for the next stage?'

'Which is?'

'Drinking the blood of Christian babies. Didn't you know?'

And, as mother and son laugh at his relief, Claudia reflects with pride on Simeon's talent for schmoozing. Is that not the perfect gift for one's children? To enable them to socialize and charm and give others pleasure, secure in the knowledge that their family is behind them, providing strength? Isn't that the best possible start in life?

Of course it is, she tells herself, as the conversation between Simeon and Robin Buckley grows ever more uproarious. She will not listen to the little pinching voice of doubt in her mind because she never does, she refuses to hear it, even as it grows louder.

*   *   *

Frances stands in the violet hush of her parents' room, watching the last of the rain. She has her back to the cot in case, she tells herself, Max wakes up and wants to play. The bedroom is warm and still. Unlike his sighing, snuffling half-sisters, he barely makes a sound. It is only by putting a hand on his fluffy hair or his fat foot that she can be certain he is alive.

But, although her job means that she barely sees him, and kissing those soft hot cheeks is surely what every mother longs for, she does not touch her son. She does not want to. She would so much rather that he stayed asleep, not needing to be dealt with. Even watching him sleeping does not come naturally to her.

This is not normal. She knows this. She worries that she will damage him, assuming that he is not already lying there cold with the cot death she visualizes so easily: her scream, the weeping, guests ushered white-faced into the street. But still she does not touch him. Another thin layer of guilt blows against the bars like a mosquito net, separating her from her baby.

Laughter comes again from the dining room. It is Claudia, whose idea of childcare during all those evenings and weekends serving her community had been cool-hearted Hilde, the ultra-competent refugee from the basement flat next door. None of the others seems to mind or even remember. If she had stroked *me* in my cot, she thinks, I would know how to be a mother. I would have absorbed the tenderness and tolerance and care. But she has ruined me and now I will ruin him.

She drifts over to the perfume-cluttered dressing table; the bed, heaped with dresses; her mother's mountainous desk. Claudia's possessions are sacred. Everyone else's are a free-for-all but no one, not even Sim, helps himself to hers. You want to bring her things, not take them. She sits like an Inca and receives tribute: jewelled gold, parrot feathers, the skins of her enemies.

Now Frances inspects the mantelpiece, where bowls of earrings and a vase of melodramatically dying white tulips compete for space with crimp-edged seventies snapshots of Claudia and Norman and their children, polo-necked, shaggy-fringed, like fierce forelocked ponies. They are all dark, all noticeably beautiful except, of course, for Frances, a plainer breed entirely, scrawnier, more easily startled, owl-eyed in scruffy plimsolls.

She looks like the perfect bluestocking, pure in mind and body. If they had known about the rest of it, thinks the adult Frances, the secret stewing world of storm-tossed cliffs and death and sex and poetry, would things have turned out differently? To think of the glorious passionate adulthood I looked forward to every night . . . well, now I know.

There is another, older, picture in the corner of the mirror: a family not yet at ease with their foreignness. Here are Gerald Simon, né Jaroslav Schulz, the handsome charmer with too much Brilliantine, his dead brother's pocket watch casually displayed; Valerie, née Veronka, wearing a

69

high-necked blouse and an air of chilly withdrawal; their two younger girls, difficult tiny Rose and schloompy disappointing Ruth, peering at the photographer with suspicious eyes. But look here at the very centre of the picture, like a strong sperm pushed towards the egg by its weaker peers. Here she is, dazzlingly straight-backed, gleaming with desirability and cleverness: Claudia Rosalind Simon, their pride, their salvation.

This photograph is not going in Claudia's book. The true past is closed. The less she will speak about it, the more certain her children are of the horrors below the surface, of their duty not to upset her in any way. The problem is that vacuums fill. Frances can barely sleep for bayoneted children and murdered great-uncles. Life feels almost too dangerous to bear.

'Hey,' says Em from the doorway. 'You look weird.' She is as delicate as their mother, but for vaguer reasons.

'No,' says Frances. 'Just tired.'

'Yeah, I'm exhausted, like, rushing around. Why are you up here?' Em is wearing a very long silvery-blue skirt with her tight black jumper. She is all breasts and waist and raspberry lips like Snow White or Rose Red, an innocent in the forest. 'I want you back downstairs. Where were you earlier, anyway?' she asks. 'I needed to talk to you. I left a message. I thought you'd come over.'

'In the day? I can't . . . I *work*,' she says and then, because she must, reins herself in from this most maddening of subjects. 'So what . . . why did you need me? Is something wrong?'

Em looks away. 'No. Things. So can you come down now?'

70

Frances follows her into the hall, past the dumping ground for Claudia's unwanted post: synagogue news sheets, cookery books, shtetl memoirs, hate mail, begging letters; a landslide of misery, threatening to pull her down. She concentrates on the back of her sister's silken head, her beautiful skull. If she cries, Em will take it personally.

'I'm going to the loo,' she says. 'I'll follow you.'

*   *   *

It only takes a minute of rolling her forehead on the calcified tiles, lowing softly like a calf, to pull herself together. She is a good elder daughter once more as she begins to squeeze her way past the seat-backs to her place, past Godson Benji's too-new corduroy collar, her mother's glossy hair, Sita Joel's jacket, very like one of Claudia's but in a duller shade. She puts her hand on her sister's hot shoulder as she forges past, reassuringly.

There is now an empty space beside Pru, a widowed schoolteacher famous for saving Sim from vodka poisoning at a bar-mitzvah party in 1985. She is one of the few non-shul friends Claudia still sees. Perhaps because of this, Frances always finds herself hoping for advice.

'So,' says Pru. 'Young Frances. How's life? Are you managing?'

Now, thinks Frances. Tell her! However, before she can speak, she sees that Leo is mouthing something at her from behind a portcullis of candlesticks and flowers. She shakes her head at him impatiently and turns back to Pru. However, her saviour has been waylaid by Robin Buckley,

71

who is discussing the attractiveness of their fellow guests.

'Over there, for example,' he says. 'Don't tell me that's not the most gorgeous man you've ever seen.'

He can't mean here, thinks Frances. Then she sees that she is mistaken. Someone new is now sitting beside her sister, tall and dark with curly hair, cut very short, enormous lashy Mediterranean eyes, a perfectly carved mouth. His shirt is bright white. He has caught her staring.

She lowers her eyes, appalled. 'Who *is* that?' she whispers to Pru.

'No idea,' says Pru cheerily. 'Friend of your sister—*gentleman* friend? She doesn't usually show them off like this. Can't say I blame her, though. What a lovely looking fellow. What are we on now? Moroccans? Assyrians?'

For her eighth birthday, when other girls were begging for guinea pigs or Victorian dolls' houses with removable frontage, Frances decided to ask for her father. She requested that he take her on a trip to the British Museum and, despite the many ways this might have hurt the others' feelings, Norman agreed. The journey involved two buses and St Pancras station in the snow. He brought provisions: raisins and a sat-upon cheese sandwich, leathery inside its cling-film wrapping like the meat Attila carried under his saddle.

'We're Huns,' she said, and he had smiled. Their conversation was a little halting but she had never been happier—except, of course, for worrying about what to do if he died here, so far from home.

He survived the journey. A little later, not quite hand in hand but standing close together, they

72

attended a demonstration in which a Florentine paper press was tightened with a wooden screw. The press itself was beautiful, glazed with amber varnish in which brilliant thoughts and poetic passions were trapped. As she watched it, she too began to tighten with longing: to lick it like a little ugly horse with a salt-lick, to write poems worthy of it, to love beauty and be loved like that. Eventually, shamefully, she had begun to cry.

'Doorbell rang a minute ago,' Pru is saying. 'You were up with the baby—bet you're glad he's over that awful colic, though your mum tells me the nights are a mess . . . So who is this new chap? Do we know?'

'Oh . . . no. She hasn't said.'

'Come on—you must know something about him.'

'Honestly.' He is wearing a dark jacket and subtly dandyish lilac tie, slightly loosened. Compared to the other men Frances knows—her father in mothy jumpers, her husband, who wears shirts from a wholesaling cousin in Wood Green—he is fascinatingly well dressed, more like a forties film star than a real boyfriend. 'Who . . . how—' He turns his head; silver shines amid the black. He is neither showing off nor cowed but simply, fascinatingly, himself. 'Did you—what's his name?'

Pru shrugs. 'No idea. Don't *you* know? And you all so close. How odd.'

Odder still is her mother, who is not shining with pride and pleasure at the sight of this handsome, suited man, as once she did at Jonathan. She is not even looking in his direction. She is talking, vigorously, to Robin Buckley, her back turned.

73

'Well, never mind,' says Pru. 'He does look very . . . desirable.'

Claudia's guests finish their dinner. Frances shrugs at Sim, who raises an eyebrow back. Their father pretends to have noticed nothing. Em, as if oblivious, stares at her plate with an expression of private rapture. The man, whoever he is, talks softly, intently to Betty Lister and then to Pru, who blushes to her collarbones. It is only to spare her further embarrassment that Frances looks away and happens to notice that Leo, whose return is, discreetly, the point of this evening, has an extremely strange expression on his face.

*   *   *

For the first time all night Leo is not being talked at. He is enjoying it while it lasts. In his mind's eye Helen Baum, slender in a female barrister's strict black suit (she is, in fact, a child psychiatrist, but that is not the point), has taken him, surprisingly, riding through the Scottish Highlands; they have dismounted in a convenient thicket of pines. She is complimenting him on his horsemanship. He is unbuttoning her crisp white shirt. Her eyes—he is obsessed with her eyes, the size of them, their Italianate straight-lashed darkness, the deep crescent shape of the upper eyelids with their transfixing crease at the top—are slightly lowered. He is trying not to think about her, he is nodding and smiling at everything anyone says, but his fingers are on her fourth shirt button and he is about to—

Part Two

ONE

Sunday 11 March

Eighteen months ago Norman had begun a short study of the wit and novelist Cedric Vickers, of all his obsessions the one Claudia most dislikes.

'But why do you care about him?' she demanded when, gingerly, he broached the subject. 'He was successful. You don't *do* successful subjects. God, he's hardly forgotten—if only he was, with his stupid post-war nostalgia and his Shires fixation and his little sneaking anti-Semitism. And all that High Church business. They loved him when I was at university, all the floppy English boys. He still bloody *sells*. Please, we need less about him, not more.'

'Well . . .'

'And whatever happened to William Flecker, the saviour of the sonnet? Or Edgar Rice and his gentle nature lore?'

'Nothing happened. I just don't want to do them any more.'

'But your audience . . . your readers *expect—*'

'You think I don't know?' he said tetchily. 'All twelve of them? They want padding for their PhDs. But isn't it maybe time I tried someone new? Someone . . . bigger? That's all. It won't change the world.'

'Well, you said it, kiddo.'

*   *   *

She thinks he abandoned it long ago. He has not exactly lied but she has assumed and, in consequence, it became harder to explain. He did not want her to feel betrayed or misled and, as a result, he has done both. Now, in this small damp room of his own, he bounces his tired bottom muscles on the seat of the hard but gratifyingly old-fashioned study chair, clicks his neck, gnaws at the pleasingly horny skin at the base of his palm where his typewriter used to rest. His newish computer has worn it glossily smooth, but Norman is not a smooth man. Then, his worn shirtsleeves rolled up, nibbling on a stray beard curl, he begins to write a feature to accompany the forthcoming publication of his findings about Cedric Vickers, in which our hero, the nation's darling, will prove to be rather more, or less, than anyone had expected. And so, at last, will Norman.

* * *

'I'm going,' shouts Claudia from the hallway a little later. She has kept to herself all day; Leo has been charting her movements from the creaking of the stairs. 'Norman, I'll be back after the Feltman funeral. Are you working?'

'Not really,' shouts her husband.

'Leo, I'll see you later. Are *you* going out?'

'No,' he calls.

'Not to chambers?'

'No.'

'Are *you* working?'

'What?' he shouts.

'Are you *working*?'

'Oh. Yes. Yes, I am.'

78

'I'll be back very soon. Be good.'

The door slams. Leo, naked and tumescent, closes his eyes.

*   *   *

'I am an abomination,' whispers Frances, and it is true.

She is supposed to be bonding with Max, her baby. They are at a steam fair on Hampstead Heath, the mere prospect of which, when Jonathan mentioned it last night, made Frances's eyes water with boredom.

'Look at this leaflet,' he had said. 'There's even a hurdy-gurdy!'

The collar of his old blue shirt was half twisted-in. Something, possibly a nose hair, glinted at his nostril's edge. It was difficult not to think, yet again, of the perfect assurance of Em's boyfriend, his skin, his extraordinarily confident smile.

'Do you really think you won't enjoy it?' he asked, surprised. 'What would you rather do?'

Thoughts of a morning to herself, reading novels in the bath, eating toast and listening to Ella Fitzgerald, began to form like a mirage. 'Well,' she began, 'there's work—'

'But,' said Jonathan with a frowny edge to his voice, 'I think the children would love it. And with school, and . . . everything, weekends are *for* them, aren't they? And for Max? So unless you really don't—'

'No, it's fine,' she said. 'I'll come. I'll come.'

*   *   *

79

So here she is, with stepdaughters who hate her and a husband who finds pistons entrancing, and the one task which every woman can perform, the adequate mothering of a baby, escapes her. Max would rather bounce along in his daddy's arms, wet grinning mouth pressed to his jumper, than be pushed in his buggy over frozen tussocks by a mother whose mind is, plainly, anywhere but here. Periodically she imagines holding out her arms and the pain of his inevitable rejection is almost a pleasure, something on which she can rely.

'You really don't want me, do you?' she asks him.

Beaming, skew-whiff, Max shakes his head.

The truth, however, is that she does not want to be wanted. She needs time to think. Her standard preoccupations—the deaths of those she loves from falling scaffolding or sudden tumours, her subtle marginalization at work, a section in her mother's new book about Frances's first period—have been washed away by a fascinating new subject: her sister's latest fling.

There is no one to discuss him with. Last night, during the clearing-up, Sim was what he calls On One: a tubthumping orgy of Rubin propaganda, policy-making and aggressive defensiveness. In that frame of mind he could ignore almost anything. Their father was evasive; Claudia frosty; even Leo, after his brief experience of passion, appears to have retreated to the world of ironed shirts and sober industry. No one, it seems, but Frances wants to talk.

In the absence of fact, she grows more curious. She pushes the empty buggy behind the others, hot with speculation, on and on across the lumpy grass until she crashes into Jonathan, who has stopped to consult his leaflet.

'Jesus!' The buggy has bitten a hole in her tights. There is icy mud all over her leg. As if she were a gigantic baby, hot tears tremble behind her lashes, waiting to be released. 'Bastard thing.'

Rebecca, with whom she has been trying hard all afternoon, opens her little pearly toothed mouth and laughs. 'Stop that,' she snaps at her poor orphaned stepdaughter. In the grey clouds above her, God puts another black mark against her name.

Jonathan is looking at her, mildly.

'What?' she says.

'Why are you so cross?'

'I'm not cross.'

'If you'd wanted to see the Victorian Waltzer, we could have. There's plenty of time. You should have said.'

She stares at the cold white sticky-paper sun and swallows hard. 'It's fine. Twisted my wrist,' she says and rubs it until it burns.

'I should have a look,' he says. 'Wrist sprains can lead to—'

'No,' she says, trying to distract herself with the candied grass, sky the deep unconvincing blue of poster paint, the nibbled leaves. Nothing works. 'It's fine,' she tells him. 'Let's get on.'

They trail around the Wheel of Fear, the Demon Grasshopper, the Monster Munch. She smiles gamely when Max looks at her, offers her stepdaughters candyfloss which they refuse and the pain that she claimed was in her wrist spreads like slow fire through her body until her jaw and fists are clenched and she finally identifies this hard tight feeling, that she has been telling herself for months is cold or tiredness or probably cancer. It is desperation. Desperation will make her need to act.

*   *   *

Leo's attempts to be good have met an obstacle.

It is a bright Sunday afternoon and, like all good lawyers, he is sitting at home in front of his desk. His Head of Chambers is expecting detailed notes on the intestacy dispute of three generations of Hendon car dealers tomorrow morning, and there is much to be done. However, his litigation bag remains unopened. His duty lies elsewhere, in a set of playing cards once contemptuously donated by Sim and never quite disposed of, on which fifty-two huge-breasted blondes beckon him hither.

'Come on,' he mutters, one hand on Casey's *Tort* and the other elsewhere. 'What's wrong with you?'

He is trying to distract himself, for his mother's sake. She has made her wishes plain. On his very first evening home she summoned him to her bedroom, where he has always felt deeply uncomfortable. Unlike, he suspects, his siblings, unlike the first-time visitors who are always trying to sneak upstairs, he has not entered it for years. It is a big blue square so murkily perfumed, so hung with intimate garments and gifts from admirers, that in embarrassment one looks away and finds oneself staring either at her desk, piled high with the secrets of the faithful and coffee-stained sacred texts, or, even more disturbingly, at the rabbi's rumpled marriage bed.

When he came in she was prowling around the

alcove, eyes shadowy with overwork and worry about him.

'Sit down,' she said.

Who could not obey? He crouched in the dust on the floor and she told him what she knew about his affair, what she thought of him and what, exactly, he was jeopardizing.

'You are the one I rely on,' she had said. 'You do realize that, don't you?'

'But—'

'Are you going back to poor Naomi, if she'll have you?'

Leo thought of the shape of Naomi's back; the thinness of her hair. He looked at the rug and shook his head.

'And the other—the affair, I assume, is over?'

'I—I suppose . . .'

'Can you imagine how often I am asked about this? How unsettling it is for my, *both* congregations, for your family? Complete strangers stop me in the street. I've had letters . . . this is not the way for one of my children to behave.'

'No, I kn—'

'Your father is devastated.'

'Has he, have you discuss—'

'Of course not,' she said, with a look. 'But I know.'

'I'm sorry. I'll—'

'And there's more. I have decided to take you into my confidence,' she said. 'I do not want to, frankly, but I can see I must.' Then, calmly, she said: 'We have run out of money.'

'Sorry?' It was as if she had started speaking in Walloon. However ropy the hand-me-downs, however uncomfortably squashed the holiday, no senior Rubin has ever mentioned money before.

'You heard,' she told him. 'We have run out.'

'But,' he said, 'I thought . . . I assumed that there was something, you know, behind us. An income from . . . your work, I suppose. Keeping us going.'

'You assumed,' she said. 'Of course you did. That was the idea. I didn't want you to worry. But keeping it all going is not actually as easy as it looks.'

'What about your, you know, salary?'

'A drop in the ocean,' she said. 'It's reasonable, although not when you think how I've increased the membership, the endless Social Action dinners and book clubs and lectures . . . But it's spread much too thinly. I know you support yourself, and Frances does too, but the others aren't as . . . well, capable. Or lucky. Not that they don't all work extremely hard, in their way, but you know that the arts aren't as easy to earn one's keep in, and four adults minimum and the house and my father . . . it's a completely unaffordable situation.'

'I thought—'

'I know you're tied up with Naomi's mortgage so I'm not blaming you. You do your best. And maybe in a year or so the clerks will give you more lucrative work. But until then . . . Leo, what I'm saying is that we need this book to work. There might be royalties, and articles and festivals— anything, frankly, with fees—'

'I didn't realize,' he murmured, fiddling with the carpet-fringe and feeling despicable.

She leant closer, her hand on his arm, blazing at him until he looked up. 'And even apart from that,

I want it to succeed, not simply for me or for us but for the shul, Leo. For the whole community. OK? I have a responsibility, exactly as you have. So, it's out in five weeks and there cannot be another balls-up. If you're still scr—'

'I'm not!' he said. 'I've stopped.'

'Screwing rabbis' wives. Or phoning, or even thinking . . . Keep away from her. No blow-jobs in back rooms. Nothing. Do you understand me? We are all counting on you. It has to be over.'

*   *   *

He has tried: truly he has. The problem is that he cannot stop thinking about Helen Baum. His heart is breaking; pieces are floating like icebergs in his chest. Of course he knows it is over. He watched her walk slowly up her little garden path, through the drizzle. He saw her hesitate and then, because she must, because of her husband's angina and son's first-year exams and the way the world works, she opened the door and went in.

To make matters worse, he has regressed entirely. Since returning to live in his mother's house and eat her cornflakes and cut his toenails with her kitchen scissors, he has become a blushing thirteen-year-old, self-conscious, obsessed with sex. There have been mornings when, startled from inventive dreams by Claudia's spare alarm clock, only the sight of his own immense shoes and underpants reminds him that he is a man, after all.

*   *   *

The naked Aryans are not working. It is as if his

mother is standing over him. He puts the cards under a pile of papers, moves them to his desk drawer, takes them out. Childhood jumpiness is taking hold. It seems entirely possible that the cards will fall unnoticed into Sandys's *Accumulation and Maintenance* or Fosset's *Disqualification Proceedings*, to be discovered at work tomorrow by Jeremy Blackstock, his room-mate and persecutor.

You are vulnerable, says the voice of reason. They will use whatever they can against you. Save and work and sacrifice. Tomorrow you may lose everything.

So, because history confirms it, because it is not so difficult to imagine Jeremy Blackstock casually wrecking his career, he places the cards in an envelope which he seals, addresses to himself and wedges securely inside *Asterix and Cleopatra*, itself once the origin of certain confusing sexual thoughts. Next, with a brisk pat at his flies to eliminate obstruction, he lowers himself to the floor by his bed and takes a handful of dried apricots from his army-surplus tin box, now emptied of his moth collection and a small plastic figurine of Princess Leia. It is simpler, given Sim's sensitivities, to forgo kitchen visits if he can. Then he sits again at his desk, moves aside the sharpened pencil whose gold HB has been distracting him, and tries to think pure thoughts.

They do not come easily. Helen Baum is everywhere, even in God's face.

Baruch atta adonai elohainu melech ha-olam, he begins, as his mother once taught him. Blessed art thou, O Lord our God, King of the Universe.

Of course he prays. He was told to and now

automatically he does: on Fridays and holy days, on tasting the first strawberry of the year, on putting on new socks, on remembering the dead who are all around, relying on him too. Now, however, an image floats against the hot pink of his eyelids: Helen Baum, on her hands and knees on a mattress in a remote Scottish hotel, with deer in the wood outside.

Baruch atta adonai, he tries again. Damn it. Baruch atta—

He is a rabbi's son whose family needs him; the house on which they all depend is crumbling; his grandfather is mad and frail in the Home for Aged Jews; and, even as he prays, a battering ram of an erection, a teenager's hard-on, is thumping against his desk drawer.

Blessed art thou, O Lord our God. He cannot have her. He cannot have her. Love is important, of course it is, but other things matter more.

TWO

'You look smart. You never wear that blouse nowadays,' says Jonathan cheerfully. 'Where are you going?'

'Oh!' says Frances, plucking at her shirt. Her sister gave it to her for her twenty-eighth birthday, and because it apparently suits her, she does not wear it, lest it should increase her husband's passion. She does not want his expectations to change.

'Only, well, to Em's,' she says, too cowardly to lie. 'I'm, I'm going for dinner. Is that all right?'

'Em your sister?' says Jonathan. 'Are you sure?'

Last night he had suggested having another baby. She should have seen it coming but, when at last the children were asleep, the remains of their nourishing dinner disposed of, a thousand hair slides and pony stickers and Princess Azandra glittery bubble-swords put away for re-scattering tomorrow, she was simply too tired to refuse him when, unusually amorous, he came to bed. Afterwards, grateful and sticky, he said it, putting his wet mouth to her shoulder and kissing her clumsily, like a dog. She couldn't pretend and she couldn't tell him the truth and so, as the night swelled fatly between them, she lay there saying nothing, until he fell asleep.

'I've hardly ever been to her flat,' she says now, zealously scrubbing the grill pan. 'Well, barely. And I think it would be . . . friendly. To visit. You know.'

'But . . . Em? She actually invited you for dinner? By yourself?'

'Yes! Well . . . yes, she did. I think she wants help with something.'

'Is it technical?' he muses. 'I wonder, that radiator . . . When did she ask you?'

'A minute ago. I—on the phone. Honestly, Jonathan, can't I just go? You know I worry about her. I haven't seen her properly for weeks.'

'Don't you think it's a bit late to be cycling over there by yourself? The roads are very icy. I saw an accident almost happen at Highbury Cor—'

'I'll be fine.'

'Even so. Anything could happen. You still haven't learned to fix punctures, and after dark . . . Besides, I'm sure she'd want us there too, love, wouldn't she?'

'Oh—'

'Bet her new man will, if he's there.'

'He's called Jay. Someone said.'

'Jay will, then. He'll need me and Max to protect him from all you scary Rubin women. Won't he, Maxie?' Max is licking snot from his upper lip. At the sight of his father, he grins. 'Of course he will. And she might, I don't know, need something explained. No, we'd better come.' What can she do but surrender?

*   *   *

She telephones her mother, who passes her Sunday evening Middle Eastern Film Club invitation to Rabbi David and greets her delighted granddaughters with videos, pogo sticks, new aprons and a recipe for chocolate cake ('But, please,' says Frances hopelessly, 'in bed by eight for school tomorrow'), and so, at seven o'clock or a little before, off they go.

'Poor Max. He's so sleepy,' says Jonathan. There is a told-you-so edge to his voice; he is driving at fourteen miles an hour. Frances stares at the road ahead, urging it towards them. 'Are you sure this is a good idea?'

Em sublets the small flat of one of the junior rabbis' dying uncles. It is in a Belsize Park fifties block, a square white box with metal-framed windows and basement storage cupboards, neatly numbered. Frances readjusts her bag and wine and beautiful costly hyacinth, and presses bell sixteen.

'You wait,' she tells Jonathan and Max behind her, hugging the pot to her chest. Max is writhing

89

in his father's arms, away from her, but she will not let tonight be ruined. 'It will be fun!'

The intercom buzzes, astonishingly loudly. She drops the pot. Max, startled, begins to scream.

'Are you there?' says a voice: not her sister's voice. 'I'm buzzing.'

'I know you're buzzing,' she shouts, on her knees amid terracotta pot shards and fibrous tufts and oozing bulb flesh. 'I'm here. I mean, we are—'

'Oh, dear,' says Jonathan. 'That pot's gone. How much did you say you paid for it?'

The intercom gives one last impatient buzz.

'Sod it,' says Frances, wiping her damp forehead with a muddy hand. 'Let's go.'

She kicks the biggest plant-clump off the step. A dark spot of blood is welling against her tights. Never mind. She shoulders open the door.

'Are you all right?' asks Jonathan. 'You're being . . . odd. You know about toxoplasmosis, don't you? It's more common than you'd think. There are disinfectant swabs in the glove compartment. You should definitely use one. And we ought to clear up that mess. I could pile the pieces neatly beside—'

'Leave it,' she says. The door is heavy and he is so slow. 'This is important. For Em. Please can we just—'

She catches sight of her face in the lift window. It is badly put together, big beaky nose, big sad greenish eyes and dark eyebrows and windswept hair. She looks too bony, too nervous. She rearranges her smile but nothing will shake that look of hot expectation.

The lift opens. Em's alarming boyfriend is waiting at the end of the corridor: a faun, a satyr in another beautiful shirt, its collar open. His smile flashes white in the strip-lighting. His eyes are watching them.

Dumbly, Frances approaches.

'Hello,' he says. 'I'm the interloper. Come inside.'

*   *   *

That night, Leo buys porn. He has no choice.

A calm analysis of the facts reveals that it is not Helen Baum he wants, exactly, even taking into account her mind, her subtle beauty, her combination of science-teacher strictness and hidden fire. No. Their affair can be explained by simple physiology. Those few nights in Scotland have somehow reactivated his libido, previously modest despite the ministrations of a fellow Sunday Draydls helper, a nervous flautist in his second year and Naomi, who had referred to sex as 'night-time'. Now, however, he is its slave. When not in the grip of lust he is imagining new and daring ways to reclaim her but this is, he tells himself firmly, destructive and dangerous. He is not like that. Given an outlet—Helen would approve, which is not the point—he can bring it under control, for all their sakes. And that, surely, is what pornography was invented for.

*   *   *

He approaches his task in a businesslike and logical fashion. First he selects an insalubrious West Kentish Town corner shop, Fags 'n' Mags, in which to buy his materials. The shop is bare and grimy, staffed by threatening youths in England football shirts. At least, he thinks, picking his way past boxes of microwaveable cheeseburgers and tins of ham in jelly, he is unlikely to bump into anyone he knows.

The porn selection is shockingly extensive. He peers up at the shelves, sweating into his good suit jacket and trying not to look like a Hassid boy in need of a kicking. There is nothing for his kind here, no *F-Cup Yeshiva Girls* or *Sachertorte Sluts*. The youths mutter and scuffle. He clearly hears one of them say 'pork'.

Stop feeling sorry for yourself, he tells himself briskly. This is a cure by masturbation. You are not supposed to enjoy it.

He has to ask for a bag. As he takes his magazines he glimpses the word **Reform** in big red letters on a shelf behind him. He holds up his hand to stop the skinhead behind the till; then notices **–atory**, just in time. Mortified, he drops his change but pretends not to have noticed. They must not think he is money-grabbing too. He stands very upright, shoulders back, and leaves the shop, a noble specimen of his race, an honourable man. Even his mother would be proud of him.

*   *   *

Later, looking back, Frances thinks she must have been blind: tonight, last night, all her life.

She and Em and Jonathan and Jay sit in the brown flat on a stranger's furniture, talking and laughing and eating delicious soup and expensive cheeses off their knees. Interesting jazz is floating down the corridor from the bedroom, which she has never seen.

'I don't like jazz,' Jonathan confides.

'Somehow I had predicted that,' says Jay, with a little grin. He moves his foot away from Max, who lies asleep, after much resistance, on a sofa cushion. 'I'd put something under him, if I were you,' he says in his smiling chalky voice. 'I think that was the masturbation area. Certain stains.'

'Stains?' says Frances.

'Do keep up,' he says.

'Is this Brie pasteurized?' asks Jonathan. 'Because brucellosis is—'

'No,' says Jay.

*   *   *

A little later, in the kitchen, Em leans close to her sister. 'Jay likes you,' she whispers. 'I can tell.'

Frances opens her mouth, then closes it. As usual they are steering the safest course through the shallows of possible arguments. Anything could alienate her. If Frances is to help her sister she will have to be careful. She must stay alert for reasons to worry and discover what she can.

There is plenty to see. Take, for example, the happy couple's similar outfits: Jay's dark trousers narrow over his hips, Em's cut more widely, her tight white shirt giving her bounce of hair and breasts a flattering frame. They even sound a little alike. And how glorious they look together, like an advertisement for sex. This perhaps is also why Frances fails to ask questions. Admittedly she is impressed too by the news that Jay is medical, which gives him a trustworthy glamour, the sense that everything he does, including smoking, is for

93

the best. Admittedly the room is delicious-smelling and dimly lit, with candles dripping on to the mantelpiece and thick paper shades from Behrens Road dimming the lamps. And, admittedly, every time Frances tries to give Jay a searching look, she is distracted by a new and fascinating detail: the beating of the pulse in his pale brown neck, the darkness of his lower lashes, his unnaturally straight nose. He looks, she decides, like the lover of a Greek conqueror, more a frontispiece than a living man. This, too, quite reasonably distracts her. She barely listens to a word he says.

That, at least, is what she tells herself, later.

Then he moves seats.

*   *   *

Leo creeps back to his mother's house, the carrier bag of shame held tightly to his coat. **TITS** is clearly visible through the white polythene but he has made it unobstructed. He is safe at last. Preparing for a sprint upstairs to his bedroom, he pulls the front door wide. There, standing on the hall rug as if forewarned, is his brother.

'Oh!' squeaks Leo. 'It's you!'

He is frightened of Sim and Sim knows it. Since childhood, certain details of Leo's life—the grandmotherly provenance of his favourite blue-velvet kippah, his membership of the Parliament Hill Fourteen and Under Knowledge Squad (PHIFUKS), his fondness for logic-problem magazines—have inexplicably roused his brother to a snarling kicking frenzy. There are still silver scars under Leo's leg hair. He flinches when cornered, even at chambers teas. Besides, he may

94

have a sailor's chest and square jaw but he is much shorter than his brother. He knows that he is unmanly beside other men.

Sim's handsome stubbled face gives nothing away. 'Where've you been?' he says.

A floorboard creaks above their heads. Leo looks up and glimpses the fringed skirt and buckled boots of his brother's latest conquest creeping upstairs.

'I said,' Sim says, flicking his dreadlocks over his shoulder, as if for battle, 'where've you been?'

Leo stares guiltily into his eyes and his brother, six foot one of unpredictable threat, stares back. 'Er,' he says pluckily. 'Actually . . .'

'You're keeping away from her, aren't you?'

'Me?'

Wrong answer. Sim extends a meaty forearm and rests the tip of his index finger against his brother's chest. So this is it, thinks Leo, whose heart is beating hard enough to hear. One little push—

Sim bends his head closer. The smell of him makes Leo's legs wobble but he cannot faint; he will drop the bag.

'Behave, you little fucker,' says Sim, very quietly. 'You've arsed it up once. Don't make it worse, puppy-boy.'

'Sorry,' says Leo, and he hangs his head.

*　　*　　*

Jay is sitting on the sofa, next to Em. Every time he wants to touch her he simply, indolently, reaches out his hand and there she is, uncurling towards him. Frances is opposite them in an armchair, enthralled by the sight of her sister, before whom men compete and schoolboys cover their loins with chemistry textbooks: entirely enslaved.

Usually all Em's flings are the same: she wears their scarves, phones them constantly, spends hours making them paperclip hearts and then they are dropped for one small transgression, one ill-judged question. Usually Frances simply ignores them, their mislaid watches and tarot cards. It saves time.

This evening, however, the flat is scattered with distracting un-Emlike objects: a tiny shining mobile phone, a black box containing brown cigarettes, a postcard of a handsome Edwardian woman in riding britches, all strangely charged with meaning, more exciting than other people's. Even the air smells interesting. Frances takes a deep breath and turns back to the conversation.

'And then,' Jonathan is telling his clearly distracted sister-in-law, 'there's boycotting petrol stations. I know your mother feels—'

She catches Jay's eye. He has a way of smiling which shuts out the world. Is this normal? His clothes are so lovely that she longs to comment, even to touch them. This is quite unlike her. I am right to mistrust you, she thinks. It's good that I came round.

'Do you want more wine?' Jay murmurs. 'You're disgustingly sober. It's quite offensive. Please.'

'Tt—are you sure you should?' says Jonathan. 'Those large glasses are two units each. My . . . Claudia,' he confides to Jay, 'says that women's livers—'

Frances sighs. Jay lowers his lids and grins. And so, because Jonathan can be relied upon to drive, because she is feeling unaccountably reckless, she says: 'I'm sure.'

Jay approaches. He sits on the arm of her chair and takes the glass out of her hand. Then he holds the bottle up to the light and squints at it, consideringly.

'It does taste like wee,' he tells her, as if referring to a joke they alone understand, 'but in a good way. Very bracing. You look like you need bracing.'

She smiles and he smiles back, right between the eyes. He bends towards her. Then she sees it.

He has breasts.

'Oh!' she says, jumping back. Breasts, she tells herself stupidly. Breasts. Like a woman. They are small, smaller than hers, but there is no mistaking them for a fold of shirt or muscle. There is even, now she looks closely, a suspicion of a bra—

'Frances?' says Em.

'What?' With an immense effort she moves her eyes away but her mind will not start working. There is a section of the equation missing. Jay has breasts; women have breasts; Jay is . . .

But Jay, surely, is a man.

THREE

It is, thinks Norman, like being in love. He goes to buy a Sellotape dispenser, makes coffee for his wife, performs his back exercises and, irrespective of what his body does, his brain has only one setting; dreaming of his future.

For Norman, it seems, is about to be famous.

97

His life has been changing, slowly, secretly. No one except his publishers, his agent and a few well-informed critics has any idea. It happened almost by accident: or, perhaps, not by accident. Perhaps he has always been a man whose time would come.

He has long been on the trail of Cedric Vickers. Vickers is the perfect subject: well known, much loved, still a big seller but slightly unfashionable. He is wrapped in nostalgia so precious that no one has ever dared to poke beneath it, lest they disturb a pillar of English self-belief. Norman, however, the boy from Paddington, has no such fears. All it took was three letters in a private collection in Sussex to which Fate led him, via a drunken lecture acquaintance on the six forty-five from Blackheath. Quick as an arrow, Norman went after them and saw at once the clue that they concealed. They gave him Cedric's heart and now, ninety-one thousand six hundred and ninety-three almost effortless words later, the unsuccessful biographer's life is about to change.

*   *   *

'What are you up to?' Claudia keeps asking him. 'Are you behaving?'

'Of course,' he says.

The problem is that she trusts him. She thinks she is only asking out of superstition, to insure herself. They have always worked well together; she shines and he has a talent for failure. No one else ever wants to write about his subjects; too late, always, he understands why. And it is better this way. Claudia, as others have noted, does not like to share the spotlight.

'It's so *interesting* that you're the less successful one,' the shul's honorary treasurer, Penny Rapaport, once commented. 'Do you find it emasculating? Or was it always part of the plan?'

Norman has never thought of himself as a secretive man. He, his children and, particularly, his wife relish his disappointments; they are his contribution to family life. Success, he has discovered, is harder to explain. His wonderful discovery has gathered lies around it, rolling more and more quickly away from him until it is too huge to confess.

This is why, he tells himself now, he said nothing; not at first; not when he knew what he had found; not even when he finished the typescript on a blazing day last July when, God's truth, he intended to tell her. He still remembers it perfectly, a much-watched scene in the film of his life: the exultant return from the post office, trailing clouds of glory; the applause he half-expected as he turned the corner of Agincourt Road and headed for home. He was looking forward to revelations, forgiveness, marital passion. 'Darling,' he hoped she would tell him, 'of course I had guessed.'

Already beaming, he opened the door. Claudia, however, was not awaiting him in their bedroom with an expression of lustful admiration. She was in the hallway, by the telephone, describing in wounded tones the latest outrage perpetrated by the secretary for admissions.

'I can't do my job like this,' she was saying to her listener: one of the children? A friend? A man? 'It's impossible with that woman. Shelley Glendel: what a name. Ugh, I loathe her. Her manicures

99

and her gazebo and her networking bagel brunches; why doesn't she go back to the fifties where she belongs?'

'I've—have you got a minute?' muttered Norman. She shot him a look of irritated enquiry. He felt his smile beginning to fade.

'*What?*' she stage-whispered. 'Oh, for God's sake, never mind. It's only Norman,' she said into the phone. 'Well, you say that, but you have *no idea*, let me tell you. The woman's a fiend—'

*   *   *

It was love, he told himself, that made him delay. He was protecting her. However, the right time to explain never came, or fear prevented him. Too late, he realized that the opportunity had passed.

Then, a fortnight later, he was telephoned by his agent, the venerable and terrifying Swithun Reece, representative of laureates and princes and, in an uncharacteristic error of judgement, Norman, believing it to be the way to Claudia's heart. For the first time in two embarrassing decades, Swithun had good news. He had heard from Norman's usually lacklustre publishers. He wanted to buy him lunch.

Norman did his best not to sound surprised. The following day, as he was led through Swithun's club to his usual table, he said—for something to say— 'I didn't know they let Jews in.'

'Nonsense, dear chap,' said Swithun airily. 'They have for years.'

Champagne arrived even before Norman had had a proper long look at the menu. Then Swithun, flushed with anticipation, made his announcement.

100

'Now, I should tell you that they want to rush it. They're aiming for the spring. Middle of April, which is when that Vickers film, what's it, *Inheritance*, is apparently coming out. Perfect timing, perfect timing. They confess your manuscript took them by surprise. Not the little book they contracted, by any means. For once they know what they've got on their hands. Absolutely top class. The film will give it exactly the springboard it needs. I told them to go ahead, of course, high production values notwithstanding. Any objections?'

The spring was to have been Claudia's. April the ninth, her publication day, is engraved on all their hearts. Nevertheless, when it came to the crunch, Norman, flawed and delighted and cowardly, said nothing at all.

*   *   *

Soon everyone who has ever scorned him will be squirming. The thought of their ingratiating efforts is a source of infinite pleasure. His moment is coming; he is going to show his peers and his family and, most of all, Claudia, whose esteem he wants more than anything, what sort of a man he is.

Yet Claudia is the problem. Not her hurt and anger at having been kept in the dark, much as he dreads it, but the possible consequences: could she, to punish him, somehow pull strings to obstruct his book, or delay it until months after her own? If that were to happen, the serial deal and features and interviews currently being set up, every new exciting step into a world that has always

101

been closed to him, would fall apart.

*   *   *

Lying beside her as she turns and sighs and tries to sleep, he has discovered something interesting. He adores her; he has always put her first, before his mother and father, his children, himself. Now, however, his heart has ballooned to accommodate another love: his book. He does not want to have to choose between them.

So he has formulated a plan. He is doing everything he can to prevent her from finding out accidentally: listening out for the post; hiding catalogues and relevant bits of the newspaper; even barking 'wrong number' down the telephone when stupid editorial assistants call him up, despite his instructions. He suspects that his reclusive grumpiness, like his marriage, may be beginning to quicken media interest but there is nothing he can do. Besides, Claudia is a busy woman with little time for literary gossip; he may yet be safe. And, if he is not, will it be such a disaster? Might she not be so excited about her own publication that she will allow him, at last, his own chance to shine?

*   *   *

Frances, wound tight with anticipation, is at her desk, dreamily cleaning her computer keyboard with a tissue-wrapped paperclip. Outside her tiny grey office Venetia and Sue, expensively bohemian partners at the agency of which she is, since maternity leave, the least glamorous element, are discussing whether to keep first editions in one's

102

Norfolk barn or in 'silly old Notting Hill'. Today, however, their glossy amateurishness, their easy chat about Whitbread parties and clangorous name-dropping, do not unnerve her. Her heart thumping like a woman about to commit a fatal indiscretion, she gazes with passionate intensity at the telephone.

She is trying to will a family member to ring. Last night, after they left the lovers together, Jonathan chatted mildly about Max's new predilection for carrot, laid him tenderly in his cot, settled comfortably in bed to read pages 211 to 220 of Bradish's *Stuart Warfare*. Still Jay was not mentioned. Any minute now, thought Frances, secretly smiling, her pulse vib-rating through the mattress springs. She had forgotten to check on Max before bed, let alone the girls, but could not risk leaving their bed even for a moment. If Jonathan failed to comment, something about him, or them, would be confirmed.

'So!' he said suddenly, closing Bradish with a bang. She jumped beside him. If he noticed his levitating wife, he did not comment. 'That was a pleasant evening. By the way, have you seen Rebecca's plimsolls? Or my calculator? I must have left it at school.'

She turned to him, her body hot and loose. This, she told herself, was how one should feel in one's very early thirties: relaxed, excited, alive. She opened her mouth.

'You're not yourself,' he said. 'I did notice you were drinking. You need a pint of water, maybe two. You're never too young for kidney care.' There was a pause. She strained her ears towards him like a sensitive silky creature, waiting for the truth to dawn. It never did. He gave a mighty congested snort and fell asleep.

*   *   *

Daylight made it impossible to tell him. Now she is marooned. There is no one at work she can discuss it with; where would she start? Leo will stammer and blush, which will embarrass her. Her friends, too, are out of the question; they are either unmarried and sophisticated or cosy and easily shocked. Besides, she has hidden her siblings' idiosyncrasies from them for so long. There is too much lost ground to catch up on now. And, obviously, she cannot ask her parents. Neither of them can quite accept that their children are old enough to sleep away from home, let alone with other people. In their fantasy of family life, puberty has barely dawned.

However, Jay's expression of amused experience, his, or rather her, daring, seem to be having an odd effect on Frances. They make her bolder. They make her think that ringing her mother—so openly welcoming to every racial and sexual and liturgical permutation, so vigorously liberal—might not be such a bad idea after all.

So she does. It feels fantastic, recklessly assertive—that is, until Claudia picks up the phone.

'Rubin?'

'It's me—'

'Can it wait? I'm up to my eyes here. Do you think I enjoy having my Liberal Synagogue Committee timetables derailed by Nicky Baum's moaning? I'm going to ask one of the under-rabbis

104

to speak to him.'

There is no point defending Rabbi Baum; since the unmentionable incident he has joined the legions of the damned. 'You know,' she says, 'you mustn't call them under-rabbis. They're juni—'

'They're fired, that's what they'll be at this rate. And if sodding Shelley Glendel—'

'Shh!'

'It's my shul, I'll say it. Shelley Glendel—if she'd stop putting her oar in . . . sorry, Vivian, over there—'

'I,' says Frances, 'I wondered . . . about last Friday night—'

'Yes!' says Claudia. 'That's exactly what I wanted to talk to you about,' and Frances jolts back to life. 'Think how it hurt your poor brother, hearing you tell Robin Buckley about your job.'

'But—'

'You know what I mean. Poor Simeon right next to him with *his* brilliant novel—why you won't show it to one of those women you work for, with, whatever, I'll never know.'

This is the greatest of all Frances's crimes. One evening a few weeks before Max was born her mother cleared her throat. From beneath her chair she took a slim green folder containing thirty heavy pages, full-colour printed, lightly scented with dope.

'We want your professional opinion,' she announced. The others were suspiciously hushed. It was a set-up; here and now, as Petey Lister was their witness, Frances would provide confirmation of what they all suspected. Sim was a genius and, with these pages, would have serious agents fighting over him by the end of the week. Frances,

105

however, failed in her task. So ungrammatical was it, so stuffed was it with coincidental meetings in Belize, cartoonish Highgate drug barons and horrible threesomes that no amount of praise could conceal her misgivings. Sim called her a fucking elitist media whore; Em began wailing; Claudia merely stared her down until she backtracked. Then, at last, Jonathan spoke. In his opinion, he humbly declared, it was a work of dazzling originality, astonishing for its daring and scope. Everybody agreed.

'I didn't mean to upset him,' says Frances now. 'We've been through all that. And I mainly do non-fiction, you know I do.'

'Well, I wish you'd think. While I remember, darling, that shirt . . . I'm not convinced. It's so . . . well, never mind. What did you want to ask?'

'Nothing. It's, I—'

'The under-rabbis are due in twelve minutes and I still haven't done Eric's memorial speech.'

'It's a silly thing, really,' she says. 'So on Friday I was upstairs, you know, quickly checking on Max—'

'Maxie,' croons her mother. 'How is his little foot?'

'His foot? Oh . . . fine. I think. And while I was up there, someone, someone arrived. Em's new, her . . .' Does her mother even realize? 'You know. Her friend.'

Silence. 'I don't know what you expect me to say,' she says eventually. 'I thought I'd brought you up to think for yourselves.'

'But,' Frances begins. 'But—'

'Enough. I have to go. If you talk to your father, will you tell him that I'll be late back. I'm sitting shiva for poor old Tibor. In fact, it would be a mitzvah if you'd bring something round to the Kayes' flat: just a casserole or something. Shall I tell them you will?'

*　　　*　　　*

In the hours that follow, Claudia grows angrier with her elder daughter. What was she doing, bringing up that person? It is unbearable to think that anything could endanger her years of work, her secret History A-level vision of the family as citadel, thick-walled and iron-bound, absolutely safe. Doesn't Frances realize that equality, openness are nothing if the family is threatened? And that is what this silly fling will do, now of all possible times. Do they not understand that I want them to be happy?

Already at shul the vibrations of disapproval, begun by Leo, are growing stronger. The congregation does not smile at the sight of her as they used to do; their muttering during services seems louder. Sometimes she hears the under-rabbis whispering outside her door. Nicky Baum has his sympathizers even at New Belsize Liberal and when, not if, they hear about this latest scandal, the ripples will spread.

Well, she will have to do something. She decides to leave her youngest child a message. While she finishes her speech for Eric Bamforth, to be delivered tomorrow to two hundred misogynists at St Paul's, another part of her brain is rehearsing what she will say to Emily's answerphone: Darling. I want you to know how much I love you. I'm worried about you. Call your mother.

Could her children have forgotten the belief for which she is most famous, that happiness has many parts? That romantic love is but a fraction of what really matters: professional recognition, financial security, moral probity, spiritual nourishment, family life? Stability, in a word: she has been certain of that through her fatherless schooldays, her frustrating time at Birkbeck and five exhausting years schlepping up the East End Road to Leo Baeck, the long time in the wilderness. Surely absolute unchanging stability is everything, the only safety?

Isn't it?

*   *   *

Lately, a tiny section of her brain has been having unsupervised thoughts. She tries to ignore it but its voice is growing stronger. Dear God, she thinks, not now. Let me not begin to doubt.

*   *   *

By lunchtime, Frances can bear ignorance no longer. She dials Sim's mobile, imagining with every ring more spilt bottles, more burning spliffs ignored; growing tighter, tenser, less suited to speaking to her brother.

At last he answers. 'Dil, man? Hey!'

'Hi, Sim.' Her voice is too bright, like a pensioner surrounded by menacing children.

'Oh, right, Fanny,' he says and then, as she is preparing the next part of her speech, he begins to mumble to someone else: 'Man, that's sick . . . I've never seen—'

'Sim? Please—can we talk?'

'Man, where are you? Want to come over and—'

'I'm at *work*,' she says. 'How could I?'

Sim, aggrieved as ever by her very existence, her affront to coolness, exhales with the disgust of a busy man. 'Go on then, Chancellor Franceleh. Talk.'

Outside her office window an intensively pierced man is selling pills to schoolgirls. He looks like one of Sim's friends. At the sight of her he gives a sarcastic wave. 'I, I was wondering,' she begins.

'Yeah?'

'Well. Er. I don't . . .'

'Fuck's sake, sis. Spit it out.'

Now the ever-alert Venetia is approaching her office, drawn instinctively to family drama. She sticks her head through the space where Frances by rights should have a door and mouths: 'Bill's file?'

'Coming. Um, five minutes?'

'You're very . . . flushed.' She eyes Frances's long denim skirt, bought when she still expected to be a capable *Little House on the Prairie* mother, building cribs with wooden pegs and hewing maple, not a woman who cries in office toilets. 'Are you having phone sex?'

'*No!*' says Frances. 'No! I'm—my brother—'

She raises her eyebrows. 'I'll speak to her,' says Sim. Thankfully, Venetia's tiny bottom is receding down the corridor. 'Is that the fit one?'

'I can't talk,' Frances whispers. 'Listen, quickly, Em and, er, Jay.'

'That!' says Sim. 'Fuck! It's dodge, if you ask me. Very dodge. Role-playing.'

109

'So you know? That's he's . . . well, a she?'

'It's not my idea of a she. You know, if they fancy each other, muff-munching and all, why don't they get on with it? Suits! Ties! Christ.'

'But . . . listen, do you think Mum knows? That Jay's not a man?'

'Er, *yes*. She's not thick. You saw her face. Don't tell me you didn't—oh my God.'

'Oh, no, no, I did . . . so you aren't surprised?'

'Nothing surprises me,' says Sim darkly. 'Down on the sites, you've got no idea.' In the background she can hear a woman murmuring; maybe two. He inhales audibly, like a Radio Three announcer.

'Is this green or gold?' she hears someone say.

'Sim! Just tell me, don't you think it's—'

'Why're you so wound up?' Sim asks. 'Bit overexcited? Tell you what, it'd be hilarious if good wholesome hetty Frances got a crush on you know, John or whatever he's called.'

'That's . . . I wouldn't! I—'

'So anyway, Frank, yeah, it's disgusting,' says Sim. 'If he comes round here again I'll deck him.'

'You can't do that,' says Frances. 'They're entitled—'

'No they're not. You saw Mum's face. Least you and me—mind the blim, man—are on the path of righteousness.'

FOUR

In this morning's post, in addition to a British Council invitation to tour Norway, of all bloody places, Norman received two interesting letters.

110

The first informed him that rights in his secret book have been sold yet again, this time to the unobjectionable Greeks, where, he is told, Vickers's wistful patriotism is surprisingly popular. He wants to tell his wife; failing that, he wants to see her, preferably over methi chicken at the Bombay Star on Haverstock Hill, where they greet him like a brother. However, he cannot. She has, as so often, other concerns, accepting first a speaking invitation from the Jewish Women's Friendship League followed by a drink with Robin Buckley followed by a dinner and slide-show with her Over-Sixties Torah Study Group because, as she put it: 'I need them all behind me. Simple as that.'

A thin night wind presses itself through the window frame, unsettling the postcard which he has, with difficulty, balanced there. He paid forty pence for this treasure, overlooked among the Bloomsbury coasters and Merovingian spectacle cases in the National Portrait Gallery shop. It is almost this room's only decoration. Claudia's prints and programmes, her signed facsimiles from Texas, Padua and Berlin have never been an option for him, until now.

If only Claudia would come home. He eats his toast in his stinking study and gazes balefully at the painting of Cedric Vickers in middle age. Cedric, bespectacled, tweedy, his secrets long buried, looks back at him.

It's you and me, Cedric, he tells him.

Then he recollects that this is not strictly true. The second letter of the morning is from a woman biographer—unknown, as Norman still is—writing yet another life of Philip Larkin. She knows that he is a Vickers expert, which is both flattering and deeply worrying. How the hell did she hear? And she is writing to ask if he would be willing to decipher something, a scrawled card of remonstrance Cedric once sent her hero, who had always been so scathing to him.

'I know you must be very busy,' she writes, 'but it would be a tremendous kindness if you were to help me. I am such an admirer of your other books and would love to discuss them further too, should you have the time.'

It is, of course, the last thing he would consider. Claudia is the charmer, the helper, the meeter of fans. Besides, he is suspicious. He has never received a letter like this. She must want something: a lead, or praise or, more probably, she is mocking him. He takes the letter from its hiding place beneath last April's *Poetry Studies* and holds it above the wastepaper basket, admiring his resolve.

* * *

Two rooms away, in the vast chipped turquoise bathtub of his childhood, Leo is sinking further into degradation.

His life is a mess. He had expected brilliance and wealth by now, evenings of delicious food and nights of erotic glory, not bus rides to his childhood home up Kentish Town Road; not arguments with his brother, who tonight took the grocery money Leo left for their mother and called him a fucking sap; not sleep in his schoolboy bed. To make matters worse, he is drunk and lying in the hottest bath the boiler can manage: an environment in which even the latest edition of *Chancery Law* does not appeal. The pornography has infected him, despite his mother's notoriously outspoken articles on the subject. The world now seems charged with erotic possibility. Women of every conceivable creed and colour jostle for his favours as he wallows in the steam.

I need flesh, he thinks, and is about to succumb to all of them at once when, reaching for his glass of unpleasant but strengthening Scotch, he knocks a newspaper supplement into the bath.

He catches it clumsily between his flippers. Since his life is unravelling, he decides, he might as well have a look. Disconsolately he begins to browse through Japanese film festivals, tattooing championships and string quartets, parting the swollen frills with increasing alienation and alarm. Then, quite by accident, he reaches the Personals, where lonely people meet.

*   *   *

Two minutes later, he is standing in the darkened sitting room: a man with a future. His hairy feet flex cat-like against the carpet; he holds his breath. The house is quiet. Sim has stamped off to the pub with someone called Giff, leaving a haze of musk and narcotics on the stairs. His father is in his study; his mother is eating walnut cake with the bereaved. This is the perfect moment. He pulls his teenage burgundy C&A dressing gown around his burly chest and, silently, stealthily, a little unsteadily, creeps to the telephone.

*   *   *

113

What harm is there, after all, in one phone call? Norman is lonely. He is longing to discuss his great consuming love, the book, with someone separate and safe. Besides, he is curious to meet his fan.

There is a telephone number hand-written beneath the rather off-putting address: *The Old Stables, Little Pareham, Pareham Stour*. How presumptuous. He frowns as he dials, as if she could see him.

She answers at once. 'Little Pareham two one oh oh?'

Norman rolls his eyes to the ceiling, glimpses damp and rolls them back. 'You wrote to me,' he says. 'Norman Rubi—'

'Oh!' she says, and laughs. 'It's you!'

She has the kind of girls' boarding-school accent which makes him shrink to a little wrinkled kernel of dark self-doubt. 'Evidently,' he says, feeling wounded. Her name, he sees rather belatedly from the letter, is Selina Fawcett-Lye.

'Thank you so much for ringing. It was the last thing I'd expected! But I'm so terribly glad you did.'

Norman is scowling so hard his forehead hurts. He is not good at telephoning women. They expect too much conversation. 'Well, you did ask me to,' he says. 'I can go.'

'Oh, no, please . . .' she says. 'Whoops, hang on—'

'What are you doing?' he asks suspiciously.

'In the bath. Oh Lord, the cordless . . . no, you're fine. Barely damp.'

He glances nervously at the door. 'In the—er, look, why don't you just send—'

114

'Hello?' says a voice, a man's voice, in his ear.

Norman jumps. Is he being bugged? 'Hello?' he says, imagining the woman's husband, riding crops, ancestral shotguns. 'Hello? Who is this?'

'Oh God—sorry—Hen?' says Selina Fawcett-Lye.

'Who—' says the man, who now sounds terrified.

'What *is* going on?' demands Norman. 'Am I the victim of a, a *sting*?'

'Dad, it's me!' says the man. 'Leo!'

'Leo!' Norman's pulse roars through furry arteries: all that cream cheese is having its revenge. 'For God's sake. What the hell are you doing?'

'Er—' begins Selina Thingummy.

'Look,' he says to his son. 'I'll be five minutes. Bloody hell. Go and have a bath or something.'

'Sorry, sorry,' says Leo. There is a click.

Everyone, even Selina, is silent.

'Sch— Christ almighty,' says Norman. He has done nothing wrong but he is sweating like a guilty man.

'Who's Leo?' she asks.

'No one . . . well, my son.'

'Mine lives with me too,' she says. 'It's ridiculous. At twenty-one! I'm chucking him out.'

'How extraordinary,' he says, beginning to sound like Dick Van Dyke imitating an Etonian. 'Good Lord. Mine's . . . older.'

'Anyway, it's still lovely of you to have rung. Do you know, I'm such a fan.'

'You should be legally protected,' he says.

'And this book of yours is so exciting. I know it's embargoed but my niece works for that awful man, Swithun, and she told me.'

115

'Really?' says Norman anxiously. He was a schmuck to fall for Swithun with his pink-and-green tie and signet ring and flabby nepotism. Too much is at stake to risk gossip on the hunting fields of Gloucestershire.

'Don't worry,' she says. 'I'm absolutely trustworthy. Look, I know this is a frightful imposition but might I send you a copy of this card?'

'Er . . .'

'Would you mind? I can't work out Cedric, you know, Vickers's, what *does* one call them, one's subjects? Anyway, his writing at all. Oh blast, I've, the soap—'

Blast? Norman rubs his knuckles under his chin. He shaved around his beard this morning and already there is stubble. He is barely civilized. As if in response the woman moves in her bathtub: water splashes hollowly around her unimaginable limbs, her rosy skin. He glances again at the door. Would a taste of the outside world be so unwise? 'I'll tell you what,' he says. 'I could meet you. Possibly. That is, obviously I'm busy, and I doubt . . .'

'Oh, would you? Are you quite sure?'

Norman closes his eyes. This was a mistake. He hates people of all kinds, smart blonde shireswomen most of all. Besides, what if Claudia found out?

'Don't worry about my discretion,' says Selina Fawcett-Lye. 'Though if you would tell me about your book I'd be so thrilled.'

Perhaps he can afford to be magnanimous. Besides, Claudia is in St John's Wood, neglecting him. 'All right,' he says. What harm can it do?

Six hundred and fifty-three women want to meet a man like Leo—or, at least, a man.

He had not expected quite so many. After a cold quarter-hour, he tries the telephone again and finds that his father has left him to it. This seems like a good sign. Heartened, he listens obediently to the advertisers' instructions, looking forward to choosing his perfect Helen-substitute: a sense of humour; vast but humane intelligence; physical beauty; moral fibre; a comfortable flat on the upper half of the Northern Line.

However, by an extraordinary oversight there are only two categories, age and sexual orientation, as if any man and any woman could, hypothetically, suit each other. He has, however, already spent three pounds and twenty pence and, he pretends to himself, you never know. With a sinking heart, he listens to the most recently placed advertisements.

It is a disaster. They are petite and bubbly; horoscope-obsessed; ramblers. They unwind in bars or by participating in combat sports. Some of them want understanding and sympathy and are plainly mad; others seek Conservatives, church-goers, fat men. Own homes seem to be an issue but not one mentions intense conversations in Royal Mile tea rooms, urgent kissing in small cars in Perivale, perfect understanding. He keeps trying to stop but the next one, or the next one, might be the one to save him, the woman he could persuade himself to love. He owes his mother twelve pounds, twenty-six pounds and it is only when his call totals thirty-nine pounds that the truth rushes coldly towards him: this is his last chance for happiness. If he cannot find a way to forget his beloved he will have nothing to look forward to but the energetic efforts of his community: matchmaking at Chanukkah cabarets and vegetarian Seder singalongs, eyelash-fluttering over the book of Leviticus, Tuesday night Older Singles Mingles. He might as well be dead.

*   *   *

So he must find someone. Diligently as he once scanned the sky in segments for constellations, he applies his considerable brain to the task of obtaining a mate. And, for once, he is rewarded. He is climbing into bed, one leg raised like a furry flamingo, when the perfect answer hits him. It is Naomi Grossman, his former fiancée.

FIVE

'When will Daddy be back?' asks Susannah, again.

Frances has been trying to entertain the girls and Max for three hours with adhesive pom-poms, a new bargain ballet video and an ovenful of disappointingly salty jam tarts. Nevertheless, each time a car slows or someone passes at street level, they all look up eagerly for Jonathan's return.

'Later. Soon,' she tells her stepdaughter, and Susannah scowls, understandably. How could a girl like she, with her interlinked gangs of friends and cool proficiency, have any use for a woman like

118

Frances? She would shun the child Frances once was, rolling herself in a plastic barrel down the nursery hill, worrying about nuclear holocaust and Anne Frank's father as human chains raged across the playground, taking more cheerful infants prisoner. She looks at her elder stepdaughter's neat brown bob, her pale self-assured prettiness, and knows that she will never be what Susannah needs.

Strangely, this does not upset her. For the first time since she became a failed stepmother, nothing, not even Rebecca's begging for a trip to Behrens Road or a carpet tack in Max's bready fist, rouses her usual wanton self-loathing. Wednesdays are generally the worst days. She works at home, reading frantically all morning and into the night to make time for the afternoon of childcare, kept stressfully secret from her colleagues, which her husband has recommended for bonding purposes. Usually it grinds past in a daze of guilty clock-watching. Not today: she is energized. She finds herself rearranging her more exciting paperbacks; sweeping crusts and toothbrushes from under the sofa; looking through the emails her mother forwards for the perfect recipe for Em and Jay, as if she might ask them to dinner. At last, at a quarter past four, when the children are on the sofa comparing their inner lips, she gives into the urge she has been fighting since Sunday, day and night. She phones her sister's flat.

'Fire station?'

'Sorry!' she says. 'I'm—'

'It's not really the fire station.' Too embarrassed to hang up or to speak, Frances makes an appalling turkey-like gobble of shame. 'It's Jay. Isn't that . . .

I know who you are.'

'Oh! Yes, it is. Sorry. Is Em there?'

'She is.'

'And . . . could I talk to her?'

'She's asleep. As so often. Are you all like this?'

'No,' says Frances. 'No, we're not. She, she gets tired easily.'

'Actually,' says Jay, 'I rather like it. It's like having a dormouse. And sometimes she's very much awake.'

'I really don't want to know.' It was a mistake to telephone; it concentrates the sense of secrets shared. 'Look. I'm not . . . I need to see her.'

'Again? Why?' Jay's voice is mocking. It is like being elegantly flayed. 'Is she at risk?'

'No!'

'I'm joking. Why are you so jumpy?'

'I'm not. I'm only concerned—'

'Why,' asks Jay teasingly, 'is no one ever concerned about me? Listen, since I've got you, let me ask you something.'

At last, thinks Frances: now they can get the inevitable Claudia-enquiry out of the way. However, it does not happen. Apparently, it is the only subject she does not want to know about. Her questions probe more and more deeply:

'What's it like having stepdaughters?'

'What does your father do all day?'

'Does that house get messier the higher you climb?'

And, lastly, 'So what's Sim on?'

'Nothing!' says Frances, comprehensively shocked. 'He's not *on* anything.'

'Well, something's up. Sex too, of course. Your sister says there's fresh blood every night.'

120

It is like being lured on to an ice rink; there is something bracing about the speed, the cold, the dangerous disloyalty. While the children roam the flat unchecked, pressing video buttons with their toes and eating plant-earth, their mother is entertained, and scandalized. Jay leaves no taboo unturned. They discuss Leo's handwriting, Sim's grooming habits, Jonathan's fondness for plastic safety corners and dental floss. She seems to know so much about them.

'Is there an order of the Poor Emilys?' Jay asks. 'Your sister is the patron saint, isn't she? And we can guess who the Mother Superior would be. The messages she leaves her, you've no idea. But what's Simeon?'

'A . . . a . . .' offers Frances insightfully.

'A simple custodian. Though even the blessèd Emily herself is in his thrall.'

It is only when Frances offers, as further fuel, the terrible secret of Leo's wedding that she realizes that she is being led astray. 'This is very unhealthy,' she says happily, already envisaging nightly conversations like this one, the meeting of minds. 'We should stop.'

'Must we?'

Something shivers between them, the tightening of a wire. She finds herself thinking of the time before Jonathan; it has sealed itself like a pearl in her mind but, lately, she has been looking at it more and more often. It was when she lived in the Angel, when the evenings were scented with nail-varnish fumes and she always seemed to be running up and down steps to unfamiliar Tube stations, alive with possibility. Sex was everywhere; kissing, or the potential for kissing, that thickening

121

of the air between you, the sense of a precipice off which you could choose to fall. It was not always, or even often, good, but it was possible. Now, of course, that time has past.

'Anyway,' she says, because there is no reason to think of that, none at all, 'my . . . you know. Claudia. What do you think of her?'

With that, Jay seems to leave the ice, leaving Frances to slide to an undignified stop without her. 'Ohhh,' she says distantly, 'the holy mother. Can't say I've given her much thought.'

'Really?'

'She's all your sister wants to talk about, too.'

'I didn't—'

'Astoundingly, unlike you lot, I'm not remotely intimidated by her.'

'I'm not *intim*—' begins Frances hotly.

'Aren't you?'

'No!' Somehow Jay has tricked her. The skates have slipped beneath her. 'No, I'm not.'

'Yes you are. Listen, I've got to go. It's been good, though. Hasn't it?'

The wire tenses again. 'Yes,' she says. 'It has.'

'Do you realize how long we've talked?' The smile has returned to her voice, that disconcerting closeness. 'We should do this again.'

Frances's mouth is dry. 'I don't know. Do you think we can?'

'Why not? Ring me at work: Royal Free ENT, Jay Marcus. Ring if you want me.'

'I don't want—'

'Fine. But you might. You never know.'

*   *   *

122

'Goodnight,' says Leo politely a little later to Jeremy Blackstock, the bane of his life.

'Off already? Early, isn't it?' Jeremy Blackstock opens his avid blue eyes very wide. His long arms are sharply striped in freshly delivered Turnbull and Asser. Casually, he puts them behind his head. The room they share is large but cramped, scented with his limey aftershave, his cigars, his occasional boarding-school belch.

Leo makes a nervous movement with his neck, like a frightened hen. His adversary lifts his eyebrows.

'Where are you off to?' he probes. There is a knowledgeable edge to his voice which the Head of Chambers, his maternal uncle, insists will take him far. 'It's not your lot's night for praying, is it? Or singing, or whatever the . . . custom is.'

'No,' says Leo. 'An, an ordinary night.'

Unlike him, Jeremy Blackstock could easily afford his own office: cooler, east-facing, overlooking the shivering trees of Lincoln's Inn Fields. However, he chooses not to. He is a man who enjoys his sport.

'So—let's see,' he says, balancing his silver fountain pen on a fingertip. 'Quiet evening in?'

'Er,' says Leo. 'Not exactly, no.' With shaking hands, he opens the door.

*   *   *

It is all exactly the same and completely different. He takes the Central Line from Chancery Lane and then the Northern Line from Tottenham Court Road, climbing the same stairs and standing at the platform end as he has always done. He

123

watches the vibrations of his grey flannel sleeve as the train bumps and slows, marvelling that he might have carried on doing this for ever, going home to first Naomi alone and then to one child and a second, not realizing the alternative life that had been lying in wait.

Then he catches himself. No, he decides as he walks down the stairs at East Finchley where, only three weeks ago, he embraced Helen Baum in the alleyway behind the station, his back to Hampstead Garden Suburb, her back to her life. He will not think like that. He is going to remake himself, pushing and smoothing the edges of the past until they press together, soft as wax, and his crime has been forgotten. He is going to start again with Naomi, if she will allow him to.

After all, he did love her, in a way. She was kind and touchingly studious and dutiful, like him. They listened to Kate Bush and R.E.M. and other familiar music; they brought their hamper to Kenwood concerts in the summer and jumped at the fireworks; they discussed popular science without fear of mockery. They were safe and happy and that, surely, counts for something. When he thinks of her, of her tears at the wedding, he feels dizzy with shame.

She is, he tries to believe, a forgiving person. Is it not possible that she might have him back?

*   *   *

He buys two, no, three bunches of lilies at the stall on Fortis Green Road and strides round the corner into Lansdale Gardens in the knowledge that he is, at last, doing the right thing. He can picture the phone call to his mother after a moving but remarkably quick reconciliation. This is his final chance to undo the wrong he has done, to be the good son he intended. He will do it, if he can.

But it is not as easy as he had expected simply to walk up to the door of their mansion block and, without warning, press the bell. He hesitates in the cold. Only one floor above him, to the left of the drainpipe, the lights of his former flat are on. The curtains are open. Naomi is indeed at home.

Oh my God. It feels as if a great ball of panic is blocking out the air. Now he sees the scale of what lies ahead: the apology he will have to make, the inviolable promises, the absolute conviction she will require from him. However, although truly sorry, he is a coward. He is not, perhaps, quite ready to face her yet.

He decides to stand on the other side of the road for a minute. It is a better observation point from which to reacclimatize. He is still going to do it, of course. This is simply breathing space. Burying his chin more deeply in his scarf, he hurries to the pavement opposite.

And there she is. Naomi Grossman, a model of gentle conventionality and caution, is standing at what she called the breakfast bar, stirring something in a green bowl: a gift from him. His heart, surprised, seems to ping. At this angle all he can see is her rounded forearm, the edge of the bowl whose durability she always mistrusted, the plump curve of her cheek and chin as she looks down; enough, one might have assumed, for certainty.

No, he thinks. I can't rush it. I need a little more time.

The difficulty is that, try as he might, he cannot quite see enough to be reminded of why he wants to come back. He hops from foot to foot but he is still too short. Competent men might fashion a periscope from wing mirrors, pull crampons from their rucksack and scale the building unobserved: not Leo. It is only as he looks about hopelessly, as if proving to an unseen audience how stuck he is, that he notices the house behind him. It has dark windows, leaflets stuffed behind the front-door grille and, leading up to it, a steep flight of stairs. No one is approaching. The street is quiet. He lays the big ugly bunch of lilies on a low wall and climbs the steps.

Clever, clever Leo. From here he can see his former living room in lurid detail: the extraordinary cleanliness, the framed poster of Haifa given by Naomi's father, the mighty fridge in which Naomi stacked boxes of chopped liver and chopped herring, fried gefilte fish and the eggs with which she made cheese omelettes two or three times a week. Leo closes his eyes. One Friday night in the desperate weeks before the wedding, he and Helen Baum lied to their families and met for dinner where they could not be found. She took him to a Vietnamese café near Great Ormond Street where the parents of sick children forked up noodles, thinking of future pain. He felt ashamed of himself for wanting her.

'They know me,' she said of the amused old couple behind the till. 'It's so close to work. And much more exciting than the canteen.'

'So are you,' he said. The thought of her coming here with anyone else at all was physically painful, like needles in his chest.

'Don't,' said Helen.

She chose. They had summer rolls with mint and basil, noodles and beef and sugarcane, unfamiliar beer, real lemonade and it felt dangerous, as if he were being given too much oxygen. He held on to the table edge to anchor himself but everything, even the grey Formica and the writing on the chilli sauce bottle, were fuel to his longings, hints of a mildly adventurous new life.

'Stick out your tongue,' she instructed him, leaning towards him with a soft green leaf.

He noticed for the first time a crease in the freckled skin above her breasts. Lemongrass sharpened her pheromones. Inadvertently, he moaned.

'It's shiso,' she'd said, pretending not to notice and, like a priest, put the food of heaven in his mouth.

Leo, now feeling uncomfortably frisky, watches Naomi consult the red plastic clock on the kitchen wall, compressing her lips and bunching her cheeks like a . . . a vole, he thinks, although his knowledge of woodland creatures is hazy. She wipes the kitchen counter thoroughly with a clean J-cloth and sits at the table to read the paper, jiggling her head gently to the radio. He is gazing at her, as into a snow-dome containing his future, when he hears footsteps. A tallish man in an unnecessarily big-shouldered overcoat is walking this way, on the other side of the street. He looks like a pleasant travel agent, with brown springy hair and an air of mild complacency. He too is carrying flowers. Jewish, thinks Leo automatically: another good son off to see his mother. Then he sees that the man has stopped outside Fortis House. As Leo was supposed to have done, he presses the bottom right-hand buzzer. The intercom beeps an electronic welcome. With a cheerful little bounce, he steps up to the front door.

*   *   *

Two minutes later the man appears in the window of Leo's former home. There is Naomi taking the flowers, smiling. She says something to him as he touches her shoulder and Leo, watching, feels the world slip beneath him.

It is not jealousy but recognition. He knows this man.

He can visualize his mother's reddish hair; he remembers a lift to a Russian Orphans' Aid Quiz Night in the family Peugeot. Who the hell is he? Then it comes to him: Saul Rose from shul, Crouch End accountant, tennis player, notoriously keen husband-in-waiting.

Oh, thank God. He is light-headed with relief, as if a bubble of helium has floated up over the Heath and straight between his teeth. He has failed Naomi but Saul Rose will not. Here, as if spontaneously generated by the heat of Leo's guilt, is his perfect substitute: a man who can be relied upon.

He watches them for only a few more seconds before scuttling down the steps, joy in his heart. Let some poor Finchley pensioner discover the flowers; he has no need for them now. He takes one last look at the flat where Saul Rose, still in his manly overcoat, is nodding admiringly at the Haifa poster, and begins to run as fast as he can back down the road. God, for reasons unknown, has

128

looked kindly twice upon him: once when He showed him Helen Baum and tonight, when He has released him into her arms. Heart pounding, he rounds the corner of Fortis Green Road and tastes at last the beautiful fumes of freedom.

SIX

'What is it?' says Jonathan. 'You seem distracted. I think you should seriously consider switching to herbal tea.'

The telephone begins to ring, extremely loudly. She jumps to her feet as if she has been expecting it all evening.

Jonathan frowns. 'This late? I hope nothing's wrong.'

'I'll,' she says. She swallows hard. 'I'd better—it might be Em.' She picks up the receiver, already smiling.

'Frances?' says her mother. 'We have to talk.'

*   *   *

Earlier this evening, at a shul Administrative (Buildings) Committee meeting to discuss the hideous new stained-glass window currently being hand-coloured, against her wishes, in Prague, Claudia had the most brilliant idea. Since the terrible almost-wedding, the ripples it has spread through the community, the pain—and the secret financial strain, and the worry—it has caused at home, Behrens Road has not felt as safe, as strong as it should. They do not discuss it. God forbid,

129

they are not that kind of family. However, she frets about it, constantly. And now, at last, she has the answer.

Pesach! Who could resist it? Everyone loves the huge Seder meal on the first night of Passover. Therein lies their salvation. She uncapped her pen and, in the margin of the extensive minutes, began a list. With that familiar gesture she began to feel herself again. Was it not, after all, at the spectacular Seder of 1968, with Frances on her breast and the walls of Leo Baeck freshly breached, that she had invited a transsexual rabbi from San Francisco, made fondue for twenty, initiated the Rubins' reputation for thrilling hospitality? Nothing soothes like continuity. If the candlelight and scorched eggs and children under the table don't do it, she will sing them into submission. Nobody can resist the mounting silliness of 'Echod Mi Yodea' for very long.

So. She would involve them all in the preparations for a truly glorious Seder, the whole megillah, cast the spell all over again. It will strengthen the fortress, bring them back to her bosom. Besides, she herself would love it. She longs for it too, the plenty, the closeness, the Passover trick of keeping sadness in sight but at bay. She is sick of the crises, of the slithering night-fears that the golden days may be over. They are not. The Rubins are on track again.

*   *   *

'You know how late Pesach is this year, don't you?' says Claudia to her daughter now. 'April the seventh! And my book's published on the ninth,

130

the Monday! A double celebration. I can't believe it didn't occur to me before.'

'But we said we'd go to Jonathan's mother's . . .'

'And not see us at all? She'll quite simply have to have the second night, when I'm doing the communal knees-up at shul. Now, we'll need those trestle tables from the shed, maybe more, and all your cutlery, won't we, and . . . Are you listening?'

'What? Sorry. How many people are we thinking?'

'Thirty.'

'Oh God. But, Mum—'

'Or even forty. If it's going to be our best, a really fantastic one, we'll have to pull out the stops. Everyone we love, everyone who needs us and then maybe a bit to help with my book . . . I was thinking of asking Robin Buckley. It could be part of his feature. Maybe he could bring the photographer . . . or, no, Simeon could do it just as well and then the press can use them. Who else? Remember Viv Feldman, the editor of *Style*? She'll want to come, and then there's—'

'But . . .'

'Please don't start being difficult. You know I need your help. Emily and Simeon will do their bit.'

'It's . . . it takes so long, and gets so expensive—'

'You can't blame them for not knowing about supermarkets,' says her mother crisply. 'Their lives are very different from yours. Anyway, I earn the money, so I decide when to be extravagant. This is important for all of us and a big chance for me. I'm not going to waste it.'

'The problem is,' says Frances carefully, 'I don't know when I'll be able . . . I don't have the time I

131

used to, not that I don't want—'

'Honestly. Give yourself the day off work. Or I could even invite them, Venetia and the other one—they'd treat you better if they knew where you came from, I've always said.'

'I . . .' Why is she even resisting? No physical mishap, no friend in need nor professional crisis, could save her now. A family Seder must come first. 'OK.' Then she finds herself saying something extraordinarily reckless. 'You will ask Jay?'

There is a short hot silence. Her betrayal settles like a puff of spores. 'There will be plenty of time for . . . niceties later,' says Claudia eventually. 'For now I'm going to ask you one question. Are you in this family or against it?'

'In it,' says Frances miserably.

*   *   *

The stars are out over East Finchley, casting their cold light over Marylebone Cemetery, the Neurological Hospital, Strawberry Vale and Coldfall Wood. It is about to be the most romantic night on earth.

His attempt on Naomi over, Leo can no longer ignore how close he is to Helen's street. He should not approach her without a foolproof plan. On the other hand, he is so very near. What harm could it do?

His previous visit almost killed him. After Scotland they took a train and then the Northern Line and then walked together to a small dim square in Highgate. The rumble of the overland train and the buses from the Great North Road rushed around them like water and there on a

132

bench they sat together, for the last time. He tried not to touch her, or even breathe audibly. In the shadows her eyes were huge silver drops of pain. They talked about her family and why she had to go back to them, her hands stroking the gloriously ugly blue skirt they bought together in an old-ladies' shop on the Royal Mile. He could only think: this is all wrong. How could he say so? He watched her hands and wished they were stroking him.

Then he walked her home, tenderly, courteously, trying to ignore the fat blister of pain pushing up through his epidermis, knowing that every hedge and shop front had been changed by her existence. Think of marble, he instructed himself: bauxite, basalt. It was useless. He would never come here again, to Ingerwood Road and happiness. However, he had been changed. His hands had touched her, his eyes had seen her naked, desperate, blissful. There is no way to remove that knowledge or change himself back.

It is perhaps because of this that, tonight, for the second time in his life, he acts without a plan. He simply does what comes naturally, a state entirely unnatural to him. Even this he fails to analyse. The crowds by East Finchley station seem to part as he approaches. No nervous trot through quiet streets for him tonight; as he approaches the home of his former mistress and her husband his usual inhibitions, his powerful and long-standing fear of being hit, disappear. All he cares about is to be near her, to walk over the same beautiful paving stones and breathe the same sparkling air.

He is not, however, prepared for what he finds. Their house is in a dark Edwardian terrace, neat, respectable, absolutely ordinary but for one unlit first-floor window. He looks more closely and there he sees slim shoulders, dark silhouetted hair, a hand resting on the wood beside it, as if its owner is talking to somebody in the room.

It is Helen, twelve icy metres away from him. At the sight of her he knows the truth. He has to have her. There is no one else in the world.

Do you think you are going to save her? asks his conscience. Are you going to knock on the door, hit the husband, rescue her? Idiot. Go home and be a good son and one day maybe—

He does not listen. As he proved outside Naomi's flat, he is a man of action. There is nothing in the world he cannot do. He opens his eyes as wide as he can, cranes his neck and sends a thought beam of supersonic intensity up to the window, towards his love.

Tell me what you want, he wills her. Give me a sign.

Then something happens. Helen Baum stirs. She turns the side of her pale face to the window and rubs her jaw, her cheek, against the shoulder of her lifted arm. It hides her eyes; if she glanced up now she would see him standing there, bright with longing, but she does not. She simply strokes her cheek, once, twice, against her own warm body. It is a gesture one could only make if one were alone, and thoughtful, and seeking comfort.

She is waiting for him to rescue her. He knows she is. At least, he thinks he knows.

SEVEN

The following evening, Norman accidentally makes everything worse.

Claudia has informed him of her Seder plans and he fears that he has under-reacted. It is hard to feign excitement when his heart and his mind are racing through the sunset towards another goal. As she talked he thought only of the days ahead: her publication and then his own, hot on her tail. With every passing hour it becomes clearer that he should keep schtum until her book is out and the adoration is flowing. Then, perhaps, she will feel happy for him. She will be able to forgive him for keeping such an enormous secret for so long.

And so he makes his first mistake. He walks into the kitchen for a strengthening handful of almonds and raisins before he goes out, not expecting to find her there, but there she is.

'Oh!' he says, grumpy with surprise.

'Have you seen my Rabbinic Conference folder?'

'Have you seen my gloves?'

'They're in your pocket,' she says. Then she sees his freshly shaven skin. 'Where are you going?'

Nothing can be straightforward with her. Over the years he has learned that her apparent openness is simply a bright surface. Even the smallest movement away from her, the least hint of a problem or lightest stretching of his ego, seems to wound her in quiet festering places she will not reveal, even to him.

'Nowhere,' he says automatically although he had intended, truly he had, to mention his meeting with Selina Fawcett-Lye, even if only in passing. Now, however, he has lied and so, to back it up, he adds, 'Only Clive,' because she has no interest whatsoever in Clive Archer, an embittered historian neighbour whom he meets for occasional moaning. It is better, isn't it, to spare her feelings? Telling himself so, Claudia's husband goes out into the night.

*　　　*　　　*

Claudia heads for central London in their smelly old car, thinking hard. The Rubins may not be an emoting, therapy-loving family but they have an understanding, don't they, that if anything is seriously wrong she will be told? Granted, the early warning system failed with Leo, but it won't again.

I'm not *frightening*, she thinks. How hard can it be?

Nevertheless, something about Norman is worrying her. Lately, observing his interest in the post, his mumbled telephone conversations with bright-voiced women, she has begun to wonder the impossible. Could he conceivably be having an affair?

It is ridiculous. The world, Norman included, agrees that he is fortunate to have her. Of course, she could go to his study and poke through his letters, monitor his emails, sift the unpleasantnesses in his pockets as other wives do. She is not other wives.

In any case, she thinks, changing into third gear as she coasts down Haverstock Hill, soon there will be nothing to worry about. She speeds over a zebra crossing, noticing rather too late to stop, but in plenty of time to smile and wave, Vera Greengrass and Carol Elfenbein, two of her stalwart supporters, clutching each other in terror on the kerb. Every time she thinks of the Seder a wave of excitement washes over her, as powerful as love: chicken with saffron and raisins, peonies and bitter herbs, companionship for the elderly and tradition for the young, Simeon's mango daiquiris, guests overcome by lust in the downstairs lavatory and rivers of candle wax. She feels calmer, more hopeful than she has for weeks. Her family can be relied upon. They are, despite recent hiccups, loyal, because they share her dream.

*   *   *

It is astonishing how unnecessary a mother can be. Not, obviously, Frances's own: the problem is rather closer to home, and more embarrassing.

Everyone wants Jonathan. His daughters have always insisted that he put them to bed, which, despite Frances's secret hopes, seems perfectly reasonable. Something, however, has changed. Whereas before they would, occasionally, tolerate clumsy stepmotherly moments, her trial period has ended. Every attempt to win them, the dazzling new toothbrushes and extra stories, is instantly deflected, as if she has been beating them in the night. Now Max too has transferred his allegiance. None of her artificial little rituals seems to soothe him. The moment she begins 'My Bonnie Lies Over the Ocean', he starts to howl.

From time to time she refers, lightly, to her

stepmotherly failings. Her friends assume she is joking. Acquaintances insist that the girls' preference for their father, for their step-grandmother and aunt, is perfectly healthy. But what will they say now that Max agrees?

She stands in the kitchen, watching peas seethe in boiling water and wishing she could talk to Jay. Their conversation clings to her mind like peach-flesh. She turns it over and over, sucking at the highlights. Isn't it time they talked again? What would she think of this kitchen, these shoes?

Last night, when Jonathan turned towards her, naked, she put a hand on his shoulder.

'You know what you said the other night?' she began. 'I . . . I don't think I'm ready for another baby, yet.'

'That's all right.' He sounded cheerful. 'We don't need to decide anything now.' His hand was moving down her back, towards her hip. She touched his chest to distract him as she inched her lower body away. 'We can still . . .'

'I'm a bit tired,' she said, quite firmly. 'Jumping about with Max and the girls.'

'Oh, did you?' he said, sounding pleased. 'Well, never mind. Maybe at the weekend? We'll play it by ear,' and, with that, he slept.

*　　　*　　　*

Afterwards her mind was tight with sex: just none of it with him. About this, too, he knows nothing. He thinks he saved her from grateful near-virginity: that her thoughts are pure. It is too late to tell him what a hungry schoolgirl can glean from her father's *Kama Sutra*, of the fuel offered by

138

Wuthering Heights to an enquiring mind.

When they are in bed together she has certain rules. She allows herself to imagine only anonymous bodies, invented faces or, in emergencies, the stars of her torrid adolescence: Keats; bits of statues; obscurely feathered swans. In the last year or so, however, it has become harder to maintain concentration. Her bedroom teems with the very last people she wants to think about: war criminals, the security guard at work, her own cousins. It happened last night. One minute she was being attended to on her mother's bimah by an eager faceless minyan; then she was in a belfry among dripping candlesticks; then, quite by accident, she was back in her sister's flat.

*   *   *

'Er,' says Norman. 'Selina, is it? We arranged to meet.'

'You're late,' says the woman before him yet, for the first time in Norman's experience of lateness and women, she is not scowling. She does not even seem to mind. 'Selina, exactly,' she says, holding out her hand.

Nothing is as he had expected. When she suggested a pub called the Fox and Hounds his heart had lifted. How satisfying to have one's prejudices confirmed. He could envisage their meeting with perfect clarity: a smoky old-man's saloon; suspicion and sour beer fumes; fifteen minutes of an amateur's woolly enquiries before, his ego punctured, he would withdraw.

However, the place she has chosen is full of flickering night lights; handsome adults flirting;

delicious-looking plates of barbecued ribs and liver-and-bacon. His mouth begins to water. His secret undergraduate passion for pork has, unfortunately, never waned.

More unexpectedly still, in place of the powdery mound of cardigans and curled index cards he had expected, he has found rather a good-looking woman. Her face seems to have done whatever women's faces do when they age well, or perhaps it is makeup. He never knows. She has reddish-blonde hair, which reminds him of his mother, and a fair wide-open face, a fresh healthiness which appeals to him. She thanks him for coming; for agreeing to meet her in the first place; for taking the trouble to walk up to Highgate on a cold evening; for writing the books ('Wonderful books,' she says; he nods, surprised) in the first place, which have given her so much pleasure.

'They have?' he asks. Good Lord.

She even insists on going to the bar while he sits there unchivalrously, enjoying himself. She brings nothing at all to eat with their wine but, in all other respects, there is apparently no limit to her consideration. 'Please don't stop,' he says after another round of compliments but, in truth, he wants her to. It is unwomanly, unfamiliar. He does not know what to do with his face.

'Oh, I'm sorry,' she says. 'I'm making you awkward.'

'I'm not awkward,' he says crossly. 'I'm always like this.' And, fatally, she laughs.

EIGHT

On Saturday morning, at precisely a quarter to eight, a newly focused Leo embarks on his mission.

Today everything will be perfect. He makes porridge, economically using the milk his brother left out all night and only a modest sprinkling of sugar. One day, when he has to carry his aged but still beautiful beloved up and down stairs, he will be grateful for his resolve.

He does his washing and ironing, showers thoroughly, scours black fur from the bathroom windowsill with the lemony chemicals Naomi used, although this batch seems less effective. He writes his grandfather's birthday card. He dewaxes his ears. He even attempts to do a one-handed press-up, as he once saw a man doing near the tumulus on the Heath. It ends uncomfortably against his bookcase but he is undaunted, invincible.

He will also be pure. Now that he and Helen are to be reunited he must conserve his manlier resources. Certain sordid practices will have to end. As if excavating the leavings of primitive man, he unearths the magazines, wraps them in a selection of unwanted financial and sports pages and buries them deep in the recycling bins of South End Green.

The next part of his quest has been planned precisely. He is going to his mother's shul. He has not been since the failed wedding: fear and shame have made it impossible. Now, however, he has a reason. Helen Baum's mother, a miniature Attila from Lake Balaton via Liverpool, moved to

141

London for her husband's brief retirement twenty-nine years ago and, apparently arbitrarily, chose New Belsize Liberal to be her shul. That was that. Nothing could make Mrs Ferencz change; not, within three months, the seismic arrival of the young Rabbi Claudia Rubin; not the appointment ten years later of her son-in-law to the shul in West Finchley, ten minutes' hobble away; not even, presumably, the disastrous collision of the two synagogues, barely a month ago. And so, on the third Saturday of every month, Helen accompanies her mother to New Belsize Liberal: synagogue-hopping as he used to do with Naomi. This is the third Saturday. Now is his chance.

*   *   *

He will arrive at a quarter past ten and sit in the Portuguese greasy spoon opposite, protected by bacon fumes, to write Helen a frank and ardent declaration. He will watch, gimlet-eyed, for the arrival of her heart-stopping navy Renault. He will admire her parking technique through the glass. And then, when she has locked her car door and, with a pre-occupied expression, escorted Mrs Ferencz up the steps towards her waiting phalanx of old ladies, he will cross the road, swift as an arrow, dash through the courtyard and brush chastely past her, pressing his note into her hand.

He is radiantly happy. He knows that he is loved. With the confidence of a man whose future lies before him, he checks his watch and sees that he has outdone himself. It is even earlier than he had realized.

Right, he thinks. I will do what young men in

142

love are supposed to. I will go for a walk.

He crosses South End Road and heads through the dappled plane trees opposite Keats Grove. He is smiling. Who would not be? It is a bright cold morning; the air is wet with life. Spring seems to have begun without him, as if that subtle incline of Helen Baum's neck had been its signal too. He passes the great sweep of gravel where the circus encamps, the huge weedy pond where the little Rubins, bonneted and scarved like Russian pensioners, begged jaded ducks to eat their malt-loaf crumbs. He strides past the Mixed Bathing Pond, ignoring the winter swimmers showing off among the grebes. Then he finds himself in the little dappled copse beneath Parliament Hill, where blackberries lead unwise children into nightmare, a tangle of robbers and wolves.

The adult Leo is not afraid. Nothing is too much for him, not even exercise. Huffing great breaths of pure clear air, he stamps to the top.

There below him is London, a golden city at his feet. He smiles benevolently at the first tourists of the morning, the extreme kite-flyers, the ornithological loners from whom in other circumstances he would edge away. Today he stands beside them quite happily to watch sunlight glinting off distant towers, rooms full of people fucking. He loosens his tie and breathes in deeply through tender nostrils. Even that small pain reminds him of Helen's body, of his own.

Don't be silly, he tells himself sternly. She won't be yours at least until after lunch. He glances casually at his watch and then, only then, sees the terrible mistake that he has made. It is a quarter to ten, not a quarter to nine: idiot. *Idiot*. She will be there already and everything is ruined.

Then something occurs to him. Perhaps he could make it if he ran. How long could it take, downhill to Belsize Park? Twenty minutes? Less? He can glimpse the dome of the church beside it, south, or is it north, of where he is standing. It doesn't look far, he thinks, ripping off his tie and stuffing it into his pocket. Running is what lovers do, and he will do it for Helen.

*   *   *

Claudia stands in the robing room, running through her sermon. She has dressed with particular care. It is not even her turn to give the sermon but she likes Lucas O'Mahoney-Lassman, today's bar mitzvah boy, and so, at the last minute, she has offered. It makes her congregation happy, impresses the guests from other shuls. And all of them buy books.

Mercy, she reminds herself, Bosnia, forgiveness; remember Lily Meyer's yahrzeit is today, or tomorrow. She checks herself, back, right side, bosom, in the spotty mirror on the back of the door: the gift of a congregation unwilling to admit, despite the bald fact of her superiority, that she would educate and unite and guide them as well as a man.

Well, she thinks, turning to view her left side, I showed them. Time for another haircut but otherwise not bloody bad. Admittedly her long black wool skirt is showing signs of moths, and there is a tiny stain on the cuff of her forties blouse. However, her gold and green kippah, her second best one, is definitely flattering. She moves the edge of her tallith a little closer to her collar; white suits her, it always has. She is too old now to wear the flashy colours of the younger women, but there are still countless ways to look dignified but exciting: a rabbi at her best.

Not bad, she thinks again, less forcefully.

* * *

This is not the whole truth. Claudia has a problem. Every time a new book comes out something unpleasant happens; a pain begins to grip in her stomach, as if a belt were being slowly tightened. It is happening now. She knows what it is: a muscular spasm caused by stress, apparently quite normal. Nevertheless, she has told no one. Illness, weakness, are not what they expect. Let me get through the service, she thinks. Then I'll decide when to go to the doctor. Nobody need know.

The murmuring outside has become more plaintive, as if God could be seduced from St John's Wood Reform up the road by a simple change of tone. Despite her many years of service, she feels the familiar squeeze of adrenaline. 'Never outgrow that,' said Seymour Bloom, her mentor. 'If you do, we are lost.'

* * *

Leo has made it. His lungs burn, his shirt is damp, it is past eleven but, thank God, he is here.

Quietly he opens the wooden doors. He had assumed that the universe would help him in his mission, that the Earth's plates would carry him closer to his love. However, he can barely push his

145

way into Landau Hall. Thanks to his mother's efforts and the O'Mahoney-Lassman bar mitzvah, it is packed. The only chair is leagues away, in the furthest corner. Of course it is. Did he think this would be easy?

For most of his life he has been the shul's pet, the most patted boy in North-West London, filling himself with Latin and clarinet lessons so that even the most tragically childless might have a good son in him. However, even before he ran off he had disappointed them. So what was wrong with our girls? they asked him. How could he have begun to explain?

Now, as he bumps his way along the aisles, his body an antenna, searching for his love, he pretends not to notice the nudges and raised eyebrows. 'Shabbat Shalom,' he murmurs, as if the people he passes are not as his extended family but strangers who have never heard of Naomi, who do not care what he has done.

He still cannot see Helen. He ignores the Ark, at which he should be praying his way back to respectability, asking for forgiveness as a good rabbi's son should. He keeps looking. Nothing has any purpose, if she is not here.

So many pointless people. He becomes more desperate, sweatier as he tries and fails to spot her. What does her absence mean? I am going to cry, he thinks and then, to make everything worse, he spots Mrs Ferencz, the wizened avenger, precisely at the moment that Mrs Ferencz sees him.

She pins him with her Medusa gaze. He gapes at her, transfixed. Then, infinitesimally slowly, his gaze slides off her and on to the being to her right: his Helen.

*   *   *

At first she does not notice him. Her head is bent so that most of her face is hidden; she is speaking kindly, intelligently, to someone in the row behind. She is wearing a grey suit he does not recognize but it does not matter; soon he will. It is enough simply to sit there, in the same cube of air, waiting for her to feel his presence. He is wonderfully certain. One look is all it will take.

*   *   *

Claudia approaches the bimah, nodding gravely to her favourites, reminding herself who will need a kind word after the service, who looks sicker and who is sad. There is Charles Jacobs, so much happier since his divorce; Leonie Freedlander despite her daughter's breakdown; oh God, Mrs Ferencz, keep your head down; dear dying Rudi, dandruff all over his tallith, whom we owe a Friday night. She gives him a wink too small for others to notice. After all that has happened, there is no room for the smallest resentment, the least mistake.

The scroll of the Torah is undressed. She helps to hold it steady for the blessings, pretending not to have just noticed the entire Gerrard family, top of her secret shul wishlist even before their ennoblement, sitting just beneath her elbow. It is only when young Lucas begins, rather quaveringly, to read the portion aloud that she allows herself to feel the quite startling pain in her stomach. She holds the handle more tightly. With medicine, in a

147

day or two, she will feel absolutely normal. A minor problem like stress-induced spasms does not frighten a woman like her.

There is nothing to be afraid of, she tells herself, ignoring the racing feeling of her heart. I will be fine, the book will succeed and we have the Seder to look forward to, once the others have shaped up. Dear Simeon: he is the only one to sense her anxiety. Last night he made her a cup of his special coffee, after which she felt relaxed almost to the point of light-headedness. With him behind her, all will be well.

Landau Hall is tense with concentration, as if movement could make the bar mitzvah boy falter. This, and the pain, and the dazzling speech they are all expecting from her, and the weeks ahead, make her jumpier than she would like. She must use her special method to calm herself. Her Hebrew is excellent, even better than her sermons, so she can afford to look away, skipping to the line ahead and trapping it in her mind. Then, as the others sing of the kingdom of Adonai and the blessings of the pasture, she thinks back to her ordination, the moment dear Seymour Bloom turned to her with the scroll in his hands and said to her words she has never revealed to anyone, which, even now, make her eyes shine bright:

'Dear Girl, I said it would be hard, and it was harder than either of us had guessed. I said you must work harder, be sharper and surer than any man, and you were. I said it would be all-consuming and that you must hold on to your self and you did, you have. But what I never said is that England's Jews are lucky to have you. Well, we are. Now, for all of us, be strong.'

148

*   *   *

It always works. Today, in pain, it fails her. Think of something, she wills herself, and then she does: a forgotten trick from childhood. She imagines her mother, pale, slender, immune to her elder daughter's charms, unable to imagine that a woman could be clever enough for A-levels or university, let alone what followed. In her mind's eye she lifts her high above Bushey Cemetery and down over the Harrow hills, the roofs of Hendon and the buses of Cricklewood, towards the scene of her daughter's glory. Then, in the instant before she smashes her through the western windows of Landau Hall, Claudia catches sight of her elder son, in the last place she had expected him, and her heart, momentarily, seems to stop.

*   *   *

Leo is no fool. What he saw four nights ago at his beloved's window was indubitably a sign. They are meant for each other.

Now, however, Helen Baum is sitting a few short metres away, apparently failing to notice him. Once, then twice, she looks his way and he tenses with excitement. Then her beautiful eyes simply glide over him and on to his neighbours, as if he is just another man. How can she not see him? He reeks with love. Pheromonal waves of longing are rolling off him like smoke from a flare. He sits as tall as he can, tendons taut, senses quivering and still she does not catch his eye.

Dimly, like a spot at the edge of his humming

149

radar, he registers Claudia's presence. He had barely remembered that she would be here. She seems to have noticed him; there is a line between her eyebrows, a certain paleness, which suggests she is displeased. But Helen Baum still has not looked at him and he is running out of time.

Hurry, he begs her telepathically. My darling, look at me.

It is surely just a coincidence that she has failed to see him, that she is keeping her body so firmly turned from his. Unless he attracts her attention in the next seven minutes she will leave with her mother and he will have to go home with his. This is not how he had intended today to end.

And so he commands himself, hotly, nervously, to be a man. He waits until his mother looks away. Then he lifts his arm high in the air, as if to stretch it and begins, conspicuously yet discreetly, to wave it from side to side. At that very moment his neighbour Matthew Schentelbaum bends forward to look for his squash partner. Leo twists clumsily to avoid him, Matthew Schentelbaum raises his hand and catches Leo's nose with his elbow.

'Help!' says Leo. He turns away, too late to stop unkosher blood falling from his nostril on to the bony knee of his other neighbour, Vera Tessler. Tissues must be found, dry-cleaning promised; he hurries and staunches as fast as he can but, by the time he can lower his head sufficiently to look in her direction, Helen Baum, his life, his light, his purpose, has disappeared.

NINE

Until now, Norman has been extremely careful. The world may be incompetent and hostile but nothing has foiled his well-laid plans: not publicity girls, not Sim's archive, not even the arrival of a vast bunch of decorative thistles from his German publishers which, with considerable satisfaction, he throws into the outside bin.

This morning, however, things are starting to slide. He has been gazing out of his study window for almost an hour, imagining another evening at the Fox and Hounds. He sees not the ferny drainpipe but a plainly fascinated Selina Fawcett-Lye, begging for further insights into his biographical techniques. And, meanwhile, as his strange new friendship blossoms, downstairs on the doormat lies the Rubins' post.

*   *   *

Claudia is dressing stealthily, willing Norman's study telephone to ring. If there is no diversion he will hear her leave, hauling open the window to shout out a question, an errand, an offer to accompany her down the road. He always senses her departures: so clingy, exactly like Frances. She could of course tell him that she is going to the doctor's but then he would worry, and there is no need to worry. No, it is better this way.

However, it is almost ten. She can wait no longer. Any later and she will be late for her visit to Nightingale House, and people will talk. She

151

walks purposefully downstairs, as if merely going to the kitchen, lifts letters from the mat and opens the front door, ears pricked. No sound, but she is oddly nervous. She thinks: you silly girl.

*   *   *

She sits in the waiting room of the doctor's surgery, trying not to be recognized. It is unpleasant to be here, conspicuous among the veiled Somali women and wan teenagers, the greedy glances of the chief receptionist. A woman her age with pixie-cut hair and ironic glasses is trying to catch her eye: television, probably, or *Woman's Hour*. She looks away.

Then she feels a knife-point nosing between her ribs and remembers her bagful of letters. They are usually all hers, a torrent of salad buffets and mentoring schemes and inter-marriage symposia and, of course, the constant efforts of her creditors and detractors to stay in touch. Nevertheless, she has the distinct impression that the entire pile was addressed to Norman. How can this be? Has he joined a new society: the Friends of Minor Poets, the Association for Scansion Research? Has he been dropped by Swithun or his publishers at last? At the thought of the counselling she will have to do a cloud of lethargy envelops her. Keeping an eye on the door through which the doctor will call her, she slips her hand into the soft folds of her bag and grasps one of the letters.

*   *   *

I am a normal man, Leo tells himself.

He is not behaving unreasonably. There is nothing wrong with jumping up from his desk at work, with dashing like a lunatic from Old Square up High Holborn, through Red Lion Square and Dombey Street and stopping at last, panting, near the Vietnamese café, deliciously close to his love. What choice does he have? He needs to contact her. The chances of anyone missing him at the chambers tea are shamefully low. Besides, he cannot work, he cannot draft or telephone or even think until he has taken the next step in his crusade to claim her.

But which of these floors is hers? Helen may at this very moment glance through one of the criminally dirty windows above him and see him down here on the pavement, undecided. It is time for action.

He leaps up the hospital steps with testosteronal vigour. The doors momentarily defeat him but he masters them. He allows a mad-looking old woman through and nothing, not even her suspicious expression, can dent his excitement. Then, in as sane and mature a voice as he can master, he approaches the reception desk and asks for directions to Child Psychiatry.

*   *   *

He has written Helen a letter. It was extraordinarily difficult. Nothing in his experience, not even the doomed applications to the judge of the Chancery Division which he so hates, had prepared him for this. Besides, he had to contend with the presence of Jeremy Blackstock, smirking every time Leo looked up, snapping shut his lever-arch files like a crocodile seeking attention. Self-expression does not come naturally to Leo. He found himself writing 'moreover' twice and it is not, as Frances has explained before, a romantic word. Are there no rules for dealing with women? Should one be gentle and humble, or masculine and forceful? He fears he knows the answer. He can only hope that his careful self will do.

Now, as he waits for the lift to the second floor, his doubts begin to blossom. Should he have spent more time analysing and rebutting her reasons for ending it? He has never been convinced by them. He thinks: what could matter more than this? She could still have her career. She could still have *me*.

After several cul-de-sacs filled with the ill and the desperate, he arrives in Psychiatric Outpatients. A vast angry child with a baby's fat cheeks and a hooligan's haircut is pouring coloured balls over the floor. In order to avoid them Leo has to perform a humiliating jig. He does not care. Helen is bound to emerge now and see him trying to dodge the balls, but the embarrassment will be worth it. They will look back in a decade or two and laugh.

However, she does not emerge. He realizes with a sudden pain that the real object of his quest, to meet her unexpectedly, has failed. He cannot ask to see her. Even at their time of greatest intimacy she made it clear that, when she is seeing patients, she cannot be disturbed. The waiting room is dim and windowless and unencouraging but he has no choice. He will have to leave his letter.

He approaches a booth in which a stout aubergine-haired woman sits, sticking down the flaps of big brown envelopes. He cranes his neck to

154

see if any bear Helen's name. She regards him coldly. Let her be very kind, he thinks, or even Jewish. 'Could I leave this with you?' he asks, holding out his own envelope with a polite and unthreatening smile.

She raises her eyebrows. If she ever knew the trials of lovers she has forgotten them. 'All correspondence must go through the post room,' she says. 'For security.'

Then she sees the name on his letter. She looks up at Leo's face.

'For Dr Baum, is it?' she asks.

He catches himself smiling. Straightening his mouth he says: 'Yes. Please.'

'You're not staff?'

'Well . . . no.'

The woman's face seems to twitch. She pinches the envelope between an extensively ringed thumb and index finger. 'Personal, is it?' she asks.

Hope, that most dangerous of emotions, is beginning to dawn. He will beg her if necessary. 'Yes,' he croaks and, to his amazement, she smiles back.

'I'll take it through myself,' she says.

He walks back through the plastic balls in a blaze of light. The world is conspiring in his favour. They will be together again, and soon.

*   *   *

'Everything all right, Rabbi?'

Claudia can feel the receptionist's beam upon her as she passes the surgery front desk. This woman, Wanda Marks, is one of hers. She entertains her neighbours during Friday night services with news of irregular stool samples, home visits, the slightest trace of tears.

'Rabbi?' she hears her calling, as if from the other side of a flooded river. 'Everything all right?'

Wanda Marks looks hungrily into Claudia's face. Claudia, undone, looks back.

*   *   *

Something strange is happening to Frances. The grey mist in which she has been wrapped for months has lifted, like a mushroom cloud, leaving the world brighter and more confusing.

She is finding it hard to concentrate. Things are being forgotten. On Monday afternoon she suddenly realizes that the Seder, which she should be helping to plan, has completely gone out of her head. Hurt by her silence, dangerously unrestrained, Claudia will be planning lobsters, dancing horses—

'Oh God,' she says, aloud.

'Did you hear me?'

Her mind has drifted. She is on the telephone to a client of Venetia's: a needy star author whose Nevada-based spiritual journeys sell in seventeen languages. 'Sorry,' she says. 'I—'

'We were *on*,' he says, extremely slowly, 'point seven of my list. Missy? Unabridged audio. Or are you losing interest already?'

*   *   *

She has also sunk to new depths of bad parenting. This morning, when she had been up with them for almost three hours, Jonathan found her standing

156

with her back to the kitchen door, behind which all three of his children screamed at her about her imperfect cereal choices. He opened the door, he embraced them, he visibly restrained himself from upbraiding her, as if she were a dangerous beast he had promised to keep alive.

This sort of thing happens all the time. As a result, it seems quite reasonable that they should hate her. She tries to sniff Max's sweet-smelling hair only occasionally, to harden her heart in moments of stepdaughterly softness. They will die or they will reject her. She must make herself strong.

Then there is last night's dream, which keeps rushing back at her like a cinema door swinging open. She had been in bed with, of all people, Pru, her mother's friend, with her steely grey hair and sensible forearms. There they were in a hotel bedroom on an unexplained business trip, unwrapping each other in a hot clutch of erotic excitement as Pru murmured appreciatively: 'Oh, look at you! You're lovely—and your skin, and your thighs, God, let me just—'

So now Frances, whose husband is growing grumpy for lack of sex, knows the feel of Pru's naked shoulders. Obviously she can never face her again. There is another problem, clearly unrelated, but equally worrying. Her mind keeps drifting to Jay, as once it did to sudden guilt-free death. She is going to have to talk to her again, purely in order to cure herself of this strange longing to be in touch. That is all. So if, for example, Jay were to ask Frances about her marriage, say, or her mother, she would change the subject. Quite definitely she would.

There is no reason to keep thinking about her. Nevertheless, she has somehow lodged in Frances's mind: a tiny scratch of sickness, a drop of poison. Kill or cure.

*　　　*　　　*

Later that evening, trouble stirs. Claudia has been out for hours without explanation, leaving Norman alone. He has been exemplary: fielding calls from unvisited nonagenarians; opening his own tins of soup; even purging the kitchen of his socks and the piles of newspaper clippings he puts aside for his children. He refuses to think of Selina Fawcett-Lye very much at all. Even when, at last, his wife comes home, stony-faced with the pinched look of Trojan helmets round her nose, he says nothing. He feels brittle as an egg, stiff with secrets, but he wants to be good.

Then, for no reason, Claudia snaps at him about an almost invisibly burned saucepan.

'Well, where the hell were *you*?' he snaps back. 'You've got a family to look after! You can't just bugger off.'

She goes very white. They rarely row. He prides himself on his endurance. His job is to tend to her, as if she is a wild unreasonable animal and he her keeper. His scratches are a mark of chivalry. However, from time to time losing his temper—or, rather, wilfully throwing it away—seems necessary, to restore balance. This had seemed one of those times.

Perhaps, he thinks now, he has miscalculated. It is too late to back down.

'You're hardly in a position to talk,' she says,

158

very quietly.

'What the hell do you mean?'

They face each other as if across a pit. She is wearing a long grey woollen skirt that shows off her haunches and a top the colour of raspberry fool. He wants to rip the buttons off it. She is breathing quickly, like a beautiful bull. If she is suspicious of him and Selina, let her be. He has done nothing wrong.

Then she does something strange. She does not begin to shout, as he would expect. Her body, instead, goes very still. She puts her palm over her face, heel to lips, fingers to temples, as if she is holding something in.

Should he say something? He has never seen this before and it discomfits him. He opens his mouth. Then he closes it. He has been struck by a terrible thought: the post.

Oh, my God. He looks frantically at the kitchen table, the pile beside the oven; there is nothing. 'I—did you . . .' She has stopped the business with the hand but he is not comforted. She simply stands, waiting for something. 'Where,' he says to her, 'what . . . where are the letters?'

She blinks at him, slowly.

How much does she know?

'Norman,' she says.

He cannot bear it. She will smell his fear. 'Er—listen,' he begins. 'Something funny. I've—they've sent me—'

'Actually,' she says, and he glimpses behind the tiredness another face: the old woman she will be. 'Can we please leave it, for now?'

*   *   *

159

She leaves the kitchen and begins to climb the stairs. Norman gazes at the place his wife has left. He is discovered, idiot that he is. How could he have thought that he would succeed?

She will not forgive him. Thanks to her shyster father she hates secrets; he *knows* this. What had he been thinking? Then something still worse occurs to him. In her fury at having been kept in the dark, only to discover the truth like this, she will punish him. She will kill his book.

Once he might have wanted it to be stopped. He has, it goes without saying, never been drawn to danger. Now all this has changed. He has scented success and cannot let it fall away. The new, victorious Norman, like a maddeningly over-achieving older brother, is almost close enough to touch.

Perhaps, he tells himself now, drawing deeply on his new reserves of optimism, there is still hope. It could be that she has found nothing conclusive. An invitation to give a minor lecture, say, could be represented as a lifetime's goal achieved, not merely a taste of things to come. Perhaps there is still time to break it to her gently; not, as he had planned, in the halcyon days after her own publication but palatably, none the less. If he can find a loose end and pull himself along it, back towards her, there may still be a way to salvage his triumph and her pride.

He wipes his hands on his faded purple trousers, bought in a moment of sartorial independence at a conference in Aberdeen. His wife and children mock them but they are precious, reminders of a Greek camper-van trip in 1963 with three other stoned grammar-school boys from his college staircase: matching chips on their shoulders, interchangeable wardrobes of suedette and flared denim. They are his Angry Young Trousers, worthy of the intellectual and romantic colossus he had thought he would be.

Lately, he has been wearing his schmutters more often. They fire him up and give him courage. How lucky, he tells himself now, one foot on the bottom step, that he should be wearing them today. He coughs nervously, rubs at an old biro-leakage on the hip. There is no going back. He is going to make himself tell her everything.

*   *   *

Claudia is sitting on the edge of the bath. Ordinarily she is doing, working, talking but now she is simply listening. She does not like what she hears. The house sounds terrible, creaking and squeaking in the wind; there is a rustling in the corner by the basin. What is worse, somebody downstairs, lighter-footed than Norman, is behaving oddly, lifting the telephone receiver, scurrying out to the hall and back again. She has heard them moving the doormat, investigating the letter-box flap. Perhaps they are—

'Darling?' calls Norman, again.

She cannot hide all night. She wants to be in bed. He has come upstairs, walked noisily up and down past the bathroom, gone into his study. He must be standing in the doorway now. Could she sneak past when he goes back inside? His hearing is not as bad as he pretends and, if he re-emerges, he will see her. He will suspect that something is

161

wrong.

This, then, is where they are, after thirty-four years of marriage. Something *is* wrong, emphatically, horribly: the disaster that they dreaded, come at last, and she does not know how to tell him so.

TEN

Where is Helen Baum's letter?

Leo had expected it by return of post: joyous acceptance, pledges, dates and times. There is nothing. He checks his pigeonhole regularly but it remains, as so often, empty. There is no email, no message on any phone. At last, after a thorough search of his work desk and chair and, surreptitiously, those of Jeremy Blackstock, he goes for help.

'I'm, er, expecting something,' he tells Neville Prior, the pink-skinned clerk whom he suspects of far-right sympathies. Leo knows that, to Neville, he has no redeeming features. Unlike the only other chambers Jew he cannot discuss football or secretaries. He is not even a very good lawyer. 'An important letter, from a client and I'm afraid, I wondered—well, it might have been, you know, mislaid. Could you, could you possibly—'

'*If* it comes,' says Neville threateningly, running his finger thoughtfully over the bristles on the back of his neck, 'you'll be the first to know, Mr Rubin.'

*   *   *

Norman is worried. His wife is ignoring him. He follows her around the house like a suitor, just catching a dressing-gown flick at the top of the stairs, the steam from her bath. If he reveals all to her now, into this silence, the effect will be catastrophic. And gradually a new belief begins to form: she suspects something but does not want to know.

So he makes a decision. If she wants to avoid him, let her. Together they will allow a thin skin to grow over her suspicion. His contribution will be to help it thicken. He will be ever more vigilant about telephone calls and letters. He will hide every trace of Cedric Vickers from her. And he will take someone into his confidence: Leo or Frances. Yes, probably Frances. She is a clever girl, he thinks, slipping a magazine photograph of Lower Keating, Cedric Vickers's country house, into a mottled box file. Sensible. Reliable. She will know how to handle her mother.

Nevertheless, isn't Claudia's silence, the way she stonewalls uncomfortable questions as, he suspects, her icicle mother used to do, proof of a deeper coolness? If he, Norman the Pure in Heart, had found something incriminating about his wife, wouldn't he have said so? Wouldn't that be fairer? So, he extrapolates, leaning his head back against the bookshelf, she has either found nothing or she is simply tormenting him, enjoying her power, for which the only explanation is arrogance, a lack of respect for him.

*   *   *

Then, high above him, he sees something which

163

makes him pause. It is the little space in which he lights his father's yahrzeit candle. He does it privately, and rarely refers to him in front of his family. This has always seemed better. Now, however, doubt creeps in.

Arguably, he has been lying to his children. It always seemed for the best. Claudia is sensitive and he is not, so, to ensure that they treat her carefully, they have been allowed to believe that her parents' past was full of unmentionable horrors, while his own mother and father, simply evaporated in a cloud of old age, painlessly, peacefully. To protect them and to support her, he has concealed the truth.

Otto Rubin knew far more of hell than her parents could have imagined. He was there. He saw things that should not be seen and asked questions that cannot be answered and although he tried to forget it for the next thirty years, there are limits to what an ordinary man can endure. And eventually, before Norman's little children were old enough to divert him, when no joke or interesting newspaper statistic could distract him any longer, he took himself off to the garage, removed his shoes and, neatly and considerately, hung himself.

Norman, who did not save him, contemplates this alone. He waits for the weight of it to shift, wipes his eyes and pushes the bulging blackness back into its place on its high shelf.

But is this fair? Why must Claudia alone be so protected? Shouldn't he, neglected Norman, be supported too? He rocks slowly against the old books, listening to the glistening sound of his hair on the spines. Fine, he thinks. If you think so little

164

of me, ignore me. Do as you like.

Or, rather, I will.

He tilts his head to the left. Here is his study: not the gracious room in which he had expected to be famous but a small damp hutch, littered with scuffed Buddy Holly tapes and the business cards of unsuccessful former school friends. There is his desk. There is the telephone, fat with promise. He seems magically to have remembered Selina Fawcett-Lye's number. Would it be, after all, so unwise to ring?

*   *   *

Leo is being watched. He keeps his eyes bent over his work but he can feel Jeremy Blackstock in the distance, like a blond moon suspended just out of sight.

He knows he is being obvious. Although he has turned off the sound that announces emails, he cannot conceal how often he checks for them. He is trying to draft a complex witness statement for a family of Greek Cypriots in Finsbury Park, but every time the telephone rings on Jeremy Blackstock's desk, he jumps and his study mate smiles.

Their conversations lower his spirits even further. Jeremy Blackstock's life is comprised of leg-ups and favours, punctuated by rural weekends with his girlfriend and brutally truncated one-night stands. Recently, after an unguarded reference to the sudden end of his engagement, Leo was invited 'as a tonic' to some sort of club.

'There'll be girls,' promised Jeremy Blackstock. 'Plenty. Even ones for you.'

165

'I, I can't,' said Leo, blushing virginally. How could he go and watch prostitutes, as apparently one does at these places, when his heart and soul are another's? How, given the state of his body, could he not? 'I have,' he said, with the good son's instinct for the unerotic, 'a family commitment. Sorry. You know, it's difficult . . .'

'Well,' said Jeremy Blackstock, aligning his cufflinks, 'I wouldn't want to get in the way of your . . . trrraditions,' and, with that, he waved Leo goodbye.

*   *   *

Now, to escape further invitations, Leo tries to look as sexually unfrustrated as possible, languorously stretching and smiling into the middle distance whenever Jeremy Blackstock turns his way. It is growing more difficult by the hour. Helen, it seems, is ignoring him. Helen, of all people, who always found ways to see him, who was willing to throw everything away, however briefly; who has been waiting, surely—he *saw* her there—for him to take her back. Could she be on holiday? Or ill? Locked in her room by fat Rabbi Baum, whom it is hard to imagine bullying a hamster—and at that thought, fatally, Leo giggles.

Jeremy Blackstock sees it. 'Dear God, look at you,' he says. He is tossing an apple hard from hand to hand. 'You're mumbling like an old woman. You're not turning gay or something, are you, Rubin?' He begins to champ at the apple with enormous schoolboy teeth. 'Is that allowed?'

At last, feeling sullied and unsatisfied after another Internet trawl for his beloved—a subscription-only article about bipolar under-fives; papers given in Reykjavik and Tucson—he does something, for Leo, very rash indeed.

*   *   *

There is a beautiful conference room on the floor below their own. It is primarily for the Head of Chambers but may, occasionally, be used when dealing with tricky clients. The persuasive power of floor-to-ceiling windows and inlaid rosewood cannot be underestimated.

Listening nervously for approaching clerks or the bark of his Head of Chambers, he creeps along the corridor. He is not quite as scared as he should be of being caught. Even the triumph of having smuggled his erection past Jeremy Blackstock pales beside the excitement of talking to Helen, of winning Helen, of their life together starting now. Nevertheless, when he sits on the slippery button-backed chair beside the telephone and begins to dial, he is almost too tightly wound to breathe. She may be seeing patients, he reminds himself, or doing her rounds, or—

He is, therefore, entirely shocked when, from the opaque medical world at the end of the line, someone picks up and announces: 'Dr Baum.'

'Darling!' he says. 'I mean—'

'Oh,' she says. 'It's you.'

Her voice! His body curls with pleasure. He is anxious but he need not be: it is his love and there is nothing to fear from her. He presses on. 'Yes. It is—it's me! It's you! Oh God. Darling. It's been so long, I—'

'It has.'

167

Her voice is restrained, more guarded than he remembered. It suits her appearance but not her soul, the sweet shadowy places. His nervousness is increasing. 'I wasn't sure— Is everything . . . is there someone there with you?'

'No, only me. Everything's perfectly fine,' she says. 'Fine. I'm very busy.'

'Of course. My love. Did—'

'Your letter came. If that's why you rang.'

There is something frightening in her tone now, a faint curl of disdain which he cannot allow himself to think about. He can visualize the little curves of her lips, the underside of her chin, the contours of each eyelid corner, but Helen, whom he knows so well, is not at the end of the line.

He rubs his forehead hard with his arm, as if trying to remember an answer. When he stood before her at his own wedding, face to face with his heart's desire, she had smiled at him and, despite the chaos and sadness, he had known exactly what she wanted. Now, for the first time, he is not quite so sure.

'I . . . have . . . but did you, you know—'

'It was,' she tells him, 'a nice letter.'

It feels as if she has slid her hand into his guts and squeezed them, not gently. He grits his teeth until he has mastered himself. 'Only that?' he asks, still trying to keep his voice light. 'Nice?'

She pauses, as she might with a difficult patient: sympathetic but no more. 'Of course it was . . . more than that,' she says. 'You said some lovel—'

'Helen. What's—what are you saying? I don't understand.'

'You wrote some lovely things, Leo. But that's not enough. Nothing's changed. We can't be

168

together simply because you wrote a letter.'

'But . . .'

'Leo,' she says again, with a catch in her voice to which he clings, arresting the sharp slide down. 'Think about it. You can't decide—'

'I have!' he says. '*We* have. Don't—'

'No. It's not that simple. I have my life, you have yours. We can't override them if they aren't exactly . . . if the people aren't exactly what we want. Other things matter more: community. Family. You know that, Leo, of all people. That was what *you* thought.'

There is a fierceness to her voice now, an exciting firmness into which he moves as towards an open hand. 'But we both agreed—'

'And when we were in . . . you know, away . . .' She pauses. Sheets and limbs and half-caught breaths balloon between them like bubbles of hope. '*Then*,' she says, as if to quell them, 'you were the one who started worrying.'

'Was I?'

'Of course you were. Naomi, and your mother, and—'

'You did too.'

'I know I did,' she says. Her voice is heavy with something. Finality? Regret? 'I know I did. And I meant it.'

Something is occurring to him, dimly, as if through sleep. 'Hang on,' he says. He is on his feet. The room swims back towards him: wood, decanters, future promise. 'What are you saying? Are you—'

'Leo,' she says. 'Stop it now. I have to go.'

Something has gone wrong as it does in dreams: a treasure lost, a window left unbarred. 'Darl—' he

169

begins but he is, it seems, too late.

*   *   *

Claudia has planned everything for this, the most difficult of mornings. To save time she has already chosen her clothes: lacy bra for courage, black suit for seriousness, greenish scarf because it works with her eyes and where is the harm in that? She has even decided on her makeup: the most difficult look of all because it is the subtlest, the one which suggests no effort has been made.

She leaves the house with her makeup bag and car keys bundled in her coat. If Norman catches her in the bathroom with her eyebrow brush, questions will be asked; the rear-view mirror will have to do. Her eyeliner catches, the concealer will not blend, she needs ten minutes and has allowed herself five and her hands are shaking but everything is fine, she is nervous but feeling fine until she glimpses her mirror-face, poised for another stroke of mascara, and sees the bones beneath it. At last she understands what today might mean.

*   *   *

Half an hour later, she finds herself walking down a long turquoise corridor. After a night spent imagining how this moment would feel, she cannot believe how suddenly she is in it. The consultant is there before her, huge forehead, old-fashioned Victorian moustache. When they look into each other's eyes it is like so many other meetings: that gratifying spark of recognition; the knowledge of

170

what, even now, her looks can do.

Then he takes her hand.

'Rabbi Rubin,' he says. 'Very good to meet you, despite the circumstances.'

She flashes him a smile. 'Yes, well.'

The ultrasound wand is cold but not unpleasant. He has warm hands; he is careful with her as, perhaps, he is with all his patients. Possibly he sees them all at such short notice, or it is because of who she is, or . . .

She will not consider the alternative. She must not imagine a parallel world in which those gripping stomach-spasms had not led her to the GP, in which her GP had not discovered, beside her nervous heart, a second pulse. She lies with her eyes closed, trying to ignore the irregular mouse-clicks as he flits over computer images of her breast, her chest, her aorta, switching, zooming in.

'I'll be frank with you,' he says.

That is when she knows. She sits in the chair beside his desk and he lays it all out before her, like a surgeon pinning open a cadaver, neck to groin.

'I understand there is no family history?'

'None. That I know of. Not my immediate family, anyway, and most of the others were killed before—'

'Quite,' he says. 'Of course.'

She cries, of course, but it feels curiously at a distance, as if for someone else. He gives her a plastic cup of warm water and she sips it as if it were brandy or belladonna and could make any difference to her at all. When he explains her options she gives her answer firmly, without the slightest hesitation.

171

He lifts one silvery eyebrow. 'You do understand what I have said?'

'I do. But I can't . . .'

'Rabbi Rubin, perhaps I was unclear. Severe bleeding from any arterial wall, but particularly from an abdominal aortic aneurysm such as this, is instantly fatal. You cannot predict when it will happen. You were fortunate that your GP felt the irregularity by chance, and that he—'

'She.'

'She identified it immediately. All we can ever do is to operate as soon as the weakness is discovered, if it *is* discovered, and hope that the grafting strengthens the artery sufficiently to . . .'

'Yes,' she says. 'I know. I know. But . . . there are other things. My book, and my, my family, and Passover coming . . . It's only a fortnight. Then, obviously, I'll—'

'Your family, I'm sure, would want you to be safe. As safe as you can be. I know you have lived with it unknowingly for a certain time but there is no way of predicting when it might—'

'Please,' she says, lifting a hand. 'I know. Thank you. You said. But I have to protect them.'

'If I may say so, this is not how I would—' He sees her expression and, thankfully, stops. 'All right,' he says, adjusting his pen pot. 'I think I'll telephone you tomorrow at the, er, synagogue. If I may. This is important. I want you to be certain.'

'Really,' she says, letting go of the tassels at the end of her scarf and putting her hands in her lap. 'Don't. I *am* certain. I'm just not sure how . . . I'd better tell them, though, what you've found and what, what I've decided. Soon. Something. Hadn't I?'

172

'Yes,' he says kindly. 'I'm afraid you had.'

ELEVEN

'Who were you talking to?' says Jonathan on Saturday evening, from behind the bathroom door.

'Oh!' Frances has been gazing in amazement at the telephone. What has he heard? 'I hadn't, I didn't, I didn't know you were lis—'

'Daddy,' says one of the stepdaughters. 'It's floating. Hurry.'

'It was simply your—' he says, his voice amplified by tiles and scratched plastic. 'Oh hang on, darling, the flannel . . . your tone.'

Through the crack in the door she can see only millimetres of husband: ribbed sock, droopy trouser knee, a tuft of ear hair. She has ten minutes in w hich to leave for Farringdon. Will he even notice? Isn't everything he needs right here?

*   *   *

Last night as she lay in the bath, letting the water close around her face, she heard a noise. She opened her eyes. Jonathan was looking with interest not at her thighs, or her breasts, but at the old-fashioned and impractical window catch.

'And Susannah's shoe is falling apart,' he was saying. 'Did you keep the receipt? And I can't find Rebecca's spelling book. And Max's rabbit lost an ear in the washing machine—we're going to have to get the drum fixed again. And did you see that email I forwarded about women being drugged in

173

sandwich shops?'

She floated before him, letting her ears slide below the surface as often as she dared. The water licked and sucked at her, puckering around her knees.

'And that hairline crack behind the pipe in the girls' room is letting in more rain; we'll have to get Gavin back to take a look. And I think your earring must have fallen between the floorboards. And did you pay that parking ticket? And don't forget it's school quiz night on Tuesday.'

There was a long pause.

'And?' said Frances with effort, watching beads of sex and longing dribble away down the bathroom tiles.

'That's it.'

The moment had come. She could see it looming above her, glinting dangerously in the taps. If she opened her mouth and said, 'Help me,' perhaps he might.

'Are you crying?' he asked, sitting heavily on the side of the bath. 'Again?'

'I'm sorry,' she said, hot tears dripping into the bath water. 'I'm . . . tired, I suppose. You're just better at it all.'

He did not contradict her. 'I'm sure it will change,' he said. 'And Max's only eight months. Do you find him . . . boring?'

'No,' she said, not meeting his eye.

'You wanted babies, though, didn't you? Of course you did.'

'*Yes*. I think. At least—'

'I know he was earlier than maybe you'd have liked, but we did say—'

'I know we did.'

174

'—that we shouldn't have too much of a gap between him and Rebecca. I worked out the ideal spacing. Don't you remember? We did agree it; to cement our family, as Claudia would say.'

Frances was sinking. 'I know we did,' she said. 'It's, it's . . .' He *is* boring, she thought, listening to the booming pipes. I don't know how to be with him. And he prefers you. And I'm damaging him, and I'm sick with guilt, and I still can't make myself give him attention. And I hate being a stepmother. And sometimes I dream of—

'Well,' said Jonathan, briskly. 'I'm sure it . . . we'll be fine. You'll simply have to try a bit harder, won't you?' He patted the top of her wet head. 'I know!' he said. 'I know what will fix it.'

Frances blinked up at him, her eyelashes clogged with tears. 'What?' she asked hopefully, thinking: He has understood how bad it is. He has found a clinic where they will make us bond.

'Your mother!' said Jonathan proudly. 'We can talk to her.'

So that was his solution. She thought of Jay, with whom she seemed to have developed an unexpected message-leaving friendship, whom she had been trying not to ring for days but keeps yielding. What would Jay's solution be?

*   *   *

'You sounded,' says Jonathan now, 'like you were talking to a lover.'

'A— Jesus!' A huge chipmunky smile pulls at her cheeks but she resists it. 'A lover? Why on earth would you think that?'

'Don't be so paranoid.'

'I'm not being paranoid! You're the one who said—'

'I'm *joking*,' he says. 'Come on, hon—of course I am. A lover! As if you would— Was that the doorbell?'

'I'll get it,' calls Rebecca from the bathroom but Frances knows already who it must be. Jay has come straight here instead of Farringdon: her rescuer. She runs upstairs. She is beaming as she unlocks the door but there is no cynically smiling Jay to greet her. There is only her mother.

*   *   *

Leo has spent the day in agonized silence, too depressed to look anyone, even the chambers spaniel, in the eye. However, seclusion strengthens him. By nightfall he knows exactly what to do.

He reaches Helen's hospital in moments. He leaps up the stairs two and three at a time, nodding cheerfully at nurses, blithely ignoring a tall handsome white-coated man with unnecessarily shiny shoes. I may not be Jeremy Blackstock, thinks Leo, or a swaggering junior doctor full of prescription drugs and sex, but I'm cleverer than all of them. I have remembered that on the fourth Saturday of the month and the twelfth of the calendar year, Dr Helen Baum will be on emergency rota on the psychiatric ward.

However, when he arrives on the second floor, he discovers that the maroon-haired matchmaker at reception has deserted him. Of course, he thinks knowingly: the nightshift. He shoots the teenager at the desk a dazzling smile.

'Emergency appointment with Dr Baum,' he

says. His tone is brisk, as if his disturbed children are just outside in the corridor, posing a threat to themselves. 'I don't have much time.'

'463,' she mumbles. 'Left at the fire doors.'

Like a salmon sensing its breeding-ground, he bounds across the blue nylon carpet to the doors. And there, his sense of direction infallible as ever, he turns right.

*   *   *

Why is Claudia here? On Saturday nights she is usually being stuffed with smoked salmon far from home, not in Frances's kitchen.

'And then,' Jonathan suggests, 'you could put Dorothy next to the Birnbaums . . .'

Frances's face is stiffening. She strains to see the kitchen clock but her view is obstructed by her great-aunt-in-law's black wooden dresser, whose simpering peasants and wheels of cheese must be treated with reverence because they are drenched in the blood of a village. Frances, however, hates it, never more than now. Endless minutes of grandchild-petting and Seder planning have elapsed already. How long will Jay wait for her at Farringdon Tube?

'Frances?' asks her husband as she stands. 'Where on earth are you going?'

'Well . . . actually, it's . . . I said I'd meet Claire, my friend from you know, from school, didn't I tell you? It's, you see, she rang and . . . I'd better get a move on, in fact. I'm so sorry. I thought I'd said . . . do you mind just finishing off bedtime? I've done their teeth and—Mum, it's lovely to see you, but I'm, I've got to . . .'

The side of her face burns beneath her mother's gaze. 'Does she often do this?' Claudia asks.

'No.'

'I'm really sorry,' Frances says.

'This is ridiculous,' Jonathan tells her. 'Couldn't you have said?'

'You did it last night. You played squash. And the night before you—'

'It's not as if he can't manage,' her mother points out, 'especially now I'm here. But to give him no notice . . . Don't you want to spend the evening together?'

'But I promised,' says Frances.

Jonathan exhales angrily. 'Go on, then,' he says. Her payment will be in barge museums, Rubin dinners, pregnancy. It is worth it. She runs downstairs to their basement bedroom, tearing off her old jumper and struggling into a blue shirt, saved for unspecified occasions: hundreds of buttons, toothpaste on the sleeve, her flushed throat exposed. She rubs a damp flannel from the radiator over her face, applies clear mascara and tinted lipsalve in Barely Raisin. What next? It has been so long since she last dressed up that she—

Then she catches herself. What is she thinking? It's not as if she's going on a date, for God's sake. She's married. She's meeting a *woman*. She's meeting Jay.

She hurries to the bottom of the stairs and there, crossing the passage above her like a frill of seawater, she sees the bottom of her mother's skirt. Claudia sounds concerned. She is saying to Jonathan: 'But isn't it your anniversary? I'm sure . . .'

'I know,' he says. '*You* remembered, but—'

178

Frances stands very still. I feel terrible, she thinks. Oh God, I do. I can't do this to him. I should put him first.

Then from the sitting room she hears a thump, a scuffle. The children have finished Claudia's lollipops. The sugar rush has begun. Max begins to cry. The chains are growing tighter. Above her, the voices of her mother and her husband are approaching the front door.

She hears: 'Is she being any better?'

'I think she's starting to settle down.'

So that is how they see her: as a child, a troublesome pet. She turns back to the bathroom and grips the basin, bright with anger. It does not calm her. Her heart is beating too quickly, as if trying to push out of her chest.

Sod you, she thinks experimentally, but her face in the cloudy mirror is not furious, as she had expected: not upset at all. It is smiling.

*   *   *

At last, after roaming like Theseus through a linoleum maze, Leo has found her. She has the most extraordinarily expressive office door: perfectly smooth, the pale pale green of bath water, with a sweetly shabby plastic sign. 463, it says, and Dr. H. Baum. He could kiss it. In fact, he does. Then, courageously, he lifts his hand and knocks.

From deep within, his prize, his heart, says: 'Yes?'

He grasps the door handle. He pushes open her door. There sits his beloved, but her expression is not what he had expected.

'What,' she says even as he beams at her, 'the hell are you doing here?'

He closes the door. He pushes his back against it, fanning out his fingertips like a tree-frog on a shaking branch. He tries to focus on the hair of the woman he loves, her centre parting and the dark strands behind her ear, rather than look lower and see her face.

'Please,' she says. 'You shouldn't be here.'

'I know.'

'So what—why are you . . .'

He opens his mouth; takes a gigantic breath; is obliged to let some out; begins again. 'Helen, come on,' he says. 'Please. You know.'

'I do not. Really. And as I'm on call, I'm going to have to ask—'

'Yes you do,' he says but, dimly, he is becoming aware that her secret signal in Finchley, the moment she semaphored her love to him, should not necessarily be exposed to air. He has no way to explain himself. Once this would have left him clearing his throat, apologizing, miserably heading off down another wrong corridor towards the exit. Now, however, he knows there are alternatives to sensible discussion. Recent events have given him an insight into how other men behave.

She is on her feet. They are face to face. He breathes in the tiniest sniff of her scent and he knows. 'Helen,' he says, to warn her. 'I want—'

As it turns out, she wants it too.

*   *   *

Frances stands in a blaze of yellow light, rocked like a happy drunk as the Tube train roars towards

180

Farringdon. She is aware of how strangely she is behaving, but only dimly: no more than of the thick grey dust crushed beneath the wheels, the grey mice trembling against the track as the train races past into blackness.

She reaches Farringdon in perfect time. Waiting in the station is unexpectedly entertaining and this, too, cheers her. It has been months since she delighted in something as simple, as hopeful, as friendship. She watches her fellow pleasure-seekers fondly as they tramp through the station in search of samosas and energy drinks, feeling almost as young and excitingly dressed, almost one of them.

Five minutes past, ten. Only at a quarter past does it cross her mind that Jay may not be coming. The butterflies in her stomach turn to alligators. Six more minutes pass. Too late, she notices that her purple scarf is liverish in the underground lighting, that her shoes bend comically up at the toes. The evening ahead seems to darken. She told too many lies to come here; she chose Jay's fencing, snappish conversation rather than her husband, who loves her.

Black clouds are descending. Her eyes are wet. Jay is not here.

And then there she is. Strangers turn their heads as Jay passes, some of them twice. She is wearing a tie again, a dark grey suit with slim lapels almost exactly like a man. She goes up to Frances and puts her hands on her shoulders.

'So,' she says. 'They let you out without your bonnet,' and she grins.

*   *   *

181

She strides along the pavement, apparently quite happy not to talk. Couples sidestep as she approaches. Frances, scampering along beside her, watches their faces as they stare. They cross Clerkenwell Road opposite a tall beautiful girl with a platinum quiff. She nods at Jay and Jay nods coolly back.

'Oh,' says Frances. 'Is she a friend of yours?'

'Yes,' Jay says. 'All lesbians know each other.'

'Er . . .'

'And the fresh ones are fitted with microchips so we can seek them out.'

'Really?'

'Not really.' Frances's words echo all the way up St John Street. Should she apologize? Her blush heats the air around her: she is Jonathan's travel-kettle element, not a suitable Saturday night companion for Jay. Dumbly she remembers this morning's conversation with her sister, when Em was already succumbing to the cold which has confined her to Behrens Road and a takeaway. She had interrupted Em's long analysis of their mother's unreasonable Seder commitments with a sudden urgent question: 'You and Jay . . . It's not serious, is it? I mean, no more than usual?'

'Course not,' said Em. 'But what's it got to do with you?'

Jay has stopped outside an ancient shop front. Tea-lights gleam from inside.

'Where are we?'

'My second favourite bar. Ready?'

'Actually, I—'

'That was,' says Jay, 'a rhetorical question.'

The bar is tiny, dark and narrow. It looks like a

bachelors' drinking den: long chalk lists of wines by the glass, no sign of food. At the door Jay turns.

'You don't need to look so nervous,' she says. 'We rarely rape.'

'I . . . I didn't—'

But Jay is already going in. Everyone looks up as they enter.

'They're . . . so convincing!' says Frances.

'Actually,' Jay says, 'those are men.'

There is one round wooden table under a bookshelf, perfect and empty and undoubtedly reserved. Jay walks straight up to it. 'Sit there,' she instructs. 'I'll get drinks.' She leans against the bar and lets the room watch her, while Frances tries to compose herself. There are so many questions she wants to ask, that she hopes and fears Jay will ask her. She tries to prepare herself but, before she can, Jay is back.

'Right.' Here are two tumblers, packed with lime and ice; here is Frances; here is the last person in the world she should be with. 'Let's get you drunk.'

'Oh!' Frances says. 'I can't—' and, with a clumsy wave of her hand, she sends Jay's cigarette lighter spinning across the table.

'Am I making you nervous?' Jay asks, stopping it with a fingertip. She keeps her dark eyes on Frances but something about her face makes it impossible to look straight back.

'No! Of course not. Sorry. No.'

'Good. Unless that's a lie.'

'Why—'

'Because at dinner the other night you weren't nervous, not at first. And then you seemed a bit . . . startled.'

It is like opening an oven door. Frances's cheeks blaze. An embarrassed smirk bakes on to her face. 'No, no,' she says. Jay grins again as she tries and fails not to look at the general area of Jay's shirt: her extraordinary open secret.

'Do you have a problem with me and your sister? Her sudden foray into—'

'No!' says Frances. 'Not remotely—I think it's . . .'

'You can skip the PC endorsements. Anyway, I'm not worried. It's just fun. Your sister's as straight as, well . . .'

*   *   *

Frances swallows.

Magically, Jay understands. She leaves the rest of the sentence unspoken, hovering between them above the tabletop. 'Anyway,' she says, 'we still have the great might of your mother to slay before I worry about you.'

'But she's very . . . very . . .' Talking to Jay is like returning to secret youthful vices: gorging on cold chicken paprika and golden syrup, confusingly polymorphic fantasies on holiday camp beds while siblings snored nearby. It is bad for you and impossible to stop and dangerously exciting. 'Open-minded. Isn't she?'

'Do you really think so?'

'Don't *you*?' asks Frances, amazed. 'Though I suppose you're right. She writes about it and campaigns for it. But in real life's not quite the, the . . .'

'The friend to homos she pretends to be? Precisely.' She is making a roll-up: quickly,

184

casually, with none of Sim's connoisseurial sniffing, his quasi-scientific comparisons of Tufnell Park skunk and Ecuadorian gold. Frances watches her brown fingers, the tip of her tongue, marvelling at this strange new outburst of friendship. Simply being out in the world is so exciting. When did she last go somewhere which did not offer toddlers peeling crayons and high chairs, where the bar staff were not at Heath Hurst Primary with her younger siblings?

Jay looks up. She meets Frances's eyes and, for one unblinking second, seems to pin her there. Then she smiles. 'Anyway,' she says, 'let's not talk about your mother, or your brothers, or any of it. Your sister is obsessed—'

'Is she?'

'Of course she is. That's the problem with you families, big in the seventies, or I suppose eighties—liberal parents, dope-smoking allowed, everyone wanting to hang out in your kitchen. Never lasts and no one ever gets over it.'

Frances sits up. 'I'm not . . .' She looks down and sees that she is digging into her cuticle. She slides her hands under the table and tries to be calm, as cool as Jay. 'We're not . . . that's not fair.'

Jay smiles. 'Fine. You're right, it's perfectly normal to spend your teens running around in corduroy smocking, discussing liturgy and begging for piano lessons and trying to bake challah like your mother.'

'Please stop.'

'OK. OK. So, let's talk about you.' She hooks her Chelsea boot through a chair and hauls it closer to rest her feet on, like a cowboy. 'Why did you want to see me?'

185

'I didn't! I thought you . . . you said—'

'I was free. And you sounded like a woman who needed a drink. Is that true?'

'No. Well, maybe. Anyway. Though this is delicious,' she says, like someone's aunt. 'What's in it?'

'Rum,' says Jay. 'Do you want another? And then I want to hear about you and your family. Your . . . husband.'

'There's nothing to say.'

'Right. I don't believe you.'

'You should,' says Frances. 'Why are your cigarettes brown? Are white ones too normal?'

'Don't be personal. They're liquorice paper. Do you want one of those too?'

'No.'

'Yes you do. Try mine.'

Frances takes it clumsily.

'Suck it,' says Jay, 'and—'

'Yes,' says Frances hastily. 'I know what to do.' She puts her lips on the dry place where Jay's have been and inhales carefully. 'Oh,' she says. 'I'd forgotten how much I like them.'

'Husband not keen?'

She gives her a look. 'No.' The second puff transports her to the belated adolescence of her early twenties: the Kilburn flat of an erratically sensitive journalist boyfriend; his chalky shower curtain; the plastic deckchairs on which she drank wine in a permanent state of readiness for sex, for splitting up, for his equally desirable flatmates to fall for her instead.

'So,' says Jay, taking the cigarette back. 'What are we going to do about you?'

A delayed nicotine high shoots through her, as if

her veins have been sliced open and air let in. Mid-gulp, she mistimes her drink. It evades her mouth completely and drenches instead her nose, her chin, her chest and an impressive hardback sticking out of Jay's book bag entitled *Italian Vogue: a Love Affair*.

'Oh God,' she says. 'I'm so sorry . . . look, let—'

'It's fine,' Jay says. 'Here,' and, as if she were alone in a bedroom, she flicks up her collar, unknots her tie and pulls it, hard, from around her neck. It flies through the air and lands in Frances's damp lap: silkily woven, blue and silver, like an exhibit from a French design museum.

'I can't use this.' She looks at Jay's neck. The tie is warm. 'Oh no, it's seeping—'

'Go on,' says Jay. 'Needs cleaning anyway. Get stuck in.'

There is nothing else for it. Cautiously, she dabs at the book, then the table, then her shirt with the end of the tie. Are there speciality shops, she wonders, floors of trilbies and sharp tailoring for women like Jay? She mops, hotly speculating about women like Jay, until the table is dry and the tie is heavy with shame.

'OK,' she says, handing it back. 'That's the best I can do.'

Jay nods. She says nothing at all. The silence thickens.

'So,' Frances says at last. 'Tell me . . . what, what do you do? I mean, medically?'

'I'm an otologist.'

'Oh. How . . . right. That's . . . isn't that uri—?'

'Ears.'

'Oh. Do you . . . like it?'

'I'm good at it,' says Jay, narrowing her eyes

187

provokingly. 'Other details you might want to know: Moroccan; Jane; always; since I was three. Any other questions?'

'No, I—'

'Good. Now tell me: what's the story with you two?'

'Us two?'

'Your husband.'

It feels as if Jay has thrown something at her, hard, like a boy: a cartoon bomb, unsafe to drop. 'Why? There's, there's nothing—'

Jay is tossing her lighter casually from hand to hand. 'You don't love him, do you?' she says. Then she smiles.

*   *   *

Because they cannot lock the door, Leo and Helen are being careful. He has pushed the desk across it in case of intruders. The lights are off. However, one peep-show glimpse would reveal everything: his hands in her hair; her lips on his throat; her door-pass swinging slowly against his shoulder; her thin white bra strap, her wedding ring. They have not spoken. The room has been quiet but for the touch of tongues, their hungry breathing.

Then Helen goes still in his arms. He lifts his mouth from her collarbone and hears what she hears: footsteps, ticking down the corridor towards them.

Her eyes are huge. He dares not breathe.

'?'

'—'

Together they listen as the steps approach their door.

188

Frances swallows. 'Of *course* I love him,' she says. Her brain feels icy and exposed, as if Jay has sliced the top off her skull and plunged her hand in. 'Of course!'

'Are you sure?'

'I . . .' All those years of imaginary confessions: now it is too late. 'I'm sure.'

'Fine,' says Jay.

'Good. So.' She should go home. She does not want to. 'I . . .' She looks up to see Jay waiting patiently: a god unleashing thunderbolts then sitting back to watch. She feels a flash of something bright and fierce and strengthening, like hatred. 'What?'

'Nothing.'

'It's all right for you,' says Frances. 'You're completely free. You can be rebellious and husbandless and . . . it's different. But some of us, some of us—'

'Are you going to leave him?'

'No!'

'It happens all the time.'

'Rubbish.'

'Course it does. It's fine.'

'How can it be?' She is staring at the table. Jay is not safe to look upon. 'It's not! You have no idea.'

She waits to be told something comforting, and waits, and waits. When at last she hears Jay's voice, she jumps.

'It all depends,' Jay says.

'On what?'

'On . . . what you want.'

Frances looks up and meets her eye. Her gaze is as hot as fingertips. It seems to unpeel her. It gives her the gift of foresight. Any second now:

Jay will say: I am falling violently in love with you. Are you sure you're straight? And Frances will say: I thought I was.

Or Jay will say: You'd be a much better lesbian than your sister. And Frances will say: It's too late. Isn't it?

Or Jay will say: Will you kiss me? And Frances will say: Yes.

*   *   *

But Jay has looked away. A woman has appeared at her shoulder, with silver-black hair like a forties pilot and huge shadowed eyes. They grin at each other. Jay pretends to inspect her: her trouser legs, her shoulders, her hands.

'So,' she says, still smiling, 'here you are.'

'I am,' says the woman. 'Very much so. It's been . . . too long.'

Frances tries to look self-contained for when they turn to her. They do not turn. They are too delighted with each other.

'When was the last time? That ridiculous party?'

'Oh Christ, yes,' says Jay. 'Ursula.'

'Chandeliers . . .'

'Whiskey. Racket sports.' Frances shifts in her seat. Her expression of savoir faire is fading. 'Did they ever fix that net?'

The small woman lowers her lashes and looks amused. 'I imagine they'll keep it as it was. A little shrine.'

'I might go down tomorrow,' Jay says, 'and take

photographs.'

'Want a porter?'

'Any time.'

As if from an enormous unclouded height, Frances understands: this is Jay, flirting. It is exactly what she has been doing with me. We don't have a special understanding. She does not want me. This is simply how she talks.

Then they turn to look at her. Jay gives Frances a different kind of smile. The other woman lifts her eyebrows. 'And who is this?' she asks. 'Not—?'

'No,' Jay says. 'Just somebody's married sister.'

*   *   *

Frances watches her own hand putting down her glass. She is hot and cold at once, like currents overlapping. She stands up, very tall and very certain. She does not even make an excuse for leaving as she finds a ten-pound note and puts it on the table. 'I have to go,' she says.

'Now?'

'Absolutely,' she says and, red with courage, she walks out of the bar.

Two shops on, she stops. She closes her eyes. If she calls me back, she thinks all the way back down St John Street, I won't stop. If she runs after me, she thinks, crossing Clerkenwell Road at Back Hill, I won't turn round. And if she rings or writes or leaves little tempting messages I will ignore her, whatever it takes I will ignore her, she thinks, as far as the Rosebery Avenue bus stop and all the long way home.

*   *   *

Helen has had to answer her telephone twice, once from under his shoulder, but, despite footsteps and trolley wheels, the wards have been quiet tonight. So far, they have been safe.

He lies beside her, listening to her computer's little sighs. His mouth is so close to her bare shoulder that he can breathe in the heat of her skin, kiss her simply by moving his lips, touch—

'Leo,' she says.

Dimly, through clouds of bliss, he beams at her. 'Mmm?'

'Put your clothes on. We need to talk.'

This moment, he had known, would come. He had pictured dim light for their leave-taking, naked skin under a doctor's coat, even a stethoscope, imaginatively used. It would be torrid, yet beautiful. However, Helen seems weirdly businesslike. She does not even help him to button his shirt. He watches her strong slender fingers refastening her bra, the way she presses her watch to her side to buckle it, and thinks of the times she has done it without him, with other men.

'Here's your shoe. Now,' she says, leaning against the edge of her desk, 'that was . . .'

'I know.' He is smiling with sexual pride, the astonishing fact that she wants him. Then he sees her serious face. He clears his throat. 'What was it . . . sorry, my love, I'm—'

'I'm not your love,' she says.

He grabs the corner of her bookcase, like an oak tree in a storm. 'Yes you are,' he says. 'Aren't you?'

'That's exactly the point,' she says calmly. Now he knows her professional face: still, impassive, revealing nothing of the woman he knows, or

192

thought he knew. Psychiatrists, he has heard his mother saying, are not like everyone else. 'Look. I don't know what you expected.'

'I . . . you—'

'Whether you thought I'd fall into your arms, or turn you away, or—'

'But you wanted me here. You wouldn't have . . . you know, done all that if you hadn't—would you?'

'Of course not. But just because I chose this, once, doesn't mean that anything's changed. Or has it?'

He is beginning to feel like a great beast of the forest, wounded, cold, afraid. 'No, nothing's changed,' he says carefully. 'Though—'

'I thought not.' She gazes at the toe of her shoe, turning it to catch a tiny smudge of light. Then she looks back at him. 'You don't understand, do you?'

They stare at each other. 'I thought I did,' he mumbles, a huge Steinbeckian dolt, bruising subtle precious things in his paws.

'You know why we, why this ended, don't you?'

At least he can answer this one. He sees her walking away up her front path, turning into someone else's wife. 'Yes,' he says, 'it was because we . . . Er. It wasn't possible, was it? For you, for me, your family—'

'*Your* family.'

'Sorry?'

'It was your family. I'd done the damage to mine at that bloody wedding. Coming back was never going to change a thing. And it's been horrible, frankly. Everyone here knows, Nicky's shul, the whole community. The way they've treated me—'

'Oh, my poor love,' he says. 'I hadn't—'

'That's my problem, not yours,' she says, her

193

face closed. 'And anyway, it's not the point. You felt . . . that we had to stop after Edinburgh, didn't you. Because of your family.'

'Well, Naomi too,' he says weakly.

'Well, no. The harm had been done to her already. It was the others, really, wasn't it? Your siblings, and your mother . . .'

Leo hears himself swallow. She seems to be waiting for him to speak. 'I, I suppose so,' he says eventually. 'Because her book—'

'Fuck her book.'

A tiny girlish sound escapes him. Slowly, he closes his mouth but he cannot stop grinning incredulously, as if he has been invited on to the bimah in his underwear. 'You can't say that,' he protests.

'I can. Why do you think, honestly, that you have to put your life, what you want, on hold for her? Actually, I know why.'

'You do?'

'Of course I do. It's my job. Lots of people . . . it's quite common. I'll give you some leaflets. The point is that you didn't seem to have realized you had a choice.'

'What?'

'In terms of your life. Your happiness. Your future, separate from theirs.'

'I can't,' he says desperately. 'I've got . . . responsibilities.'

'Yes,' she says. 'To be thoughtful. To love them, if you can. But not to . . . to *trash*—'

She moves her head and he realizes that the pink glint on her cheekbone is not a heavenly aura, as he had vaguely assumed, but tears.

'Oh God, don't—'

194

'It's fine,' she says, wiping her hand across her eyes. 'Let me. Look, do you understand what I'm saying? I can't bear us both to go about the rest of our lives—'

He is fumbling for a handkerchief. Does she mean separately? he wonders. He holds it out towards her and, only then, notices the boxes of tissues on the desk, on the low table and the windowsill. Everybody cries here.

'—with you thinking that you had to do this, end this. You didn't have to. I loved you and you loved me and if you hadn't been such a sodding good boy we could have found, we could have managed . . . oh God.' Her face is in her hands now; she is beginning, horribly, to sob. He stares, his arm still extended, worrying about the soundproofing. Then, with infinite slowness, the truth dawns.

He lowers his aching arm. 'Are . . . are you saying,' he says, 'that after Scotland I could have had you, we could have been together, if I'd only said that's what I wanted?'

'Of course! God almighty, do you think I'd have walked out on my husband, my son, everything, so bloody publicly if I hadn't meant it? Loved you? I don't make grand gestures. I'm a grown-up. But if you weren't, if I'd always be doubting that your wants and our needs would come first, what future would we have had? I didn't want to marry your mother. And I'm too old to be a daughter-in-law again. As if all this hasn't been painful enough . . . Why would I choose that?'

My God. He tries to look wise and intuitive but the truth is that none of this has ever crossed his mind. Do people really defy their families and act on their own desires? Even people like him?

195

They do. And perhaps he too can do it. With that, as if cherubs have peeled away a curtain and revealed another, bluer, world, he understands what he, Leo Rubin, Love Commando, must do. He will pretend to be someone else: decisive, daring, ruthless, and prove to Helen that he can. However upset his mother is, she will understand eventually. They have all the time in the world to make it up to her.

Now he knows what Helen wants from him. He wants it too. Beside her ear is a fat blue book: *Fifty Ways to Leave Your Mother*. Almost smiling now, he says: 'I'm certain. About Mu—, my mother . . . Claudia, all of it. I will behave like an adult and you will come first.' There is something else to add. If he says it, joyriders will kill his elder sister on

a zebra crossing, his mother will develop rheumatism, his father will be kicked to death by skinheads. No good son would ever say it, but he must. 'Nothing matters more than you.'

She smiles, at last: a hatch in a nunnery wall. 'Are you sure?'

TWELVE

Sunday 25 March

Rabbis know about trouble. Much as Claudia's congregation likes to kvetch about her famous friends and avoidance of bridge nights, they also need her. She has become a woman-shaped septic tank, a jewelled repository of misfortune, of

196

neglect and grief and slow excruciating decline. In times of crisis, most people want to hold a hand.

She is not most people. Besides, there is an alternative. Other women, whom she admires, have handled this, mortality, differently. They told no one even when in pain—not that, of course, she will experience that. They were private and proud; they kept their families from suffering for as long as they could. With a handful of them she, Claudia, had been the only person on earth to know. One or two, including her own mother, had hidden enormous tumours, the most horrible treatments, from everyone until the very end.

Weakness is a luxury, like fur or Porsches. She has never been drawn to it. Besides, eggs cannot be half broken. Even the smallest caving-in is disastrous. If the massed therapists of Hampstead and Highgate disapprove of such attitudes, stuff them. When she thinks of the thin brown hands of the brave ones, she knows whose side she is on. Like them, she, Claudia, is going to be strong. She has decided to tell no one, do nothing. And, by sheer willpower, she will make it go away.

*   *   *

That, at least, was the plan. But at four in the morning she jolts awake. Her nightdress is stuck to her breastbone with sweaty fear. Her mind clashes with unimaginable horrors. Nothing, not even Norman's warm hairy body, or the rustle of the trees outside, can soothe her.

Is this it? she thinks. Is it tonight? Must I tell them, after all?

*   *   *

Five hours later, full of coffee, shaken by an overlooked letter from the bank but still, thank God, alive, she descends. Norman is already in the kitchen, looking self-conscious. He does not turn round. She gathers milk, spoon, a bowl: no reaction. She approaches the muesli jar.

He is eating his bran standing, like a penitent. She watches him turn the newspaper pages in silence, uncharacteristically ignoring the columnists' anti-Semitism; his rivals' presence in the birthday lists; the television programmes which have snubbed him. He is pretending not to have heard her. A valve seems to open in her chest, letting panic in.

'Norman?' she says.

*   *   *

Norman woke this morning in decisive mood. He has been feeling wounded and, yes, misunderstood, which he has always felt to be an unfairly mocked condition. Indignation, however, suits him perfectly. If he is to ring Selina Fawcett-Lye, it will spur him on.

After all, what does Claudia expect? The secrecy surrounding his book is eating away at his nerves, as visualized in biology O-level textbook red and blue ink. How can he face another day at his desk without one little ego boost? Besides, he has been thinking resentfully, man cannot live on whatever it is alone. Some of us need support, encouragement. For God's sake, even she does.

And now here she is, feeling sorry for herself.

198

Too late, he thinks, blindly flicking through Travel, his back turned to her. The corner of the Books section, hastily stuffed down his trousers, is beginning to pierce his side. The ink will give him septicaemia; now, of all times, when success is so close.

'Don't you have a confirmation class to teach?' he says, not looking up. He can hear her making her private gesture of comfort, rubbing one foot with the other like, he always thinks, an erotic cricket. He ignores it. 'A tombstone to consecrate?'

Although she says nothing he can feel her, watching. Just go, won't you? he thinks, feeling satisfyingly brutal.

Then he looks up and sees her face.

*   *   *

A little later, at their father's summons, the younger Rubins begin to gather. There is no sign of either Norman or their mother. Leo looks like Frances feels, with the stunned glaze of the profoundly underslept. Em is resplendent in a tiny jumper and shaggy jerkin, her hair in little bunches like a child's. It feels strange to kiss her, stranger not to say Jay's name. However, Frances cannot risk mentioning her. She has made her decision. If she is to purge herself of this strange friendship, she must not think of Jay again.

Leo is smiling at something on the floor. 'Why are we here?' she asks but, before he can answer, there is Sim's smell, a fug of rolling tobacco and dirty tie-dye, and he is beside them, wiping his nose with his wrist.

'What's up?' he says, one hand possessively on

Em's shoulder. 'Bet you know, one of you two. Bit of a tip-off from Daddy? Have they decided who gets what when they croak?'

'No!' she says. There is an awkward silence. 'Doesn't anyone know where they are?'

Jonathan would know what to do but, today, even he is not family. He is staying at home with the children, overseeing the baking of Sim's supplementary thirtieth-birthday cake. When she came in last night, he was asleep. Don't other men wait up for their wives, even to argue? Never mind, she thinks. All that is over. I am a good wife and mother and daughter and sister again. It does not matter now.

*   *   *

Claudia's children bite their nails and find things to eat, pretending not to watch Sim preparing his breakfast: pumpernickel, gherkins, horseradish and their father's private Czestochova herrings, bought at great expense from an Ealing restaurant supplier. Leo sits down suddenly, overcome by acetic acid and troubled desire.

'Are you all right?' asks Frances.

He smiles. He wants to tell her. He opens his mouth, then sees their father standing in the middle of the hallway, scratching his scalp like a tired silverback.

'You'd better come through,' he says. 'Your mother is waiting.'

Leo files out behind the girls, Simeon at his back. His stomach is full of melting ice. Heresy, hubris, are always punished. He will lose his family, or Helen, probably both. Behind him Simeon

200

breathes quietly, like a man with a knife.

Their father stands in the sitting-room doorway, gnawing at his palm. He looks like a Roman sentry, nervous and badly trained. They troop past him and there, on the hard chair beside the fireplace, sits their mother.

She looks tired. She does not smile at them but at her hands, clasped in her lap. Embarrassed, Leo glances at the others. No one will meet his eye. This, he thinks, is where the punishment starts.

'I . . .' begins Claudia. 'I asked you to, to come . . . God, where do I start?'

*   *   *

It is only now that she understands what she has begun. If she tells them the truth, they will cry. They will try to delay her book and the Seder, thinking that it is for the best. They will treat her as if she is flawed and finite, as if she is the one who needs protection—and that is before one of them confides in a friend, who tells another, and by tomorrow the whole of London will know.

She cannot do it. She was wrong to try. And what if the doctors are mistaken? She could have years ahead, a decade, two. Perhaps, she concedes, if all goes well, she will try to slow down, a little. But, in the meantime, why upset them? Why not stick to her original plan, despite what the specialist said, and keep this to herself?

Every eye is upon her. She tries to look solemn but she feels buoyant, as if she has pulled off a startling, glamorous crime. There is, too, the unmistakable satisfaction of holding an audience, hot in the palm of one's hand.

'So,' she begins.

She catches Simeon's eye. He is feigning relaxation on the sofa but one of his square knees is jiggling. She has frightened him. He shifts uncomfortably. How tired he looks. If only Leo were to move on to a chair he could lie down properly.

Time to begin. 'There's a reason I've gathered you all,' she says. 'It's to say thank you.'

They gape and blink. Emily whispers something in Simeon's ear.

'Why?' says Frances.

'Well, why shouldn't I? I do realize what a strain it all is, the interviews and so forth, me so tense. You've all been brilliant and it's looking so good, it really *is* going to be big . . . You know about the documentary, don't you? That it's going ahead?'

'No,' says Frances. 'What documentary?'

'Hello?' Emily says. 'Wake up. Of course we know.'

'But I know it's hard,' Claudia continues. 'So I wanted to say that it is appreciated, darlings. By me, and your father—'

'Hrrhrm,' agrees Norman.

'And also—I know this sounds silly . . . It means so much to me that you're all behind me now.'

'Yeah,' Simeon says, lifting his head to scowl at his sofa-mate. 'Not saying any names.'

She beams at him and goes on. 'I know that if we can only get through this together, it'll be worth it. We've always been a team, haven't we? And this is our chance to show the world that we're still on top form: the Seder and the book together, bang bang bang. Don't you think?'

'Nice one,' says Simeon, and they smile at each

other.

*   *   *

In the silence that follows, their father harrumphs. 'Coffee, anyone?' he asks. 'If that's all?'

'Of course it's all,' their mother says. 'Thank you, my loves.'

Something is wrong, thinks Frances. As the others begin to drift out into the hall, she puts her hand on Leo's arm. 'What's going on?'

He actually jumps. 'What? Me?'

'Something is. Come on, you can say.'

'Say?'

'You sound demented. Just answer me. What's up with her?'

'Her?'

'Mum!'

'Oh. Oh, right. Phew. Er, is something?'

'Hurry,' shouts Em from the kitchen. 'I need you!'

'Why?' whispers Frances. 'Is something else wrong?'

'Nothing!' Leo says. 'I—'

'It's an emergency,' their sister calls. 'My phone's in the washing machine . . . Come *on*,' and, when Frances answers, Leo slips away.

Her next hope is Sim. Her brother, however, usually so alert to the tiniest hint of neighbourly disrespect, for whom every road-bump is a government plot aimed at him, claims to have noticed nothing.

'Dunno,' he says, viciously decapitating a banana with a Magimix blade. The muscles beside his ear tighten, release, tighten. 'If something was wrong she'd say.'

'But maybe she wouldn't. You know what she's like.'

'I do,' says Sim. 'I live here. Do you?'

'Well, hang on. I do know—'

'She's stressed about her book. And probably stuff at 'gogue, Pesach stuff and that.' He throws the rest of the banana in the sink and rubs his hand along his jaw, as if testing its sharpness. 'You want my advice, you'd leave it. You heard her. We've all got to be behind her. I've had enough of this crap.'

'Well,' she says, 'I'm sorry, but—'

'And don't say sorry all the time either.'

Then only Em and she are left. They always seem to be on the brink of real sisterhood, about to discover stepping stones across the waters of oversensitivity and the torrent of ego. Perhaps, she thinks, now is their chance.

She opens her mouth and sees that, already, Em's eyes have grown bright. Tears begin to fall from her lower lashes, dripping off her lips.

'Oh no,' she says, 'oh no, what's wrong?' But she knows. Excitement flares in her chest. It must be Jay. She takes her sister's hand. 'I know,' she says.

'No you don't! You have no idea.'

'What's happened?'

'Nothing. I feel bad, that's all.'

'Why?'

'You heard. Me and Jay, the, you know, girl thing, it's bad for Mum. The book, everything. We've got to get behind her, not mess about. You know. Close ranks.'

'But if you like her—'

'I do, but not . . . not that much.'

'Are you sure?'

204

'Course I'm sure.'

Frances tries to think of something elder-sisterly to say. 'Well,' she says, then stops. Where Emily's lovely neck meets her shoulder, on the soft crème-caramel skin, is the biggest, clearest, freshest love-bite she has ever seen. Jay, she thinks wonderingly. So that is what they—

'I so hate the thought,' sniffs Em, 'of you lot at the Seder, and me by myself—'

'You won't be,' Frances says soothingly. 'We'll all be there. But the only thing is, well, you don't have to end it, you know, just because—'

'Why not?'

'Well . . . Jay's good for you. Isn't she? I mean, she's quite a . . . Don't you think you're more yourself when you're with her? Happier?'

'I don't know,' says Em thoughtfully. 'What do you mean, more myself?' She smoothes back her hair from her face, looking interested. 'What do you think I am?'

'But you can't let it happen,' Frances says. 'What's the worst she can do? If she's putting pressure—'

'Crap.' Em is beginning to cry again. She wipes tiny stars of snot across her jumper sleeve, dampens a finger to smooth down her eyebrow, inspects her reflection on the oven door. 'I don't want to be brave,' she says. 'We've got to be *closer*, us lot. Even closer. We owe it to her.'

*　　　*　　　*

It has been a mystifying day. Claudia's sudden instruction to gather the children frightened him. She seemed on the verge of revealing something awful which never came. But now, after a brief interval of relative cheerfulness, she has returned to her newly distant self. She made two boiled eggs for lunch and took them both up to her desk, leaving Norman feeling foolish and hungry in her wake. He tried to console himself with toast, with the thought that, yet again, the bad news he had been braced for never came. It did not work. She isn't interested in you, he kept thinking. She doesn't care what you do.

Three large sandwiches later, he is feeling more confident. Well, he thinks, if that's how she feels, tough. Tough: what a pleasing word. He waits until she has left for shul. It requires effort not to follow her upstairs to the front door, to ask where she is going and when she will return but, newly macho, he manages it. Then, like a wounded general, he makes plans.

Selina, he discovers, will be attending a meeting of the Chelsea Scientific and Literary Society this very evening. She could leave now and be in London in an hour. What could be nicer than a walk? Groping beneath his desk for the *Ham and High*, Norman locates the Lauderdale House café closing times. He calculates a schedule to allow for minimum walking time, maximum cake. Then he agrees.

*   *   *

The weather has cleared by the time he begins to bound towards Waterlow Park on springy soles, thinking of coffee cake for him, something paler— Victoria sponge, a Bakewell tart—for her. She will be late, presumably, so he has brought to their agreed bench Cedric Vickers's *Nature Studies*: his own little Bible, full of love and hate. And something else, charmingly wrapped in a carrier bag: a Larkin pamphlet, of which he has two copies. He does not intend to give it to her, not at all. If it is worth anything, which he doubts, his children will need it more than she does, with her stables and her spoilt wastrel of a son—

She is there already. In Norman's experience women are generally called away to last-minute interfaith symposia; they divert to buy flowers for dinner parties full of smiling Aryans; they bump into flirtatious poets when crossing the Heath. As he approaches his hand slides around the plastic, pulling it tighter.

'Hrumph,' he says, by way of greeting. Everything about her—the old gold chain round her neck, her healthy freckles, the conker sheen of her bag—proves that he was mad to come. It can be only a matter of time before she says something terrible about the tendency of his race to meanness, hirsutism, oversensitivity, world domination; before *The Protocols of the Elders of Zion* falls out of her bag.

But it appears that she has left her Klanswoman hood at home. She smiles as he approaches, stands, offers him her cheek. Naturally, he kisses it. He is at least partly civilized. Her skin has a fascinating texture: milky and very soft, with none of his wife's firmness, her zaftig sheen.

'What's that?' she says, startling him. 'Under your arm?'

'Oh, nothing. Nothing. Well . . .' He shoves it at her. She recognizes it at once. Her delight is delicious. 'Keep it,' he tells her, 'if you want.'

207

'Oh no,' she says. 'No, you mustn't. Honestly. I can't—'

'Fine,' he says gruffly. He cannot help interrupting her and will not try. God knows how many of her other Cheltenham Ladies' rules he must have broken. 'Leave it if you don't want it. I don't care.'

'No, no, it's a thrill, that's all.' He looks at her sharply but she does not seem to be mocking him. However, one never knows. 'I'm not . . . it's such a pleasure to dip into your world.'

'Nonsense,' he says lightly, but her words are ominous. Which world: failure? Semitism? What on earth can she mean? He thinks of National Trust tea rooms, cagoules and Christmas carols, Little Lord Fauntleroys with tiny tweed jackets. Any minute now she will bring out her comedy-Jew accent. 'You know, maybe I should g—'

'No, it's true. The people I know care about Waitrose parking and church fetes and, and, *tack*.' Norman smiles knowledgeably. 'They aren't interested in Leavis, or bibliographies from 1980. I, well, I can't tell you what a relief it is to encounter, well, a sympathetic mind.'

A curl of beard has clamped itself between his teeth. Discreetly, he lets it go. It occurs to him to tell her that he, too, dreams of sympathy. Sex he has, yes; mental stimulation; friends of sorts; grown children. But has there been anyone else who cares for Cedric Vickers's world as he does?

Not until now. He looks into her eyes: the unremarkable blue-grey of unvisited northern seas. 'I,' he says solemnly, 'feel remarkably similar.'

*   *   *

All at once he seems to be telling her everything: his third of a century in the biographical wilderness, his devotion to the unpopular Vickers—'and I am, you see, Jewish,' he says to get it over with, carefully examining his knuckle, 'so he wasn't an obvious choice'—and a hint as to the nature of his discovery, although of course not the whole truth. There can be no question of trusting her but, oh! The pleasure of a little showing-off.

Then matters grow more complicated.

They have ended up outside the café, on the bench dedicated to a pair of aged Nussbaums, P. and C., with a Shakes-pearean couplet in German underneath. He usually finds it strangely moving, although if he ever meets one of the presumably wealthy Nussbaum children he would hate them, without a doubt. Today, however, he barely notices their ghostly presence. The cake he failed to order sits inside in the dark, almost forgotten. They have not stopped talking for two and a half hours and, somehow, in the course of their discussion, one of them has taken hold of the other's hand.

He is refusing to consider this fact. The hands lie between them on the silver wood like leaves might, dry and without interest. Any number of explanations is possible: literary camaraderie, encouragement, cold, but he prefers to think of it merely as an accident which has befallen a stranger's body part.

However, young stud as he likes to think he

once was, he has never been cool with women. He cannot quite help sneaking glances at their knuckles in the dim light, glowing faintly together like underwater stones. Then, as he lifts his eyes once again, he meets hers.

'Dear Lord,' he says, a little abruptly, 'what do we think we're doing?'

Her mouth twitches. She takes her hand away. 'Are you not—'

'A hand-holder of strange women? Oddly no, not usually. Not,' he says gallantly, 'that you are.'

'Strange? Or a woman?'

'Oh, no, no, I meant—'

'I'm teasing,' she says. 'I've no idea what we're doing either.' She beams at him and he smiles back. He cannot help it. 'I think we've fallen in friendship,' she says.

His libido, piqued, flicks its tail. 'Is that what this is?' he hears himself saying. His words float between them, as if pulled along by an aeroplane.

She hesitates. 'One thing, though. I'm curious. Your son, that man on the phone . . .'

'Not a *man*,' says Norman, before realizing that, strictly, this is what Leo is. 'I mean—'

'Well. I hope you don't feel this is prying—'

'No, no, not at all . . .'

'But are you, do you . . . it sounds so silly to ask this. But, do you have a, well, wife?'

The garden falls cold and quiet. Birds which, to his faint irritation, have been shouting in their ears as dusk descends, choose this moment to be still.

'I, I have, yes,' he says, after a time. 'Ahem.' It feels as if the bench has been ripped away, taking his trousers with it. Well, he asks himself, what did you expect?

'And she's . . . ?'

He swallows audibly, like an adolescent. It is confession time. 'She's . . . well, you might have heard of her, actually. Er. Claudia . . . Claudia Rubin?'

Astonishingly, she shakes her head.

'She's a rabbi,' he reminds her as, all over Waterlow Park, listening Jews hold their breath. 'Claudia Rubin. Rabbi Claud—no?'

'Honestly,' she says. 'Sorry to be an idiot. I really haven't the faintest idea who you mean.'

'Good Lord,' he says. He squints to get a better look at her. 'Do you really not know?'

'I'm afraid I don't. Sorry. I never see the news—'

'Well.' Ordinarily he would be bristling on Claudia's behalf but, today, it strikes him as rather funny. Rabbi shmabbi, he thinks but, of course, does not say. 'Do you have a husband?'

'Yes,' she says. 'But I never see him. Don't like him much.'

'Really?'

'Absolutely. Long story. We bred. That's it. You know how it is. Basically,' she says cheerfully, 'I'm my own woman.'

Norman finds that he is stroking his beard, like a panellist on late-night television. He wedges his hand beneath his thigh, the warm dense muscle. 'Interestingly enough,' he finds himself saying, 'I know exactly what you mean.'

THIRTEEN

Wednesday 28 March

My brother, thinks Leo, is not normal.

For weeks they have all been pretending not to notice that Simeon is being himself, only more so. He leaves his room infrequently; the dark Simeon-scent as you approach the stairs, the tangle of sex and drugs and dirt and danger, has deepened; he listens to his enormous headphones even on the way to the bathroom, and closes his eyes if Leo appears. He has begun keeping the oddest things for his Rubin archive—old negatives, shopping lists—and insists their father stores them in the safe. Most ominously, he is eating only at night, when his family are in bed, his diet confined—Leo excavates the table each morning—to omelettes from the Bombay Star, chips from the Chinese on Gordon House Road, and pints of milk.

These habits are familiar. In Simeon's late teens, after months of muttering and unpredictable rages, their mother sent him to a psychiatrist neighbour for, as she put it, a friendly chat, which lasted ten minutes and was never mentioned again. This time, however, it seems worse.

Sometimes Leo thinks of talking to one of the others, probably Frances.

Sometimes he thinks of telling Frances everything, even about his side of their childhood, even about Helen.

Sometimes, when he lets himself in after work at night, the air seems thickened, like aspic. It feels as if everyone is waiting, as if they have rushed out over a cartoon cliff and haven't yet looked down. He thinks of it again momentarily at lunchtime, standing naked and absolutely still in Helen's holidaying colleague's flat near Russell Square, both inside and outside her, not breathing. Then he forgets it, because other things matter more.

*   *   *

Oh, my darling, thinks Norman. You are beautiful.

His book is here. His publishers have been expressly forbidden to send the usual twenty gratis copies of *A Hidden Man: The Surprising Life of Cedric Vickers* to Behrens Road. He has, however, allowed them to post him a single finished copy. See its blessed blue endpapers; see his name in gold upon the jacket and beneath it, indelibly, on the spine. See the copy: this book is revolutionary. Its author is acclaimed . . . Well, I should be, thinks Norman. And see, on plate four, his treasure: the reproduction of a battered group photograph, kept with the Sussex letters but never identified, until now. Probably no other Vickers scholar had ever entered the basement off Baker Street where extra boys from Marylebone Reform had, even in his day, endured Religion School, counting every whitewashed brick, dreaming of girls and breakfast. It paid off, as Norman's parents always said it would. With those background bricks identified, microscopic gaps in Vickers's apparently ordinary Anglican childhood, lacunae in letters, suddenly made shocking, glorious sense.

Norman turns to page six. He runs his stubby finger over the sentence which will bring delight or horror to so many, over the beautiful words, in Garamond (he asked), which reveal the truth that only he could have discovered:

'Because what nobody realized, then as now, is that he had not always been Cedric Fergus Vickers. He had been named Karoly Felix Cantor because he was, of course, secretly a Jew.'

*   *   *

Frances needs somewhere to cry. It keeps happening, as if all the thoughts she must not think are condensing inside her, and leaking out. Today, at least, she can find one. Susan Bourne, a sweetly unpleasant editor with pendulous breasts and a distracting mole, has cancelled their lunch. Frances had come in specifically to meet her. Now she has a whole hour to herself.

'I might run to a . . . a bookshop,' she tells Jerry, the assistant, unnecessarily. 'See what's coming out, er, up.'

But she is lying. Smiling madly into the middle distance, she passes reception, currently staffed by a Booker-winner's daughter, and slips downstairs.

*   *   *

Mercifully, the basement meeting room is free. She spreads out the new publicity stills for *History Under the Microscope*, covers her eyes with her hand and lets a great wave of hopelessness, uselessness, pointlessness wash over her and gather her in.

Then Magnus Brill, from Film and Television, opens the door.

'Sorry,' he says. 'Looking for my diary,' and notices her face.

Magnus Brill is a certain type of man. Women think they alone have discovered him. He is tall, thin, balding, terse in meetings. He does not immediately try to be their friend. Frances, however, has seen his flashes of charm. She knows that there is always a moment under a shared umbrella, at a publishing party by the coats, when such men seem to unfurl and focus. It is then that you notice the intensity of their dark-lashed eyes, their rumbling accent, the fact that, of all people, they have chosen to talk to you. Besides, Magnus Brill allegedly writes, which does wonders for a man.

Generally she treats him with an amused distance, to signify how unmoved by his charms she is. Today, however, mottled and snotty, it is harder to maintain reserve.

'You,' he says. 'Christ, what's up?'

She swipes at her face with her hands like an animal discovered in its burrow, which is not the ideal relationship to Magnus Brill. She lowers her heavy head and sees that he is passing her a square of tissue from his pocket, as if perpetually prepared for women in distress. He shuffles a chair next to hers and, rolling a forbidden cigarette, asks her if she has ever noticed the fascinatingly penis-shaped tip of the agency's most eminent novelist's nose. Then he begins to tell her a scurrilous story about Venetia at a Canadian literary festival, caught with two naked poets by a hotel fire alarm.

He seems quite happy to entertain her, neither anatomizing nor ignoring her misery but simply letting her be. That is why, when he says, 'It's

215

lunchtime, anyway. Come and have a drink,' she simply follows him.

*   *   *

She feels desiccated with crying. Salty crystals make the skin of her face itch. He gets her drunk in a maroon pub on a side street, quite openly. It is, he says, her cure. At first it feels like charity and then, when she is past caring, it feels like something else.

'Gins and tonic are fantastic,' she declares after her third. 'It makes nothing matter.'

'Nothing?' he says. 'At all?'

They order each other's sandwiches. With editors or authors, lunches are harder work and almost always sober. One does not laugh this much.

'Why have I never noticed you?' she asks. 'As an office accomplice?'

'I've no idea,' he says. 'Well—'

Then he catches her eye. She remembers, as if hearing an echo, the instinct she had a glass ago: that sexual frustration and gin and truancy do not mix. She smiles, uncertainly. 'Oughtn't we to go back?' she asks. 'I mean—'

'Too late,' he says. 'Have to pretend we're at a meeting now. Have to pretend publishers did this to us, this terrible drunkenness thing.'

She starts to eat his sandwich. He says: 'Let's go for a walk. Rude not to. Primrose Hill is inches away.'

*   *   *

Despite a lifetime of nightmares simply about being late, going AWOL comes naturally. It is only as they walk through the trees, free and coatless, breathing the alcoholic air, that she remembers that she has children. Or, perhaps, she says it, because when she turns to look at him he gives her a sideways smile. She is in a bubble of irresponsibility.

So, she thinks delightedly, this is how liberation feels.

When they are very near the gate they see a taxi. 'Let's get in it,' he says.

'We don't need to. Aren't we—'

'I have an idea.'

The taxi drops them outside an old print works on Copenhagen Street. After a lot of stairs he lets her into a white room with a sloping glass roof through which the sun shines, thick and hot.

'Whose is this?' she asks.

'Mine,' he says. 'And look—wine.'

'I like it in here. But don't you have a flat? A house?'

'Of course I do,' he says, giving her a glass. 'But this is for the writing.'

'Writing.' She leans against the window and notices, under curling piles of papers, a blanket: a bed. She chooses to ignore it, concentrating instead on the delicious, horrifying fact of their escape. 'We're being very illegal,' she tells him.

'We are. Venetia will sense it with her budgetary radar.'

'Oh God,' Frances says. 'I bet she can,' and the thought is unfrightening, almost, just as she is almost not thinking of Jay, all the time.

'I tell you what,' he says. 'You look amazing.'

217

'Rubbish,' she laughs but, inside her, something hungry and longing and lonely turns towards him. Her hand reaches up to her hair.

'It's not. Look at you.'

'I have,' she says, breaking his gaze. 'It's a horrible sight. Anyway, don't—'

'What?'

'I suspect your motives,' she says and raises her eyebrows, or tries.

'Mine?' he says, smiling at her from the desk chair. His long legs are resting on a telephone directory from 1992, before she knew that Jonathan or Jay existed. 'I don't have motives. Why would I?'

'But you—you're always—'

'The fact that I talk to women doesn't mean I carry them off to my lair.'

'But here I am,' says Frances, trying not to think of other lairs.

'You came of your own accord,' he tells her. 'Besides, that doesn't mean anything. You're much too sensible and good for . . . that.'

'Oh,' she says. She is sitting beside him, on the bed, by accident. She is seriously drunk, although she had not meant to be. That, in any case, is how she will later rationalize what happens next. 'Sensible. Is that how you—how I seem?'

'You'd never do anything so . . . unbuttoned.'

It is that word, unbuttoned, which does it. She grins, childishly and so does he, in a different way. The air between them glistens. He leans in his chair towards her, releasing that smell she had forgotten: the aromatic reek of unfamiliar men. Maybe, she thinks, it will cure me.

'So,' he asks, still grinning, 'are you what

218

everyone thinks?'
'What.'
'Buttoned-up. Disciplined.'
'Is that a challenge?'
Magnus Brill smiles.

FOURTEEN

*The first day: fish, candles, Greek shop, tablecloths,
napkins, Afikomen covers, folding chairs.*

One week to go. Not all Passovers require lists but
this year's, apparently, does: even two. 'You never
know,' Claudia said in her message. 'The spare
one's on my bedroom mantelpiece, just in case.'

Frances hurries to meet her after the Saturday
morning service, as instructed, unable to give this
aberration the thought it deserves. All she can
think of is discovery. The familiar smells of kosher
canapés, damp hat, tuberose perfume and Brasso
clog her nostrils like mashed potato. The mosaics
and marble and parquet reflect scarlet As—tiny
ones, admittedly, but only because she stopped
him—straight into her eyes. She fights her way
upstream as stills of her with Magnus Brill, her
body and, worse, her mind, are projected on to the
walls. Thank you, God, she thinks, humbly, for not
making Magnus Brill a Jew.

'Shabbat shalom,' say those she passes,
squeezing her cheeks. An old woman she cannot
even name criticizes her ironing. Her mother's new
assistant's uncle tries to interest her in the poetry
of his teenage daughter. She nods and smiles but

219

the bifocals conceal X-ray vision, there are lie-detectors in the cardigan pockets. She is not safe.

She is also late. She is due at Vivien's in Swain's Lane in an hour, for a day of pale sofa-covers, cautious reminiscence and begging the children to play quietly. She has also agreed that, this year, she and Jonathan will host the second night of Passover: for Vivien, for Jonathan's silent sister and her silent family, for the parents of his blessed dead first wife and for any shul overspill, the students and widows for whom no other family can be found. 'We'd love to help,' Jonathan told her mother. 'They're our responsibility too.'

Then there is more participation in family life, more help with Susannah's homework, more effort to keep the flat tidy and the children nourished and, as Jonathan tactfully put it: 'A little more us-time. We don't want to leave it too long for another baby, do we?'

Too late, she thinks and, here in God's house, she blushes. She tries to breathe calmly, but by the time she reaches her mother's glossy door she feels naked and horribly nervous, almost as if she were about to confess.

'You're late,' says Claudia. 'And you look knackered. Is Maxie still waking up?'

'Well—'

'You're doing something wrong. I don't know. Anyway, you should be used to the mornings by now. When you lot were little I'd be up before you and writing a chapter,' she says. 'Even on holiday. Now, where shall we start?'

*   *   *

220

Claudia is trying to be patient, but really. 'For God's sake,' she says at last, quite gently, 'darling, concentrate. Please. We should be able to do this like clockwork. You're being very . . . peculiar. You only have to remember our usual and think more spectacularly.'

She grasps her fountain pen and begins again, determined to ignore this strange sensation of being on a moving walkway, set slightly too fast. It is, Claudia tells herself, the hidden terrors of publication, that painful surrendering of control. She had quite forgotten how it feels. She must master herself.

*   *   *

Indeed, once Frances has gone she feels calmer, although there remains so much to do. On the way out to order the salmon she thinks of Norman, for whom she left a to-do list this morning before he was up. Will he have seen it? She doubles back into her office and picks up the telephone but it rings and rings. Where on earth can he be?

Never mind him. Back outside, into the car, off to Steve Hatt's on the Essex Road: salmon, she thinks. No, sea trout; more dramatic. There, her high green suede shoes splattered with ice chips, Linda Gruber in the queue ahead trying to buy tiger prawns quietly, as if anyone cares, Claudia finds that she will need at least five sea trout for forty. It will mean a kitchen full of fish-kettles. No, screw the semi-vegetarians. It will have to be chicken.

'Pop round to the butcher's and warn them,' she tells Frances by mobile. 'We'll need, say, three to a tray . . . so ten? Twelve. Or—where are you?'

'On the way to Swain's Lane,' says Frances. 'Like I said.'

'Well, that's no good. You're supposed to be buying walnuts, ground almonds, blanched almonds. Let's see, what else? And *I* can't do it. I'm supposed to be meeting the Muslim Brotherhood League at the Imperial War Museum in half an hour.'

'Look, I can't—'

'Well, you have to. Once and for all, Frances, don't let me down.'

FIFTEEN

The second day: kiddush cups, candlesticks, Haggadot, cutlery.

Where are the Haggadot? Leo pulls open drawers and cupboards with increasingly damp palms. The box is enormous, a cornucopia of stray kippot and chocolates and children's plague-wheels. How hard can it be to miss? But it is not on the bookshelves, or under the squirrel-store of raisins and crispbread in his bedroom, or among the mysterious Czech china in the dining room, which can neither be used nor asked about but simply sits there, looking haunted.

Could it be in his mother's room, tangled in her confusing underwear?

Could it have been lent to a community in distress?

222

Could Simeon have sold it?

Then the answer comes to him: his father's study. Thankfully, Norman is out. The air is rich with bar-heater dust and little extinguished thoughts. So preoccupied is he with images of Helen that he does not notice that the usual leaf-mould of perished rubber bands has been swept away, that the newspaper stalagmites around his father's desk have disappeared. He sees only shelves of poetry he has disappointed his father by not reading. Not the new coloured folders, not the expensive highlighters like insect casings, light and dry.

A postcard has fallen on to the rug; the draught from the door must have blown it. He picks it up and it turns over in his hand. Thick blue-black letters push themselves towards him like fleshy petals, seeking light. The letters say:

Still thinking of Sunday. Let's fail to have cake together more often. Talk soon. S.

*   *   *

Norman is on his Saturday afternoon Heath constitutional, soon to be rewarded by a slice of something creamy at the Italian café. It is a pleasure to be out of the house, where no one can glance his way and suddenly deduce either of his secrets. He is striding down his favourite of the paths which lead home, where a bench dedicated to someone called Adolf P. Schlossen is as ever unsat-upon. Nettles grow up through the slats. No one wants to sit on a Nazi. All is right with the world.

223

Recent events have energized him. The wind whips saplings beside the path, the grass is luridly green and as he feels his calf muscles tighten he knows that he will handle the coming days masterfully. Selina is proving a pleasurable distraction. More importantly, in the brief moments when they do see each other, Claudia's love, her need for him, seems unexpectedly to have increased. All he had dreamed of has come to pass. And, if he continues not to think too closely about after the Seder, when he will actually tell Claudia about his own book, he is enjoying the build-up. He is coasting on a wave of excitement, sleek in the knowledge that in a fortnight's time he will be the envy of his peers, his children's hero and the idol of his wife.

How different his life could have been, he thinks, feeling in his coat pockets for a wizened apple. He could have married a girl from the Marylebone Reform Social, of whom his parents would have been unafraid. He could have gone into work they knew: not barbering, not with his education, but the rag trade, envelopes, cord and string: something useful. Or he could have been a lonely old schlemiel, mooning after neurotic girls like this one, he tells himself now, watching a particularly windswept cat-fancier, swathed in a long black scarf like a gloomy present, stamping her way up the slope towards him.

Oh dear. Women like this make him nervous: watercolourists; missionaries. What they need, he always thinks, is a damn good fuck, although not, please God, with him, and then they'd stop muttering to themselves, forget their gluten allergies, eat a proper—

Oh my God.

It is his daughter.

*   *   *

Frances has not even noticed him. She is attempting to blow her nose with a pathetic scrap of tissue, patching together holes and ribbons into a grey little pad for her nose. Norman hesitates, goes on. The wind lashes her scarf-end and hair across her face. She pushes it away, looks up, pink and rained-on, and sees him there at last.

'Dad?' she says. 'What—'

It is not rain. His Frances, whom he has dared to love almost as much as her mother, is crying bitter tears.

His own eyes sting. He swallows and holds out his arms. However, things have changed. She does not come to him but huddles further into her horrible overcoat, scrubbing the tears from her cheeks with her shoulders like a child. His chest tightens. My heart, he thinks; here we go. Then another, deeper dread begins to grip him. He has caused this by his ungodly smugness. How could he have relaxed? How could he have forgotten that something bad is always about to happen, that the evil eye—tu-tu-tu—simply bides its time?

'What is it?' he asks urgently. 'Franceleh? Who has hurt you?'

'No one. Nothing.'

'Don't be stupid. Tell me. What has happened?'

'Nothing,' she repeats, shrinking further into her collar. 'Please, it's fine.'

Her face is so thin, he thinks, such a clever nervous face but sweet too—oh God, forgive me.

225

Into his mind comes a prayer of atonement but, like everything these days, it is jumbled up with something else. He fills his lungs with clean air and tries to pull himself together for his daughter, who looks so mortified that her shame burns him too, like steam.

'Come here,' he says, holding out his arms again. 'Come on, love. Come here.' Should he divert her with a joke? An accent? 'Tell Papa vot's wrong.'

She pulls away. 'I have to go,' she says and begins to hurry down the slope, towards the ponds.

'Frances!' he shouts. 'Stop!'

But she ignores him. She pushes through the long grass like a stranger. He should go to her, he knows he should, but up here in the cold wind he feels exposed and guilty. He has not been the father he meant to be. So he hesitates and, as she slips away from him, he realizes what the Yom Kippur prayer was mixed up with: the prayer on a death.

SIXTEEN

The third day: ingredients, kosher wine, children's prizes, macaroons, Elijah's cup, visible rooms.

Claudia stands in her larder. Nobody knows she is there. Until half a minute ago she had been checking, more for comfort than efficiency, her supplies.

Gherkins (4 jars)

Mustard (2 big pots)
Oil (olive, sunflower, walnut (old))
Salt (plenty)
Mayonnaise (buy more)
Vinegar (7 bottles, various, from Sim's culinary
    experiments)
Grape juice (so expensive but more needed)
Potatoes (sack)
Tinned tomatoes (27 tins)
Tea bags, coffee (if only the Seven Sisters Cash
    and Carry still existed)
Honey (huge jar from grateful Bulgarians)
Rosewater (evaporated, bugger)
Cinnamon (sticks)
[oh God, is that a mouse-hole?]
Garlic (never enough)
Matzoh meal—

Then she registers, almost as clearly as if he is in
the room with her, her husband's voice.

'I told you,' he says. 'No, never. How many
times . . .'

My God, she thinks. For once he has thought
ahead and is ordering the kosher wine himself. She
opens her mouth to call out. How funny, she wants
to tell him, that in all these years we've never
noticed how audible the hall telephone is from
here, with the little airbrick and the rotting
wood . . . and then she stops.

'I've told Kath,' he is saying, 'I don't want a
part—no, nor a dinner. Same thing applies . . .
Does she? Are you sure? That seems very
strange—oh, the *Telegraph*? Really, does he? Oh,
good, good . . .'

His voice tails off. Is he still there? She puts her

ear to the damp whitewash: soft as seawater to the drowning, offering itself, suggesting rest. She closes her eyes.

'Well, I'll consider it. How many? No, fewer— twelve. Ten? If you're sure—but I'll have to, er, check with, er, my wife. Not now. Nearer the time. Week after next. I know. Quite, quite. Nevertheless—'

Claudia, running her fingertip over the plaster, thinks of skiing. A terrible sport: the ice, the pain, the slicing metal. It has, however, one thing in its favour. It demonstrates perfectly how best to lead one's life. Simply the image of herself speeding over metaphorical moguls while other people, more earnest and dangly earringed, plough through the snowdrifts, emoting, discussing, sharing, has always cheered her.

At least, that used to be the case. Now she sees herself on a ski slope, dressed in old-fashioned black salopettes, a tight glamorous polo neck and her mother's green mittens. Before the war Veronka skied, like everything else, perfectly. To her left glints a sheer drop, thrilling and treacherous. To her right is the slower softer way through the trees, which others take. Ordinarily she would not allow herself time to think. She would head for the drop without question. However, since her hospital visit she has felt herself sliding towards it, faster and faster, even before she has chosen to go. For the first time in her life, she is afraid.

'Norman,' she makes her lips say. She touches the cold handle of her larder door. Her mouth is dry. Should she ask for help? Should she say: Stop me from falling? Or is it too late? Has steadfast

Norman, who cannot know how she depends on him, already moved away?

SEVENTEEN

The fourth day: trestle tables, macaroons, tablecloths, kippot, make/freeze stock.

Leo is in trouble. He has been making promises which he cannot keep. Helen has been meeting him; not in her office, which has become in his dreams an ever-expanding idyll, with grassy banks, cushions, even a swing. She favours less encouraging surroundings: the Urology fire escape; a bench; the coffee shop of an empty church. There, discreetly holding hands over hard cakes and strong tea, feeling so many pains throughout his person that he must be dying of desire, he has found himself describing his mother as surprisingly tolerant, not remotely grudge-bearing: a woman who will forgive him for what he is about to do.

He has been frighteningly successful. Desperation has given him voice. Helen now apparently believes that at any moment he will call her to say that the truth is out, his bags are packed, an extra place has been laid at the Seder table. She thinks that Claudia, despite her fierce reputation, is waiting with open arms.

*   *   *

The reality, however, is a little less straightforward.

229

The tension in Behrens Road is mounting. His timing, he now realizes, is perhaps not ideal. At eight, tired and anxious, he enters the kitchen and finds his younger sister sobbing; no milk for his cereal; their mother counting candlesticks. Her face is thunderous. She looks like a pirate dissatisfied with her hoard.

'Er,' he begins, hoping for the courage to reveal his promise. She ignores him. At least I cleaned up last night, he reminds himself, a good boy to the last, before noticing that stock is bubbling all over his gleaming hob and that the table top has already vanished under Simeon's leavings: open bottles of wine and Coke cans and cartons of papaya juice; smashed chocolate muffins and hollow sausage rolls; and Leo's own hat, a graduation present to himself, which seems to have been used as an ashtray.

'Have *you* seen the cheque for the gas board?' asks their mother irritably. 'I left it out last night.'

'Is it . . . could it be here?' offers Leo, helpfully poking about by the toaster. 'What did it look like?'

'A *cheque*, Leo. Words. Pound signs. You know.'

Em lifts her head. 'I wish I had a cheque,' she says mournfully. Then something occurs to her which Leo has not dared say. 'You had filled it *all* out, hadn't you? Even the name?'

'Well,' says their mother, 'maybe not every bit of it. But I left it here to remind me when I went to bed. Before Sim and his frien— Oh. I see.'

*   *   *

At work Jeremy Blackstock asks Leo for help with

his accounts, presumably on racial grounds. Both his youngest siblings telephone and try to borrow money. Leo finds that his own wig has vanished an hour before a rare court appearance and has to borrow a colleague's too-tight one, which clutches his scalp like a crab and gives his already dismal performance a hysterical edge. His mother rings to remind him loudly about the Haggadot, during an unexpected visit by Giles Blackstock, Head of Chambers. He bites through his fountain pen and drips ink all over a freshly filled-in claim form and witness statement. By the time the telephone rings yet again, his endurance has worn thin.

'What?'

'I've done it!' says Helen.

'Sorry . . . you've done what?'

'I've told him. I've left him. I'll stay with Petra or someone and . . . Leo, are you listening? I've asked for a *divorce.*'

*　　　*　　　*

Tonight the Haggadot can wait. The postcard on the study floor must remain his private concern. Instead he must do what all sons must when their sisters are shockable and their friends are worse. He must speak to his father.

Time passes, very slowly. He cannot work. He can barely eat; at least, he does not have seconds. At last, when dinner is over and his mother is organizing something on the telephone, he goes to the place where, on the fifth night before Pesach, all Jewish patriarchs must be.

He climbs up the shaking attic ladder, stair by rotting stair. He turns left at the T-junction and

231

fights his way through tinsel, broken lampshades, *Peter and Jane* books and plastic fruit. There, squatting on a bale of underlay, searching through chipped wine glasses, is Norman Rubin. Clouds of toxic fibres swirl under the light bulb shining from the rafters. There is something powdery on his forehead, an ominous dark smear on his thumb.

'So don't just stand there,' he says. 'Help me move this bookshelf.'

'Oh—yes, sorry.' People have probably suffocated in such an environment, or contracted lethal lung disease. All Leo wants to do is take off his jacket, wedge himself between tea crates and hide in here reading mildewed joke books until everything is solved.

But he would lose Helen. 'Er,' he begins. 'Dad?'

'Bugger,' his father mutters. 'If some fool hadn't packed the cases—'

'Um. Could I . . . actually . . .'

His father snorts through his mighty nostrils. He lifts his head. 'Nu?'

Leo's own nose is filling with asbestos fibres and cobwebs and fear. There is too little air for them both. 'It, I,' he says. 'I was wondering—'

'For God's sake. Can't you see I'm busy? Find the bloody serving plates, at least.'

'*Dad*,' he says, like a weedy schoolboy. 'I have to ask you something. Please, will you listen?'

Only now does Leo realize the import of what he is about to say. 'Er . . .' he begins. 'Er—' His father's inky eyes, his screech-owl eyebrows and enormous ears, seem to be focused upon him, as if he has evolved antennae for spotting unrighteousness. 'I . . . Dad. How are you?'

'*What?*'

232

'You know. Are things . . . how are you and Mum?'

So gross is this breach of family etiquette that his father, at first, remains silent. He opens his mouth. He closes it. He gives a great ripple-browed scowl, reminding his son of the belly-dancing display he attended with Jeremy Blackstock, where not even utter embarrassment and a bottle of Turkish red could prevent his person from responding in certain shameful ways.

'Fine,' Norman mutters at last, sticking out his leg as if about to dance the cossackski. 'Bloody thing,' he says, flexing his ankle. 'Why? How are you?'

'I . . . I thought maybe—' Leo swallows but no saliva comes, only the first tickles of a nervous cough. 'It might be difficult, for you,' he says, inspecting a frayed piece of string, 'you know, with, with the book, and everything, the Seder—'

'With the *book*?' his father says. 'Who said something about a book?'

'Mum's book . . . you know. Everyone's a bit, well, tense . . .'

'Oh! Oh, no, no, it's fine. It's all fine,' he says. Then his face clouds over. 'Why? What are you telling me?'

Leo totters. 'No!' he squeaks. 'I'm not, it's fine, really. Fine, fine . . . everything is fine!'

His father peers at him. His antennae quiver. 'You're not . . . you're . . . behaving, are you?'

'Yes!'

'Good, good,' he says and they nod at each other, but Leo knows that his father knows that he has lied.

Sweat is trickling down the back of Norman's shirt. His knees are beginning to give way but something, some hitherto hidden jungle instinct, tells him to stay down here on the underlay, apparently at ease, as long as he can. He watches Leo fidget and a suspicion, no, a fear begins to grow within him. Is it conceivable, likely, even, that his elder son's life is not, well, quite as it should be?

My God, he thinks: not now.

'Because, you know . . .' As a young father in the seventies, Norman had tried to do well. He added parenting manuals to his handbooks on yoga, compost and Arabic. He read up on the chemistry of the adolescent brain and liberal education. Now, after decades of snappishness, across synapses perished with disuse, he remembers something about the Teachable Moment. This is, perhaps, one of those. 'In a, hem, man's life, S-Leo,' he announces, prodding the torn skin of his knuckle, 'there are moments—'

'Dad . . .'

'Let me finish. There are moments when one has to, ah, put on hold what one might, you know, one's own needs and, well, delay. I know things might, must have been tough after the wedding . . . though God knows it was worse for your mother. Anyway . . .'

'Actually—'

'Just listen. Look, what I'm saying is . . . if it's, if you're still, ah, thinking, at all, of her, whatshername, Nicky what's-it's wife, hold off. All right? In a while, maybe, when the dust has cleared, you know, five years from now, you'll still

234

be young.'

*   *   *

It does the trick. His son smiles, weakly. He turns and begins to descend through the trapdoor, chastened but, thinks Norman, slightly wiser-looking. Thank God, he thinks, wiping the foul sweat from his eyebrows. Leo is back on the straight and narrow for five years at least, knowing him probably to the day. This leaves his father to behave, well, a little more freely.

Besides, he thinks, because it's all connected to Claudia, this isn't being unfaithful, not really. I still love her. Even when I kissed Selina, Claudia was the one.

EIGHTEEN

The fifth day: matzoh; seating plan; place cards; crockery.

Frances is usually a terrible driver, checking her mirror more often than the road: not tonight. She signals decisively, as if giving a demonstration. Her corners are swift and precise. She is being careful because on black evenings such as this, mothers like her—she cannot be the first—drive into conveniently located oak trees and end everything, tactfully.

Jay, who had seemed the answer, has now become the problem. She leaves drily flirtatious messages on her work telephone, when Frances is out at lunches or at home. Lately Frances has begun to return them. She does not want to want to. It makes no sense for her to feel this, to keep checking her answerphone, to jump guiltily every time it rings. This does not happen to people like her.

So why has it happened to me?

Magnus Brill's bony nose keeps looming at her. She can feel his long fingers on her breast. It has been a week since her lunatic act and no one has noticed but they will, they will.

Oh God. She stops the car. She gazes at the enormous embarrassing red mobile phone bought at her parents' insistence, as if she is in the secret service and could be needed at any time. She should call Jonathan for a logistical catch-up, except that they're not speaking. Or are they? The rows have merged into each other. They can barely keep up. Besides, he is not the person she wants to speak to.

'Ring,' she commands the telephone. 'Now. Please.'

But it does not ring. She turns the key and waits for the engine to return to life.

*   *   *

Forty minutes later she reaches her destination: the gates of hell. Brent Cross is too suburban-Jewish for the Rubins; they roll their 'r's when they speak of it, to show it is a place where others go. Its weak point, however, is food, so today it will be almost empty. Given the huge well-stocked supermarkets at Camden and Chalk Farm, the kosher glories of Frohweins and Golders Green

Road, no one she knows will be here.

So Frances is safe, but also out of her depth. So sensitized is she by weeks of extreme self-consciousness, by the certainty, every time she goes anywhere near the Royal Free (and it is amazing from how much of North London it can be seen), that she will meet Jay, that she can think of little else. She becomes hopelessly lost among tiny waistcoat–bowtie combinations, barbecue aids and pineapple-scented teenage perfumes. The aisles are fragrant with salt beef but she cannot find any actual food. She bumps into a cousin to whom, because of an old broigus about a baby shawl, her family does not speak. The American Tan tights, the pregnant frummers are beginning to close in on her. Is this, she wonders, how people at work, or Jay, or Magnus Brill, see me?

At last she spots a cluster of knowledgeable-looking women, gathered around what may be something non-edible but vital.

'Excuse me,' she says. 'Sorry, I'm sorry, could I . . .'

But the crowd will not part for her and when, hot and humiliated, she reaches the front, she finds only julienned courgettes and a man demonstrating the fully stainless Dice 'n' Slice Electric Mandolin. 'Your dinner-party guests will envy you,' he promises. 'Your husband's boss will thrill—'

No wonder everyone hates Jews, thinks Frances, trying to push her way back through the glowering women. I hate Jews—except Dad, she thinks superstitiously, and Leo, and of course the children. She bolts down an unappetizing passage, where the fumes of lo-salt pastrami baguettes and

237

triple-choc almond cookies compete violently for dominance and finds herself, at last, at the supermarket, twenty minutes before closing time.

Its skimpy Pesach stock is clearly intended for last-minute extras, not for the entire festive requirements of leading London rabbis. However, she tracks down small piles of Rakusen's matzoh, matzoh meal and Californian kosher wine so expensive that for a moment she is paralysed. Seder shoppers are clearly being targeted. No time to worry about motivations: back to the vegetables where, thank God, she discovers among the movingly English carrots and celeriac a single wizened horseradish, a concession to those fools who do not do their food shopping in Temple Fortune. Then, as she weighs it in her hand with what she hopes is an experienced air, she has a terrible thought: shank bones.

Oh no. She rushes her trolley to the tiny meat counter. There are no bones left. She begins to beg.

'Please?' she asks. 'Under the counter? In, er, the fridge?'

He shrugs. His hygienic bonnet and apron are entirely bloodless, like a butcher in a children's book. 'Clean out,' he says. 'Like locusts.'

She stares at him. 'What—what can I do?'

'What's it used for?'

'Burning. Well, baking. But it's got to be bare,' she says. 'And lamb.'

'No chance,' he says. 'Pity. Ten o'clock this morning I had a nice—'

Despairingly she hangs her head and sees before her, in the little plastic pasture behind the glass, an oddly shaped piece of meat, in which something lies embedded.

It is the perfect bone. She looks him straight in the eye. 'Yes!' she says. 'That! Yes—that's what I need!'

'Well, you say that, but—'

'No, really, that's it.'

'Are you sure?'

'Sure. Please—can you wrap it? Really well?' She is keeping her head up; it is perfectly possible not to see the animal-shaped labels, the helpful identification of parts. Jay would approve, she thinks, and feels her mouth twitch. 'I'm, I'm vegetarian,' she hears herself say.

*　　*　　*

Later, when Jonathan is in bed catching up on Stuart weaponry and she is standing by a pan of boiling brine, prodding the ham with a fork, the urge to telephone Jay and confess her latest crime overwhelms her.

But Magnus Brill, she tells herself. I'd have to tell her about Magnus Brill and, unless I explain why I think I did it, wouldn't that give her entirely the wrong idea?

Her red mobile phone lies on the table but she keeps her back to it. She hoists the meat from the pan and on to a plate, begins to tear the pink fibres from the bone. The phone hums behind her like Kryptonite. She picks it up. She puts it down. She imagines burning it, boiling it, losing it, as if anything could save her now.

239

NINETEEN

*The sixth day: cleaning; hametz; cakes; Seder plate;
charoset; everything else.*

On Thursday, thankfully her day off from shul,
Claudia:

— removes a year's worth of shul newsletters,
yin/yang pendants, diabetic kosher cookbooks
and invitations to charity quiz nights for the
disabled orphans of Belarus.
— telephones her friends about their duties:
bringing candlesticks; giving Simeon their
publisher neighbour's phone number; avoiding
the subjects of cancer and miscarriage,
depending on their place in her complex seating
plan.
— throws out two loaves of bread, almost all
Simeon's Wagon Wheels, four open boxes of
stale crispbread and, in her distraction, the oven
glove.
— takes prizes for the Afikomen-hunters from her
enormous store of presents: no Hebrew
flashcards or wooden puzzles here but
glamorous picture frames, sacks of Hershey's
Kisses and, for the little ones, an amusing new
book called *The Dragon that Pooed*.
— collects the trestle tables from Dmitri's down
the road and hauls them into place, cursing as
every year her tiny kitchen, the narrowness of
the dining room, the impractical shape of the
space in which she is expected to do God's

240

work.

—fetches kindling and logs so they can do without
the broken boiler, which cannot be fixed until
her publication advance is paid.

—gets down on the floor and, ignoring the knee-
pain, the back-pain and the painful absence of
children or grandchildren, sweeps up two
dustpans' worth of hametz, mainly Rizlas and
shrivelled peas and onion skins but also,
satisfyingly, several pieces of toast and, to save
time tomorrow, burns it in the grate. How her
eyes sting. Do not think, she commands herself
as she stands up, about ash, about dust. Who
does that help?

—buys grape juice, potatoes, chives, emergency
gherkins, seven pots of Greek yoghurt, twelve
Romaine lettuces, two kilos of green beans,
onions, lemons, grapes, courgettes, parsley,
cheese, six bags of oranges, dates, walnuts,
apples and, as a reward to herself, a brick of
marzipan.

—boils eight of the oranges for two hours and,
when they are cool and soft as death, mixes
them with ground almonds, cocoa, sugar and
eggs, pours the speckled goo into cake tins and
bakes them until the house smells as it should.
Blessed art thou, O Lord our God, King of the
Universe, who has kept us in life and preserved
us and enabled us to reach this season, she
thinks, and then she stops, and then she carries
on.

—makes vinaigrette: so familiar, so prosaic, but
oh, the pleasure when it emulsifies.

—realizes that no one has remembered the Seder
plate and adds it to Norman's as yet undone list

241

of tasks. If only, she wishes, her confidence briefly punctured, there was a way to attract good fortune, as at Rosh Hashanah. Could she include extra sweet things, more charoset than usual, in case?

— whisks the egg whites and mixes them with yolks and soaked squeezed matzoh and garlic and parsley, shapes it into ninety-odd balls which she chills and then simmers until they are both boring and delicious, exactly as they should be.

— turns the radio up and simmers onion, garlic, spices, raisins, pine nuts, spinach and matzoh meal to make the stuffing for which she is justly renowned.

— roasts the prettiest egg and the bone which, imperfectly wrapped in kitchen towel, glistening with an unexpected knob of gristle, Frances has posted through the letterbox—odd, thinks Claudia but she is, by this point, too richly busy, too lulled by routine, to worry.

— and then, at last, her evening's highlight; the making of the charoset. One is simple, Ashkenazi, her mother's; she will put it on the table but she will not eat it, she never could. The other, half-stolen from Iranians and Italians, stands for the life she has chosen: dates, wine, cinnamon, prunes and almonds, so many happy Seders simmered down. Please God, she thinks, with unaccustomed nervousness, let this one be happy too.

*   *   *

If Leo is to succeed in tomorrow's act of daring, he must avoid any opportunity to confess. He will

242

hide from his family until the last possible moment and then, hand in hand with Helen Baum, he will spring his surprise.

*   *   *

At first it seems easy. He waves a cheery goodbye from behind his desk to Jeremy Blackstock, who conspicuously rearranges himself through his trouser pocket and bids him a suspicious goodnight. He attempts a casual chat with Neville Prior, the last clerk on duty. He browses the day's cases on Lawtel, until forced to accept the absence of references to child psychiatry and Ingerwood Road. He contemplates a brisk walk around Coney Garth or a lime soda at the Seven Stars, but the thought of bumping into a now drunken Jeremy Blackstock puts paid to that.

He eats the greasy apple and hard roll he has saved from lunch, thinking of his mother's kitchen. The building grows still and cold and quiet. He begins to feel uncomfortably alone. This part of London is thick with history, most of it bloody, and it is crowding in. By nine o'clock it seems as if the darkness is massing against him, as if the persistent scratching from the stairs is not Trelawney the chambers spaniel, or a perfectly reasonable mouse, but something more frightening. Perhaps it is time to go after all, where there is warmth and food. For now, at least, Behrens Road is still his home.

*   *   *

However, as he trots through the drizzle from Belsize Park Tube, up Lawn Road, Cressy Road,

Agincourt Road, his sense of foreboding thickens. It is a bright night. A single star wobbles above Chalk Farm, where Helen has a friend from work with whom she may now be staying. She has not told him. He only knows that she will meet him at the White Horse in South End Green at seven o'clock tomorrow evening, from where he will take her to the Seder.

As he approaches the front door, his stomach squirming, he hears the faint murmur of voices. Something tells him to be careful. Nervous, he presses his ear to the wood. Then, because it pays Simeon's siblings to be cautious, he pushes open the letter-flap. There are the spare umbrellas; his father's comfortingly rank black overcoat; the tweed cap he wears, despite Simeon's derision, on the Heath. And there, he sees with a little squirt of adrenaline, is Simeon.

He is sitting on the stairs, his legs bare. The curly telephone cable stretches across them. Close by is a pink striped garment, dark hair, their younger sister's shoulder.

Could they be looking straight at him? He jerks his face away but he cannot let go of the squeaky flap, although the brass is cold and the spring is strong. He must stand there like an idiot, fingers trembling, trapped.

'But I explained,' Em is saying into the telephone.

'Unbefuckinglievable,' says Simeon.

This door, Leo remembers now, has a fatal flaw. The latch is too weak. Strong winds have been known to blow it open. Protect me, Lord, he thinks.

'Shh . . . no,' his sister is saying. 'It's me who's

244

behind this, not Sim. It's . . . but it's not what I want.'

'Say: "Bog off," ' advises Simeon.

'Well, I'm sorry too,' she says into the phone. 'But . . . no, that's not fair! I'm not doing it *for* Sim but of course he's import— Yes! Even in this—'

With a horrible wrenching crash, Leo's world collapses.

'Help!' he squeaks. His arm is yanked from its socket. The flap bites down on his fingernails. He sprawls on to the doormat, wincing up at the colossal crotch of his brother.

'You *freak*,' says Simeon.

'Er . . .' He touches his bristle-burnt cheek. Em, who could help him, has turned her back. Normally, he would have leapt up by now, grovelling out of harm's way but, down here, spreadeagled, he feels curiously safe. He always expects the worst but nothing is wrong after all, no fights or drug-dealing. Sim has not even hurt him. It was merely his usual fearful paranoia.

In twenty-four hours, he thinks, at a conservative estimate, Helen Baum will be mine. Surely this is the right way to do it, bringing Helen into the very heart of my family. Then, because he is on the brink of happiness, he allows himself to entertain a tiny forbidden hope for the future. Why not babies? Forty-year-old women have children all the time. Chambers is full of them: grim, relentless, combining gyms and plaintiffs and school concerts with apparent ease. Tentatively, he lets himself creep a little further to the edge. He sees his parents, snowy-haired and joyful, dandling the infants Helen has borne him on their aged but almost Scandinavianly healthy knees.

It is possible, he tells himself. Such simple happiness is possible, even for me.

TWENTY

The first night of Passover

'Frances,' says Claudia. 'Tell me you haven't forgotten the chickens.'

The day had begun well. She had spent far too much on flowers, soothing herself with the gorgeous stink of wet flower-paper and twine, the sight of excess. She had gone home; she washed the lettuces and chopped gherkins and chives for the potato salad, simmered green beans in tomato sauce, defrosted the stock, roasted three trays of aubergines, peppers, thyme and feta for the bloody vegetarians, chose and ironed the least stained tablecloths. She gave a telephone interview to the *Ham and High*, whose pet she is, and after hurried grooming let in Philip, who is painting her portrait for an exhibition on faith at the Tate. Then she rested. Then she realized.

'Frances?' she says.

*   *   *

Frances shoots through the traffic light like, she imagines, a Walthamstow greyhound. She has never pedalled so quickly in her life. Her tangled brain has been scooped out and replaced with one simple image: the Seder ruined, because of her.

She is on Brecknock Road before she thinks to

gather reinforcements. She snatches the phone from her bag, skidding dramatically. 'Listen,' she pants, 'I need you—'

'Who is this?' Leo says.

'Me! Your sister. Listen—for God's sake, stupid buses—what are you doing?'

'I'm working.'

'Where?'

'Well . . . in Sachertorte. I wanted a cup of—'

'You have to help me,' she says.

* * *

At two o'clock, the senior Rubin children converge outside Hampstead Heath overground station. Frances's face is very red.

'I need . . . I need to sit down,' she says. Leo holds out the fruit of his labours: a single striped carrier bag. 'So what did you find?'

'Thighs,' he announces proudly. He has been looking forward to this moment. 'Forty of them. God, they were expensive. But there was nothing else. I tried Haverstock Hill, and Safeway's, even that meat-products place on Fortess Road, and they'd all sold out. So I was, well, ingenious.' Her head has drooped. 'I thought you'd be pleased.'

'It's . . .' she says, 'I was meant . . . Oh, sod it.'

'Really?'

'She'll have to manage.'

Leo blinks at her. You sound like Helen, he thinks. 'What did you buy?'

'Nothing for ages and then . . .' She nods at the bench where three bloody paper-wrapped parcels lie, as if left by a crocodile. 'A scary shop in Camden. They're not necessarily edible. Do you

247

think that's OK?'

'Of course it—' Her hands are shaking. 'Look, are you all right?'

'Will you sit with me for a minute?'

Oh God, thinks Leo. In barely five hours he is meeting Helen and there is so much pacing to do, so many tactics to work out for the Herculean task ahead. Then he looks at his sister, her thin shoulders and lovely anxious eyes, and thinks: She is the one of all of them I could not bear to lose.

They sit side by side. He watches a pigeon pecking, the glint of its oily neck, and longs for Helen.

'It's,' his sister begins. 'I mean—'

No, no, not tears: he waves his hands to ward them off. What time is it? 'Please. Don't.'

'It's all right. It's only . . . Listen,' she says. 'If something happens—'

'Why? Will it?'

'No, but . . . I want you to, to know that I . . .'

'What?'

'I love you.'

'Ah,' he says. 'Right. Yes. Um.' Say it back, he tells himself but finds that he cannot. He pats her knee awkwardly instead and fiddles with his sock elastic and so the moment passes.

*　　　*　　　*

With difficulty they work out the steadiest possible arrangement of birds and bags and gravity. 'I'll be there soon, to help with everything,' he says, like a bad defendant. 'See you at the, er, you know—'

She is frowning down at her handlebars. 'See you,' she whispers. He pats her again, this time on her shoulder, and waves her off up Constantine Road and then, although he had meant to return to Sachertorte, he stands there, watching her. It is only when she is out of sight that something occurs to him.

Maybe she was asking him for help.

*　　*　　*

Six thirty: never an easy time. The preparations have speeded up. Here is Frances, in a strange long grey belted cardigan that makes her look like a teacher at a charity school, throwing knives and forks around the table. Here is Leo, who has spent the afternoon energetically underfoot and now is polishing candlesticks with commendable vigour. Here is Simeon, his hotdog obediently dumped in the outside dustbins, arranging the elements of the Seder plate with extraordinary care. Norman is upstairs, which is to be expected. He has performed his duties: the relatively bearable Passover wine on which he prides himself; the Afikomen on its silver plate; the four large jugs of salt water which—provided that the salt and jugs and spoon are laid out by the sink—he always mixes with such care. Look at us, thinks Claudia, all you doubters. Look at us and envy.

*　　*　　*

'You didn't forget the travel cot, did you?' calls Jonathan. 'You said you'd put it in the car before you left.'

Of course she forgot it. For days now her mother's brilliant suggestion that they all stay the

249

night at Behrens Road ('The girls will love it, and I'll need you to help clear up') has been oppressing her but not, it seems, sinking in.

'Can't we put him somewhere else? I don't know—Mum's bed?'

'Frances,' he says expressionlessly. 'You know as well as I do that children die rolling off adult mattresses.' He sighs and looks away. Then his face brightens.

'Hooray!' cry the girls as Claudia approaches, holding up their pyjamas for her approval. Max stops wailing and launches himself at his grandmother's knees. 'Wow,' says Jonathan.

*   *   *

Claudia looks perfect. Her tight orange apron clutches at her breasts and hips. A strand of hair is stuck becomingly to her brow. She is holding a large rubber locust. 'So who's ready to find the Afikomen?' she asks.

'We are.'

'Who's ready for the Four Questions?'

'We are!'

She crouches before them. She scoops her grandson on to her thigh, puts one hand on Susannah's shoulder, one on Rebecca's head. 'Who,' she says quietly, seriously, as if revealing a sacred truth, 'is ready for an enormous scoff?'

'*We are!*'

Frances leaves them to it. The guests are about to arrive and the air prickles, as if a smear of ice has settled over them and at any moment may start to crack, or thicken. She goes as far away as she can, up from the sanitized ground floor and the

250

charmingly disordered first to where the dark heart of the house becomes audible, the stairs leading up to the second floor where empty vodka bottles, CD cases, bin liners and tampons and mouldy crockery crunch underfoot, like bones on the forest floor. She clears a space with her foot and sits, her chin on her knees. She thinks: I cannot face tonight unless I phone her.

Do not phone her.

She hauls herself to her feet, walks down the corridor to the window at the end, presses her forehead to the cool glass and tries to compose herself. A man is running down the road towards South End Green. Downstairs someone's voice is ominously raised. Frances is wearing a truly horrible skirt because it has a pocket. She puts her hand on her phone.

I have to ring her.

Don't do it.

I have to.

Blood bangs in her ear. She can already see Clerkenwell and Soho, smell the washed-out restaurant bins and star anise and urine and excitement. She takes a deep breath, sick with self-disgust and anticipation, like a furtive child in the dark.

She dials the number. But it rings and rings into emptiness and Jay does not pick up the phone.

TWENTY-ONE

'An olive?'

Rabbi Rubin holds out the bowl to her latest

251

arrival, a handsome but smelly Russian cellist brought by Francesca Birnbaum, and smiles, dazzlingly. She is wearing a new dress, somewhere between black and silver and cut just tightly enough. It was also horribly expensive, but that is not the point. It is a champagne bottle smashed against the side of her book, a monkey gland, a human shield and it is becoming more and more apparent that she was right to wear it. She takes a deep sniff of garlicky chicken and wood smoke and closes her eyes for a moment.

But someone is missing. Be calm, she commands herself. The guests are here: Robin Buckley and his tiny boyfriend in festive gingham shirts; Sita and Hugh Joel, with their tray of Gujarati relishes. Beryl London, the secret Jew, is awaiting her annual dose of culture before returning to the vicarage. Betty Lister hovers with a well-used Tupperware of bready matzoh-kneidl. Francesca Birnbaum laboriously translates every word for her cellist, who gratifyingly ignores her. Godson Benji helpfully fetches tonic water, hoping for a chance to report on his recent Israel trip: the youth hostels, the very small climb on Masada. Overexcited children, already almost at the limit of their staying-up-late good behaviour, play killing games behind the sofa. Faithful friends attend to Norman's irritating elder brother and Claudia's sister's prolapse. The noise and heat and jollity are extraordinary already, exactly as they should be. Everything is as it should be, a normal homely family celebration with, because it is Claudia's, the famous actress and newspaper editor and novelist whom everyone pretends not to have noticed, releasing little puffs of suppressed excitement wherever they pass.

The doorbell rings again. Graciously she welcomes the Lancasters, whose grandson is even iller, and Clive Archer's newly divorced brother, currently recording a documentary about London's cultural future. He has hinted, only hinted, that her paperback may play a part. Next is Gerard Tucker from All Hallows whom nothing, not even talk of blood libel and impending messiahs, can shake from his devotion to her. Norman has appeared at last, in a grey shirt she does not recognize. Frances's girls are passing around the cheap champagne, obtained cleverly by Simeon from a friend at the Forum.

But where is Leo? Her heart flutters against her breastbone, almost audibly, as she waits for him to come home.

Seven forty passes. Seven forty-five. The olives have run out. They cannot wait any longer. Her children keep glancing in her direction. Norman's eyebrows are raised.

'It's time!' she announces bravely and, like ducklings, she leads them out of the sitting room and into the hall.

*　　　*　　　*

They are hungry, excited, emotional already. They think they know, minute by minute, page by page, exactly what the evening has in store. They follow their hostess and falter only when she does, at the sight of her elder son and his mistress standing together by the long white table, hand in hand.

*　　　*　　　*

253

Simeon is right behind his mother. He moves first.

'You fucker,' he says and steps into the room. It is Claudia who stops him. She shoots out a hand, grabs his forearm, grips it as tightly as she can. At the pressure of her strong fingers he turns his head slowly. She looks into his eyes and he looks back. She thinks: I will remember this for ever.

*   *   *

Leo has tried and tried to plan this moment. He has struggled to imagine the emotions, the consequences. He even covertly drew a diagram on the back of a legal pad which, to avoid detection, he was obliged to Tippex over while Jeremy Blackstock sneered. None of this, however, has prepared him for the gulping panic, the shaking legs or, unexpectedly, the thrill.

I am, he thinks, a crusader. This is my chance to prove myself.

He forces himself not to glance at her, at Helen, the miracle in his mother's kitchen. It would be his undoing. Besides, she has assured him that she will be fine, a little nervous but fine. Who is he to doubt her?

Simeon takes a step closer. His big dreadlocked head seems to swell. Do not look at him, Leo commands himself. Don't panic. Look at Mum.

Claudia is a lioness, dangerously still. His throat is dry. 'Er,' he begins. However, now he understands that his clever speech about the traditional hospitality of the Passover table misses the point. Love is the point. With Helen's hand in his, he knows that.

'I realize that this is . . . unexpected,' he says to Claudia. 'I do know. But I would like, we would like to stay for dinner. To have Seder with my family. That is what we'd like.'

His mother hesitates. The air seems to shimmer, as if before a fire. Her eyes rest on Leo's right nipple and, although it burns, he lets her do it, pinching his palm between thumb and forefinger rather than brush her gaze away. He watches her stony face and thinks of how once he would have done anything to keep her from anger, or disappointment.

Not any more. He is emitting little compressed exhalations like a troubled dragon. He must not faint. Helen is beside him, her body and mind and soul radiating warmth. The very thought makes him fainter. Be strong, he commands himself, and he is, for her. When, at last, his mother lifts her eyes to the general region of his face, he knows that he has won.

'Well,' she says. Her voice has edges but only those who love her can hear the tightness, the shiver of pain. 'Here we all are, then. Let's sit down.'

*   *   *

Norman takes his rightful place at the opposite end of the table, as far from his wife as it is possible to be. Wedged in as he is against the window, his back an easy target for lurking skinheads, rather nearer the children's table than he would like, there is nothing he can do to help her. He can only sit here in lordly discomfort, his heart aching, watching her struggle to master

255

herself.

Fortunately the others understand what is required of them. She gleams as they praise her; 'God, Claudia,' says good old Petey Lister, 'it looks incredible in here.'

And it does. An enormous uneven table top stretches the length of the house, from the kitchen sink up the little step into the skinny dining room, all the way to Norman's lap. It billows with white cloths, it shines with silver dishes and candlesticks, vases of flowers, Chinese kiddush cups from well-wishers and coverings embroidered by grateful oldies, junk-shop serving spoons, wine glasses and soup bowls: a mini-synagogue's worth. Beauty, tradition, the happy prospect of food: Claudia has excelled herself. It makes him feel even more of a shit than before.

*   *   *

He consoles himself with the amusing sight of the younger guests taking their seats. How jealously they note their distance from their hostess or, failing that, from the recently damed Diana Lancaster, née Dorrie Schub, for whom he always had a soft spot, or from one of the other excitements; not Norman though, as if he cares. And, as they admire her tulips, offer compliments and jokes and proofs to each other of how at home they are, they tell themselves that they are almost family.

Norman settles into his chair and permits himself a quick leaf-through of a children's Haggadah, so much more exciting than his with its fire-and-brimstone red-and-black type, the impressive breasts of the Egyptian women. He turns for old times' sake to the translators' names that Frances loves, the dedication to the mysterious Auntie Bashie, but when he tries to catch her eye she is prising matches from the baby's fist and does not notice him. Well, never mind her. There is too much to look forward to: even hunger. All that waiting, punctuated by as much charoset and horseradish and matzoh as you can lay your hands on, makes the meal more of a pleasure. He would never admit it—God forbid that he should, and put off his children—but he loves Pesach. Tonight he is not a disappointingly inattentive rabbi's husband but an old-fashioned patriarch, as he always wanted to be.

So he forgets about Frances. He decides he will think about bloody Leo tomorrow. Even his recent . . . forays, which now seem reckless acts of folly, he puts out of his mind. Tonight he will concentrate on simple pleasures. Admit it; of all the Seders in London, isn't this the one to be at? Who could not admire Claudia: the spectacular cheekbones, as if her innate superiority is pushing up through her skin; the greenish eyes, narrow with intelligence and sex; the curves which, even as he touches and admires them, he is assessing for tiny fatal changes; her infinitely exciting mind? He thinks of Seders past with his sweet good parents, who thought he was a genius, who believed that knowledge and inconspicuousness were all, and his heart is full.

Because, for the first time in months, Norman knows he is blessed. He watches as she strikes the first match and begins to light the candles, leaning forward between pairs of guests to bless them with

257

a sniff of her perfume, a silhouette of breast. He is still mystified as to why she objected to his candle-choice, forty turquoise tapered beauties with an interesting green twiddle at the base.

Well, too late now, he thinks cheerfully. Look at her. How on earth did he ever persuade her to go out with him? This absurd life lived in semi-public, watching her flirt with prospective members, fighting for a share of her at weekends; it was worth it all.

'Hello, Norman,' says a voice.

He blinks, turns his head and sees that, in flagrant contravention of the seating plan, the wrong person entirely is taking the place beside him. It is Betty Lister, with malice aforethought.

*　　*　　*

Claudia is getting into her stride. The first minutes are always tricky. She must guide the clueless without patronizing the learned, include and inform, give unto each of them spiritual sustenance, a sense of community, self-respect. Other, worthier rabbis claim that the community Seders are the highlight of their year. Bullshit. What could be better than leading those you love through a little service in the house you bought, using liturgy you helped to modernize, with food in the fridge, noisy children everywhere? Is this not what she was created for?

Baruch atta adonai, she begins, lifting the first cup of wine and leaning dramatically towards dear cousin Henry. Elohainu melech ha-olam, borei p'ri ha-gafen. Yes, thank God for the fruit of the vine. She rinses her hands, dries them on a faded square

258

of dishcloth bought in Haight-Ashbury in '72 and, as she dips the parsley in salt water and lets its green minerals nourish her, she tries to forget she has anything to worry about. Everyone is here, at least. She looks good and, what is more, she trumps them all, even her dear colleague and rival rabbi Evelyn Hellmann, with her subtly inflected soprano, her tendency to delve a little deeper into the Megillah than she might. Tonight Claudia is father and mother to them all as she lifts the three matzohs and intones the old, old words:

'This is the bread of affliction which our ancestors ate in the land of Egypt. You who are hungry, come and eat with us. You who are in need, come and celebrate the Passover with us. This year we are here. Next year may we be in our own land. This year many of us are still as slaves. Next year may we all be free.'

And her guests shout, 'Amain,' and nod and cheerfully bicker, and pinch bits of sweet charoset, and sigh to themselves. How they love their annual bittersweet submission to tradition. At least, she frowns, let's hope they do. She has subtly interleaved the trickier relatives between her more tolerant friends, as far from the stars as possible. However, she cannot legislate for lavatory visits or lifts home and God only knows what disastrous combinations might ensue. She flashes them solicitous smiles, tries not to wince when Norman's chippy brother offers to whiten Robin Buckley's teeth, when Francesca Birnbaum recommends Muswell Hill Baths to Diana Lancaster with her secret mastectomy scar, but all the time she is worrying, worrying. She is never more on duty than when pretending not to be.

Still, for now they seem happy. What's more, because she is the Queen of Multi-Tasking, all this intellectual merriment is doing wonders for her book. Robin Buckley, having abandoned all attempts to keep his place in the Haggadah, is taking notes beneath his napkin. She has tried to see what he is writing, whether he is still with her or is lost, but she has failed. Should she have invited a critic, or someone from radio? Is every base covered? The newspaper editor she met in the green room at Bush House has been joining in with gusto, despite being, she suspects, rather less Semitic than he says. 'We'll certainly be doing something with your book,' he told her on arrival. 'The question is: what?'

Exciting as that is, merely the thought of how much can still go wrong makes the walls flutter with panic. Her eyes prickle as if ash or earth were already pressing at the lids. I am dying, she imagines saying to Henry, her favourite cousin, who would summon every relative, sort out her children, even have words with Norman, if she asked.

No, she thinks. No need. We are strong and happy. Danger comes from outside. Nothing here needs to change.

*   *   *

'Why is this night different from all other nights?'

As young Susannah launches herself at the Mah Nishtanah, her emphases a little off, Helen Baum smiles at Leo and begins to edge behind the disapproving and the curious towards the downstairs lavatory. Leo is surreptitiously counting

260

the pages left until dinner when the empty chair scrapes beside him. Em has taken his beloved's chair.

'Shouldn't you—' he murmurs.

'On *all* other nights we eat hametz or matzoh,' notes Susannah in apparent astonishment. 'Why tonight do we eat only *matzoh*?'

'Shut up,' hisses Em. 'You're not one to talk. What the hell are you doing?'

'What?'

'Turning up with her like that.'

'On all other nights we eat all *kinds* of vegetables,' Susannah shrugs. 'Why tonight do we only eat maror?'

'I didn't *just*,' he whispers. 'I thought about it a lot. I . . . I had to do it.'

'Crap.'

He thinks of Helen's face and it strengthens him. 'I did have to,' he tells her, stepping nervously on to the thin and uncharted crust of sexual openness, 'because I love her.'

'*That*'s not love.'

'On all other nights we don't *even* dip our vegetables once. Why tonight do we dip them twice?'

'It—'

'I'll tell you what love is,' Em whispers furiously. 'Love is changing your life for someone who needs it. Who deserves it. *I'm* doing it.'

'Who for?'

'Idiot. *Mum.*'

'But she doesn't need you t—'

'I've decided. No more going out with people. I can't do it to her.'

'On all other nights,' observes Susannah

261

incredulously, 'we eat sitting *up* or leaning. Why tonight do we only lean?'

'But she's not *ill*.'

'That's not the point! You hardly see her! You don't know her like I do.'

'But,' he whispers, 'she wouldn't want you to have no one. No, you know, boyfriends, or, er, girlfriends, or, or, *se—*'

'She hates it,' snaps Em. 'Jay was a mistake. They all are. And if it upsets Mum I don't want it either.' She turns her head, her jaw set, her eyes sparkling. She looks like a romantic heroine, fierce with love. 'I can't hurt her like that,' she says.

Susannah, beaming like an Olympian, lets her Haggadah snap shut. Everyone cheers, or claps, or helpfully criticizes as, behind him, Leo senses a presence. It is Helen, and her expression is concerned. Does she, he wonders for the first time, see his family in quite a different way to him?

'Ahem,' he begins, raising his voice over the collective recitation of the Mah Nishtanah in Hebrew. 'Er, darling, this is . . .'

However, Em does not hold out a hand, or even acknowledge her. Instead she leans very close to her brother, so that her words pour into his ear alone. She says: 'You're a traitor. I'll never forgive you, fuckface.' Then, smiling sweetly, she returns to her chair.

*   *   *

'You know,' whispers Betty Lister to Norman, who is still worrying over Susannah's performance (shouldn't she be reading better at seven?), 'I should tell you something.'

'You should?' He pretends to be extracting a matzoh crumb, pressed into his Haggadah spine like an Edwardian flower. Discovering last year's leavings is one of the private pleasures of the Seder, like the increasing desperation for dinner, the cloudy mess of salt water and egg yolk and matzoh crumb, the fantastic names: Laban the Syrian; Og, King of Bashan. She will not rob him of it.

'Norman,' Betty Lister taps his forearm. 'Concentrate.'

As slowly as he can, he turns his head. 'What is it, Betty?' he asks. She is smiling at him. There is a cold feeling in his legs, like hemlock. He looks at her clogged eyelashes and wrinkled lips and tries to smile. 'Enough already. Tell me. What?'

'I saw you,' says Betty Lister.

*   *   *

It is not working. Claudia's heart is heavy, because she cannot ignore the section of the table inhabited by Leo. Tonight is different from all other nights. She tries to draw courage from the sight of her edible youngest child, free of that awful boy-woman at last; from her grandchildren's familiar struggles to float Moses across the Nile with a cardboard tab. She winks at her neighbours like a happy woman, but the Haggadah is speaking of hidden thoughts and misery and sorrow and Leo is sitting there gleaming with the sheen of sexual fulfilment on his forehead. While whispering crossly to one of the girls, Frances's bony elbow knocks over her wine glass, perilously close to Robin Buckley's sleeve. Even Simeon is a source of

263

worry. He may look like a handsome savage but there is a pinkness to his eyelids tonight, an edge to his voice which alarms her. She can smile for all she is worth and pray for her book and her babies, but she is filling with an unmasterable fear and cannot shake it.

'Blood,' she recites, dipping her finger for a drop of wine. Her guests are smiling. Everyone loves the plagues. 'Frogs. Lice—'

'I've got those!' says Rebecca.

Not again, thinks Claudia, catching her son-in-law's eye. Frances is neurotic about chemicals. She will have to have a word. 'Wild beasts,' she continues. 'Murrain. Boils. Hail. Locusts. Darkness. Death'—do not look at Leo—'of the first-born.'

'Yay, finally, singalonga Egypt,' she hears Simeon say over the clattering of glasses, the perpetual scraping of chairs as the guests try to make themselves comfortable. She leads the table in 'Dayenu' like a vigorous, healthy woman, beaming equally at the faultlessly traditional and the dramatically off-key. We would have been content, they claim together, with the smallest of God's kindnesses.

'As if,' she mouths at Evelyn, who alone knows the complaining force of Jews en masse, and Evelyn smiles.

*   *   *

Then, as Betty Lister embarrasses the goyim with stories of their medieval forebears' paranoia, and Clive Archer offers his mad geographical interpretation of the four parts of the soul, Claudia

264

jumps to her feet and plops ninety matzoh balls one by one into the pans of chicken stock. She returns to the table in time to read the one hundred and thirteenth psalm herself, neatly sidestepping the awkward fact that Vivien Archer, whose turn it is, is unlikely to 'live as a joyful mother in her house' because she is clearly in love with her brother-in-law. She winks at Francesca Birnbaum, whose husband they are all pretending is not about to leave her, catches Simeon's eye at the line about mountains skipping like rams because they always laugh at this bit, and always will. She rests her eyes on the dear kind profile of Seymour Bloom and thinks of the words with which he ordained her: 'be strong'.

Leo came back, she tells herself. We are all alive, not schlepping bits of pyramid, not starved in a shtetl or raped or burned or, God forbid, in Jerusalem tonight.

'Blessed art thou, O Lord our God, King of the Universe, who has redeemed us and our forebears from Egypt and kept us alive, until now.'

And there it is again, like the distant vibrations of a Tube train, at first inseparable from one's own breathing, the press of life: the rumblings of trouble. Where is it coming from? Norman is conducting his customary noisy seminar on the significance of the Hillel sandwich, to divert those for whom thoughts of the bitterness of life may be too much. Isn't he a little louder, more urgent-sounding, than usual? Simeon, whom she discovered a little late in the day has shaped the Seder plate charoset into rather a brilliant caricature of Leo, is glaring ferociously at his brother, who is gazing . . . well, elsewhere. And

Emily is flirting with the French biochemist to her left, ignoring both poor old Charles Levine, who thanks to his heartless sons has nowhere else to go, and the documentary-maker to her right, who has such power. And as for Frances—well, if the idea of tonight is control in the guise of relaxation, Frances, biting her fingernails, picking at her napkin, is endangering it all.

Claudia's hostessly pleasure recedes a little further. She straightens her aching back, licks her lips discreetly, checks the soup pans, announces, to cheers, that because the little ones are growing sleepy they will now sing either 'Chad Gadyo' or 'Echod Mi Yodea', to be decided by a vote. The cramped rooms are growing hotter. The roar of her guests' voices raised in song must be audible halfway up Parliament Hill. Let's get through the meal, she thinks. Please. Just grant me that.

*   *   *

Betty Lister will not say what, or whom, she has seen. She merely smiles, and admires the horrible yellow rock her husband the Hosiery King has bought her, and pretends to be busy chasing her hard-boiled egg around her bowl as Norman's life, like the yolk, is steadily mashed.

Everything is ruined now. So much warmth and security wasted and he is the reason. What was I thinking? he asks himself. What have I done?

He gazes at his finger ends: flattish, roughened and trembling with his heartbeat. It seems dangerously fast for anyone, let alone a man of his age and weight. What if he dies before making amends? The thought of losing Claudia's love, even after his death, even mixed as it is, is unbearable. I will ensure that bloody Betty Lister does not know what power she has, he vows. I will stop seeing Selina. I will make it up to Claudia.

Let my book fail. Let her forgive me. Please God, let nothing change.

TWENTY-TWO

The bowls and serving plates and boards, slick with vinaigrette and chicken fat, are being passed up to Claudia's end for stacking in wobbling piles around the sink. Simeon, on guitar, is leading an acoustic rehearsal of 'Who Knows One?'. It has been more a triumph of catering than culinary heaven but Claudia, slicing up chocolate almond cakes and ladling out sliced oranges, is feeling . . . well, nothing so reckless as hope, but a little more cheerful. As she looks down the narrow stretch of wine-stained tablecloth and sees her guests reaching out for a little more salad, one last potato, she allows herself a small shrug of pleasure.

However, even before her shoulders have settled, she hears an unexpected sound.

*   *   *

Who could be telephoning tonight? Ordinarily Leo, perpetually prepared for disaster, exposure, shame, would be rigid in his seat. But, today, why worry? Helen is here, not only safe but with his family, where they both belong. His parents, his

267

siblings, even his step-nieces are all accounted for. Probably double-glazing, he thinks, his focus returning to the question of Helen and in whose bed, tonight, he will thank her for her bravery in coming here and, he hopes, be thoroughly thanked in return.

*   *   *

Dear God, thinks Norman, let it not be for me. Nothing, not even cheese, can distract him. As the hall telephone rings and rings his mind flutters with panic as, for example, an epileptic's might, not that he is one of those. At least, not yet. Someone is bound to have cocked up, he thinks, phoning him here at home about the book or, God forbid, Selina. No one can be trusted. In his distress, wedged in here between Betty Lister and wily old Seymour Bloom, who has always looked on Claudia as a daughter—or, in his dreams, as something more—what can he do but listen? Beneath the table he pulls out an arm-hair, then another, and waits to see into whose hands his fate will fall.

Don't make me answer it, thinks Frances.

'Who the hell is that?' her mother mutters, although her smile remains. 'Make them go away.'

Heavily, hopelessly, Frances dodges past her mother's guests and slips out of the kitchen door. After the fierce heat of the dining room, the hallway is cool as water. Everything feels heightened, swimming with meaning: the air too cold to breathe, the telephone's ring astoundingly loud. Why is it so hard to lift the receiver? Slowly, Frances presses it to her ear. 'Hello?'

'Hey, you,' says the voice at the other end and her heart, unprepared, leaps with love.

*   *   *

Tell them to leave us alone, Claudia commands her daughter silently from the kitchen, where the freshly conscripted Francesca Birnbaum is making a pig's ear of the cakes. What bloody stupid timing. Why is she taking so long?

*   *   *

'You can't . . .' Frances whispers. The horrible truth that her heart revealed circles above, winged and cobwebbed and laughing. 'I mean, I don't think—'

'But I'm the cavalry,' says Jay. 'I knew you needed me.'

Frances leans against the doorway of the dark sitting room and listens to the noise across the hall, like a television turned up very loud. 'How did you—?'

'Your little distress signal showed on my phone. I'd been thinking, anyway, what a nightmare it must be over there,' says Jay as, beneath the sounds of cake appreciation and social contest, Frances detects her mother's voice. 'That violent little mummy's boy tossing his dreadlocks, the mutual masturbation. And after all those messages you've been leaving me . . .'

'*You*'ve been—'

'Whatever . . . I thought you'd like to hear my voice.'

Frances swallows. 'But,' she begins, as one of

269

the dining-room chairs scrapes aside. 'You mustn't—' The door which had been keeping her safe, forgotten, is creaking open. They are discovered.

'Frances!' hisses her mother. 'Hurry up!'

Lies slide on to her tongue so easily. She puts her hand over the mouthpiece and offers the only excuse her mother would sanction: 'It's the childminder. She thought Max was coming down with something today—she wanted to warn me. Hang on.'

'For God's sake,' says Claudia but, although a whiff of rebellion hangs in the hall, she seems to believe her. She does not snatch the phone from her hand and tell Jay to keep her world of wonders to herself. She does not even, yet, insist that Frances fire the childminder immediately and offer Em in her place. She simply returns to the kitchen, to the marvellous hellish family celebration, leaving Frances suspended between the two.

*   *   *

Leo's mistress's palm rests on the meat of his thigh. Its warmth and subtle pressure have been distracting him from what he has done. There may have been other, less brutal, ways of uniting those he loves tonight, but they have not occurred to him. His mind is focused on one thing only; how, using muscular twitching and his own hand if necessary, he might coax her fingers a little higher, further, deeper, to where he needs her most.

Simultaneously, through the pulsing haze, he is growing aware of a problem. Where is Frances? Without her here the entire weight of this evening

270

will rest on his misleadingly broad shoulders. Helen sits calmly beside him, full of faith, absolutely naked but for her clothes. A sickening tide of lust and worry and chocolate cake washes over him.

'All right?' whispers Helen.

He smiles weakly at her, as one might to a lamb one was leading to its death. He can hear a strange undercurrent to the guests' loud conversation, a flicker of unrest.

'I think—' he begins, but she has already turned away. She is looking at his mother who, despite her radiant smile and apparent hostessly interest, is clearly not listening to the conversation around her. Like him, she seems to be wondering how long Frances's phone call can possibly take.

*　　　*　　　*

As Jay talks, a certainty, at first soft and tremulous, begins to set in Frances's mind. For too long everything has been more than she can cope with: sibling chaos, marital rot, maternal failure. This strange fascination with Jay has seemed the last thing she needs. Now, however, that the fascination has a name, the balance has changed. Suddenly she knows what she has to do.

*　　　*　　　*

'Is something wrong?' Helen asks.

'Why?'

'You're squashing my knuckles. I think it's time to go.'

'What?'

271

'You've made your point. We shouldn't push—'

'Hang on,' he says. He has caught his father's eye. He shrugs. Norman shrugs back. One of them is going to have to do something and it looks like it will be Leo.

*   *   *

Frances heads into darkness, to the dim entrance hall beside the front door, where cold breaths of night and handbag exhalations form little scented pools. She is invisible. The door is caught on its metal latch and with every gust of April wind it moves towards her, as if it is alive. The smallest push would slide it open. Anyone could come in here and attack them. They could snatch a bag, even hers, and go. Disaster is so easy.

Behind her, in another orbit entirely, her family will be growing angrier. She can, however, barely hear them, what with the whistling wind through the hinges and the firing of her blood. She thinks of going back there: not any more.

*   *   *

Standing, despite the lack of space, is fairly easy. Leo is, however, trapped on the wrong side of the table, as far from the hallway as it is possible to be. Quickly, with a mind honed by Dungeons and Dragons, he compares his escape routes. To his left nineteen chairs, seventeen occupied, and numerous tired children block his path out of the dining room. To his right, only fifteen lie between him and the kitchen door.

Beside him, Beryl London looks disapprovingly

272

over her frameless glasses. Love gives him strength. He touches Helen's shoulder for luck. Then, with a simple, 'Excuse me,' as a knight might murmur when off to slay a dragon, he smiles at Beryl and pushes past her chair. He squeezes up the step into the kitchen, pressing onward as a geomorphologist bores through rock: Cousin Lou's husband; Rabbi Evelyn Hellmann; Jonathan ('What's wrong?' Leo shakes his head and he understands not to follow; a critical mass of Rubins must be maintained); Godson Benji's girlfriend; Harvey Lancaster; a gap; American Henry, who winks at him; his mother's place; Russian Cellist; Francesca Birnbaum; Rev. Gerard; Diana Lancaster; keep going, keep going; Robin Buckley; old Charles Levine from shul; Simeon—and then, released, he bursts into the hallway.

It is like entering a cave, in which something waits. But no one waits. A strange chill covers his jaw and legs and forearms, as if the back of a razor is sliding over the hairs. He hears a burst of noise behind him and whirls around to see not Sim, thank God, or even Helen—his groin twitches in disappointment—but his younger sister, looking furious.

He begins to creak open his mouth in Frances's defence.

'Where's she gone?' says Em. 'Mum's freaking. We'd better look.' But although they expect to find her in every room, she has vanished. The first floor is cold and quiet.

'We're taking too long. Where is she?' asks Em. 'How could she?' Her tears fall on to the carpet like a trail.

'I'll wait here,' Leo says at the bottom of the

upper stairs. When Em comes back down her face is grim.

'Not here.'

'Are you sure?'

They stare at each other. 'She . . . she must be getting something from the car,' he says eventually. 'I'm sure it's that.'

'Of course . . . Yeah, must be that. Or went home for something they need for the night?'

'Maybe. I'll, I'll find her. You go back down. That's best. Do you think?'

Em is biting her fingertip, like a child. A fibre of sympathy creeps out from his heart and begins to stretch its way towards her. Then she speaks again.

'Bloody cheek, though. Is she going to miss the benshing? And the singing?' Her mouth is hard with disbelief. 'How's it make Mum look?'

The fibre retracts. 'I'm sure it will be—'

'Well, *I'm* not clearing up.'

Leo swallows. 'Well, we should . . . whatever you think.' Helen, alone in the dining room, is pulling him towards her. 'Don't worry,' he says. 'I'm sure there's a perfectly reasonable explanation.'

However, there is no explanation. Frances has simply disappeared.

Part Three

ONE

Tuesday 10 April

Frances looks, on the outside, perfectly normal. The kitchen in which she sits is cold and she is shivering. Her bra, hastily bought near Victoria station, is a little tight. But, in all other respects, she could be any other woman with time on her hands.

In the National Gallery shop this morning she found a cheap book full of her teenage favourites: prodding spears and lascivious vines, Bronzino's depraved Cupid, holy gleams of flesh. She has made it the base of a little temple to pleasure: postcard of Battersea power station, disappointing red bean-paste cake from Chinatown, the paperbacks she has prescribed herself: *Emma*; *The Curse of the Woosters*.

As long as she guards herself against thoughts of home, of what she has done and whom she has left and what she is going to do, she is coping perfectly well. Time stretches before her like a gift. She can eat and sleep and bathe and read as much as she wants to and, slowly, she is coming back to life.

*   *   *

On an evening three nights ago which she is trying not to remember, she walked through the drizzle to Belsize Park and bought a ticket and took the first Tube train. It was extraordinarily easy. The train shot through Chalk Farm and Mornington

Crescent and, although her mind seemed to have stopped entirely, at Euston her legs obligingly carried her up the escalators and out of the station. She could see, as if through a tiny hole of light, the scene at Behrens Road. Jonathan would notice her absence but assume nothing more serious than that she had, rudely, selfishly, gone back to their flat to sleep. This is precisely the sort of un-family-minded behaviour they had been arguing about. He would decide to have words with her in the morning. For now, he and the others would sing their hearts out, to keep the guests unaware, and then settle down for a cosy family sleepover, so much better off without her.

Meanwhile, in the dark and secret night, Frances was unaccounted for. She crossed the Euston Road carefully, her flesh as light as dust. She wandered down Upper Woburn Place, holding her bag tightly, as if she or it might smash. Then, outside the Bloomsbury House Hotel, whose palms and Dallowayburgers the Rubins have laughed at on every journey home to North London for thirty years, whose doubtless extortionate airless boxes no one known to the family had ever entered, she took another step into nothingness. She decided to stay the night.

She lay in her clothes on the bed, closed her eyes and, like death, sleep came. When she woke twelve hours later, no time seemed to have passed. She pulled herself upright. She took her bag and left. When the receptionist smiled at her she ducked her head, wrote a cheque and went out into the unbearable brightness of the street, the stinging air. She walked down a gauntlet of squealing tourists' cases and roaring buses until

278

she found herself on Southampton Row, where as a student she once shocked her sister by suggesting they try an Indian restaurant other than the Bombay Star.

What now?

There was a café, its windows papered with posters for musicals and visiting gurus. The pavement appeared to be shaking. Gently she escorted herself inside. She drank sweet lemon tea. She ate a rock cake. She waited until the hairy-eared old man at the next table had finished his paper and then she reached over and picked it up. She looked politely at every page, like a visiting alien. Then she came upon the To Let pages and, as she browsed, she began to imagine alternative lives: rich vegetarians in Palmers Green; students in Elephant and Castle; feminist house-shares in Stoke Newington. All the short-let rooms had reasons not to live in them, she noticed, not that she was looking, and then she found a little row of three that didn't.

*   *   *

In Behrens Road the children would be awake. Soon they would drive back to the flat to fetch her, or phone to summon her to Gospel Oak. She could hurry back and they would never know the scale of her crime. However, for having left at all she would be punished, and the guilt or anger or indifference she would have to face loomed above her like foothills, too icy and perilous to climb.

Try the numbers, said a voice: Jay's, or her own. So she did.

The first was a youngish woman. 'The rent's

gone up,' she said. 'And we were hoping for a bloke.'

The second was a horrible old man who said: 'You come round and I decide. All right? You'll have to clean.'

She finished her tea and made herself try one more. The third, another woman, was unoppressively friendly. 'Do you think you could come today, after twelve?' she asked. 'Or I'll have to let it to my neighbour's son and he's revolting.' She told her which bus to take from Haymarket and how to identify East Dulwich. 'See you there,' she said, by which point it was too late to explain.

So Frances went. Lordship Lane was a huge roaring tunnel full of double-deckers and minicab offices. The house was stained pebbledash with a paved garden and orange curtains. 'Not beautiful, is it?' said the woman. She had pink cheeks, bright blue eyes, dark sensible hair, and wore a navy Guernsey, sleeves rolled to the elbow. She looked as if she should be in Africa, inoculating cattle. 'But it came with the job, luckily. No heating—that's why the rent's so low. Do you mind?'

The fluttering feeling in Frances's chest was giving way to felty deadness, as if she were filling with cement. She saw again an image from the Seder: when Helen Baum passed behind Sim's chair on the way to the loo, he suddenly reached back, as if stretching and, apparently innocently, whacked her on the arm.

Now, in this stranger's kitchen, she winced and heard her saying something about furniture.

'The thing is,' she said, 'I . . . I've brought nothing. I don't know how long I'll stay . . .'

The woman did not blink. 'Well, you seem very

nice,' she said cheerfully. 'I'll risk it, if you can put up with the grot. My bad husband's got all my furniture. This stuff's mostly cast-offs—doesn't bother me. Does it bother you?'

'No,' said Frances truthfully. She could see nothing immediately threatening: no BNP leaflets or samurai swords. The embossed wallpaper, the tins of soup beside the barleycorn toaster, were oddly comforting, as if she were staying with a kindly aunt.

'Good, then.' A tiny space hung in the air between them. She felt hot and hollow, an invalid in need of broth. Should I warn her, she wondered, about what I've done?

'I can pay you for a week,' she said. 'Is that all right?'

'Perfectly.'

'Even if I only stay a night? Or, or two?'

'Then I'll give it back. We can play it by ear. Let's see it, anyway,' and Frances and her handbag and bloody hands were led upstairs.

She admired the clean carpet and plain walls of her little room for as long as possible, delaying the awful moment when she would be left alone. When at last she thought of a question, she said: 'So you moved for work?'

'Well, yes. I mean . . . things were going wrong, so I applied for this job.'

'And what, what do you—'

The woman smiled. She looked perfectly normal. 'I'm a vicar,' she said.

TWO

Wednesday 11 April

Anyone would assume, thinks Leo, that after all she has witnessed, Helen Baum would wash her hands of him. However, he is beginning to suspect that psychiatry is not a job for normal people.

So here he is, outside Russell Square Tube station, pretending to be adult. He has, he hopes, so far concealed from her the fact that he is completely out of his depth. Even the flat he shared with Naomi was bought from a cousin, vetted by his mother. However, Helen's calm confidence about finding somewhere to live together, without anyone's assistance, moves and excites him, perhaps more than it should.

*　　　*　　　*

'I think you're fantastic,' he whispers as they cross Woburn Place and wade through the wet billows of blossom that clot Tavistock Square. 'I'm lucky, aren't I.'

She smiles at him. 'Definitely,' she says.

He closes his mind to thoughts of Frances, hanging from a rope. He is in Bloomsbury, two and three-fifths of a mile from Gospel Oak and possibly even further from her. Besides Helen has assured him that Frances will not hang herself. She claims that running away is not unknown and that, 'provided she seeks help', she will be fine. How this can be? he wants to ask her. Don't you realize that, in my family, nobody except me ever runs away?

They are waiting for an estate agent outside an oldfashioned council block on Wharton Street. Pensioners croak approvingly at them, as if they represent the future, a bright new blast of love. However, it is a dramatically ugly building of milk-chocolate tiles and grey cement, stained with the soot of ages, its official name, Arthur Court, emblazoned in gold and green above the door. Someone seems to be throwing clogs down the rubbish chute. Perhaps, he thinks anxiously, we will have to live in her office.

'You know,' he says, privately impressed by the scale of his devotion, 'I'd live in a, a shoebox with you. Or that flat we saw with a rat-trap.' The scent of her hair always makes him think of having sex underneath a piano. Maybe, he thinks, we could *buy* a piano, and—

'Well, my darling,' she tells him, 'I would build a tree house with you, behind the public toilets in Russell Square. And it may come to that—oh, Lord, what a suit. It must be him. Let's just have a look, to be polite. Besides, you never know.'

*   *   *

Claudia's needs are growing more specific. She cannot tolerate references to Leo's domestic plans, to the house or her younger children's prospects, or to Norman, or to Frances, most of all.

Six days since the Seder and her head still aches. Even now, when she thinks of Frances's vanishing, of how close they came to absolute disaster, the ground seems to lurch beneath her as in a dream. But this is no dream.

Fortunately, when Emily and then Leo returned and told her that their sister had gone home, she thought quickly. She told the gossips that Frances was upstairs with a headache. Jonathan, accustomed to schoolyard crises, concurred. With a face like his, who would not believe him? They ate the cake, redistributed the Haggadot, arranged sleepy children on willing laps and launched themselves energetically at the rest of the service, still unaware of the shock that would greet them tomorrow.

To their credit, they pulled it off. Frances's invisibility, her non-participation, made it possible for no one to notice that she had gone. Robin Buckley was diverted with a swift introduction to Diana Lancaster, who had him captivated in thirty seconds with a story about Gielgud in the bath. Meanwhile Claudia talked on. The Listers and the Birnbaums tried to catch her eye. Helen Baum coughed and everyone looked up. The chair Simeon had allegedly fixed that morning broke beneath Betty Lister, so Jonathan had to do what he could with a meat tenderizer and fuse wire. And, when at last they neared the end of the Night of Watching, when they filled the goblet for Elijah, bearer of good news, and the children opened the door to let him enter, in expectation of hope, redemption, life, what should Simeon shout over their heads but 'Come on in, you fuck'?

Every time something went wrong she stretched her smile a little tighter, and everyone else relaxed. She still shudders in the night at the thought of it. However, the others claim it was a triumph. The Birnbaums' cellist agreed to play at shul. All the food was eaten. And, better still, Robin Buckley's glowing profile of her appeared yesterday, its odd spiky asides only visible to those in the know, her book described as a potential bestseller in paragraph two.

Perhaps, she thinks now, he is right. Four hundred copies sold already won't save the roof, but the bills will be paid. They can have a new boiler at last. You have pulled it off, she thinks, you clever woman, but, because of Frances and the doctor, how can she enjoy it?

*   *   *

Only on days like today does her horizon widen and the terror recede. She is just back from Radio Four, which she enjoys more than anything: the introduction (today she was 'the writer, broadcaster, pioneer'); the sycophancy her book inspires in her fellow guests; the amniotic peace of that dim hot little room. But now she sits at her desk at work and can think of nothing but what she has lost, or is about to lose.

*   *   *

This is, thinks Frances, like being dead.

She has left her job. 'No notice?' said Venetia, bracelets clanking, as her girlish haphazardness fell from her like a mould. 'And half a week AWOL? Didn't you get your mobile messages?'

'No,' said Frances truthfully, thinking of the bins beside the Karachi Curry House on Norwood High Street.

'How strange. Well, I think you'll find that your authors won't w—'

'I don't want my authors.'

'Well! That's professional. Most agents—'

'I don't want to be an agent any more,' she said and, as the words left her lips, they solidified. 'I can edit freelance.'

'Edit?' said Venetia, with an interestingly panicked tone. 'What do you know about editing?'

'I edited all my authors. Endlessly. That's why their books earned—'

'*Did* you? Christ.' Hastily she rallied. 'Anyway, freelance will hardly keep you.'

'Well,' Frances said, 'that's what I'm going to do.'

*   *   *

Her first job, restructuring the rambling memoirs of a wild-eyed Sixties singing sensation whose editor is about to have twins, begins next Tuesday. It will, in theory, pay a month's rent, although neither she nor Gillian, her landlady, have mentioned the future. They float past each other, smiling vaguely, like the gentle kicking of swimmers in warm and salty waves. This is her life now: reading creased newspapers in Bosnian cafés, roaming the tiny cemeteries and parks of South-East London, drugging herself with tiredness and the small pleasures of parsimony, gorging on sleep. Isn't this coping? She now has a toothbrush, a library card, an umbrella. She is successfully impersonating a normal person.

And, provided that she sandbags her mind against almost every thought of what she has done, the choice she did not know how to make, she can feel the first pricklings of life returning. The melodramas of Behrens Road must take place without her. She worries about Leo and Max and pines for her father but, she tells them telepathically, it was better than the alternative, however scarred the children will be. Believe me, it was. They are better off without me, either way.

So when what she has done rears up at her, as she is sinking into sleep or when walking among the rubbish and pound shops of Peckham Rye, she stops up her brain. Shaking and crying are, she tells herself, a perfectly natural reaction to shock, as someone rescued from death might shake and cry. This is my cure, she thinks. It had to be dramatic and painful to work. There is no reason to think that escape was not the answer, after all.

THREE

Friday 13 April

Claudia is sitting in her annexe, busying herself with a comment piece for *The Times* when, behind her, she hears a creak. Usually she refuses to be a fearful woman. Everyone likes this about her, particularly Norman, and she has laboured to maintain it through thin and through thinner and even now, with her great hidden terror sitting like an ice cube in her chest. Now, however, she feels a chill of fear, as if a hammer is swinging above her, tearing the air as it falls. She whirls round. There, in the doorway, stands Norman in his pyjamas, looking extraordinarily sheepish.

'My God,' she says, slapping her hand to her

breast. '*God*, Norman. What are you doing to me?'

'Sorry, sorry,' he says, trying to smile at her. She knows him too well to smile back. Clearheaded, even now, she slides her hand up to her throat, so that he will not suspect her.

'Darling,' he says. 'Sweetheart. I . . . I know you're busy.'

'Mm.'

'The thing is . . . There's— We ought to talk.'

But, she thinks, that is not what we do. She is sensing, as others claim to have a feel for snow, the advent of a confrontation. She must make him stop. 'Do we have to?' she says.

It sounds sharper than she had intended. She sees him wince. Poor Norman, she thinks, but it passes. 'I know it's not the best circumstances,' he says. 'But . . . you see, it, it can't wait.'

As he invokes Frances, she notices, he averts his eyes. Is this one of our odder principles: the privacy of pain? Is this where we went . . . well, less right than we intended?

'What is it?' she says.

He clears his throat, unsuccessfully. A film of shame has gathered there. Marriage is about self-preservation, the reading of signs. What wife could not have suspected him? He has been looking over his shoulder for months now. Does he think she notices nothing?

'My darling,' he says. 'Claudia. I . . .'

She sits back in her chair, as far as she can before her hip hurts. His face is imploring.

'I'm not going to make this any easier,' she says.

He hangs his head. His shoulders wobble. As the strangled sounds begin, she thinks of the tears he wept at Frances's birth: the first girl, the only baby he really wanted. Strength, she commands herself. Her own face stiffens as he collapses. Do not think of Frances now.

'I have done something terrible,' he says eventually.

Her first thought is: an interview. He has told the press everything. Her pride cannot bear it. I would rather die, she thinks, than be exposed.

'I feel awful,' he offers. 'If you knew how difficult it's been—'

With that the horrors of the last few months rush at her. Her ears fill with their roar. She jumps up. She is a flood of lava. Norman is falling over himself to escape.

'Don't give me that rubbish,' she spits, rounding the edge of her desk. 'How dare you?'

'But,' he says, 'you don't even know what I've—'

'I can imagine! You stupid . . . you prick! As if all this wasn't bad enough.'

'I know,' he says, his face in his hands.

'Come on, then. What? Who did you tell?'

Now, at the moment of revelation, he falters. 'Maybe,' he begins, 'we could . . . I don't know. Could we . . . maybe we should forget—'

'For God's sake!' she roars. '*Tell me.*'

His voice cracking, Norman spells out the truth. He has betrayed her with, of all people, Cedric Vickers, writer of little poems for little people. He has taken her belief in privacy and turned it against her. Her faith in him was wrong.

There is a galloping in her chest, as if the adrenaline on which she usually coasts has been mismeasured. It should energize her but it does not. She feels sick, like the women she despises, those who let their bodies rule their minds.

She lets him give her names and places, endless worthless justifications. If she is to be armed she needs the facts. Over and over again he tells her that he is sorry. She can hear the excitement leaking out around his words. You jellyfish, she thinks, you worm. If my rock has betrayed me, what is left?

She sits on the corner of her desk, holding on, breathing. She waits until her mind is like a laser, burning into him.

'Norman,' she says and her voice is like a hand beneath his chin, forcing his head up. 'Enough. Just tell me when.'

'It's . . . All right. All right. It's . . . Oh God. Monday.'

She feels it in her stomach. Strike back, she thinks. Do it now.

'I know,' she says, and sees him flinch. 'I've always known.'

*   *   *

Later, replaying this moment, it will seem to Norman that the ground drops beneath him. He gropes backwards and finds only wobbly books, on to which he clings. 'What?'

'You heard.'

'You can't know.'

'Why not? Did you think you'd covered your tracks that well?'

'But—'

'You're not infallible. And clearly I'm not. I thought you were trustworthy and obviously I was *completely* wrong about that. You know how I feel about secrets, about being certain of someone. To think how often you must have lied to me . . .'

'Don't,' he says, waving his hands weakly. 'Please. I didn't mean to hurt—'

'It's a little too late,' she says, 'for that.'

*   *   *

In silence he endures her stare until, eventually, he begins to squirm. His scalp, his chest, every fleshly masculine appendage, grow bald and contemptible beneath her gaze. He is in her hands as, once before, at twenty-one, he took the beautiful and terrifying Claudia Simon upstairs at a party and confessed to having inadvertently slept with her cousin Bernice, whom she despised. Other men love the solvent whiff of power that infidelity gives them. Not Norman. Then, as now, he feels only fear.

Eventually, when he can bear it no longer, he asks: 'What . . . so what do you want me to do?'

'Me? Nothing.'

'But . . . It's too late to stop the book, though, isn't it?' Anyone could hear how pathetically hopeful he sounds, how much he wishes that she could put out a hand and save them.

'Why should I?' she asks. 'Although my book's doing well—perhaps you haven't noticed—we still need the money, Norman. And it's good for your career. It's fantastic. What happens within a marriage is not the issue here.'

Never has an indefinite article frightened him more. He rubs at his beard like an anxious beast but she is Beauty, with his testicles in her hand. He wants to say: I need you. Nothing else matters.

Even he knows he is far too late for that.

291

'And if you want to know how I knew,' she begins.

'Yes?'

He expects her to say, 'Tough,' and smile, or lead him through an agonizing list of his errors. However, even now she has not lost her power to amaze. She only looks at him strangely, sadly, as if all the disappointments and small treacheries of their life together have suddenly overwhelmed her.

'Nu?' he says.

But his wife, who bears such passionate grudges, whose boycotts last for decades, whose broiguses are passed lovingly to her heirs, is wearing an expression he has never seen before. It is acceptance.

He tries not to stare. 'I'm sorry,' he says cautiously. 'I thought . . . it was so difficult . . . I mean, how do you say—'

'It doesn't matter.'

'What?' No, he wants to say: it does. Of course it bloody does. You should be raging against me, making me suffer, sacrificing nothing if you love me at all. Dear God, he thinks, dear Claudia, don't forgive me now.

She shakes her head, as if he has apologized for a mislaid teacup. 'Let's forget it,' she says. 'At least, tonight. I'm very tired.'

'Really?'

'*Yes*.'

Now he is irritating her. Is that a good sign? 'So, we'll talk again tomorrow. Shall we?'

'Fine.'

'We . . . I don't want it to fester. I'm sorry, my darl—'

'Enough already, Norman.'

Yes, he thinks, enough. Tomorrow we'll talk and then, maybe, please God, we'll move on. Is it too much to hope that he, Norman the nebbish, has been lucky? That he could have his book and his wife, that Frances will come back, that the world will look kindly on him, after all?

FOUR

Saturday 14 April

Norman wakes, mildly surprised to be alive. His body feels bruised and brittle after their argument. He holds himself still but cannot hear, over the squeaks and rustlings of his bristly body, whether Claudia is lying beside him. How, after all these years, can he not be sure? Tentatively he stretches out a hand, an arm. Her side of the bed is cold.

He must go to her. He dresses in those of his garments she seems to prefer: a grey flannel shirt in which he feels like a well-dressed mental patient, a pair of greenish woollen trousers from Palermo whose purchase, he has always dimly suspected, involved another man.

She hasn't guessed about Selina, he mutters to himself, as if simple repetition can thicken the ice beneath their feet. Stop feeling sorry for yourself and do something. Build bridges. Shore up ruins. Act, you idiot, act.

He sticks his head into the hallway. While he slept, insensitive lout that he is, his dreams were curiously noisy, as if an orchestra had been assembling nearby. But now, when he wants comforting kitchen sounds, spatulas, a radio play, there is only silence.

So where is Claudia?

She is, he tells himself, at shul, gliding through the Saturday service as if nothing at home is wrong, least of all him. But what if she has gone, like their daughter? He stands in the corridor, hobbles across to his dark study like an invalid, leans against the desk for a moment, cold hands in his armpits. Superstitiously, he touches the calendar Frances made him in nursery, its sequins now vanished between the floorboards, its pasta wheels and bows providing secret nourishment for God knows what creatures in the night—probably Simeon. He does it for love but then he sees, brazen and beautiful, the date he has been hoarding in his soul: his publication, only two days away. Slowly, like creeping sunlight, the golden haze of his secret begins to revive him. I have worked so hard on my book, he thinks. Am I to be robbed of this pleasure too?

*   *   *

He makes himself go downstairs: no toast, no coffee and—oh, the disappointment—no Claudia. Perhaps it is hunger, or the strains of the night before but, like an infant, he starts to wobble. His nostrils sting. I'm not, he thinks . . . but yes, he is. He sits down suddenly on the table edge and, as tears begin to fall on to his old man's hands, there is a commotion by the garden door.

Frances's children burst into the kitchen and stop dead, their little mouths open.

'Be extremely careful not to sli—' calls their

father.

Then he, too, stops. Pink-cheeked, bright-eyed, extremely well wrapped against the mild spring air, they stand frozen in horror at the sight of their grandfather, disintegrating.

Then Jonathan swings into action. 'Girls,' he says, with maddening calmness, 'go upstairs. Start your unpacking. And take Maxie to find his yellow brick.'

His daughters retreat slowly. His father-in-law attempts to find a handkerchief. The men are left alone.

Norman blows his nose loudly, like a baboon establishing territory. His trumpetings hang on the air. There is something particularly embarrassing about this relationship, with its potential for advice-seeking and skin-crawling revelations. He lives in fear that this keen young man, for whom he feels nothing beyond mild suspicion, will one day call him Dad.

Jonathan rolls back his shoulders. He refines a caring yet masculine smile. 'Er,' he says. 'Golly. Are you OK?'

Norman busies himself with a protruding nail-head, as if he could flatten it with a tap of his mighty thumb. 'I'm fine,' he says.

Jonathan clears his throat. 'I know,' he says, 'this week's been pretty tough for you and, er, Claudia. I mean, God knows, it's been hard on us all.'

Norman frowns. He does not want to think about how this man may miss his daughter. Theirs are hardly the ties of blood. He is about to snap at him when something crosses his mind. 'What did you mean, a minute ago, about unpacking?'

Jonathan glances away, not quite quickly enough to hide a little smirk. Everything about him—his wholesome haircut, his chinos, his wedding ring—emanates sensible satisfaction. Oh, Frances, Norman finds himself thinking, you deserved more.

'Ah,' says Jonathan. 'Didn't you know? She, Claudia, said that I, we could . . . we . . .'

Black ungrandfatherly thoughts scuttle across Norman's mind. 'You could what?'

'Move in.'

'What? That's ridic . . . Where?'

Jonathan scratches the side of his nose. 'Well, we've been wanting to move for months, as you know . . .'

'Do I?'

'Yes. And if we clear the attic—'

'The attic's fine!'

'Well, Claudia's been wanting it cleared, of course.'

'She said nothing to me.'

'Er . . . well, anyway, it makes sense. We've only lost a month's rent, and the children will be with all of you. It's perfect.'

'Hmm,' says Norman. 'So this is . . . permanent?'

'Yes.'

'And you think that's what Frances will want?'

'If she comes back.'

Norman buries his fists deep in his pockets. 'Of course she will,' he says.

*   *   *

So this, thinks Leo, is how rebellion feels.

It is Saturday evening, a week after his sister's

296

disappearance, when any normal son, surely, would be in his family's bosom, worrying: not Leo. How can this be? The more vigorously his younger siblings try to involve him, by means of tearful accusations on the stairs or painfully misspelled ('But who's counting?' his father would say; actually, thinks Leo, I am) poison-pen notes stuffed under his bedroom door, the more desperate he becomes to escape them. His mother, after an interrogation about Frances's whereabouts from which only utter ignorance freed him at last, has vanished into her work and her book, apparently furious with them all. His father, whom he has been avoiding, cornered him in the front garden yesterday morning. The excruciating telling-off Leo had dreaded was over in two minutes.

'Let's sit on the wall,' said Norman, where he veered into a weird monologue about literary endeavour and artistic seclusion which left Leo, his thoughts more on the cold damp curve beneath his bottom, mystified but curiously aroused.

It is surely reasonable, therefore, to want to escape. Soon he will. The Wharton Street council block contained the perfect flat: a cube of light and built-in cupboards, unglamorous enough to be almost affordable, available with a month's notice from the heirs of its previous owners, Mary Moss and Mr Moss, who within a year of their golden wedding anniversary had both died, apparently fulfilled.

'Good precedent,' whispered Leo, trying not to skip down the estate agent's steps too obviously, and Helen, thrillingly, had agreed. Six hundred and twelve hours to go until the flat is theirs: almost six hundred and eleven. Love has made an optimist of Leo. Surely, if he works constantly and goes for strengthening walks on the Heath and cleans the bathroom, the time will pass with almost no further sibling interaction?

He is sitting at his desk, his eyes on Ramsay's *Trusts* and his mind on wall-to-wall carpeting, when, with a bang, his door flies open. It is Em and, for a change, she is crying.

It is easy to forget that his siblings do not have a Helen. There is no one to comfort or reassure them about Frances, to give them a sense of perspective. For the fifth time today he tries to imagine his life without his love and fails. It is too horrible.

'You can't do this,' says his sister.

'Do what?' he asks but, of course, he knows.

'Come on.' There is a warning sheen in her big bright eyes. 'Don't pretend.'

He feels himself about to sigh and tries to hide it. She will take offence. 'You mean move?'

'You're so stupid. *Yes*.'

'But,' he says, 'I've got to do it eventually. Mum knows that. This was never going to be permanent. And N-Naomi's selling the flat and moving back to Woodside Park so the mortgage—'

Em inhales sharply. Financial references, like housing or work, are traditionally avoided before the younger Rubins. It is, everyone agrees, hardly their fault that worthy employment never quite came up. Now, however, Em simply takes another long-suffering breath and explains: 'You have to think of her *feelings*.'

'But,' he says, sounding plaintive, 'I can't stay here for ever.'

'Why not?'

'Because I have this whole new life—'

'You never *think*,' she says furiously, grabbing a clean sock from his drawer and wiping her eyes.

'Er, please—' he begins.

Too late; she is wiping her nose. She ignores him. 'How can you? You're meant to be so bloody perfect but you're as bad as her.'

You can use her name, he thinks, but is too cowardly to say. 'But . . . so what am I supposed to do?'

'*Stay*. Durr. You can't move out—'

'You did.'

She takes a step back. Her mouth is open. 'What's wrong with you?' she says. '*I'm* moving back. She needs us all.'

'But Frances will come back,' he says. 'And Mum's book's doing well, isn't it?'

'Er, yes . . . hadn't you noticed? How could you not? She's all over the pape—'

'So why can't we do what we want, too? Does she have to be, you know, the centre of everything?'

'Yes!' says Em, outraged. 'How can you even *say* that?'

'But we . . . aren't we grown-ups?'

'I'm not!'

'You're twenty, what, twenty-seven . . .'

'Twenty-eight! And that's not grown up.'

'But don't you want things? Er, you know: affection, outside interes—'

'Are you mad? I don't want a bloody *hobby*. She's our mother! You can't just treat her like an ordinary person. God, Leo, I knew Frances was rubbish but I never thought—'

'Stop that,' he says. It comes out more loudly than he had meant but, he thinks, now it is said. He licks his lips. 'Please don't say that about her.'

There is a sticky silence. When, at last, Em speaks she sounds absolutely cold, as if he is a stranger. 'We thought you were on our side,' she says. 'We thought you understood what matters, even when you screwed up. Both times. But you've been faking it, haven't you? You've been getting the cred for being the good ones, both of you, our whole lives. But you're not, are you? You stupid fucks. You've been lying all along. You never were.'

*   *   *

It is coming, thinks Claudia in the night. She puts out a hand for Norman, close enough to feel his animal heat. She is too frightened for it to calm her. Oh God, she thinks, no. Please not so soon.

This evening, for the first time since their fight, he offered her a cup of coffee. She paused. It felt as if she were ice and he were a burning wire, pushing through her: painful, ruinous, but a relief in the end.

'Yes,' she said. 'All right.'

His smile was so happy that she felt a troubling flash of empathy, despite all that he has done. How, she wondered, does being married to her feel?

Now, millimetres from waking him, she hesitates again. If she tells him what is wrong, he will not be able to bear it. He loves me so, she thinks. A slow tear begins to roll from beneath her eyelid, over her cheekbone, down towards her throat. Better that he should not have to live with fear like this.

FIVE

Monday 16 April

Publication day. Norman wakes to find his body tense with excitement, already. His cells, it seems, sense something. They are no longer mere elements of his toenails or chest hair but part of something greater: a famous man.

Yet, as he lies there on warm cleanish sheets, determinedly revelling like a millionaire in his own success, something begins occur to him. The world has not stopped. Cars can clearly be heard in the street outside. The man with the inexplicable rag-and-bone handcart still rings his irritating bell and shouts his mysterious cry. Even the radio at someone's open window—is it the end of *Today*?—makes no mention of him.

Oy, his heart says. His brain thinks: never mind. He hauls himself out of bed and wanders to the bathroom for a thorough inspection of his snowy stubble, his father's nose, the skin-tags whose progress he watches with panicky fascination. You've done well, he tells himself in the mirror and, although he still cannot quite believe it, he feels a smile begin at the words. The sight of it makes him smile harder. Baruch atta adonai . . . there must be a b'racha on a son's success, however belated. His mother and father would have been so proud.

301

Because, he reflects as he dresses in relaxed yet faintly distinguished clothes, lest he be photographed when buying the papers, of all possible literary coups what could have pleased his parents more than this? Without those endless evenings in front of the radio, the pale Bush and then the darker, smarter Pye whose dust-gold mesh seemed to smell of the future, listening to their gentle arguments about which matinée idol was secretly surnamed Blinsky, which politician started as Frankenburger, the truth about Cedric Vickers, bard of suspicious, sentimental Middle England, might never have been revealed.

Sorry, Cedric, old boy, he thinks, and smiles sadly to himself. He goes down to the kitchen, reminding himself to expect nothing, in the circumstances. Nevertheless, a medium-sized part of him cannot help but hope for glory, lox and champagne, his proud wife cheering, his children carrying him aloft.

So where are the flowers? The clapping? There is only his grandson, blood of his blood, with whom he has never spent so much as a minute alone.

The child is battering at the toggles of its little orange jacket. Norman harrumphs. He considers suitable subjects for conversation: the unpleasant secretions on its jacket collar; breakfast; yesterday's marvellous discovery of 'sharopnikel', New Yiddish for a comfort object, such as the repellent fluffy yellow brick his grandson is holding in his grubby paw.

Where, thinks Norman, is that schmendrick, your father? Carefully, hands braced against his thighs, he creaks downwards. He is expecting the child to wail but, remarkably, it does not. It—

young Max—actually lowers his fists. He seems to compose himself as he looks up at his grandfather's grizzled chops, perfectly calm.

'Why are you here?' enquires Norman. 'Shouldn't you be at . . . you know, school? With people your own age?'

Slowly, with an air of wry amusement, his grandson's little red lips open, revealing the wet tip of a tiny tongue. Norman too begins to smile. The baby beams. He looks, thinks Norman, somewhat like his own father's baby brother, whom he glimpsed only once in a now-lost photograph. That strangely square head and the black cowlick are exactly the same.

Still the tongue emerges. 'What are you doing?' asks Norman.

Instinct tells him to move his big bristly face closer. He sees sleep, snot, spittle, a spark of life in those shiny eyes. The tongue protrudes further. Norman moves closer still.

At that moment, his grandson's lingual muscles give a final push. Silently, moistly, nose and tongue-tip come into contact. It is not horrible, as one might expect, but delightful. Frances would understand, he thinks, this urge to taste but, almost before he has had time to miss her, he hears a voice.

'Oh!' it says.

Norman jumps up. It is not Frances but the baby's father, no substitute, waving a red plastic book.

He has, as he explains in some detail, popped upstairs for the medical records before taking Max for his jabs, which are so important. 'Don't you think?'

'Well,' begins Norman, but it seems simpler to agree. He stands aside, the dot of saliva cooling on the end of his nose, while his son-in-law buckles the child proficiently into a complicated-looking pushchair.

Life is painful, he tells the fluffy curls of his motherless grandson. But I will comfort you as I tried to comfort Frances, with jokes and etymology, with as much culture as I can sneak past the others, who will allow us so little time. I will be maddeningly even-handed, as my father was. You may be moody and oversensitive, like her. But because of that moment of silliness, that spark and that cowlick, you will be my secret favourite, just as she was.

Only this time round, I will make sure that you know you are.

*   *   *

In the evening, Frances falters.

Hard as she tries to prevent thoughts of what she has done and why she did it, as a person dying of cold might seal up windows and doors, it is becoming more difficult to keep them out. It begins with her hands. She finds herself stroking them comfortingly in the oddest situations: buying fruit by the bowlful on market stalls, returning library books, making enterprising soups. Then, in the National Gallery, she finds herself avoiding the Madonnas, not that those creepy Christ-children with their old man's pectorals have anything to do with her. Her long nights are laced with dreams of terrible decisions, and she always chooses wrongly.

Today she has walked too far: all the way to Fulham, for no particular reason, and all the way back. Her defences are lowered. She lies in the flimsy pink bath and suddenly an image of her son's knees, sweet silky moons of flesh, floats above her. She begins to cry, then to sob. Howls of pain bounce off the fibreglass until she remembers that her landlady is home and ducks under the water, letting her mouth fill until at last she is quiet.

Too late. When she emerges, Gillian, who has been kind and clever and not asked a single question, is speaking to her through the door.

'Sorry?'

'Are you in labour?'

'Oh, no . . .'

'We're not trained for it, you see.'

'I'm sorr—'

'Unless you're dying. I can do death, at a push.'

And then it hits her. All the thoughts she has not been thinking, the dreams of scented springy skin and apricot plumpness, pour in like poisonous waters over her pathetic walls. While she has been trying to forget him for his own sake, because she does not know how to be natural, because she must be fair, because, most of all, he will die and she will go mad, she has been hurting him, as she has always feared.

Isn't it too late?

Not for me, she thinks. He isn't cold and dead and buried. He is alive and she can try again. However many days have passed since she left, however much harm she had done to him already,

305

it is not too late to find him, to hold and sniff and stroke him. If she hurries.

She sits up like a corpse revived, water pouring from her hips and nipples.

'Sorry,' she calls, struggling into her clothes. 'I'm all right, but I've . . . I've got to go out. And when I get back I might need to talk to you.'

Gillian's voice comes to her from very close by, as if her forehead is resting against the door: 'Don't worry. It's fine. Do whatever you have to do.'

*   *   *

Ten minutes later, Frances bursts on to the echoing forecourt of East Dulwich station and races towards the ticket machine. Her hands seem to have jellified. She can barely hold her purse, let alone extract the coins, but there is no time to spare. She must not miss this train.

'Easy,' says the man behind the Plexiglas window as she asks for a ticket. She nods and smiles at him like a lunatic, throws the change into her bag and stampedes up the stairs to platform two. No one spits at her as she waits, or points to Wanted posters. She stands in the little shelter unassaulted, jiggling against the cold, feigning interest in a notice about the University of the North Downs while she awaits her train: six minutes. Five.

There is a payphone at the end of the platform, shielded with perforated metal as in her student hall of residence on Maple Street. She has trained herself to ignore telephones now. She will pay it no attention.

Change slithers at the bottom of her bag. Above her head, the monitor blinks: four minutes. She needs an activity.

She begins to walk. She floats along the platform like an astronaut, one way, then the other. Oh, she thinks. Here's that phone.

Nobody is looking. She steps into the booth and finds, to her surprise, that the bloody smell she remembers is there beneath the grime and urine, as if she is standing inside a metal horse. She presses her fingertip against one of the holes: white, then pink, then white again. She remembers this too, and the weight of the receiver in her hand. She drops in coins and dials a number, simply to see—

Jay answers.

'Oh!' says Frances, unmoored. 'I—oh . . . I . . .'

'Hel*lo*. Good Lord. You'd gone silent.'

'Sorry?'

'What's up?'

'Sorry?'

'Frances. Are you drunk?'

'I . . . no.'

'So . . . ?'

'Um, right. OK. Then you haven't spoken to Em? Not recently?'

'Nope. Nor am I likely to. Didn't you know? I assumed there'd been some sort of Rubin crisis summit: Rescue Em from Degradation. Why? Is something up?'

'No—'

'Well, I'm glad you rang. Now tell me, what can I do for you?'

So here it is, thinks Frances, her forehead cold against the metal, breathing again the scent of possibility she had thought was lost. This is the moment I've been waiting for.

Then distantly, as if through swirling galactic dust and cold starlight, she sees the train barrelling into the station. She could jump beneath it. She could climb on board. She could ask Jay to meet her.

She does not.

* * *

Overground through dirty terraces, underground through windy tunnels, Frances crosses Brixton and Victoria. She holds a newspaper in front of her, its pages trembling.

Euston.

Camden Town.

Archway.

Here she is.

* * *

Nu? thinks Norman.

He is a reasonable man. He acknowledges that, in the circumstances, telegrams, banquets and copulation were unlikely to be his. However, try as he might to feel nobly Spartan, to persuade himself that he lives only for his art, it is difficult not to feel hard done by. What, after all, was this effort for, if not to be repaid?

As the day progresses, his mood darkens. There is nothing for him in the post from Selina, of whom he still had dim hopes despite his rather formal letter of disengagement. Nothing even from his publishers, the bastards: he should have guessed.

308

However excitedly the press girl chirps of widespread coverage this weekend, it gives him no pleasure. He needs immediate proof of his success, of his cleverness and, without that, the day is dust.

*　　　*　　　*

Worse still, Claudia is avoiding him. Is it too much to ask that she invites her husband out for lunch? Could she not have lowered herself to send him a manly bouquet, a helium balloon, even? Evidently not. By seven o'clock, his day of glory wasted, he decides to escape his son-in-law's offer of a nutritious stir-fry and go for a walk.

I need some air, he tells himself, not bloody sunflower seeds. I'll take myself out to dinner.

Worse is to come. He has chosen, he thought cleverly, to wear his most grippy shoes as defence against fallen blossom. However, as he crosses the road he steps in something soft and unpleasant, in full view of Roger Griffin, Professor of Smugness, as he climbs out of his executive car. A sticky spring drizzle begins to fall. Several houses on Constantine Road, about which he feels competitive on Behrens Road's behalf, exhibit annoying signs of prosperity: major scaffolding, dazzling windows, skips containing perfectly serviceable-looking furniture whose minor flaws he does not know how to fix.

By the time the unconvincing and probably dangerous Cressy Road Working Men's Social Club comes into view, his spirits are low. He is worrying constantly about Frances. It hurts even to imagine her face. Perhaps because of this, he is also fretting about her son, his new responsibility, although babies, he reminds himself, are terrible things.

What did you plan to do with him, anyway? he asks himself. Offer him a hairy nipple? Build a little crib?

Most depressingly of all, he is beginning to imagine how hard the years ahead—even the decades, please God, if he lowers his cholesterol— will be. The Selina guilt will be with him for ever, at every family occasion, each mention of Cedric Vickers's name. As if that wasn't bad enough, he must lie in bed beside his wife—the one person in the world who, if she has time, can analyse anything to its very nucleus with that beautiful satisfying brain of hers—and not talk to her about any of it: not a single word.

If he is lucky, this will be his only punishment. After an extremely difficult conversation with Betty Lister he has established that all she saw was a little feature about his book in the trade press, helpfully sent home by her middle son. But someone, he keeps thinking, still might have seen him and Selina together. Lauderdale House, of all idiot places; every time he thinks of their kiss he wants to bite the table with embarrassment and fury.

I have ruined my own marriage, he thinks now, gesturing dramatically and scratching his hand on some fool's hawthorn hedge. Growling, he turns and sees a happy couple walking hand in hand towards him. They are nothing like him and Claudia but at the sight of them he feels even worse, as if they represent a time when he was randy and hopeful and Claudia was still unbetrayed. Then they turn to face him.

310

Usually Frances dreads Holloway. Today she is not afraid. She slaloms expertly around abandoned mattresses, the car-window leavings which carpet St John's Grove. Potential murderers walk by her on the way to collect their pizzas and she does not flinch. She runs the last metres to her front door like a perfect mother, hungry with love. Then she notices that the house is dark.

'Max?'

All is silent. With one sniff of the communal entrance she remembers why she left in the first place: doll celluloid, sour sofa cushions, secret despair. I am free of all that, she reminds herself. This is what I wanted. Her key turns in the lock.

Something is wrong. The hallway is piled with neatly taped boxes, dismantled shoe racks, toy potties and textbooks and Junior Monopoly. First she thinks: this is not our flat. Then, underneath the damp, the chemical reek of takeaway flyers, she senses something else, sweeter and warmer than the rest. It makes her mouth water, more like a lover than mothers are meant to be. She takes a deep, deep sniff and then she locks the door.

*   *   *

Norman says: 'Are you following me?'

'I can assure you,' says Leo's rebbitzin, the Baum woman, 'that we're not. Actually, *we* were ahead. Were you following us?'

His mouth feels completely dry, as if she has emitted a defensive cloud of talcum powder. She

311

is, he notices now in the street-light, unexpectedly good-looking, like a Latin teacher one might spend one's adolescence loining for. Somewhere deep within him, admiration for his son begins to stir.

'We haven't . . . officially . . . I'm Norman Rubin,' he says, holding out his enormous crêpey hand. 'As you probably know.'

'Mm,' she says with a wry little smile. She takes his paw with warm and certain fingers. Beside her his mute son gives a ghastly grin.

It is definitely time to turn back. A crate of champagne from Swithun may be being delivered at this very moment; Frances may have seen his name in the paper; Claudia may be home, baking soufflés. 'I—' he begins.

'Dad—' says Leo.

'What would you think,' asks his girlfriend calmly, 'about joining us for a drink?'

*   *   *

Immune to stitch, blind to the enormous youths who dawdle on the kerb, Frances runs back down St John's Grove, races through Dartmouth Park and, panting, crosses into Gospel Oak. It is only when she reaches the corner of Behrens Road that she remembers her bicycle, that she thinks of the plans she could have made. By then it is too late.

Sixteen houses away . . . fourteen . . . The Shaughnessys have a new car, she sees; there, by the post box, Hugo Silverstein, the twelve-year-old model, takes advantage of his psychologist parents' absence to readjust his genitals. Ten houses, eight: spring smells like spring here, of wet leaves and rickety tree houses, of sodden earth criss-crossed

312

by the tracks of educational toys. Seven: now, despite the humming darkness, she can identify the bushy hedge with which her parents wage war on Camden council; the flowering cherry in the Momsens' front garden to which she wrote impassioned poems in her teens. Five. Although her legs move, it grows more and more difficult to imagine ever arriving. The house has become an enormous magnet, repelling her with its rays.

Nearer still: close enough to see the curtains into which she once tried to sew five pounds and a rubber frog to keep them safe from Simeon. Four: what if Jay, thoughts of whom she has been keeping at arm's length even now, or only a little closer, senses that she is back? Three: the patterned path; two: the front door; one: a bright segment of kitchen at the far end of the dining room, in which her husband aeroplane-swoops her laughing baby into Claudia's open arms.

She stands by the rotting gatepost, growing colder in the drizzle, biting at the grainy inside of her lip. She must do what is best, but what is? Would it be better for Max if she went in and claimed him and tried to become a patient baking mother, or if she left them to be happy without her, as they truly seem to be?

Then something occurs to her. What does she want?

She cannot tell. She understands 'ought' and 'should' and the subtle arts of delayed gratification, but reading her own heart comes less naturally, if it ever comes at all.

Well, she thinks, now it has to.

Like a murderer, she creeps up the garden path. Like a stranger, she presses the bell. The door swings open. There, in a blast of familiar air and the *Princess Azandra* theme tune stands one of her victims: her elder stepdaughter, damp-haired in new fairy-patterned pyjamas. She looks at Frances with an expression of perfect blankness.

'Oh,' she says. 'You.'

'Hi—hello,' says Frances. 'How are . . . things?'

'OK.'

'I've been . . . staying with a friend,' she says. 'Sorry I rushed off. I, it's difficult to expl—'

'OK,' says Susannah. She looks back towards the sitting room, beginning to turn on her bare pink heels.

*   *   *

It would be less painful to let her go. Don't, Frances tells herself. She bends down and touches her stepdaughter's shoulder. 'I need to tell you something,' she says. Rebecca keeps her face averted but tucks her hair behind an ear. 'I'm going to . . . it's not going to be the same for you and the others. But I think it'll be better.'

'How do you mean?'

'I won't be, you know, nagging . . .' Rebecca does not smile. 'I know I've been . . . not how I wanted to be. I'm sorry. But I . . . there might be a different way of doing it. I can be a sort of long-distance person. I'd be better at that, I think.'

'OK.'

'I am sorry. But I think you're . . .' Close like this, as they never are, she can see the down on her stepdaughter's soft earlobe, the freckle beneath her left eye. She seems younger, and reachable. 'I love you, you know,' she says.

'Mm,' says Rebecca.

Stiffly, Frances stands up. 'So shall we do that? If you want me to?'

'Maybe. If you like. Susannah will.'

'Oh! Really? Will she?'

But that is all the reward she will have because Rebecca asks, 'Can I go now?' and, at a nod, she does.

*   *   *

When Frances pushes open the kitchen door, the room goes quiet. Even Max, suspended in his father's hands, stares. His chin twitches but he does not recoil, or even cry. Is it possible that he wants her? She holds out her arms and then, before he or anyone else can change their minds, for the first time she can remember, she simply takes him.

Oh yes, she thinks. She breathes in his hair, grips his hot surprising weight as she tears at his Babygro poppers, searching for skin. This is a hunger she has never known before, or not for him. Her mother's eyes are upon her but she keeps her own on him.

'What are you *doing* here?' says Jonathan.

The Babygro is free. She rips up Max's vest and here, at last, is his stomach, a hot round sun; his strong little back. With her hands on him she can look up.

Jonathan first. He is standing beside his mother-in-law, gripping the back of her chair. He looks both cross and puzzled, as if his difficult wife has rebelled against her true nature by coming back. Nervously, Frances lowers her gaze to her mother.

315

She will not look at her. She offers only the side of her face, the cheek, the jaw; she is preparing her strike. Her perfume thickens the air. Although it feels like a tiny act of matricide, Frances begins to breathe through her mouth.

As if she senses it, Claudia turns her head. She looks exactly the same as usual, glossy hazelnutty hair, perfect bones, stony composure. Her frightening eyes meet her daughter's and, as Frances's legs begin to shake, she says: 'Obviously you can't do this.'

Frances moves backwards, as far from her mother's pulsing magnetic rays as the cramped kitchen will allow. She reaches the sink and perches on it, hugging Max half-standing to her, his warm chemical-spiked nappy perfectly aligned with her nose. Only then does she address her mother. 'That's what you think,' she begins, 'but—'

'I don't think it. I know it. Of course I know.'

'I'm—'

'We don't,' says Jonathan, 'want to hear that you're sorry. We've discussed this, haven't we, Claudia? That isn't the point.'

Claudia nods thoughtfully, as if they are at a conference and he has made a fair and flattering point. 'Exactly,' she says, still very calm. 'Listen to him.'

Frances looks at the floor. Her body feels scaldingly hot but her mind is cool. She presses her heels against the sink cupboard until her knees stop trembling. Max's hot moist breath roars gently in her ear. 'I'm still his mother,' she says. 'It isn't up to you.'

The room itself seems to gasp, as if the air has combusted. Max's fat feet shift on her lap.

Claudia's mouth opens with a tiny click.

'You are being,' she says, her eyes narrowing, 'utterly ridiculous. Jonathan, make her see sense.'

Frances grips Max more firmly around his absence of waist. He puts up a sticky hand to steady himself, clutches at her hair a little too tightly, but he still has not cried. A miracle, her father would say.

Where is her father?

Ordinarily she would not ask. Her mother, her siblings, must feel that they alone are enough. Today is not ordinary.

'Is Dad around?' she says. Jonathan and Claudia exchange an ominous look. 'Oh my God,' she says, seeing blue flashing lights, his lonely coffin. '*What?*'

'He's fine,' snaps her mother. 'It's the rest of us who—'

'Can we please focus on the issue at hand?' says Jonathan loudly. 'Frances, don't you realize that this . . . this isn't on? You can't simply leave and come back whenever it suits you. It's unsettling. I mean, not that we haven't been, you know, managing, but *psychologically* it's very disruptive. Maxie's been quite perplexed, haven't you? Yes, you have . . . shall I . . . All right, you hold him, for now. But I must say that the girls . . . well, they're fine, it goes without saying, they're absolutely fine, but Simeon and Emily have had a terrible time, really, you can't imagine how . . . And that's another thing—' He talks on and on and, after some time, Frances drifts away. She has Max and her father is safe. Now she can look down on them all and marvel.

*   *   *

Jonathan, she realizes, is completely paralysed in front of his mother-in-law. He cannot be rude or furious with Frances because she is one of Claudia's children, and nothing matters more to him than her good opinion. And, since they obviously haven't made a plan, since—she can see it now; she is growing angrier—they've clearly decided that they're the perfect little family anyway, he doesn't know what to do. He's waiting for his instructions.

The future, she thinks, is up to me.

She turns back to face him. She has Max's arm around her neck and the warmth of it, the springy plumpness, encourages her. Jonathan hesitates. He takes a breath. Now? Never?

'I want to take him with me,' she says to him.

Claudia snorts through her nostrils. 'Well,' she says. 'You can't.'

*   *   *

Frances had always believed in the survival of the fittest. She had assumed that evolution, quite reasonably, had reserved Claudia's ferocity, her crusader's zeal, for her stronger, lovelier son and daughter. Now, however, at the thought of the flat and fearful life behind her, the dim compliant future ahead, fire starts to roll through her. She stands up, sword in hand.

'I don't care,' she says.

'Er,' says her husband, looking stunned, 'there's no, no need to shout . . .'

'Yes there is! There bloody is! *He's* all right,' she

318

says, pointing her chin at Max. 'And the girls are fine. They've got you, anyway. I know this isn't good. I *know* that. But what do you expect me to do? Stay for ever, getting more and more miserable?'

He lifts a finger, as if she is contesting the date of the Stuart accession. 'You weren't exactly miserable,' he begins.

'How can she say that?' interrupts Claudia. 'You were *lucky*. Think how the others would have wanted such a wonderful li—'

'Well, they could have had it!' she says. 'I wasn't stopping them. Anyway, what the hell have they got to do with this?'

Her husband and mother exchange a look of alarm. Frances is galloping away from them now, shedding money and food and children as she picks up speed.

'They're your brothers and sister,' offers Jonathan, reverentially.

'I know! And they can do what they want. That's up to them. But . . . but it's not what I wanted.' She is crying, she realizes. So, at the sound of the shouting, is Max. She ought to stop but she can't. 'Neither of you,' she says, 'neither of you have the faintest idea how I felt.'

'What you felt,' Jonathan tells her, 'isn't the . . . We're a family, Frances. You have to make sacrifi—'

'*Why?* Listen to yourself! You sound like a Mormon! It's unbelievable. I'm not a bloody *good* you can pass around. You're making this sound like an arranged marr—'

Then she stops. My God, she thinks, of course it was.

319

'I can look after him,' she says, more quietly now. 'I know what to do, and I love him. I'm his mother.'

Jonathan smiles, coldly. He looks happier now. 'I think you'll find,' he says, 'that it's more complicated than that. If you walk out on your children, your child, then in the eyes of the law—'

Frances swallows. She removes Max's finger from her mouth. 'Wait,' she says. 'What are you saying?'

'What he's saying,' begins her mother as the kitchen door swings open.

*   *   *

'Hello, hello,' says Norman, struggling with his jacket zip. He is bright with damp fresh air and cigarette smoke and self-satisfaction since Leo's rather clever, er, girlfriend, quite casually mentioned reading a large and positive review of his book this very morning. He is also agreeably diverted by the question of how to enable the young couple to meet, et cetera, under his family's roof. He does not, therefore, notice the composition of this little scene, at first. Then he lifts his head and sees his daughter, come back to him.

'Frances! My God, my Franceleh! Come here.'

He blunders towards her. Only then does he notice that Claudia too is present. Mid-stride, he weighs her general irritability, her current touchiness, her sensitivity about the younger children against the joy he feels at his Frances, home at last. In this family it takes courage to ignore one's wife.

He will do it. He clasps Frances to him, touches her hot cheek with his own, bats her little boy clumsily on the head as a bear might and, only then, his arm on his daughter's shoulder, turns to meet Claudia's eye. However, even before she can speak, at this most beautiful, most important of moments, his son-in-law interrupts.

'As a matter,' he says, 'of fact—'

Family! Hierarchy! Could any son-in-law not see that this is a private matter? 'What?' barks Norman. 'Listen, Leo-Sim-Jonathan, could you kindly leave us to—'

Then something unexpected happens. The schmendrick stands a little straighter. He puffs out his chest. 'Norman,' he says. 'If I may . . . you see, your, my, Frances's return does bring some complications.'

'What complications?'

'Er, pertaining to child-rearing. We have to decide whether she is, you know, ready for it.'

Norman, upon whom the sanctity of motherhood has long been impressed, gives a frown: minor, then major. His vision obscured by eyebrow-hair, he does not at first realize that Frances is crying, hard. He glares at his son-in-law.

'Course you're ready,' he tells his daughter. 'Aren't you?'

'Yes . . . I . . . Yes. I am.'

'It's not bloody easy, is it, childcare?' he says and, as his reward, she gives him the sweetest imaginable smile. So moved is he that he can almost ignore the woman who sits amongst them, like an ancient statue foretelling war. Be brave, he tells himself. He squeezes his daughter's arm and prepares his next rhetorical flourish.

'But,' says his son-in-law. For God's sake, thinks Norman, can't he be quiet? 'Fathers can . . . they can bring up children too—'

'Well, only if they absolutely have to. Feh! I'd have killed you all,' says Norman cheerfully, as if the thought of raising his four alone hadn't regularly given him nightmares. It still does, even now.

'You know, research has shown—'

But Norman is watching his daughter and grandson; her hand on his little baby tochus, his fingers in her hair. He gives her thin shoulders a shake and thinks: this is as it should be, mothers and sons together. If she needs help we'll give her help. So she went. Well, didn't she come back?

But Claudia has still said nothing. Her eyes are closed, as if she is merely enduring a dull play. Time, he thinks grimly, to face her. 'Darling?' he says. 'This is better, isn't it? Don't you think?'

How ravishable she looks. If only she would agree with him. 'Darling?' he says again.

She opens her eyes. He holds his breath. They all do. Isn't this exactly what they need to cement this happy moment: the considered warm-hearted view of a mother, a rabbi, the leader of them all?

Claudia, however, disappoints them. 'Do whatever you think is best,' she says, and shrugs.

What the hell is going on? Norman sucks a fragment of salted pistachio from a molar and straightens his back. My daughter has returned, he thinks. My son is happy and I am about to be famous: well, famousish. And so, because today he feels entitled to a little respect as the nominal head of the family, he takes her word as his due.

'Right,' he says. 'Exactly. What I think is best. Well, what I think is . . . Frances? Let me get this straight. You want the baby or you don't want him?'

'I wa—'

'Good. Of course you do. You're his mother,' he points out regally. 'Next: you're coming home?'

'I'm . . . No, I'm not.'

Norman swallows. 'Ah. Right. Fine. So you, you have somewhere to live? Nice? Nice enough for my Franceleh?'

Frances smiles. Her eyes are bright. 'I think so,' she says. She leans her head against his arm and there it is: their happy moment, after all.

SIX

Sunday 29 April

Despite their lovely day at Kenwood and their extensive lunch and tea, Helen is not happy. 'But I don't want to fuck in your mother's house,' she says.

'Why not?'

'Oh, Leo.' It is eleven and a half days until they move into their flat: two hundred and eighty hours, sixteen thousand and . . . oh, never mind. It remains, as far as he can tell from several pilgrimages to the street outside, a wonderful flat, still daringly unsanctioned by his mother, the Mosses' gleaming linoleum and geraniums intact

323

and waiting for them. But, until it is theirs, their options are limited and, as he is slowly beginning to realize, his tolerance for Behrens Road is rather higher than hers.

*   *   *

They are in the damp passage which leads to the garden. It is one of his favourite places: spotlit with lichen, scented with the fascinating decay of next door's wall. Not even Leo, so bad at seduction that he once, as his siblings like to tell, offered to show Jessica Lister his telescope and actually meant it, expected sex right here. But upstairs, he had hoped, perhaps . . .

'Tell me,' he says, unable, despite the pepper in her voice, to resist brushing the edge of her breast with the backs of his fingers. It is a small but, he hopes, irresistible, invitation. 'Am I doing that thing . . . what *is* that thing I do?'

'Do you really not know?' They are standing very close together, close enough to kiss. 'Not at all?'

He ignores the drip of rainwater from a mouldering gutter, the private mumblings of woodlice in their powdery beds of brick. Because she wants him to, he tries to understand. 'Do you mean . . . that it shouldn't be exciting?'

'No. Not that. It's perfectly normal, although one would hope that it would grow less so . . .'

'I'll practise.'

'But, my love,' she says, leading him out of the passage and into the garden, where almost every dark hidden place of his childhood has been overwhelmed by rampaging clematis and brambles,

324

half-dead jasmine, vines and nettles and blossom, blossom everywhere. 'You're a clever boy,' she tells him as together they wander towards the creaking shed, and stop. 'I'm sure you can understand that I just don't *care* about them as you do. Do you see? For me it would be an uncomfortable nervous grope on your horrible teenage grey geometric duvet cover: not scary, not sexy, not important. At all.'

'But Dad—my fa—you know, Norman did say . . . And anyway, until we've got the flat—'

'My love,' she says. 'Let me put it bluntly. You either look backwards or forwards. "Us" means you and them, or you and me. I know it's painful, but you're going to have to choose.'

*   *   *

Dusk falls noisily on Behrens Road. Frances pushes a large rickety buggy towards the front door of number seven. Inside, on the first floor, Claudia draws the curtains and lies down on her bed. And, down at the shadowy end of the garden, among the bamboo canes and carcasses of abandoned pot plants, Leo, finally, makes his choice.

Frances unclicks the straps, quietly. What if, despite her careful preparations, Jonathan has not taken the girls to Swain's Lane as he agreed? Or the Beth Din has decreed that her mother can keep her grandson? Or at the first sight of someone he knows, someone who has not damaged him irreparably, Max holds out his arms and refuses to come back?

She lifts him out. The buggy crashes to the hall floor. She holds her breath for a voice, a squeaking floorboard but there is nothing. Then she sees that Max's face has darkened.

'Shh, shh-shh,' she whispers, stroking his hair shyly. Gradually, painfully, she is getting the hang of him. He cannot choose to go to his father and she cannot pass him over and so, slowly but definitely, she is beginning to glimpse how competence feels. 'It's OK,' she says. 'They're all out. We'll quickly find your things and go.'

She begins to creep upstairs, thanking God that Sundays mean weddings or stone-settings, keeping her mother from home. Max is heavy and the enormous canvas bags Gillian insisted she bring entwine themselves lovingly around her legs, trying to keep her back.

No, she tells herself. Don't think like that. She will carry them with pride, she decides as she climbs on and on, although the others would mock them. If they laugh at her self-chosen clothes, she thinks, holding her head up selfconsciously, or at Max's second-hand-shop baby garments, let them laugh.

The smell of her younger siblings' floor is terrible. She lowers her nose to Max's deliciously unwashed-scented head and tries not to notice the filthy carpet, the knee-deep drifts of misbegotten keyboards and cracked bongs, the mouldy plates, the encrusted loo. As she approaches the wobbling ladder to the attic, she feels, if possible, even worse about her stepdaughters than before.

However, Jonathan was right. Emptied and thoroughly de-cobwebbed it is quite big enough for the girls. 'All it needs,' as he said on the phone to her, 'is a little window. And when Simeon and Em have had a tidy-up of their floor—don't laugh—it

326

will be lovely. We're starting this weekend. You wait.'

*   *   *

In fact, it is wonderful. Strange as it is to see their little beds and chest of drawers installed up here, to imagine the cot and marital futon below in the sitting room until Leo moves out too ('I do think,' said Jonathan, 'that it's a little insensitive of him. Even now you're, well, found'), they will love living here. The wall is already painted the Calamine pink which she, their wicked stepmother, most hated. Bradish's *Stuart Warfare* will be lying downstairs on Jonathan's pillow. They are home at last.

'I can't carry much,' she warns Max. 'Next time we'll fetch some more. Now, can you wait?' and, while he sucks at a musical eggbox, she sorts through her mother and sister's comedy T-shirts, a tiny Rasta poncho from Sim, the creamy mounds of lemon-yellow knitted jackets and complex leggings sent by elderly well-wishers. 'Never forget,' as her father pointed out when the bales started arriving, 'you will always be their child.'

There is room only for essential babyware: not his towelling bath chair but a chewed spider book; the favourite pyjamas she has not allowed herself to dress him in, lest he became sweeter and she more vulnerable; a selection of hedgehogs and elephant seals because she does not know which will comfort him when he misses the rest of his family, when the terrible wound she has inflicted begins to show. She resists the queasy urge to look through her own things; her father, during an

327

awkward but affecting telephone conversation, has promised to drop a selection—oh God—of them round.

Then, because Max, although almost too swaddled to move his limbs, is miraculously still not crying, because she cannot hesitate any longer, she goes over to her stepdaughters' little beds. She reaches into her landlady's navy shoulder bag ('St Paul's Retreat, eh?' Sim would say but she does not listen, or not much) and leaves on each pink pillow a letter.

*   *   *

Gillian, her landlady, is the reason for this. The letters, at her suggestion, explain, apologize, invite the girls, when they are ready, to Imax cinemas, cake shops or anywhere else they might wish to go. Gillian is extraordinarily unrufflable, even with deranged parishioners, or her own mother, who rings in a weekly drunken rage from Wolverhampton. Frances finds herself hanging around to observe it, as if her calm strength, her sympathetic cleverness, were things one could catch. Meeting her, being allowed to spend her evenings discussing novels or being made, painfully, to laugh, is beginning to feel like the most extraordinary piece of luck.

Because even when, almost a fortnight ago, Frances appeared with a hitherto unmentioned baby and her coat pockets full of bibs and nappies, Gillian took it in her stride. Mother and infant spent the next day wandering dazedly around Stockwell, clinging to each other in Portuguese coffee shops and wondering how they would manage. Eventually, after a long cold scary day, they returned to find that Gillian had procured and somehow erected an old-fashioned white cot, decorated with smiling chickens, at the sight of which both Frances and Max began to cry.

Having Gillian behind her is like going into battle with a superior gun, thinks Frances. She strokes her stepdaughters' pillows clumsily, as if her feeble good intentions could be absorbed while they sleep. She dresses Max in as many more layers as he will tolerate. The house is still quiet. This visit has been so much easier than she feared. Amazed at her own good fortune, she begins to go back downstairs.

*　　　*　　　*

Down by the compost heap time has passed, deliciously. Now Leo is hungry. 'Are you cold?' he asks Helen. 'Shall we go in? Have you tried Mum's walnut cake?'

'Let's not.'

Wow, thinks Leo. He pokes modestly at a broken pot with his shoe, pretending not to notice the earwigs. Here he stands, a man able to pleasure a woman so extensively beside a garden shed that she will resist cake. And, as his father would say, vot a voman.

'Believe me, I'd happily stay out here for ever,' he says. 'But hypothermia—'

'No. I meant let's not go in. Why don't we find a café in South End Green?'

Something previously repressed, for the sake of peace or pleasure, begins to emerge. 'Look,' he says, quite patiently. 'They're my family. And even if you have . . . ambivalences, and ideas about what would be healthier, you can't expect me t—'

'I'm not expecting anything.'

'Yes, you are.'

'No, Leo. I just don't want to participate.'

They are glowering at each other, but with difficulty. Her features are becoming mere distinctions of tone. Evening is falling and the air hums with pollen and sex. 'Shh! Please!'

'They won't hear,' she says.

'They might. Look, I don't want to hurt them.'

'Well,' she says. 'Maybe you will.'

*   *   *

As Leo and Helen begin their first row, but not their last, Frances is feeling her way back downstairs. Birdsong pours like sunlight through the hall window. The dusk feels alive. She keeps thinking of the day she moved away from here, into a student box off Tottenham Court Road, to the noisy disgust of her siblings and her mother's wet-eyed silence. It was impossible to make them understand why she might not want to commute to lectures from home, or be brought stuffed cabbage by her mother at midnight in warm silver-foil parcels, or have her twenty-first-birthday party not at shul or in Behrens Road but in a nasty hired room of her choosing. How her stomach had fluttered every time she tried to resist them. How quickly she gave in.

Her foot creaks on the stair. 'Who's there?' calls her mother from the bedroom.

Frances freezes. Why is she even home? Something must be wrong. She cannot see into the hall from here. Could they sneak past?

'Ka,' says Max loudly, stretching out his arms towards the bedroom door.

Frances lowers the baby clothes. She shifts Max to her right shoulder.

'It's us,' she announces, steeling herself against her mother's expression at the sight of her unglamorous trousers, her wholemeal South London bags. She pushes open the door.

Her mother is lying on the bed. She is dressed as for work but here she is, her profile fizzing in the darkness, her rings and hair and ankles reflecting the last smears of light from the sky outside.

'Hello,' says Frances. Mothers should be vertical. It does not suit hers to be so reduced. 'Were you asleep?'

'I think so,' says her mother. 'I don't know.'

Frances, frowning, approaches. She puts Max on to the bed like an offering. If he cries, she promises herself, I'll go. That will be my sign. As she bends to kiss her mother, dipping into the parental fug of sheets and scattered shirts and comforting perfume, she notices a strange new smell: pheromonal, nervous.

She stands up. 'What's wrong?'

'I had a headache. I came home.'

'Really?'

Claudia moves her head. 'Hello, Maxie,' she says. 'Hello, darling. How are you?' She strokes his cheek with a finger. Max begins to make his way closer, parting the lavender peaks of duvet as if swimming through a cloud.

'I, I was getting some things,' says Frances. It is extraordinarily difficult not to tell her Max has missed her, not to put up a hand to civilize her own

331

hair, but she resists.

'All right.'

It must be the twilight. As Frances looms over her beautiful mother, stretched on her bank of pillows and dressing gowns, she cannot judge her mood. 'There's more to fetch,' she says doggedly. 'I, I think I'm going to stay there, um, yes, I am, for a while at least, and I need to make him happy.'

'Can we not talk about this now?' says Claudia. Then she is quiet. Into the quiet, Frances says:

'I'm going to make things all right.'

'You must.'

'I know I must. I'm moving jobs.'

'About time,' says her mother.

'Not . . . not somewhere flashier. But better for me. It's—I'm reading submissions for editors. And that agent: Malcolm Dickens.'

'Oh, that one you like.'

'Well,' she says defensively, 'he likes me. He's independent now, and really busy . . .'

'You know, I should ask the Waxmans' son, Allan, if he can—'

Frances's saintly intentions, her resolution to keep this visit calm and bright, dissolve. 'Mum. Please don't. He's a rubbish agent. Why do you always—'

'So this might be OK?' She puts her hand on Frances's wrist and begins to stroke it, slowly, with her thumb.

'Yes,' she says at last. 'I suppose so.'

'And the place you're staying, they're mensches?'

Frances moves her hand away. 'It, she—'

'Yes, I know she. Daddy said. So, is she?'

Frances sighs. '*Yes*. Why—'

'That's fine, then. Fine. Let's not argue now.'

*   *   *

Frances rubs her eyes. The twilight thickens. It occurs to her, looking at the familiar sights of her parents' room—the tangled jewellery, the stolen hotel notepads, the metal bedstead bought in Paris before her birth—that she could explain herself now. She could tell Claudia what she has only now realized, torn between kissing Max's head and wincing with impatience: that she will always be a little distracted, selfish, unrelaxed, but that she wants him, absolutely. Instead of waiting to be the mother she thought she should be, this is her, Frances, being a mother, and she can do it reasonably well.

But she cannot say it. She thinks: you don't deserve this from me tonight.

'I'm sorry you're not feeling well,' she says unconvincingly. She reaches for Max and, as he writhes, she finds herself grasping moist dungaree. He has wet her mother's duvet.

So you were wrong, she thinks. You can't do it at all. You don't even know where to put his penis in his nappy. Apologize, hand him over and get out.

No. Not again. She will take him and his sin with her. She thinks of their bedroom, the hard work and cold kitchen, the painful necessary distance from here. Gillian will be waiting. At the thought of that, she smiles.

Her mother is looking. 'Is there someone?' she says.

'Sorry?' The room seems hotter. 'No!' Does she mean Gillian . . . that she and Gillian . . . it has not

333

occurred to her. Then she thinks of the odd expression she has caught once or twice on Gillian's face, or felt on her own, and wonders if, perhaps, it has.

'I'd better go,' she says.

'I just want— Oh, never mind. Kiss me,' says Claudia.

So Frances does, and then she leaves. But a moment later, as she retrieves her bags in the gloom from the hall rug, she hears her mother saying something.

'I love you,' it sounds like. Of course, she cannot be sure.

*　　　*　　　*

Norman stands in the Hampstead Village Bookshop, entirely at a loss. He has nothing whatsoever to complain about. Piles of his Cedric book are larger than he had feared, although naturally smaller than he had hoped. Moreover, the booksellers, in whom he has so little faith, have put it under both New Non-Fiction and Jewish Interest, which shows that some of them have even read it to the end. Thanks to his new sport of literary onanism he knows it has sold five copies at least, out of a thrilling fifteen. This almost consoles him for the Highgate bookshop he visited earlier this evening: only one copy, which they asked him not to sign.

Never mind them. This morning at the Heath café he spotted P. I. Trethewey, biographer of Auden, snob and probable anti-Semite, reading the Books pages. When he caught Norman's eye he nodded: only once, but enough to make his life complete.

As for home, he still cannot understand quite what has happened. Has he won or lost? Frances has taken his grandson into the wastes of outer London ('South,' she said, as lightly as 'the desert' or 'the stars'), leaving nothing: no key, no telephone number, only a painful tenderness in his heart and a promise to visit as often as she can. Well, thinks Norman, his warm haze of success consoling him, at least there is that. Better this way, even for Jonathan and those little girls, than . . .

But there his imagination falters. Life, after all, is not so bad, if he ignores the fact that he nearly ruined his marriage, for which he will be punished by having to carry guilt and fear to his grave.

Only last night, when Claudia climbed into bed he turned to her and found himself saying: 'We're all right, really, aren't we?'

'Yes,' she had said, pressing her face against his. 'Darling, I . . . I'm sorry too.'

Surprised and touched and puzzled, he had kissed her. 'It's fine, fine,' he said, hoping to suggest that he knew what she meant. Then, because he can never leave well alone, he had said: 'We weren't perfect, but we tried. Didn't we? I don't know if we could have done better, with the children, even if . . .'

He had expected her to demur. For Claudia, good enough has never been good enough. But she had said, 'I think so too,' quietly into his neck like a child, and he had thought his heart would break with loving her.

Will you ever forgive me for not telling you about Cedric? he had wanted to ask her again. Are we all right? But he had stopped himself. Yes, he decides now, wondering if he should buy her a book, a little present. Yes, we are.

*   *   *

Leo lets himself into his parents' house. He is not at his best. Arguments unnerve him. Besides, he has the uncomfortable sense that he was wrong. Helen has 'gone on ahead', which means that she will be staying with Petra or Suzanne or one of her other unmet friends, who probably hate him, and he will be confined, alone and frisky, to his single bed.

Now he is cross, sorry, uncomfortably excited all over again. Something is singing loudly in the sycamore tree in the garden. Sap rising, he thinks. God, that is all I need.

He will do some work and perhaps afterwards he will ring Frances on the number she gave him when she first called him at work. It had surprised him so that he jumped to his feet, upsetting a huge pile of Mercer's *Legals* and Jeremy Blackstock too, not that he cares. 'It's just for you,' she said and he had understood. He has written it into his address book in code and consults it frequently. Thank you, he thinks, for bringing her back to us.

Then, he decides as he reaches the first floor and sees the windowful of leaves and blossom at the end, perhaps he will go for a little walk in the garden to sniff the fertile air down by the compost heap and think about Helen, who—

'Norman,' calls his mother from her room. 'Is that you?'

'It's me.' Leo keeps walking. He puts his hand

336

on the handle of his bedroom door. Then he hesitates. 'Oh, isn't it Sunday? Why aren't you—'

'Come here and see me,' she says.

He pushes open the door. Her room is soft with navy light. He looks towards her alcove, at her dressing table. Then he glances at her bed and realizes that the almost perfect woman-shape of clothes on her duvet is his mother, flat on her back.

He gives a little weakling's gasp. What should he do? He cannot ask if she is all right because he knows she is not, because of him. He cannot touch her because it would be too strange.

'Do you need an aspirin?' he asks, eyes averted.

'Not really. Leo . . .'

'Yes?'

'Look at me.'

'I am looking at you.'

'Look at my face.'

Slowly, as if lifting a huge block of stone, Leo forces his head up. He identifies her neck, her hair. Then, tentatively, he moves his gaze to where her eyes gleam blackly at him, the only living things in the room.

'I want you to impregnate her,' says his mother.

'Mp!' says his mouth. He gives a little idiotic laugh. 'I can't . . . I don't . . . er,' he says. 'Helen, you mean?'

'Obviously. Doesn't she want to?'

'I, we . . . yes, I think . . .'

'Well, then.' His body gleams with embarrassment and pride. This is, he realizes, the perfect moment to ask what he has been longing to know for weeks, months, the year and a half since he first laid eyes on Helen Baum, his forbidden fruit. 'Um, actually I wondered—'

Because she is his mother, she knows. She says: 'Do you want me to say whether I could ever like her?'

'Well, yes.'

'No,' she tells him. 'I could not. But she will be good for you.'

*   *   *

Later, when Leo has gone next door to his bedroom and the night is a little blacker, the house seems strangely still. Soon Jonathan will be back with the girls, and Norman. What will they find?

I was right, thinks Claudia, not to have told them. Besides, if her instinct about tonight is correct, it is too late now. She has seen a lot of dying. Whatever the doctors say about this particular weakness, the impossibility of knowing when it will strike, she knows how the sick change when they feel themselves beginning to fall. That, she thought, was how she felt today.

But what if she was wrong?

Will there be pain? Where will I bleed? Oh God, Norman, she thinks, what have I done?

And what if she has made a mistake; if she should have told them?

If I am spared tonight, she thinks, I'll go straight to the surgeon and he can graft me or laser me or do anything he wants to save me. After all these awful secret years of not-believing, maybe God has looked kindly on her after all. I . . . I have made a mistake, she thinks. It was terror that made me resist help, not courage. I need to write more books. My family need me. I must have more time.

Then something occurs to her. Tonight, if it is

338

going to happen tonight, there is no time for news of bicycle accidents or heart attacks. For the first time in her life she is safe from fear. Her own death is the worst thing she has to face. This is, at last, happiness.

And if she is wrong and can still be saved, well, happiness can keep.

So, although she knows that the relief she feels may be simply endorphins, although even now she cannot shake the feeling there are other things to do, she reaches cautiously across the bed for the Hotel Davos pad and pen on Norman's table. And there she makes herself do what she, Claudia, whom everyone thinks of as so brave, has never yet dared. She begins to write—who knew that it would be quite so difficult?—Emily, Simeon, Frances, Leo and Norman, most of all Norman, the love letters that they deserve.

GLOSSARY

Afikomen—a piece of matzoh hidden during the Seder for children to find

auf ruf—a blessing for a prospective bride and groom before the wedding day when the man, with or without the woman, is called up to the Torah

b'racha (*plural* b'rachot)—a blessing

Beth Din—Rabbinical court

bimah—a platform in a synagogue on which the Torah is read

bris—circumcision ceremony

broigus—angry/a row or grudge

bubeleh—little baby, darling

challah—plaited rich white bread eaten in honour of the Sabbath

Channukah—eight-day festival of lights in December

charoset—a mixture of apples, nuts, spices and sweet wine, eaten at the Seder to symbolize the mortar with which Jewish slaves built the houses of their Egyptian captors

cholent—a stew containing barley, beans and goose or sausage

chuppah—a canopy under which wedding vows are taken

Cossackski—a kicking dance with arms crossed and legs bent, cf. 'To Life' in *Fiddler on the Roof*

frummer/frum—a religious person/religious, orthodox

goy/goyisher—a non-Jew/non-Jewish

Haggadah (*plural* Haggadot)—the story of the

341

Jews' exodus from Egypt, read aloud at the Seder

Halachah—Jewish law

hametz—food containing yeast, which must be removed from the house before Passover begins

hillel sandwich—a little bit of horseradish between pieces of matzoh, eaten during the Seder

Kadimah—summer camp run by Liberal Judaism; kadimah means 'forward'

ketubah—a marriage document drawn up under Jewish law, in Hebrew

Kiddush cup—the cup for wine used during the blessings recited on the Sabbath and festivals

kippah (*plural* kippot)—the skullcap worn by observant male Jews, and some female Jews

klezmer—folk music from Eastern Europe, usually clarinet or violin

k'nayn hora tu-tu-tu—expression said superstitiously to ward off the evil eye, meaning 'let there be no curse'

kvetch—to complain or moan

Leo Baeck—London's rabbinical college (non-Orthodox)

Mah Nishtanah—the beginning of the Four Questions asked during the Seder by the youngest child, meaning 'why is this night different from all other nights?'

maror—horseradish, eaten during the Seder to symbolize the bitterness of life under slavery

matzoh—thin sheets of unleavened bread eaten during the eight days of Passover

matzoh-kneidl or matzoh balls: dumplings for chicken soup

megillah—a complicated palaver; originally

meant a long scroll

mensch—a decent person, a good egg

meshuggener—a mad person, anyone with whom you disagree

milchedik—food classified as dairy by Kosher laws

minyan—the ten male Jews required for religious services in Orthodox Judaism

mitzvah—a good deed, a religious obligation; literally a commandment, a duty

nu?—So? Well? And?

Pesach—Passover: at which Jews commemorate their ancestors' escape from slavery in Egypt

rebbitzin—a rabbi's wife

schlemiel—a clumsy, foolish or unlucky person

schlep—to haul or move laboriously

schluf—sleep

schloompy/schloomp—frumpy, drippy, droopy/someone who looks a bit of a mess

schmendrick—a particularly puny schlemiel

schmooze—to chat, or chat up

schmutter—rags, clothes

schnorrer—a scrounger

schtick—a routine, a sketch or riff

schtum—quiet

schtuppable—fuckable

Seder—a ceremonial feast, with prayers, on the first and second nights of Passover

Shabbat—the Sabbath

shiva—a period of mourning, usually lasting seven days (shiva means seven) and hosted in the house of the bereaved

shul—synagogue

tallith—prayer shawl

tchotcke—a little silly plaything

tefillin—leather boxes with straps containing biblical passages, used by Orthodox men for morning prayer
tochus—a bottom
Torah—the five books of Moses
yahrzeit—the anniversary of a death
yeshiva—rabbinical college; cf. *Yentl*
zaftig—juicy, sexy